ALL
I'LL
Ever
NEED

Other Books by Harry Kraus, MD

Could I Have This Dance?

For the Rest of My Life

HARRY KRAUS, MD

BESTSELLING AUTHOR OF COULD I HAVE THIS DANCE?

ZONDERVAN®

All I'll Ever Need

Requests for information should be addressed to:

Zondervan, *Grand Rapids, Michigan 49530*

Library of Congress Cataloging-in-Publication Data

Kraus, Harry Lee, 1960 -
All I'll ever need / by Harry Kraus.
p cm.
Sequel to: For the rest of my life.
ISBN-13: 978-0-310-27283-0
ISBN-10: 0-310-27283-1
1. Women physicians – Fiction. 2. Euthanasia – Fiction. 3. Hospital patients – Crimes against – Fiction. 4. Virginia – Fiction. I. Title.
PS3561.R2875A79 2007
813'.54 – dc22 2006039496

Interior design by Nancy Wilson

Printed in the United States of America

---

07 08 09 10 11 12 • 10 9 8 7 6 5 4 3 2 1

Acknowledgments

Sincere thanks to Aaron Cook, criminal defense lawyer, for his expertise. And thanks to Natasha Kern, my literary agent, for her support of this project.

ALL
I'LL
Ever
NEED

Prologue

1992

Ami Grandle clutched the stuffed teddy bear to her chest and watched her house burn. Acrid smoke enveloped the waning moon overhead. Hungry flames licked at her bedroom curtains, the blue and white ones that her mother let her pick out at K-Mart in downtown Brighton. Soon the second floor dissolved into a sea of orange. Her mother's screams penetrated the night, muffled from inside the inferno. Certainly, she thought, her mother would make it out alive. "Mom!" she screamed. Should she go back for her?

But in a moment, the front door opened and her mother ran into the yard. "Ami," she gasped, stumbling forward into her daughter's arms. "I thought you were trapped."

She shook her head. "I'm okay."

Ami tried to pull her mother back into a comforting embrace, but she pulled away, the outline of her slender form silhouetted by flames reaching up to challenge the darkness of the summer night.

"What's wrong?"

Her mother grabbed Ami's wrist, lifting her hands to her face.

The kerosene. She smells the kerosene.

"What have you done?"

Ami looked away. "I didn't want anyone to know. The police would take you from me."

"I could have told them the truth. He was a monster," she whispered. "It was self-defense."

She didn't care what her mother said. Ami needed the house to burn, needed him to burn. "Mom," she said, trying to steady her voice. "Tell them I was filling the kerosene lantern Grandma gave me. Tell them I stole one of your cigarettes." She turned to face the sound of an approaching siren. "It was all an accident."

Her mother wrapped her arms around her and began to cry. "Ami, Ami," she cried. "What has happened to my little girl?"

She let herself relax in her mother's arms.

"I'm so sorry, Ami. I'm so sorry."

Her mother lifted her head to face the distant siren. "Go around to the spigot near the shed. Wash away that dreadful smell."

Chapter One

Claire McCall closed her hand around the pistol's grip, snapped off the safety, and stared into the darkness. The room was midnight black except for the digital alarm clock that cast an eerie green glow across her pillow: 3:00. The numbers mocked her inability to sleep. Her heart pounded as she tightened her grip and waited for another sound to break the silence.

She mouthed his name. "Tyler." It had been six weeks since the assault, six weeks since the violent intrusion into her bedroom by Tyler Crutchfield, a former employee who had gone by the name of Cyrus Hensley. She stared at a dim slit of light beneath her door.

A creak from the old floorboards whispered a different message. She sat and listened, nodding her head in quiet resolution. She weighed the pistol in her hand and thought about the last time she'd used it. Right there, at the foot of her bed, she'd defended herself against him. Claire steadied the handgun, lifting it up and steeling herself for a shot toward the door. *I won't just wound him this time.*

Outside, a peaceful blanket of night cuddled Stoney Creek and the surrounding Apple Valley. Beyond her home sang the comforting noises of the country. The barking of the neighbor's dog. The wind rustling pine branches against the roof of the small ranch house. A summer locust. The soprano chorus of the frogs seeking food or love or both.

But she'd heard something else. Inside. A noise in the hall and then in the kitchen. Footsteps. Willing the old box springs not to squeak, she rose and crossed to the door. She twisted off the dead bolt, lifted the locking chain, and turned the doorknob to unsnap the lock. Opening the door, she slipped into the hall with the gun lifted at arm's length in front of her.

She paused at the end of the hallway and listened. A glass clinked against the counter. She stepped quickly into the kitchen with her arms extended, pointing the gun in the direction of the sink.

After a few seconds, her eyes adjusted to the dim light and she could see a woman, facing away, looking through a window into the night. Claire lowered the pistol to her side and took a deep breath. Her mother turned around. "Oh," she gasped, sloshing a glass of water on her nightgown. "Claire, you startled me."

"Mom." She followed her mother's gaze to the gun. "I — " She halted. "I thought you were an intruder."

"Put that thing down before you kill someone."

Claire slowly uncurled her blanched fingers and laid the weapon on the counter.

"This isn't rational."

Claire knew that. She couldn't dispute it. She shrugged. "Fear is irrational."

"Tyler is in prison, honey. He can't get you anymore."

"I hear you. Just tell that to my gut."

Della stepped toward her daughter and enveloped her in a hug. "Don't you think you should talk to someone?"

"We've been through this." Claire broke away, and touched the pistol again. "I just feel safer if it's near me, that's all."

Della lifted gray-streaked blonde hair behind her ear. "How did someone so stubborn come out of me?"

Claire squinted back at her mother, feeling the sting of her accusation.

Della laughed. "Don't look so hurt," she said, turning back to the sink. "Want some coffee?"

"I want some sleep."

"It won't kill you to get some help."

"I just need some time."

"Want to know what I think?"

Claire shook her head and sat at the kitchen table. "When have my desires ever stopped you from giving an opinion?"

"You're not afraid of Tyler anymore." Della snapped on a fluorescent light over the sink. "How many locks do you have on the bedroom door?"

Claire didn't answer. They both knew the answer.

"Tyler is locked away. This is Stoney Creek, one of the safest towns around. It makes no sense for you to have to protect yourself this way."

Claire sighed. "I told you fear wasn't rational."

"You're trying to protect yourself against the future. Ever since you got the results of your Huntington's disease gene status, you've grown more and more withdrawn. You've had locks installed on the doors, alarmed the house, have Mace under your pillow, and a gun on the nightstand."

"He tried to rape me, Mom. Forgive a girl for being afraid."

"I know you. You've been through similar trouble before." Della threw up her hands. "Brett Daniels," she said, speaking the name of a troubled resident who stalked Claire during her internship. "He spray-painted threats on your door and tried to run you off the road."

"So?"

"So?" Della shook her head. "You didn't react this way then."

"Maybe this is different. It was here. In my own bed. Maybe I should move."

"Maybe you should admit that you're trying to defend yourself against the future."

"So now you're a psychologist."

"I'm your mother. That qualifies me to make a judgment."

Claire huffed.

"Tyler is only an excuse. There is only one thing stalking you now."

She looked at Della, silhouetted by the light behind her. "Huntington's disease." She spoke the name of the disease she'd inherited from Wally, her father. She couldn't keep the sarcasm out of her voice. "And you think that I think that this gun is going to keep HD at bay?"

"Of course not. But your fear that HD will strike and spoil your future is manifested in your need for that gun."

Claire felt like cursing. Was it anger over her mother's insight? *Or has Huntington's already started to affect me, altering my personality so that I'll be less inhibited and more likely to ...* She closed her fist and counted. *One, two, three, four, ten!* "And where did you get your psychiatry degree?"

Della stared at her daughter. To Claire, it was the look you give a stranger who has mayonnaise on his cheek and doesn't know. Pity. Embarrassment.

"I need some sleep," Claire muttered. She stood and walked toward the hallway, but not before picking up the pistol from the counter.

"Claire," her mother said softly.

Claire looked back at Della without speaking.

"I saw a beautiful wedding dress in Brighton last week. I want to show you."

She smiled. That was Della. Always trying to get Claire to look at the bright side, reminding her that John had only recently popped the question after learning that Claire carried the HD gene. "Okay, Mom," she whispered. She paused. "I'm supposed to see my genetics counselor today. Maybe I'll see what she thinks of your theory."

Claire walked back down the hall to her room, locked, dead-bolted, and chained her door, and set the pistol on her nightstand. She reached her hand beneath her pillow and closed it around a small canister of pepper spray.

She lay awake wondering about whether she'd ever be able to follow through and marry the man she loved. *Mom wants me to look at wedding dresses.* Her eyes flooded with tears. *Is it fair to doom his future just because mine is ruined?*

By 9:00 a.m., business at Medical Records Solutions raced forward at a hectic pace. Ami Grandle sipped her second cup of coffee and looked up as Bob Estes walked past her desk. "Valley Orthopedics called," she said. "They want you to give a demo on our e-patient software."

Bob poured himself a cup of coffee and slapped a newspaper on her desk. "Check this out. Give Cerelli time off for sick leave and look what he does."

"Are you listening to me?" she said. "Dr. Smith said he— "

"I know, I know," he groaned. "Look at this," he said, pointing to the paper. "Cerelli must have really injured his head in that accident."

Carol Dawson walked in, clicking her high heels against the floor. "That's old news. Cerelli's been dating that girl for years."

Ami studied the small engagement announcement in the *Brighton Daily.* She felt her stomach tighten. She'd known of John's on-again, off-again relationship with the Stoney Creek physician, but the last time John had talked with her before his accident, he'd said he'd given up hope on a future with Claire. "This can't be right," she muttered.

Carol tugged on the upper edge of the paper. "You're blushing."

Ami threw the paper in the trash.

Bob hooked a finger in his belt and leaned against her desk. "Another one bites the dust."

Carol moved closer. Ami looked away, wishing the duo would leave her alone.

"What's wrong, Ami?" Carol asked.

"John's too sweet to be treated the way that woman jerks him around."

Ami watched as Carol and Bob exchanged glances. She felt heat rise in her face. John had been so friendly since she'd started working in his office. She'd allowed her hopes to rise too high. She pretended to busy herself with a stack of files on her desk, avoiding the examining eyes of her coworkers.

Carol took Bob by the arm, nudging him from his perch on the desk. "Come on, big boy. Give a woman space to work."

Ami waited until the others disappeared from her office, then turned her attention to the picture of the happy couple in the newspaper. Opening the top drawer, she retrieved her scissors. As she cut out John's picture, deftly separating him from the smiling blonde on his arm, she whispered, "I know how you feel about me, John." She placed his photograph in the drawer and crumpled the rest of the page into a wad and tossed it into her waste can. "I'm not giving up that easily. Dr. McCall is no match for me."

Later that morning, Claire sat in the genetics department at Brighton University across from her counselor, Ginny Byrd.

"Huntington's disease changes everything." Ginny's statement hung in the air like the threat of rain.

"Everything," Claire repeated.

"Knowing you carry the gene for a deadly disease can empower you or crush you." The genetics counselor folded her arms across her lap. "In many ways, what happens is up to you."

Claire nodded. That's what she loved about Virginia Byrd. She never held back. She cut through the fog straight to what mattered. *You would make a good surgeon.*

Today was to be her last scheduled session with Ginny, a closure encounter to see how Claire was dealing with the new information that she carried the Huntington's disease gene. Ginny seemed a transplant from the sixties. Gray-streaked blonde hair pulled into a long braid, an African-beaded necklace, and a long denim skirt graced her almost-five-foot frame with a charm that warmed her to Claire from the start. She tapped a legal pad with a pencil before storing it back in her hair at the base of the braid. "How has knowing affected your relationships?"

Claire felt heat rise in her cheeks. "I'm engaged now."

Ginny leaned forward and took Claire's hands. "I heard. So it's no rumor?"

"John didn't want to ask me until he knew the results of the test. That way I wouldn't think he'd asked me before, only wanting me if I wasn't a carrier for HD."

Ginny beamed. "I like his style." She pulled her hands away.

Claire thought back to her early morning conversation with Della. "I'm struggling to be upbeat. I want to use my gene status as a reminder to live each day to the full," she said. "John and I may not have a long lifetime together, so we have promised to not let a dread of the future spoil today as well." She looked down, afraid of betraying her feelings. *Okay, so I believe it in my head, but what about my heart?*

"Good for you." Ginny smiled. "If there is anyone I know that deserves a little taste of happiness, it's you."

Claire attempted a smile. "We're already planning the wedding." She shook her head. "There is so much to do." She lifted her hand to count off her fingers. "A florist, photographer, caterer ..."

"A church, a vocalist," Ginny added.

"A hairstylist, a manicure ..."

"A videographer, invitations." The duo ended their list together and laughed.

They sat together for a moment as comfortable in silence as they were with shared laughter. "That's good. Everything's great," Ginny said.

Claire nodded, wanting to believe it. "Yes."

"You don't believe it."

"Am I that transparent?"

"Let's call it translucent. You're pretty good at putting on a happy face."

"Maybe I'm a little scared of commitment."

Ginny shook her head. "Maybe you're afraid of letting someone else take care of you."

"John doesn't need to suffer too."

"Maybe you don't realize that trusting your life to him may mean humbling yourself to let him care for you."

Claire frowned. "He loves me like I am. What if he doesn't love me when I look like my father?"

"Sometimes love finds its sweetest expression in illness."

It sounded like a platitude. Claire didn't want to argue, so she forced herself to smile. A happy face. "Sure."

"So what about Wally?"

Claire's smile melted. Leave it to Ginny to launch another probe. "Daddy?" She shifted in her seat. "He's getting so thin."

"I want to know about your feelings. How has knowing he passed the gene to you changed your relationship?"

Claire took a deep breath. Ginny's pick-a-scab approach to counseling was effective and painful. "HD seemed to settle a lot of issues for me in terms of relating better to Daddy. Once I knew about HD, I was able to forgive him for his erratic behavior." She paused. "I was able to put some of the hurt behind us." She dabbed the corner of her eyes. "He tells me he loves me now."

"But?"

Claire didn't want to uncover this scab. She pressed her eyelids with the fingers of her right hand. She opened her eyes and raised her head. "How do you know there is a *but*?"

"There always is with HD."

A tear escaped the corner of her eyes. Her voice cracked as she spoke. "For the longest time, I was able to be so positive, even around Daddy. I suppose down inside I always held out the hope that I'd be negative, so I didn't let it get to me."

"And now?"

Claire paused. There was no polite pretending with Ginny. "I hate seeing him now. As long as I am at work, or busy with John, or planning the wedding, I'm okay. HD is in the background somewhere, but I'm not thinking about it." She shook her head. "But when I'm with Wally, all I see is so horrible. He can hardly speak a clear word anymore. His head, arms, and legs are constantly banging against the padded bed rails. It's like a cruel glimpse into the future."

"So what do you do?"

"Avoid going very often."

"Are you angry?"

"At my dad?" Claire thought for a moment. "It's not his fault. He didn't even know he had a disease to pass along."

"So where's the anger coming from?"

"Who says I'm angry?"

"You're clenching your fist. You started when you mentioned your father."

Claire looked at her right hand and uncurled her whitened knuckles.

"I'm not judging you for being human, Claire. Anger is often a normal response to finding out about HD." She shrugged. "You blame the parent who passed it on to you. You blame God."

Claire nodded. "So what do I do?"

"Do?" She leaned forward. "You're such a doctor. You want to fix everything."

Claire held up her hands. Surrender.

"This isn't something you fix."

"I sleep with a loaded gun by my bed." She decided not to mention the three locks on her bedroom door and the pepper spray. She looked into Ginny's face. "My mom says I'm trying to protect myself against the future."

Ginny leaned back and crossed her legs. "Is she right?"

Just like a counselor. Answer a question with a question. "I have nightmares about the rape attempt," she said, shrugging.

Ginny nodded and didn't speak.

"Okay, maybe she's right. I know no one's after me, so maybe my fears represent something else."

"You're good at looking strong, Claire. In fact, I think you're a very strong woman."

"But."

"But you're human. Women who've been victims of sexual assault often benefit from talking things out."

"Two against one. No fair."

Ginny looked puzzled.

Claire explained, "My mother said the same thing. I don't suppose you do that kind of counseling too?"

"Outside my league, kiddo. I can make a referral if you'd like."

She sighed. "I'll think about it."

Ginny pulled the yellow pencil from its resting place. From Claire's angle, it looked like she pulled it straight out of her brain. The effect was chilling.

The counselor tapped the pencil against her lap. "Wally is dying." She paused, perhaps to be sure the words had a chance to penetrate. "Now begins the final chapter in your relationship to your father. Avoiding him now is losing something you'll never regain."

"Maybe you don't get it. Wally can't walk anymore. He can barely swallow. His arms and legs swim over the sheets like a drowning man. He can't get to the bathroom, so he pees in his diaper. The constant movements keep him in a stinky sweat. I get nauseated just going in the room." She hesitated, locking her eyes on Ginny's. "And all I can see is me in his place."

"I know, Claire. It must be horrible."

"It's worse than that. I hope somebody puts me out of my misery long before I look like my father."

Ginny nodded with understanding and spent a moment with her hands folded in her lap before speaking. "May I make a suggestion?"

Claire tilted her head. "Find a silver lining."

"Am I that predictable?" Ginny laughed.

She grinned. "Maybe."

"Tap some of that Claire McCall optimism. Make every visit with your father a reminder to live today to the fullest, not an excuse to dread the future."

The thought resonated with her. She wanted to do that, longed to do it, in fact. She and her father had been too far down a healing road to let her own fear spoil her final months with Wally.

She looked up at Ginny. “It’s a plan.”

Claire hugged her counselor and walked down the hall wondering how all the talk was supposed to equip her for the future.

I’m engaged to marry John Cerelli. I should be delirious with joy. So why do I doubt I’ll ever walk the aisle for him?

Chapter Two

The next morning, Claire awoke before her alarm at 6:00 a.m. She uncurled her blanched fingers from the small can of pepper spray and groaned, working her fingers, wondering how long they had been frozen in flexion. After taking a warm shower, she made coffee, allowing the first cup to drip straight into a large purple mug emblazoned with the name of a drug used for treating acid reflux.

After adding a large dollop of French vanilla creamer, she looked up to see her mother.

"Morning."

Claire forced a smile, not wanting to hash over yesterday's early morning encounter.

Fortunately, it appeared Della didn't want to either. "Shall we go to Brighton to the bridal shop Saturday?"

"John wanted to go to the mountains."

"That man is in no shape to hike."

"Not hike, Mom. He just wants to meander along Skyline Drive to clear his mind. Sitting around his parents' home in rehab is making him stir-crazy."

Della poured herself some coffee. "Give him some time in the afternoon. We have a wedding to plan, remember?"

Claire smiled. "I remember." Leave it to her mother to bring some joy into her life.

"It will be the most beautiful wedding Stoney Creek has ever seen." She'd used this phrase so many times that it had become a joke.

"Mom!"

"I'm serious."

"I'll talk to John. I'll let you know." Claire touched her mother's arm. "Did Wally talk to you yesterday?"

Della shook her head. "Not a word. It's like your father goes into his own world. Maybe he'll talk next week." She shrugged. "He's done this before." She put her hand on Claire's. "There's a second patient on his wing with Huntington's disease, you know. The nurses tell me he does the same thing."

Claire busied herself at the sink, washing a lonely supper dish. She knew the next request before her mother spoke it.

"Maybe you could visit Wally."

She paused and leaned against the counter. Why did Della have to continue to poke the tender spots in her life? What may be a joy to her father often left her sullen and depressed. "I'll think about it."

"He loves you, honey. It will brighten his day."

Claire locked eyes with her mother. "Don't you understand that every moment I spend with that man is like looking into a crystal ball for me? I see the future." She threw the dishrag into the sink. "I watch him lying there twisting and turning, barely able to utter a comprehensible word, and I wonder when my dance will begin."

Della's gaze was unbroken. She wouldn't unlock her eyes from her daughter's face. "I know. But for now, you're okay, and your father needs you."

"Thanks for the guilt trip."

Claire saw the sting in her mother's eyes.

"I'm sorry, Mom." She hesitated before adding, "Maybe I'll drop by to see him after work."

Della nodded without speaking.

John Cerelli looked in the mirror and turned on his father's electric beard trimmer. It was time to try to do something with his hair. The trauma surgeons had given little thought to his hairstyle when they shaved a diagonal stripe across his head to repair a jagged laceration sustained in his accident. Now, with his long brown curls falling away from the stripe on both sides of the shaved path, he looked like someone with a kind of reverse Mohawk.

He set the guard to clip everything to one length, one-half inch from the scalp. In ten minutes, he was done. His thick hair stood on end like a Brillo pad in an electrical storm. "Ugh," he sighed. "Claire is going to kill me for this."

John was at the home of his parents, recovering from a serious car accident in which he'd sustained a head injury and fractured his thigh bone. He'd careened off the road in front of Claire's Stoney Creek home while in the process of rushing to her side after she'd had emergency surgery for appendicitis. His rebound from the head injury had been too slow for John and scary for Claire, as John had manifested a loss of some of his social inhibitions. Fortunately, his conduct improved, and John's only knowledge of his misfit behavior came from Claire's jokes about his actions.

He frowned at his reflection. *Claire's going to think this haircut is evidence that I'm still not thinking straight.* He loved his physician fiancée, and chuckled at his next thought. *She'll probably insist that I get a head CT scan when she sees what I've done.*

He put on a baseball cap emblazoned with an "A" for the Atlanta Braves and hobbled out past the kitchen, hoping his mother wouldn't see him. He was recovering nicely from his left femur fracture, thanks to a sixteen-inch metal rod supporting the shaft, but he still used a cane, mostly to speed his progress when he walked outside. Today, he ventured to his parents' mailbox.

Inside, he found a small envelope addressed to him. He opened it standing next to the road. The return address said only "Ami," spelled with the "i" dotted by a little valentine-shaped heart. Inside was a short encouragement to get well and was signed, "Yours with love, Ami." Again, the "i" was dotted with a heart, but also small hearts formed the "o" in *yours* and *love.* She included a copy of a small digital photograph taken a few weeks earlier at the corporate office of the software firm where they worked. Ami had grabbed his elbow as the picture was taken. They had all the appearance of a happy young couple.

John shook his head. Ami Grandle was a nice young woman, a new secretarial assistant to the sales force, of which John was a part. *She probably oozes loving care over everyone who gets sick*, he thought.

He looked at the picture. Ami had dark eyes, wide with mystery and beauty, and the slender figure of a woman addicted to exercise or calorie counting or both.

He shoved the photo into his pocket and moved slowly back to the house. There, he dropped the card into the kitchen trash. It wouldn't do to have Claire drop by and see the heart note. John didn't want to have to explain when there was no explaining to do.

Claire McCall pressed through the morning with the assistance of an efficient nurse and two more cups of Kenyan AA coffee. By late morning, she paused at her desk to sign her charts and to initial the lab work results she'd ordered in the last few days.

Ms. McCormick had high calcium, probably a disorder of her parathyroid glands. Claire checked a box on a sticky label beside the words, "Call for appointment."

Jeff Richardson had red blood cells in his urine. Claire scribbled a note to schedule him for an IVP, a special X-ray of his kidneys.

Blake Stevens turned fifty. Claire dictated a referral letter for a screening colonoscopy.

A hand-addressed letter in her in-box caught her eye. The return address just said, "Women Care." Inside was a brief letter of introduction to a new counseling service directed to women who had endured sexual assault. It included a business card with a phone number of a licensed social worker. Claire held the letter over the trash, but retrieved the business card and slipped it in her jacket pocket. The address was Brighton, but the phone number of the counselor was a cell phone.

Claire shrugged. Perhaps Ginny had contacted this counselor and told her about Claire. Or maybe this was an ambulance chaser who'd read the news of the assault. At any rate, it seemed too timely to be a coincidence. Maybe God really wanted her to do what her mother had been bugging her to do the last two weeks. Get some help. Talk to someone.

It would be just like God to drop such an obvious clue. She withdrew the card and nodded. Maybe calling this counselor for some information wouldn't be such a bad idea.

By midmorning, the temperature in the Apple Valley rested at a balmy seventy-five degrees. *Perfect golf temperature,* Jimmy thought. He squinted down the fairway and sighed. He hated this hole. It was 420 yards with a dogleg left. He lined up his shot, paying attention to every detail, trying to remember just what the club pro had instructed. He'd taken up the game to please his wife. *"You need some fresh air. Why don't you take up golf like other doctors?"* He hooked the ball into the woods.

He shook his head and wondered if she would force him out of the house when the weather cooled. Soon, the air would carry the scent of firewood and the promise of a respite from the moisture of summer. The leaves would color and camera-toting tourists would photograph the transformation of green to a palette of paint that rivaled the bright lights of Times Square. Dr. Jimmy Jenkins had purchased his own digital camera for the event. Now that he was retired, he was determined to capture just the right reflection of the morning dew from a red maple leaf.

He had risen, unable to sleep at 5:30. It seemed his internal clock had been forever programmed by a career that groaned under the weight of the town's medical needs. For thirty-five years as the only family doctor between Stoney Creek and Carlisle, Jimmy pushed himself to his own limits and beyond. Now, several months into retirement, the free time he'd craved began to give rise to a listlessness in his soul and a desire for meaning beyond the pursuit of rest.

He'd made coffee and stared at the thirty-page manual for his new digital camera. After ten minutes, he tossed it aside and took sixty-seven (he had time to count) pictures of his sleeping black Lab, experimenting with just the right angle to capture the light reflecting from the edge of the dog's nose.

That, however, was two hours ago. Now he cursed his lack of golfing skill and watched as he hooked another ball toward the forest on the left of the fairway. He muttered about the amount he'd spent on equipment and set off in search of another lost ball.

Twenty minutes later, he trudged through ankle-deep grass pulling his golf cart beside the fairway between holes five and six at the Apple Valley Country Club. In one hand, he lugged a large plastic bucket brimming with golf balls. Once he was just shy of the green, he detoured into the woods, all-too-familiar territory for a golfer of his stature. Twenty yards from the fairway, at a spot overlooking the North River, he teed up his first shot, aiming for a spot on the opposite rocky bank two hundred yards away.

Plink. Splash. Plink. Splash. Dr. Jenkins sliced and hooked his way through the first fifty balls, exhilarating himself and scaring the trout. He sat on the ground and wiped the sweat from his forehead. After a few minutes he practiced his way to the bottom of the bucket, never once reaching the far bank. With that, he fixed a sticky note to his golf bag, indicating the set would belong to the next amateur who ventured this far off the course in search of a ball.

He shook his head. Golf was not Jimmy's game.

He struck out from the parking lot of the club, lighter for the absence of his gear and the burden of needing to golf his way through retirement. But a nagging anxiety remained. So far, with all the extra time on his hands, he hadn't been able to squelch the inner voice critiquing his life. He had dreamed of years spent traveling with Miriam with the freedom that accompanied the escape from responsibility, but after so many years of a demanding career, he found he hardly knew the woman he'd married.

He had time to know her now, but an open, loving relationship was a long way up a steep path that Jimmy seemed too tired to pursue.

He knew the way back into a stronger relationship with Miriam. Honesty. But after so many years, uncapping the well of hidden secrets he'd kept seemed too painful. But necessary. He sighed. He'd counseled too many couples over the years of his career to know he couldn't sing a different tune for his own marriage.

He slowly drove the streets, his Jeep Cherokee following the pattern they'd taken together almost daily since retirement. Through Stoney Creek, up to the next town of Fisher's Retreat for coffee at Fisher's Café, and back through the center of the small town. There, he passed the small brick ranch belonging to Mabel Henderson. He'd probably made a hundred house calls to the diabetic Mabel over the years, and he found himself wondering how she had adjusted to a new face in his office. He had been so significant to her once. Now, instead of stopping to check her blood sugar or clean up a foot ulcer, he just slowed and stared at the windows as he passed.

Two doors down was Charlie Lambert, a manic-depressive who always stopped taking his hypertension medicine when he was up and overdosed when he was down. Next to Charlie lived the Smiths. Gladys Smith always brought her doctor oranges from Florida in January. On the corner was Jake Yoder's place. He'd lost his wife to melanoma two years ago and came in almost monthly to have Dr. Jenkins look at a mole or two "just to be sure." He always had dirt under his fingernails and a manicured lawn as a result. Jimmy saw Jake standing in the side yard by an azalea bed. Jake wasn't wearing a hat, but hopefully was wearing his sunscreen.

Jimmy drove with the window down and with classical music on the radio. Once he passed Community Chapel, he pulled over by the cemetery. There, he climbed the hill and weaved his way between the headstones, many bearing the names of patients he'd once loved and treated. But memories of old patients did not draw him to this place. He looked to the far corner of the field where the canvas awning of Lindsey's Funeral Home had been erected over a freshly dug grave. He checked his watch. Thankfully, he was alone. Likely, mourners would gather later in the day for the ground to receive the dead.

He was not there to gather with others to honor a common friend. Driven by his sorrow over a past secret, he stopped at a small stone bearing the name of his only child, a boy he'd not helped raise, and his mind drifted to the time of his son's birth. Clay McCall was the first baby of twins, a fact that had taken both Dr. Jenkins and his clandestine lover by surprise.

I deliver the head and suction the nose and mouth with a bulb syringe. The shoulders come next, and soon, I am holding the screaming infant, a boy, cradling him against my body. For a moment, I am frozen in thought. There is a special energy I feel, holding this infant, an unseen bond as real as anything I've seen with my eyes. I cannot describe it beyond that. I am warmed. And frightened. But I cannot reveal it.

I look at my patient, no longer able or willing to avoid her searching eyes. I see her and I am speechless. We communicate without words, the way we did at our first meeting. She knows. I know. But there is no one else who will ever know the truth about this baby.

Jimmy kept his secret for twenty-seven years before Claire McCall pried open his vow of silence when she investigated her own genetic past and solved the mystery of the Stoney Creek curse, a scourge of Huntington's Disease that had long haunted the area. Since Clay's death, the likelihood of Miriam learning the truth was small. But Jimmy couldn't seem to escape the thought that his lie was a stone dropped into a pond. And the ripples had spread far and wide from his first cover-up to affect his whole pattern of communication. If his marriage to Miriam was to survive into their golden years, it would be because he decided to make some things right.

He had been so naive, overconfident in his ability to keep himself from crossing a professional boundary. But Della was so beautiful. And so lonely.

I watch as Della gently lays baby Margo in her crib and pushes a rebellious strand of strawberry blonde hair behind her ear.

"Give her one-half teaspoon four times a day," I say, handing her a pink bottle of aqueous penicillin.

Our hands touch.

Electricity.

Our eyes meet.

She smiles a perfect smile.

She holds my gaze. I have a lump in my throat. "Don't worry about your bill. I know things are tough without Wally."

"You shouldn't. This is the fourth time."

I nod. "It's okay, really."

Della kisses my cheek. "Wally's been gone a long, long time."

He wiped the sweat from his eyes. It seemed odd. How was it after all these years that his sins were the things that were etched most deeply in his memory?

"Dr. Jenkins?"

He stumbled backwards at the sound of the voice and clutched his chest. He looked up to see a lean, well-muscled woman with gray-streaked black hair. He clutched his chest. "Nancy, you startled me."

Nancy Childress nodded. Her eyes were narrow and her long fingers seemed to be knotted in a tangle across her lower abdomen. She stood staring at him for a moment.

He tried to discern her question. Was she wondering why he was standing by Clay's grave?

Her voice seemed frayed with fatigue. "I thought I might find you here." She looked down. "I've been seeing you around town." She cleared her throat. "I've seen you come here before and I wanted to catch you."

I've become boringly predictable too soon in retirement. "What is it, Nancy?"

Her eyes bore in on his. "I want you to help Richard die."

Jimmy frowned but said nothing.

Nancy Childress made a despairing gesture. "Dr. McCall only allows Richard to have a small prescription of pain pills at a time."

Dr. Jenkins shook his head. "I'm retired. There's nothing I can do for you now."

The woman sighed. "Come and visit us. Then you'll see."

He shifted his weight from foot to foot. He'd never had such a request in all his years of practice in the Apple Valley.

"He's dying a slow miserable death. He just lingers day after day. He can't take it anymore."

Jimmy looked at her, trying to see beyond her set, stubborn jaw. *Or is it you who can't take it anymore?*

"Please."

He took a deep breath. "You still live off Spring Creek Road?"

She nodded. "Just after the Burner Towing Company."

"I know the place. I'll visit after lunch."

Nancy looked into the distance beyond Jimmy. When she spoke again, her voice cracked. "I never dreamed it would come to this."

"What if I would bring Miriam? She has a practical wisdom about things. I'd like her perspective." He hesitated as she continued to stare into the sky behind him. He found himself tempted to turn to follow her gaze, but he knew she was focused on something only she could sense: a slow pain that comes with months of fatiguing illness.

She nodded again without speaking. She turned and walked away, the normal pleasantries of hello and good-bye having been brushed aside by the seriousness of her request.

Jimmy watched her go and thought about how illness had crept in upon the Childress family uninvited, how it had slowly become everything in their life, defining their communication and every waking thought. He looked back at the headstone capping his secret past and resolved to make today a new start with Miriam.

He traveled home, contemplating what to say to his wife. He may have excelled at communication with his patients, but silence had ruled the Jenkins's home for the past few years. Sure they talked, the polite interchanges of strangers, but heart-to-heart communication faded from their lives soon after the lies began.

He found her in their bathroom, behind a locked door. Miriam was always so private. The fan was running. He knocked softly at the door. "Miriam, I'm home."

He heard her sigh. A deep gasping breath, the sound of someone heart-weary of the charades. Perhaps Miriam had been doing some soul-searching of her own. She did not speak.

"Look," he said, leaning his forehead against the door and closing his eyes. "I know we haven't really talked for a long time." He paused. "I want things to be different. I want to start over."

He knocked again, softer. "Miriam?"

He heard her sigh again.

"I don't blame you for being angry. I haven't been the husband I should."

He waited a moment longer. "Won't you come out so we can talk?" He sighed and tried the handle.

He decided he could wait. He leaned against the wall, defeated by her silence. Miriam could be stubborn. Well, downright brick-wall unyielding. But Jimmy supposed that it wouldn't be easy. He slid down the wall until he was seated on the carpet next to the door. If that's the way she wanted to play this, he could talk to the door, make his confession just like he did growing up in the Catholic Church.

Forgive me, Father, for I have sinned. Is that how I should start? Forgive me, Miriam.

He leaned against the wall and let his hand fall to his side against the door. But as he drew his hand along the lower edge of the closed door, he startled. Something sharp had scratched his hand as he pulled it along the carpet. *What?* Something was sticking out from beneath the door.

He squinted to see the tip of a finger, a long, red-painted nail that belonged to Miriam. He gasped and withdrew his finger. "Honey!" He reached out and touched it, then gave it a little tug. "Miriam!" He stood and shook the door. "Miriam, speak to me!"

He rested his ear against the door. Her breathing was coarse and deep. "Miriam!"

He shook the doorknob again, cursing.

He ran to the front door and retrieved a key hanging on a small rack. Back at the bathroom, he unlocked the door and pushed it open against the weight of his wife's body. She was sprawled on the floor wearing only a nightgown, facedown against the tile with her arms over her head and one hand extended to the undersurface of the door. Instinctively, he shifted his focus, doing a rapid assessment of her breathing and pulse. Respirations deep and gasping, pulse 120 and thready. Her pupils were wide, her gaze unfocused.

He stumbled out of the bathroom to a phone on the nightstand. He dialed 911.

"Nine-one-one. What is the nature of your emergency?"

"It's my wife," he yelled. "She's unconscious!"

Chapter Three

The afternoon came and went as Nancy and Richard Childress waited for Dr. Jenkins.

"I don't think he's coming," Richard said, his voice just above a whisper.

Nancy rubbed a warm washcloth over her husband's back and dipped it into a small basin. "Maybe I misjudged him."

With arms made strong by caring for him, she lifted him to get off his diaper.

She turned her head away from the putrid smell of his diarrhea. When she looked back, she frowned. "There's blood in it again."

"Careful," he said as she pulled the diaper away.

She wiped him with the cloth, wincing for him as she blotted the mucus away from his buttocks. A waitress by trade, she'd gotten her nursing skills the hard way, by cleaning and dressing her husband's wounds as the colon cancer ravaged his body and robbed his strength.

"There," she said, attaching the sticky tape to secure a new diaper.

"I hoped Dr. Jenkins might feel differently than Dr. McCall."

"Should I call him?"

Richard shook his head.

Nancy walked around to face him and touched his brow with her hand. The whites of his eyes were yellowing, a sign that the cancer was taking over his liver. "It's time for *Wheel of Fortune.* Shall I turn it on?"

Another shake of his head.

"Do you feel like listening to a book? I can read another chapter of— "

He groaned, interrupting her question. "Just help me get back in my chair. It's easier to nap there."

She nodded and assisted him to the recliner they'd positioned next to the bed. He was too weak to walk but could help bear weight to pivot into his chair. Once he was seated, she shifted his weight so that his buttocks were in the opening of an inflatable donut cushion.

With that, Richard closed his eyes, and Nancy plodded to the front room, where she lifted a frayed curtain from the front window. *Come on, Dr. Jenkins. You were my only hope.*

Claire finished work at the Stoney Creek Family Practice Clinic by six and groaned as she mailed a student loan payment that was two days overdue. Having finished medical school $120,000 in debt, she'd begun the slow process of digging out of her financial misery. *Let's see, at this rate, I'll have this loan paid off by the time I'm fifty-three ... if Huntington's doesn't strike me before that.*

She punched the pound symbol followed by a "3" on her cell phone and smiled. *At least I know John Cerelli doesn't plan to marry me for my money.*

John answered after the first ring. "Hello."

"Hi, sweetie. I'm on my way to see Daddy. I just wanted to see how you're doing."

"Rehab is boring, Claire. Are you sure you can't talk my orthopedic surgeon into letting me drive? I'm getting stir-crazy."

"You're not roping me into that, cowboy."

She heard him sigh, then ask, his voice quiet, "And what about you? When you left on Sunday, you looked like you'd seen a ghost."

She remembered the moment too clearly. She'd been trying to leave for fifteen minutes. John's kisses had moved from good-bye to slow and dangerous. An eerie anxiety seized her. It was more than a prick of her conscience. This was a body memory, a dread she didn't understand. She stiff-armed him and pulled away.

"I'm okay, John, really. I think I put so much of my energy into making sure you were okay that I haven't completely put the attack out of my mind."

"Della told me about the gun."

Claire hesitated. "It helps me sleep, that's all. John, it's not like I was really raped or anything. He didn't even ... well, you know."

"He attacked you in the night, in your own bed. He ripped your clothing. He— "

"Stop it."

Another heavy sigh. John wasn't happy.

Claire slowed to turn into the lane leading up the hill to Pleasant View Home. "I've invited Kyle and Margo to a cookout Sunday afternoon. I want you to have a chance to spend some time with my family."

"Sure."

She heard him tapping the phone with his fingers, a sure sign that he was irritated with her change of subject. "I'm at Wally's place. I've gotta go."

"Sure." The one-word answer of a frustrated male.

She pulled her Beetle into the closest open parking spot. "Be patient, John. If it makes any difference, I'll admit it. I know I need some help working through this whole attack thing. I just wanted it all to go away." Her voice thickened. "I have the name of a counselor. I'll call her tonight."

"That's my Claire. You aren't one to run from a fight. I love you."

She sniffed. "You too."

Claire hung up and took a deep breath. Dabbing her eyes, she studied herself in the rearview mirror. *I'm going to bed early tonight. I just hope the dreams will stay away.*

Once inside, she inhaled the clinical deodorizer that typified the nursing home and walked the hallway to her father's room. Even before entering, she could hear his legs whistling their way across the sheets. She watched him from the doorway, his little world framed by the padded railings on his bed. He was a man in constant motion, his arms, legs, and head in rebellion against the brain that once controlled them.

She'd given up trying to embrace him. A kiss with Wally was a black eye waiting to happen. Instead, she stood back and tussled his hair. "Hi, Daddy."

His eyes seemed to flash recognition of her voice. He was concentration-camp thin, his constant movement now burning more calories than he was able to consume. A glass of thickened lemonade sat on a table by his bed. She turned a crank at the foot of the bed to elevate his head. "There. Want something to drink?"

She didn't expect an answer. Wally may decide to talk today, or next week. In the meantime, Claire would continue, talking as if he understood.

She shoved the end of a straw into his mouth, carefully guarding the lemonade container from his hands. He slurped the thickened liquid, pausing several times when his swallowing muscles refused to obey.

She kept her voice firm and steady. "John and I have picked a day for the wedding. How does the first Saturday in May sound?" She paused and sat down in a chair beside the bed. "I hope the weather will be warm enough. Spring is so unpredictable here, you know."

She crossed her legs. "John would like to get married tomorrow, but I told him to quit whining. Just like a man to rush through the most important time of my life, huh?

"Work is about the same. I'm busier than ever. It seemed like even that story in the paper about a rapist targeting my patients wasn't enough to scare them away. I was hoping for a little breather.

"John is doing so well with his rehab. He doesn't really need his cane anymore. He just uses it for long walks."

Wally coughed, apparently choking on a little bit of lemonade that just made it to his throat. Claire wiped his mouth and frowned. "There. Feel better?"

She sat back down. "Kyle and Margo are coming down to our place on Sunday. Won't that be nice? I want John to get to know his future nieces. He and Kyle haven't really hit it off, but I think it's because they haven't had a chance to talk."

As Claire rambled on, she had the sudden thought that talking to Wally felt like prayer, all one-sided, and her hand went to her mouth in dismay. *Oh, God, I know prayer isn't like that at all!*

She finally tired of telling him about the local happenings and sat quietly, paging through a *Reader's Digest* that Della had left behind.

When she stood to leave, her father spoke for the first time. "Cl–cl–claire."

"Yes, Daddy." She touched his ashen face, which was wet with perspiration from his constant dance.

The cadence of his speech was halted, as he struggled to control the uncontrollable relationship between his breathing and his voice box. The frustration often drove Wally to complete silence, or to aggression and anger at his inability to speak.

Claire was prepared to have him repeat the words until she understood. If he was going to speak, she would be patient to help him communicate. But today, when the words finally tumbled out, it was as if he suddenly dislodged a boulder from its perch atop a hill, sending it down in one speeding event.

He slurred, "I want to die."

That evening Kyle Stevens brought a bouquet to Margo and planted a noisy kiss on the foreheads of his three daughters, Kelly, Casey, and Kristen.

Margo looked on from the kitchen as her gut tightened. Displays like this were too typical for her husband, a product of his struggle with self-esteem. It was a pattern she'd seen before. Early in their marriage Kyle spent lavishly on her to make up for their fights. Then, earlier this year, when he'd learned of Margo's risk for the Huntington's disease gene, he'd had a brief affair with a college coed. When Margo tested negative for the HD gene and Kyle wanted back in, she'd relented, partly because of their children, but also because she still loved the man who'd swept her away from her dysfunctional family. Predictably, a week after Kyle's return, Margo found a new minivan in the driveway and a husband who seemed willing to give anything to buy her affection again.

It had taken months of counseling with Phil Carlson from Community Chapel to help them come to an understanding that would serve as a foundation for a new relationship. Kyle even showed some interest in faith, but struggled with the concept of grace, seeming more comfortable in his work-harder, work-longer-to-please-God mentality. Margo saw the same attitude mirrored in his relationship to her. He couldn't seem to comprehend that she could be willing to give her love away.

For Margo, forgiveness of her husband's affair hadn't come without tears. After drawing clear boundaries, she'd let Kyle back into her life and willed herself to love him again. In the end, it was as if her own belief in a forgiving God seemed tied in some way to her ability to forgive her husband. If God could really allow her to forgive Kyle, to *really* forgive him, then maybe God could forgive her too.

So now, as she saw the flowers in his hand, she found herself wondering. *Is it devotion? Or another installment to purchase my love? Or has he done something else to test my mercy?*

He kissed her.

"You shouldn't have," she said, taking the flowers from his hand.

"I know."

"We can't afford it, silly."

Kyle opened the refrigerator and frowned. "Relax. Someday, you'll inherit enough for me to bring home flowers every day."

"Do you know how much it costs for Wally to live in Pleasant View Home for just one week?" She placed the flower arrangement on the kitchen table. "We'll be lucky if anything is left."

Kyle raised his eyebrows but didn't reply.

Margo sighed and watched him disappear into the den to read the paper. She didn't question him about why he'd brought the flowers in the first place. She knew he had a debtor's mentality. She worried he'd never get over it in his struggle to believe in a loving God.

She leaned over and sampled the fragrance of the bouquet. *Maybe I should stop worrying why he buys me flowers and start worrying that he might stop trying to keep me in love.*

Bracing for the next standoff she'd anticipated, she opened a bottle of beer, an offering to soften the impact. As she handed him the beer, she kissed his cheek. "I accepted an invitation for a barbecue with Claire and John at Mom's on Sunday."

She scurried back to the kitchen as she listened to him groan. Opening the oven to retrieve a baking pizza, she heard him say, "At least Wally won't be there."

Della's hands were on her hips. "That's it? That's all he said?"

"The only words he spoke during my whole visit." Claire shook her head. "He's depressed."

"Who wouldn't be?"

Claire thought of the life her father lived, trapped inside a body in constant motion. It had been months since he was able to walk, and years before that since he could walk and speak normally. Inevitably, when she thought of her father's life, her mind traced a well-worn path to a dread of her own future. As a carrier of the same gene that produced his agony, every new misery he manifested thrust a dagger of fear into her own heart.

Claire pulled herself back from the downhill slope of self-pity. "Is he still taking an antidepressant?"

"I think so. Although the nurses say he doesn't swallow the pills very well."

"He's going to die soon. I watched him choke on his own spit today. It's only a matter of time before he gets another bout of pneumonia."

"If he's going to die soon anyway, why not— "

The phone interrupted Della's thought. Claire held up her hand, not wanting her mother to finish the sentence. She watched as Della picked up the phone.

"Hello."

Della's hand went to her open mouth. "Oh, Jimmy, that's terrible ... When? ... Okay." Della seemed to hesitate. "Bye."

"Mom, what is it?"

She replaced the phone in the cradle. "That was Jimmy Jenkins. His wife just died."

After sunset, Nancy Childress stopped by the Food Mart at the local Exxon to pick up milk, bread, and adult diapers. It was a special-order item, but Ned Brown had always been willing to go out of his way to help an old friend. On her way home, she swung by Hillcrest Drive and saw that Dr. Jenkins's place was brightly lit. In fact, the whole block seemed abuzz. Cars lined the street like Nancy hadn't remembered since the July Fourth fireworks display at the Ruritan Club.

She slowed, noting the extra cars in the driveway. *Richard always loved a good party.*

She looked at the stack of diapers on the passenger seat, conscious of a growing lump in her throat. She inched along, watching as a man escorted a woman carrying a casserole dish across the lawn. Then she sighed and sped off into the night.

Chapter Four

The last guest left condolences and a casserole at eleven, leaving Jimmy amazed at the speed of small-town hospitality. He'd cared for the whole town for so long, it seemed that half of them had shown up just to let him know they cared.

He looked at the dining table and shook his head. He had enough food to feed the football team at Ashby High School. Patsy Underwood, a patient he'd seen through twenty years of hypertension, left country-ham biscuits. Jimmy stretched plastic wrap across the plate. *I told her to cut back on the salt.* Barb and Sam Stackhouse, both of whom had been on twelve-hundred-calorie diets since he'd retired, brought three dozen cookies. "It's nothing," she said, resting her hand on her generous waist. "I keep 'em in the freezer so I'm always ready." *No wonder all the diets I prescribed never worked.*

He walked from room to room aware of every little noise. The creak of the old oak kitchen floor. The ticking of the grandfather clock. The barking of the neighbor's dog. How often had he walked these same rooms after Miriam had gone to bed, and yet now, the rooms seemed larger, empty without her. He touched the edge of a picture frame. Miriam posing next to the door of the motor home they'd purchased, but not yet used.

At one, he hung his pants and shirt on a hanger, just as Miriam would have wanted. Then he lay on their king-sized bed, pulled her pillow to his face, and wept.

Claire startled awake at two, launched into alertness by nighttime terror. She reached for the pistol and pulled it to her side, gripping it tightly until the feeling passed.

Eyes open, she traced the outline of her small room. Ceiling, corners, furniture, all the same as it had been for years. Except for the absence of posters on the wall, this room hadn't changed significantly since she'd left home nearly a dozen years before.

She set the gun aside and sat up, rubbing the back of her neck. A memory long pushed away, buried by will or her own defenses, seemed to perch beside her, just beyond reach. She touched the surface of the bed, the same bed where just a few weeks before, she had been brutally yanked from slumber by a man in her employ. Although his attack had been unsuccessful in its violent intent, it had wormed its way beneath the cap she'd kept on a bottle of old hurt.

Something else had happened here, something dark, which whispered its pain from a lost time. A violation of trust? She closed her eyes and stared into the darkness of her eyelids, willing herself to see images from the past that held the secret to the dread that floated within her.

Nausea prodded her to her feet. She walked to the bathroom and lowered herself over the commode. After she surrendered her stomach's contents to the bowl, she was struck again by a sense of familiarity with an event long hidden. *I was sick here that night too.*

She remembered the pain. A throbbing headache. The fuzziness of a hangover. Feeling the strain in her lower abdomen from vomiting so hard. *Or was it more than that?*

It was an evening of teenaged rebellion when her disdain for her father's drinking was overcome by her own desire to escape the torture that her home life had become. It was before she'd dropped out of school. Before she'd moved in to take care of Grandma Newby.

Claire looked around the bathroom from her position with her head just above the commode. From that angle, the room felt small, oppressive. She remembered seeing that the undersurface of the blue cabinet had never been painted. She remembered vowing that she'd never ever lose a night in the fog of drink.

She walked back and studied her room from the doorway. *I remember going out with Tommy Gaines and Shelby Williams. Shelby's brother Grant was old enough to buy beer. He gave me cheap wine and told me he had things he wanted to teach me.*

Claire rubbed her eyes. *I remember giggling out of control. Kissing Grant while lying in the bed of their pickup.*

I remember slapping him and telling him to quit.

But I don't remember getting home.

At 6:00 a.m., a dull ache in John Cerelli's left hip nudged him from sleep. Although the acute pain from his femur fracture was gone, he had more stiffness in his hip than before the accident. If he tried to sleep more than six or seven hours, he had to get up and move around to work it out again.

He made strong black coffee and sipped while he logged on to check his e-mail. He had six e-mails from an AmiAmi@aol.com. They were from Ami, his secretarial assistant. Two were work related, reminders to the sales force of upcoming meetings. One was a forward, a stupid message he was to send to five friends to ensure good fortune. Three were personal. One was a wish for his rapid recovery, one a positive thought for the day, and one just said "thinking of you." John highlighted each letter and pressed *delete.*

Then he held out his father's digital camera at arm's length, took a mug shot of himself with a goofy grin, and downloaded it on an e-mail to Claire. He entitled it "My new haircut" and typed a quick note to "My dearest fiancée" and signed it "Love, John 'the Barber' Cerelli."

He smiled. That should brighten Claire's morning.

Claire opened her eyes to the sound of Della in the kitchen. The night was over. She took inventory. The tightness in her gut was gone, but the impression of suppressed pain remained. She looked over at the array of weaponry on her nightstand and felt a stab of remorse. *We've been through so much together, God. You'd think with each new trial I'd begin, instead of just ending, by trusting in you.* "Forgive me," she whispered as she unloaded the pistol and returned it to a box on the shelf of her mother's closet.

With that, she returned to her bed and opened her Bible. She ran her fingers over the inside cover where she'd copied something from C. S. Lewis. She'd dated the quotation two weeks before she learned she carried the Huntington's disease gene. "We are not necessarily doubting that God will do the best for us; we are wondering how painful the best will turn out to be."

She had penned a reference beneath it. Isaiah 64:8. Claire turned to the passage and prayed the words she read there. "I am the clay. You are the potter. I am the work of your hands." She paused, and then added, "Give me strength to accept your way." She read for a few more minutes until a renewed peace settled into her road-weary soul.

When she walked into the kitchen a minute later, Della smiled. "You look rested."

Claire shrugged. "It wasn't the hours in bed that did the trick." She set her Bible on the table. "Trust."

"That's it?"

Claire poured creamer into a tall mug of steaming coffee. "What do you mean, that's it?" She laughed. "Sometimes I wonder if I'll ever face a difficulty without the anxiety that comes from taking it on in my own strength."

Della shook her head. "Not if you're like your mom, you won't."

Claire leaned over and kissed her mother's head. "I'd be thankful if I turned out like you." She lifted a strand of hair. "What's this? The bombshell Della McCall is finally going to gray?"

Della batted her away. "Oh, stop."

Claire laughed again as she pulled out a loaf of bread to make toast.

"I want to visit Jimmy Jenkins today. Shall I wait until after work so you can go with me?"

Claire thought for a moment. "No. Go without me." *Now that I know just what you two went through, I find it hard to talk to him.*

Kyle finished his morning coffee, picked up his keys, and had his hand on the doorknob when he heard Margo. "Do you mind stopping for a few things after work? There's a list on the refrigerator."

He groaned. "Whatever."

"Kelly has a soccer game in Carlisle at six. I suppose I could go after that."

"No. I'll stop." He hesitated. "Maybe I'll see you at the game."

He looked back at the bouquet on the kitchen table. *Would she forgive me if she knew?*

He grabbed the list from the refrigerator door and glanced at the items. *Maybe I'll grab another bunch of cut flowers too. That's bound to please.*

Midmorning, after two well-baby checks and a hypertension medication adjustment, Brian Dickson interrupted Claire's schedule. Brian, a twelve-year-old extreme skateboarder-wannabe, performed a 360 face-plant onto the edge of a Fisher's Retreat fireplug. After thirty minutes, Claire smiled at her job and pulled off her gloves.

"How many stitches did I get?"

Claire counted. "Fourteen."

Brian closed his fist. "Cool."

His mother sounded alarmed. "Fourteen?"

Claire nodded and pointed to a fine line above her patient's right eye. "But most of his scar is going to be hidden here in his eyebrow. No cosmetic worry for a tough guy like Brian."

She handed Ms. Dickson a prescription for an antibiotic and checked the chart to see that Brian was up-to-date on his tetanus prophylaxis.

Outside the room, Claire's nurse drew a line through a name on the daily patient list. "Good news," Lucy said. "We had two no-shows, so you're still on schedule."

Claire nodded. Whereas she might make most of the clinical decisions, she counted on Lucy to point her in the right direction. She raised her eyes in a question.

Lucy answered the unspoken request. "Yes, you can have five minutes." Then she whispered, too quiet for the patient in the next exam room to hear, "The coffee's fresh."

Claire cleared her throat. "You've worked in this community a lot longer than I have. Do you know of a Joanne Phillips?"

Lucy nodded. "Dr. Jenkins referred patients to her for counseling. I know he liked her, but I never had a chance to meet her."

Claire mouthed a silent "Thank you" and retreated to her office. If this counselor was good enough for Jimmy Jenkins, she'd be good enough for Claire. She sat at her desk and called the number on the business card labeled "Women Care."

"Hello, Joanne Phillips."

"This is Dr. Claire McCall. I received a letter describing a new counseling service for victims of sexual assault."

"Is this about a patient referral?"

"Well, yes, but, well, it's for me."

The voice sounded young. Too young. But soft, concerned. "Oh, well, I'd be glad to set up a time when we could talk."

"My work usually occupies me up until five. I could make it to Brighton by six if you ever set up evening appointments."

"Why don't I come to you? You're over in Stoney Creek, is that right?"

"Yes, but—"

"I like seeing physicians on their own turf. As a rule, they feel more relaxed. I'd like to come to your office, if that's okay."

"Sure."

"Is Thursday alright?"

"Anytime after five."

"I know the area. You're at the Stoney Creek Family Practice Clinic?"

"That's right."

"Great. I'll be there." She paused. "And, Doctor, don't worry. This will all be very low-key."

Claire nodded, willing the knot in her gut to dissolve. "Okay."

Chapter Five

Della arrived on Jimmy's doorstep just as he opened the door. "Oh," he said. "I was just on my way out." He paused, then stepped back. "Come in."

"I don't want to interfere."

"Oh, it's nothing. I was just— " He took off his hat. "Well . . ." He motioned her inside. "Maybe I should explain."

She held up a plate of cheese and crackers. "I thought maybe you'd have guests to feed."

"I think you hit a lull in the parade."

"I just came to say how sorry I am." Her eyes met his.

He nodded and cleared his throat. "Sure."

She walked to the kitchen and put the covered plate in a crowded refrigerator. When she looked up, he was staring at her from the entrance to the dining room. "So how are you?"

He seemed to know better than to just say "fine." He looked down. "Shocked." He looked around. "I can't believe she's gone." He looked at his watch.

Della didn't know what to say. "I should go."

He seemed to be puzzling over something. "Maybe you could help me."

Della smiled. "Of course."

He sighed. "I was on my way to see Richard and Nancy Childress. Maybe you could go with me. Help me think through something."

Della sat at a wooden kitchen chair. "I don't understand."

He placed his hands on the back of a chair. His knuckles trembled, then blanched as he gripped the chair back. "I promised I'd go to see them yesterday, but then, well . . ." His voice weakened. "Anyway, in the midst of everything, I forgot about my commitment. I need to get out, to think about something else, so I thought I'd just go see them. I was going to take Miriam yesterday."

"Okay." She studied him for a moment. He was uncharacteristically fidgety. Perhaps it was just the shock of losing his wife. "Are you sure you want to make a social visit? I mean now? They'd understand. You just— "

"Richard is very sick, Della. His wife claims he just wants to die."

"Are you sure you're up to encouraging him?"

"Della, Nancy asked me to help Richard die."

Her hand went to her mouth. "Are you? I mean, what— "

"I just told them I'd come by to see him. I wanted to bring Miriam for her opinion." He shuffled his feet. "You've faced terminal illness with Wally." He looked up. "Would you want to go along?"

"Jimmy, are you sure you want to think about this now?"

He ran his hand through his silver hair. "Della, if anything, I need to think about something else besides Miriam right now." He picked up his hat. "But I'd understand if you were uncomfortable. You'd be crazy to get involved." He shrugged and faked a smile. "I should get going. I'm sure the break in the parade won't last long."

Della stood. "Wait up, Jimmy. I'm coming with you."

Looking like a statue, Nancy Childress stood on the front steps of the white-sided ranch house. Her cheeks were pale from too little sun and the apron around her waist was stained with ketchup or worse. She didn't smile when they arrived. She just ushered them into the front room and closed the door. Della knew of Nancy's devotion to her husband. The way the town talked, she practically worshiped the man who'd rescued the single mother a decade before. The lines on her forehead belied her age, but witnessed to the strain of dealing with an abusive first husband and a schizophrenic daughter.

The room was dim, the light of the morning sun blocked by yellowed venetian blinds. The air carried the musty scent of illness and sweat. Della edged closer to a small window in the front door and squinted toward an empty hospital bed in the center of the room. Della's eyes met Nancy's as Jimmy made the introduction.

"Nancy, this is Della McCall. She's a friend. Her husband has been ill for a long time. I thought she might be able to help me."

She nodded slowly. "Richard's been having headaches. He likes it dark." She looked at Jimmy. "Dr. Jenkins, this is a bad time for you. You shouldn't be having to think about us when— "

Jimmy held up both hands. "Nancy, it's okay. I needed to get out of the house. Really." He offered a half smile. "How's your daughter?"

Della watched as the creases deepened from the corners of Nancy's eyes. "Hard to tell with her. She tells me she's got a boyfriend now. A new job." She shook her head. "I'm afraid she's still not right. Delusions, her shrink says."

"Too bad," Jimmy muttered.

"She don't come around much. Richard ain't her real father, you know. But he treated her like she was his own. If you ask me, I'd say most of her problems are because of the things her biological father did to her."

Jimmy let the comment fall. The trio stood in the little room as silence gathered around them. Nancy didn't seem to know where to start. She pointed to a couch crowded up against the front wall by the bed. "Thanks for coming. Have a seat."

Della cleared her throat and sat on the edge of the old couch next to a blue absorbent pad that occupied the center. Nancy pulled the pad away. "Sometimes Richard likes to lay on the couch when he tires of being in the bed."

Della felt like an intruder. She examined the couch cushion beside her and wondered about whatever secretion the pad was supposed to collect.

Nancy touched the tip of her chin with her hand. "McCall?" She said the name slowly as if trying to make a connection.

"Dr. McCall's mother," Jimmy said.

Nancy straightened. She diverted her eyes from Della and spoke to Jimmy. "You should have come alone."

Della stood. "I can wait in the car if—"

Jimmy shook his head. "I asked her to come."

"Dr. McCall didn't look too kindly on our request. She refused to help us."

Della felt her dander rising. "Jimmy, I'd better go."

She turned as Jimmy gripped her arm. "No." He looked at Nancy. "Anything that happens here is just between us. Dr. McCall won't know anything about this." His eyes bore in on Della's.

She nodded. "Of course." Della's stomach knotted. "It's confidential, just like any doctor visit."

Nancy sat on the edge of the hospital bed staring at her hands. She stayed quiet for a moment before looking at Della. "You can stay."

Della shuffled her feet and sat back down, careful to avoid the center cushion.

"Richard is in the bedroom. He divides his time between this bed and the one in the bedroom." She paused. "We should talk before you see him."

"Sure," Jimmy said.

Nancy began a saga of Richard's decline, beginning with a long battle with Crohn's disease, a bowel blockage, three surgeries, radiation, and chemotherapy. Della found her mind drifting as Nancy detailed the spread of colon cancer to his liver and his multiple visits to the oncologist. When Nancy began to describe his vomiting and diarrhea and the drainage from openings near her husband's buttocks, Della forced her mind away, willing her own stomach to obey. She closed her eyes. *Mountain views with fresh air, the salt smell of the ocean in the morning, meadows with spring flowers.*

Nancy's voice intruded. "Sometimes he vomits until I see blood ..."

Riding in a convertible with the top down through the country.

"He cries every time I have to clean the raw areas of ..."

Crisp autumn, sweater weather with morning frost.

"... his body is so thin that the diapers won't even conform to hold in the ..."

Della put her hand to her mouth. Her diversion tactic had been overcome. Not knowing where the bathroom was, but knowing she needed to be somewhere quick, she broke for the front door and the fresh air beyond.

Outside, she lowered her head behind a bayberry bush and surrendered her morning coffee. A few moments later, Jimmy crouched beside her. "I'm sorry, Della."

Embarrassed, she spat into the mulch and wiped her mouth with a tissue. "I'm okay," she said. "I just didn't know what to expect." She looked up to see Nancy standing on the top of three steps.

Her face was without expression. "I'm sorry. I've kind of gotten used to things after so long."

Jimmy whispered, "Do you want to wait in the car?"

Della shook her head. "No. I'm okay now." She hesitated. "I feel better."

They walked back into the house, following Nancy down the hallway to the room where Richard lay. His skin was yellow gray, the whites of his eyes pumpkin orange. Della remembered pictures of starving children in Africa who looked vigorous compared to this. Bones on the side of his face seemed determined to erupt to the surface, tenting up the skin like moles in spring grass. He looked over at Jimmy and slowly raised a hand covered with purple blotches. "Hi, Doc."

Nancy looked at Jimmy. "It's been three years this month since you sent him to a surgeon in Carlisle."

"You're the one who diagnosed me, remember?" Richard said.

Jimmy nodded. He stepped closer. "Mind if I take a look?"

Della watched as Jimmy pulled down a sheet and raised up the shirt-tails of a tattered pajama top. Richard's stomach was bloated like a tick after a meal.

"Are you in pain?"

"Here," he said, placing his hand over his stomach. "Cramps all the time." His fetid breath hit Della's face as he coughed. She stepped back, wondering if she would need the bayberry bush again.

She edged closer to the doorway as Jimmy looked at Richard's back, diverting her eyes completely as she heard him pulling away the sticky tape of his diaper.

In a few minutes, they were done, and retreated to the front room. "I need some air," Della said.

Della sat on the front steps and waited, trying to make some sense out of Richard's current life. *Is a life like Richard's worth living?* She thought about Wally. *Is it ever right to hasten death to relieve suffering?*

She'd grown used to Wally's misery, but this was different. She stared unseeing across the yard. Was she shocked because of her newness to Richard's condition? Could she have grown calloused to her husband's grief? Confusion and despair played tag team against her belief in life's sanctity. *Why now, God? Why am I suddenly faced with another soul asking for death as a healing?*

Five minutes later, Jimmy emerged. He took a few deep breaths, coughed, and cleared his throat. She watched as he shook his head slowly and reached for her hand. He didn't speak. Instead, they drove away in a contemplative silence, with Richard's wretchedness hanging between them like an impenetrable fog.

Claire closed the clinic during the memorial service for Miriam Jenkins, expecting most of her patients felt loyal enough to Dr. Jenkins to pay tribute to his wife. She was right. As she sat in the back of the Presbyterian church, she recognized most of the people from the files at the clinic.

Miriam died from a ruptured cerebral aneurysm, a silent killer that had given the Jenkins no warning until its fatal rupture. Claire studied the backs of the heads that lined the pews. Odds would have it that at least one or two of them harbored a pea-sized bubble on a blood vessel that would seal their date with the grim reaper as well.

Claire had gone for the sake of her mother. And of course, as the new replacement physician for Dr. Jenkins, she supposed everyone expected her to be there. Certainly Jimmy Jenkins had been there for her over the years, cheering at Claire's basketball games, and providing her work in his office when she showed an interest in medicine.

It all seemed so odd to her now, looking back from the vantage point of the last year's discovery. As she'd diagnosed her father with Huntington's disease, it became important to trace blood inheritance of the illness from generation to generation. In doing so, she put to rest the folklore about the Stoney Creek curse, the mysterious illness that weaved its way through the families of the Apple Valley. In the middle of her search, her twin brother Clay died from injuries sustained in a car accident. During her review of his medical records, she made an unexpected discovery: Clay's blood type revealed that he could not have been fathered by Wally McCall. That, of course, prompted Claire to question Della about an affair. Her mother confessed to an intimate relationship with Jimmy Jenkins, the town's family doctor, but stopped short of providing the details. Claire's discovery initially gave her hope that she had also been fathered by Dr. Jenkins, and that in fact she may not be at risk for inheriting the Huntington's disease gene. But that was not to be. Further digging into her family's troubled past revealed that she and her twin had different fathers, a rare but possible situation because her mother slept with Wally and Jimmy within a few days' time. Knowing that her mother had kept a dark secret that was confessed only when forced, Claire's mind wandered through the possibilities. Who seduced whom? Was he a one-night stand or a regular lover?

Looking back with the new knowledge that Dr. Jenkins had fathered her twin brother, Clay, she felt funny about her connections with her long-time mentor. She respected him as a successful professional, but found that when she was around him, her mind drifted to questions about his relationship to her mother, questions that intrigued and troubled her. She told herself that she didn't need to know. She wanted to forgive, forget, and go on.

The service was one hour by the clock. Three of Miriam's favorite hymns. Memories by Janet Brown, a close friend. A tribute by Dr. Anderson, her pastor.

After the service, Claire answered Emma Harrison's questions about her bursitis and Fred Smith's need for home oxygen. After dodging a brittle diabetic who always wanted to show Claire her most recent blood sugars, she managed to give Jimmy Jenkins a polite hug and told him to stop by the office.

The afternoon was crowded with three work-ins who had food poisoning after a family reunion. At five, Claire exited an exam room to see Lucy. She wasn't smiling. The staff rarely did after five.

"Joanne Phillips is here. She claims to have an appointment to see you. I don't have her on the books and I told her we don't schedule after five."

"It's okay," Claire said. "Just send her back to my office. The staff can go." She lowered her voice. "It's a personal matter."

A few moments later, Claire looked up from her desk to see a young woman with shoulder-length dark hair, smartly dressed in business chic. She stood and extended her hand. "You must be Ms. Phillips."

She smiled. "Call me Joanne." Her eyes scanned the room. "Am I interrupting? Or are you ready to begin?"

Claire took a deep breath and shoved a file aside. "Ready." She winced. "I guess."

"Why don't we sit out here," she said, pulling around two chairs so they faced each other. "An open posture."

Joanne gestured to the other chair and sat. "I take it from our phone conversation the other day that you're dealing with some issues of your own?"

Claire nodded. "Perhaps you saw the story. It was splashed all over our local press. An employee of mine, Tyler Crutchfield, was taking advantage of young women who were physically disabled, several fresh from operations that made them vulnerable to attack." She paused. "I was his last victim."

Joanne opened a notebook and tapped a silver pen against her chin. "I did read about that."

"I fought back. He did not rape me."

"How is it affecting you now?"

Claire looked at the floor. "Trouble sleeping. He attacked me in my bed." She looked up and met Joanne's dark eyes. "I've been sleeping with a loaded gun on my nightstand."

"What else?"

"It's weird. It's like the whole experience has brought up a memory I'd shoved away, hoping to avoid."

"A memory?"

"Let's call it a partial memory. I remembered a night when I was about sixteen. I wasn't a big partier or anything. I'd grown up with an alcoholic father, so I'd tried to steer away from the stuff."

"What happened?"

"I remember getting some wine with some friends. I got totally smashed. I had no tolerance whatsoever. I don't remember even getting home."

"What's the first thing you remember?"

"I was sick in the bathroom. I remember looking up at the ceiling ... feeling pain ... thinking I'd gotten myself messed up. I remember crying because I thought my virginity may have been taken away."

"But you don't remember what happened?"

Claire shook her head. "I was so drunk."

"You think you may have been raped?"

"I know this sounds weird. But I've been having horrible dreams. A few nights ago, I sat up after a dream and I had this horrible déjà vu experience. It was like I knew something dark had happened to me in that place. It was so terrifying that it made me sick to my stomach. I went to the bathroom, and that's when the other memory came back."

"Claire, this isn't weird at all. It's very common for one bad experience to stimulate memories of other pain in our past." She leaned forward. "Let me see if I understand. You were attacked in your own bed a few weeks ago, but the rapist wasn't successful with you."

"Correct."

"But you have a vague sense that something else happened to you in that same place. You remember being sick and worrying that you may have been with a man, but not really remembering."

Claire nodded.

"Can you remember why you thought you may have been raped?"

Claire looked down, feeling reluctant to explain. "I remember waking up and someone was touching me. My breast." She pinched the bridge of her nose. "I'd never been with a man, you know, had sex before. So I didn't know what to expect. I wasn't sure."

"Were you bleeding?"

"A little."

"Did you tell anyone?"

Claire shook her head. "I just remember thinking I'd better not tell my mom."

"You were afraid?"

"I think so."

"What did you do?"

"Nothing. Well, I worried about it for a while. I wasn't sure what had happened, so I finally just put it behind me."

"Until now."

Claire looked up as Joanne reached for a small framed picture on her desk. Her eyes seemed to savor what she saw. "Your boyfriend, I take it?"

"My fiancé."

"How has the rape attempt affected him?" She ran her finger over the top of the frame. "Men can be funny about this kind of thing. Has he been angry? Jealous?"

"No. But he was badly injured in a car accident around the time of my attack. I think he's been pretty focused on getting better himself."

"How have your memories affected your relationship with him?"

"I'm not sure." She thought back to their last good-bye. "There was a time when we were kissing." Claire felt heat rise within her cheeks. "Anxiety suddenly seized me. I didn't understand it. I pushed him away."

"Maybe another memory trying to surface?"

Claire shrugged.

"What other men lived in your house during the time of your memory? Brothers, uncles, perhaps?"

"Only my father. My twin brother was living with a cousin at the time." Claire stared at her counselor. "Why?"

"I'm just trying to determine who may have had access to you in your own bed." She seemed to hesitate. "Sometimes those who are closest to us can hurt us the most."

The thought sickened Claire. She looked back to her hands in her lap. "So now what?"

"Realize a few things. You're safe now. Whatever memories are surfacing come from a long way off. Whatever hurt you then cannot hurt you now, unless you let it." She leaned forward and took Claire's hand. "You're in a safe place to remember. And whoever hurt you then is not hurting you now."

"So what do I do?"

"Give yourself plenty of time to remember. And give yourself permission to think about that night. For some reason, perhaps even as a defense against your own pain, you've chosen to forget. Give yourself permission to remember."

It sounded like psychological mumbo jumbo to Claire. She had been attracted to surgery because these were problems she could get her hands around. And for the same reason, she had avoided psychiatry. She mumbled the phrase back to Joanne. "Give myself permission to remember."

Joanne didn't hear the sarcasm. "Exactly."

Claire turned her hands palm up. "I'll try."

"It may help to spend time in the places that carry the clearest memories. Lie on the bathroom floor if that's what it takes."

Claire raised her eyebrows. She could just see Della walking in on her. She'd better keep the bathroom door locked.

"And concerning your boyfriend. Perhaps you ought to lay off the physical contact until you get this sorted out."

The advice seemed old-fashioned for such a chic professional. *But maybe old-fashioned is good.*

Joanne stood up. "You're going to get through this, Claire. Lots of women have. Can we meet again in two weeks?"

"Sure."

"Same time, same place."

Chapter Six

After work hours on Friday, Claire startled at the sound of a key in the back door. *Who could that be?* She initialed the lab result in her hand and set it in her out-box before standing in response to footfalls in the hall.

A second later, Jimmy Jenkins appeared. "Oh, Claire, I didn't realize you'd be working late."

"Just signing off on test results and finishing my dictation."

He nodded and fumbled with his keys for a moment before moving down the hall with his back toward Claire.

She followed, puzzled by his quiet manner. Normally, he'd have taken the opportunity to chat about old patients or ask how things were going. Perhaps he was overwhelmed because of Miriam's death.

He opened a large closet where the clinic kept its drug supplies.

She leaned against the wall to appear casual. "How are you doing, Jimmy?"

He glanced over his shoulder as if surprised that she would bother watching him. "Fine, really." He opened the lock on the refrigerator. "I'm just here to get some medicine for a friend."

She watched as he picked up a vial of morphine from a small box. He squinted at the label, then put the vial back in its container and lifted the whole box.

"That's a lot of morphine for one patient." She stepped forward as he locked the refrigerator and backed out of the closet. "You're not planning to—"

He must have read the alarm in her eyes. He smiled. Too broadly. "Oh no, Claire. It's not for me." He reached in his pocket and pulled out a crumpled prescription. "This is for the patient record."

She took the paper and read the script he'd penned for Richard Childress. It was written to give one to five milligrams every thirty minutes as needed for pain. She shook her head. "Jimmy, I don't know how much you know about Richard. He's very depressed. This amount of morphine in his hands could be dangerous."

"I know what I'm doing, Claire. I didn't really want to get you involved."

"I'm already involved. He's a patient of this clinic."

"And they called me for help." He took a deep breath. "Look, if you need to know, they called me because I've treated Ricky for years. I made the diagnosis of his cancer. They just ... well, they just didn't think you were being responsive to their needs."

"He wants to die."

"He doesn't want to suffer."

"So deal with his pain."

"That's what I'm doing. Read the prescription. That dose isn't even close to lethal."

"So why dispense so much? And why give it to them?"

"They have no insurance. They are living off of what little she can make part-time at McCall Shoes." He said *McCall Shoes* as if he tasted sour candy.

Claire stepped back, uncomfortable challenging her mentor. She touched her forehead and sighed. "Look, there are other issues here. I'm concerned about you. You've given up your malpractice insurance. If you write a prescription and something goes wrong, a lawsuit could bring down the whole practice."

He nodded. "Then there goes everything I built for this community."

And there goes my job!

She watched as his knuckles seemed to whiten over the box of narcotics. "There is another option, Claire. One that would protect the practice."

She locked eyes with him.

"You write the prescription, sign it, and put it in his record. Document that you are writing the prescription for pain relief only." He paused. "Then you're covered."

She puffed her cheeks and exhaled slowly with her lips pursed. "I don't know."

He touched her shoulder. "I'm going to tell them exactly what a safe dose is."

She nodded, knowing that the unspoken double meaning would be communicated. *If they know the safe dose, they will know a lethal one.*

"He's terminal soon, Claire."

She plodded to the file room and pulled Richard Childress's file. She couldn't let Dr. Jenkins write a prescription, especially one like this when he had no malpractice coverage. After scribbling down the prescription, she made an entry in the chart. *This will be the last entry in this file.* Her eyes met Jimmy's again. "Please, please tell them only to use this dose." She shook her head, knowing she was playing a dangerous game with her conscience. *It's only for pain relief.* She held out her hand. "You've given him too much. They can pick up some more in a few days."

Jimmy tightened his grip around the small package. "If he uses five milligrams at a time, this only represents twenty doses. He'll be through that in no time." With that, he turned, but paused at the door. "Thanks, Claire. You've done the right thing."

"He's weaker today," Nancy said.

Jimmy watched as Richard seemed to work for every breath. "It won't be long now."

Richard tipped his head in Jimmy's direction as tears spilled on Nancy's cheeks.

Jimmy handed her a small paper sack. "Here's the pain medicine. A milligram or two should be enough to keep him comfortable if you give it straight in a vein. You can use up to ten milligrams if you give it in the muscle." Jimmy pushed away the sheet and pinched up the skinny flesh on the top of Richard's yellowing thigh. "Here."

She nodded.

"I've included some syringes and needles. Are you sure you can do this?"

"My daughter taught me how to give intravenous injections when Richard had pneumonia. She was in nursing school when she ..." Her voice weakened.

Jimmy put his hand on Nancy's shoulder. "It's okay." He remembered well how Nancy's daughter had her first psychotic episode during her first clinical year at Brighton University. She was home on vacation when Nancy brought her by the office, a young woman completely out of touch with reality.

He looked up when Nancy squeezed his arm. "You should get back to your family."

He nodded. "It's a zoo over there," he said, smiling. "My brother from Michigan brought his three boys." He shook his head. "I've forgotten how much teenagers eat."

Not knowing what to say, he took a deep breath and reached for Richard's hand.

Richard looked up, his eyes locking on Jimmy's. He communicated with a weak hand squeeze what he couldn't verbalize.

Perhaps it was the fact that he sensed death was standing at the door. Perhaps it was the stress of dealing or not dealing with his wife's sudden departure, but regardless, Jimmy suddenly found himself on the edge of tears. His throat tightened. He squeezed Richard's hand and looked away.

Pulling his hand away, he backed toward the doorway. He steadied his voice against the sorrow that rippled through his surface calm. "Say everything you need to say, Nancy."

She lifted her hand to her mouth.

"You won't have many chances to get it right."

That evening, Della found herself in the familiar role of servant. She'd stopped by Jimmy's place to pick up her plate, began talking to the neighbors and Jimmy's brother, and soon was sharing in the abundance of food which had been contributed by nearly everyone in Stoney Creek. Now she had retreated to a comfortable spot for her, the kitchen sink.

She scrubbed a persistent bit of crusted macaroni from the bottom of a casserole dish and looked up as Jimmy entered. Noise from the other room mingled with the clink and splash of her work. It seemed that his nephews had come to comfort their uncle, but found it more interesting to sit in front of Jimmy's widescreen TV. "You have a nice family."

He leaned against the counter and sipped a glass of wine. "I do. But tomorrow I'm giving them the boot." He laughed.

She turned her attention back to the dishes, thankful to have something to occupy her hands. She glanced at Jimmy, aware that he seemed to be watching her. "Don't worry," she said. "I'm getting them clean."

"No, it's not that." He became quiet, looking at his glass as he swirled his drink.

She found herself wishing that his talkative brother Bob would join them. She didn't know what to say to fill the silence between them.

"It's ironic."

"What?"

"I kept the secret about us from Miriam for so many years."

"It was a long time ago, Jimmy. We don't need to talk— "

"I finally knew that the right thing to do was to 'fess up. Work on opening up communication with Miriam so we could go forward in our retirement years with a fresh start." He sipped from the goblet in his hand. "So I came home and talked to Miriam through the bathroom door." He sniffed. "I thought she was mad at me, that she wasn't talking back because she was angry." His hand trembled as he set the glass on the counter. "But she was on the floor the whole time." He wiped the back of his hand against his nose and his voice dissolved as he spoke again. "I wanted her to forgive me, but she never heard me say, 'I'm sorry.' "

She squeezed the water from her dishrag, laid it in the sink, and opened her arms to receive him. There, with him falling against her chest, she hesitated, then placed her wet hands against his back. She held him as he wept, a man broken by loss and by his too-little-too-late repentance.

She looked up to see Bob in the doorway of the kitchen. Their eyes met before she closed hers and laid her head on Jimmy's, letting him purge his grief in deep, hot sobs against her neck.

Chapter Seven

Outside of town, down Spring Creek Road, just beyond the corrugated steel fence surrounding Burner Towing Company, the serene appearance of the Childress home belied the sorrow within. Nancy watched as her husband's gasps for breath slowed to a stop. She held his head in her lap, stroking his forehead and promising she'd see him again. Then, mechanically, she rose and called Lindsey's Funeral Home.

After that, praying that the stress of Richard's loss wouldn't break her daughter's fragile psyche, she telephoned to give the news.

"Hello."

"Ami, it's Mom." Her voice quivered.

"W–what's wrong? Is it Richard?"

"Yes, honey. He just died."

She listened as her daughter gasped.

"It will be okay. We all expected the end was near."

Her daughter sniffed. "I know. I know. Should I come over?"

"No. I think not right now. I'll let you know about a memorial service."

Silence separated them. Nancy could hear her daughter cry.

"It's going to be fine. I'll be fine." She listened for a response. "You'll be fine. He told me he loved you just before he left."

"Oh, Mom."

Nancy pressed the phone into her forehead and closed her eyes, as if she could hold back the tears. "I'd better go. I have some other calls to make."

"Okay, see you soon."

Nancy set the phone in its cradle, looked back at the body in the hospital bed, and cried.

Claire pushed aside another bridal catalog and moaned. "I didn't know it was going to be this expensive."

Della smiled and looked toward the front of the Bridal Gallery that bustled with Saturday morning clients. "Just take a take a deep breath, honey. You're the only one I get to plan a wedding for. I don't want to have regrets because we cut every corner."

"Tell me that again after you've been eating rice and beans for a month."

She watched as Della's forehead wrinkled for a moment until she met Claire's gaze. Her mother laughed and pointed at a picture. "Oooh. I like this one."

"The neckline's too low."

Della winked. "You've got it to flaunt, dear."

Claire reached over and shut her mother's book. "Grow up, Mother." She pulled her hand through her blonde hair. "Besides, I've got it narrowed down to three."

"Okay. Shall we get something to eat?"

"Something quick. I want to look at a few houses with John this afternoon."

"I thought you were going to the mountains."

Claire laughed and started walking to the front of the store. "That was John's idea."

That night, after hours of house hunting in Stoney Creek and a late dinner at Claire's house, Claire yawned. "I'm beat." She looked at John, who was already stretched out on the couch. "So are you ready for the little McCall family reunion?"

She knew John was dreading it. Past pain fractured the McCall family so that they were never really the cozy unit that Claire longed for. But she hoped that little efforts like her planned cookout could be the start of some mended fences.

John just smiled. It was a good smile. She almost believed it meant he was happy about it.

She kissed his forehead and pointed to a pillow and a folded blanket. "I hope you enjoy the couch."

He pulled her to him and kissed her mouth leisurely. "I love you."

Her heart thrilled every time he spoke those words. "I love you too." She pushed him away. "Now don't you even think about getting off that couch until morning."

She talked in jest, but it took every fiber of her strength to keep from falling into his arms. *Help me, Lord.*

A few minutes later, she exited the bathroom and passed John in the hall. "Night," she said, before slipping into her room and closing the door. Then, with a slight hesitation, she pushed the button to lock the door.

Collapsing onto her bed, she thanked God for bringing John Cerelli back into her life. Floorboards creaked in the hallway as John passed by, and she curled away from the door, pulling her comforter over her shoulders. She had not yet undressed. In that condition, a memory tickled at the edges of her mind. *I remember sleeping with the light on. Sleeping in my clothes, just like this.*

I remember being afraid.

She turned over and looked at the door. *I remember watching for shadows under the door.*

She shuddered and thought about the question her counselor had asked about men in the house. *Certainly my father couldn't have. But sometimes he was crazy drunk.*

The thought sickened her, spurring her heart to a gallop. "God," she whispered. "I don't want to remember. I can't deal with this."

But even as the words escaped her lips, she knew she didn't have to. *Trust, right, God? That's what it's about.*

She thought of the phrase Joanne had used. *Permission to remember.* It sounded so simplistic, yet she realized that perhaps her will stood in the way. If there was more pain in her past, she didn't want to dig it up.

That's when she remembered a phrase her pastor used as an illustration. He talked of God dealing with our pain layer by layer, like the peeling of an onion. Done too quickly, the aroma makes us cry. *Maybe I just need to peel back one layer at a time.*

She closed her eyes and tried to focus on her past. Had she locked away painful events in defense of her own sanity?

What happened that night?

I remember drinking with Tommy and Shelby and Grant. I remember someone pulling at my jeans. I remember resisting.

Claire fought a sense of rising panic. *I can't remember what happened next. My next memory is of being in my bed. Waking up in my clothes. Knowing someone had touched me without permission.*

I remember the smell of alcohol on his breath. The next thought pierced her soul like a knife. *Daddy came to my room that night.*

"Oh, God," she whispered in the darkness. "I don't want to remember this."

She shook her head, brushing her hair against her pillow as a memory solidified. Fragments coalesced. *A hand groping beneath my shirt. Daddy was here. I remember Daddy being here.* Her mind whirled with the shock of discovery.

She sat up and covered her mouth with her hand. *I think I'm going to be sick.*

The next afternoon, after church, the Wally McCall family gathered in the backyard for grilled hamburgers, potato salad, fresh veggies, and homemade ice cream. In all, Claire felt the event had gone well. Kyle seemed to warm up to John, although they never seemed to dive much deeper than the current slump the Atlanta Braves were in.

After dinner, Della teamed up with Casey to face Kyle and Kristen in a fierce game of backyard badminton with John sitting in a lawn chair on the side, raising his cane to indicate points for each side.

Claire looked on with glee before retreating to wash dishes in the kitchen with Margo. She took a deep breath. "I've been trying to sort through some things in my past," she began. "I was having so many nightmares after this rape attempt that I finally contacted a professional to talk things out."

Margo set aside a drying towel and sat down, her face reflecting concern. "I hope it helps."

"This attempted rape seems to have unearthed some old pain."

Margo squinted. "Old pain?"

"I remember something happening in that same room." Claire looked away from her sister's searching eyes. She was ashamed to say it. She stuttered forward, tiptoeing into waters swelling with hidden pain. "I think Daddy may have been inappropriate with me."

Margo's mouth dropped open. "Inappropriate?"

"I remember being touched. I remember resisting."

"What are you saying?" She leaned toward Claire, reaching across the table. "Daddy?"

Claire shut her eyes, willing back the tears. "Yes. I remember bits and pieces. I remember knowing that something very bad had happened in my bed."

Her sister's voice was soft. Too soft for the harsh word that she spoke. "Rape?"

She nodded.

Margo stood and put her arms around her sister. "Claire, that's horrible. But how do you know?"

"I remember enough. I'd been out with Tommy Gaines and Shelby and Grant Williams. We stayed out drinking and I got so plastered." She felt her voice thickening. "I can't even remember how I got home. But I was so drunk I couldn't defend myself.

"I remember being so sick the next morning. I remember the pain I had." Claire looked up at her sister. "Did he ever—I mean, with you, did he ever—?"

"No," she said. "But I left before things got too bad, remember?" She shook her head.

"Maybe his problems ran deeper than we ever knew."

"Have you talked to Mom?"

"No," Claire said softly. "She's been through too much pain with Wally to bring this up." She hesitated. "I'd need to be sure."

"Claire, Daddy was a violent drunk. But there were certain lines even Daddy wouldn't cross."

"Rape is violence. Rape isn't about sex."

Margo sighed. "Do me a favor. Don't share this with Della. I think she'd kill him if she thought he'd ever touched you."

Claire looked up to see Kyle enter through the back door holding an empty bowl. "Any ice cream left?" He paused, his eyes on the duo. "Did I interrupt?"

Claire turned her face to the wall.

"Here," Margo said. "I put it in the freezer."

In the den, Della put her hand to her mouth and slowly backed away from the entrance to the kitchen. *I remember that night. I was so worried about Claire. It wasn't like her to stay out so late. I remember Wally getting up, telling me he was going to check on Claire.*

She retreated back down the hallway and into the bathroom, where she studied her worried expression in the mirror. *Wally?*

She took a deep breath, forced a smile, and bounded into the hall. "Anyone for a rematch?"

An hour later, Claire and John were on their way back to Brighton. John touched her arm. "I want to stop by Pleasant View," John said. "I want to see Wally."

Claire kept her eyes straight ahead. "You're kidding me, right?"

"No, I'm not. I haven't seen Wally for a few weeks. I just want to say hi." He sighed. "We talked about this last week."

Claire hadn't had a chance to share her discovered memories with John. She'd wanted to process them with Margo first and see if she'd had any similar experiences. "I don't really feel like seeing my father."

"You stay in the car then. Just let me go in."

She stayed quiet.

"What's wrong?"

She recounted her counseling session with Joanne Phillips and the recovery of her memories.

John sighed. "Man oh man oh man."

"Is that all you can say?"

"I'm sorry, Claire." He let the apology hang without further comment. They drove along in silence for a minute until he spoke again.

"If something really happened between you and Wally, it was a long time ago, buried beneath years. You visited last week. Nothing is really different about today."

"*Everything* is different about today." She hesitated. "Today I have feelings ... memories about my father that I can't ignore."

He drummed his fingers on his knee and looked out the window. Claire could see the hurt on his face. But how could he be so insensitive to her feelings?

"Look," she said, "I wish I could make it all go away. I wish I'd never been attacked. I wish I didn't have hurt locked away that has come creeping out to mess up today." She pressed her right hand onto her upper lip.

"I'm sorry."

She didn't know what to say.

"Don't discount the way God has worked things out between you in the last six months. Do you remember how significant it felt to finally have him say, 'I love you'?"

She drove on, fighting an internal battle. He was right. She had seen improvement and healing in her relationship with Wally since she'd uncovered the mystery of the Stoney Creek curse. And she liked the fact that John had such a great relationship with Wally. She loved John for relating to him, even in his present condition, as if he was just a normal guy. She felt guilty for wanting to stay away, but she couldn't deny the fresh wound that had opened in her soul.

When she got to the entrance to the lane leading up to Pleasant View Home, she yielded to her desire to please John. She turned and headed up the hill.

She glanced at John. Surprise registered on his face. "You don't have to go in."

She parked. "I'm going with you." *Maybe looking at him will help jog my memory.* She took a deep breath. *Okay. I can give myself permission to remember. I'm safe now. The pain was a long time ago.*

They stayed for twenty minutes, with John chatting on about the boredom of rehab and the army-sergeant therapist he had to deal with in the hospital. Claire looked on as John assisted Wally with some thickened lemonade.

She tried to remember. *Daddy, did you ...? Could you ...?*

How could you?

Wally stayed expressionless, seemingly trapped behind a dull mask some cruel playwright made him wear in a play called Huntington's. He was quiet for John's entire one-sided conversation.

As they said good-bye, he spoke the same words Claire had last heard him speak. His voice was weak and the words were punctuated in a rhythm matched by the bumping of his limbs against the padded rails of his bed. "I want to die."

This time, Claire's first thought troubled her more than her father's deadpanned statement.

You deserve it.

That night, Margo tucked the girls in bed and tapped on the back of a thick book that hid her husband's face. "Night, honey."

He lowered the spy novel. "Are you going to tell me what was going on between you and Claire?"

She sighed. "Claire's been seeing a counselor, trying to work through some of the issues that have come up as a result of her recent assault."

Kyle raised his eyebrows. "Issues."

"Claire thinks Wally abused her as a young woman."

"And that's news? How many times did he swing at you when he was drunk?"

"I don't mean in that way. I mean sexually."

"Wally? That sounds like rubbish to me."

Margo sat on the edge of the bed. "That was my first thought. But Claire has some pretty strong memories of being touched in her own bed." Margo shook her head. "She remembered well enough to tell me the exact day."

Kyle stared straight ahead. "I'm listening."

"She says she'd been out with Tommy Gaines and Grant and Shelby Williams. They got her pretty drunk. She thinks Daddy came to her when she was back home in her bed and unable to defend herself."

He lowered his head onto his hand and rubbed his eyes. "Oh, man."

"Kyle, what should she do?"

"Do?" He set aside the novel. "Nothing. She should stop digging up memories that are long buried. What good can it bring to accuse Wally and upset your mother?"

Margo nodded. "I told her not to tell Mom. I don't think their relationship could stand a blow like this. They've come so far in reconciling in recent months."

Her husband yawned. "What'd she say?"

"I think she'll keep it quiet. But knowing Claire, that doesn't mean she won't need to get to the bottom of it before she moves on."

"Will she take your advice? Tell her that memories that drift back through the haze of alcohol aren't reliable." He stood up and walked to the bathroom, muttering as he left, "Innocent people could get hurt."

Chapter Eight

After a weekend of wading through unnerving memories, Claire welcomed Monday morning's business to occupy her attention. She toiled through the load that included three sports physicals on Ashby High football player wannabes, an asthma follow-up, two blood pressure medication adjustments, and a biopsy of a suspicious skin lesion on the bald spot of a golfer.

At noon, she retrieved a can of chocolate Slimfast from the fridge and sat at her desk to catch up on dictation.

"Here," Lucy said, placing a form on the desk. "The guy from the funeral home dropped off another death certificate."

Claire sighed. She was responsible to certify the official causes of death for her patients.

"Do you need the patient record?"

Claire read the name on the certificate. "Richard Childress." She shook her head. "No, I remember Mr. Childress. I won't need the record."

Her stomach knotted as she read the date on the certificate. *Saturday. The day after I wrote a prescription for morphine.*

She looked at the lines highlighted for her to complete. *Immediate cause of death. Other factors contributing to death.*

What do I write? Sarcasm tempted her. *Assisted suicide from narcotic overdose?* She shook her head. *No. I don't know that. If they took the morphine as instructed, there would be no reason to think the morphine contributed to his death.*

She propped up her head with her hand. *So why do I wonder?*

She penned in the diagnosis. Metastatic colon cancer.

I wonder if a blood test could reveal a narcotic overdose? Should I call the funeral home and see if a sample can be taken?

Should I call Mrs. Childress and ask?

What's the point? Do I really want to know?

Richard Childress was going to die anyway.

So why do I feel guilty?

Claire chided her sensitive conscience.

Would it really have been so bad to shorten his suffering by a lethal injection?

On Monday afternoon, Jimmy Jenkins sat in the driver's seat in his new Winnebago motor home and cried. Last week the camper on wheels had been full of retirement dreams, but now he felt like leaving it on the curb with a sign like he'd left on his golf clubs.

On Tuesday, he stayed in his pajamas until supper, something Miriam would never approve of. Wednesday, he passed her walk-in closet and rested his hand on the door. Thursday, he opened the door and peered in. Friday, he entered her sanctuary just long enough to bury his nose in her favorite blue dress. It still carried her scent. After a few minutes, he rubbed a spot near the collar, wet with his tears, and retreated from her closet with the dress, which he gently placed in his own closet, hanging it closely against his gray suit, the one Miriam liked. She said it brought out the gray in his hair and made him look dignified.

On Sunday, he visited Community Chapel. He supposed death was supposed to make you think about eternity, but the truth was, he felt so guilty for hiding a secret from Miriam for so many years that he thought he'd give church a go again to see if anything good would stick. *Kind of like walking through a smoky bar*, he thought. *Maybe the fragrance of the place will rub off on me.*

From the back, he strained his head to look for Della, but to no avail. Maybe she had gone to Brighton to see her future in-laws.

The next week he took the Winnebago back to the dealer who accepted it back, given Jimmy's sad circumstances. With the refund check in his pocket, he took the bus to Brighton, walked three blocks to the Harley Davidson dealer, and bought a Fat Boy motorcycle along with a matching shiny black helmet. He took it right from the showroom floor, waiting an hour for them to add the leather saddlebags that had classic leather strings hanging like a little waterfall around the fringe.

Riding back to Stoney Creek with the wind in his face and the throaty growl of the engine behind, Jimmy thought about the warnings he'd given his young patients over the years. He'd called them donorcycle riders, because they so often ended up donating their organs after a brain-deadening crash. Now, with a growing sense of freedom, he chuckled at his new image. Sails to the wind! He twisted the throttle and held on as the bike responded, pulling forward against his hands. He tightened his grip. He should have done this years ago. *Of course, then Miriam would have stroked sooner.*

He whispered an apology to his wife and conquered the twisted highway over North Mountain toward Fisher's Retreat. Red, orange, and yellow leaves passed in a dizzying blur of fall color. At noon, he stopped at the café to order greasy french fries. Then he drove by Della's three times, but didn't stop because the driveway appeared empty.

On the third pass, he contemplated turning in, but told himself it would be better to get a leather jacket first, one like he'd seen Steve McQueen wear in an old motorcycle movie.

That's a plan. Just wait until Della sees me now.

Joanne sat in a cushioned chair across from Claire and adjusted the picture of John Cerelli toward her. It was just a slight gesture, a bump of the hand, an accidental knock of the photograph with the edge of her notepad. But Claire noticed that Joanne's eyes went to the photo again and lingered. It was just a second or two, but enough to see the flicker of enjoyment that moment brought.

"How are you doing, Claire? Are you busy with wedding plans? I can't imagine the stress."

Claire's eyes had followed Joanne's to the photograph. "Oh, yes." She looked back at her counselor, who sat on the edge of her chair. "It is a bit hectic."

Joanne slid back and crossed her long, slender legs. Her skirt edged up. Her thighs were fit, without a hint of age-related dimpling. Claire was sure she must spend hours in the gym. Joanne picked up her notebook. "So how goes the memory trail?"

"Okay, I guess." She explained how she'd laid on her bed and remembered sleeping in her clothes with the lights on. "When John slept over the other week— "

"John slept over? I thought we'd talked about limiting physical contact for a while."

Claire looked up. *You interrupted me.* "I was saying that he slept over, but not in my bed. John sleeps on the couch when he stays in Stoney Creek."

Joanne nodded. "Good girl."

"Anyway, while I was lying on my bed, I heard the floor squeak as he passed my room. I remembered lying awake on my bed, years ago ... being afraid, listening to noises in the hall."

"Listening for the creaking floor?" She paused. "Listening for someone walking to your room? Was it your father?"

Claire grimaced. "It might have been. I remember turning off the lamp and staring at the sliver of light coming from under my door. I watched for shadows of feet."

"Do you remember being attacked?"

"I have memories of being held down in my bed. But that's what Tyler did to me, when he tried— " She halted. "You know."

Joanne nodded. Her face was kind, like she knew how hard it was for Claire to even say the word.

"Anyway, the memories of that attack are so vivid to me. So when I remember that, I don't know if I'm mixing it with recall from another attack or not."

Joanne wrote something down on her yellow notepad. They talked again about safety issues, about how it was okay if Claire felt safe to have a gun around, how normal it was to feel anger toward her father, and how she may even want to facilitate a confrontation at some point. "It's good to get everything out. It's painful, but it can do a lot for closing this chapter in your life."

Claire shook her head. "You don't understand. My father is very ill. Huntington's disease debilitates him. He doesn't even respond to me half the time. I'm not sure if it's a true decline in his intellect or just personality changes. Besides, if he abused me, I'm sure he was drunk."

"Hmmm. There may be some alternatives."

"Alternatives?"

"Mock confrontations. Let me give it some thought. It's a technique I've used before when my patients' fathers are already deceased."

Claire wrinkled her nose. It didn't sound too pleasant. She took a deep breath. "Sometimes I wonder if any of this is real. What if none of this ever happened?"

"You told me yourself what you experienced the following morning." Joanne leaned forward. "And fear doesn't come out of nowhere. Girls don't normally lie awake at night quivering at the sound of the floor."

It sounded reasonable. Claire looked at her watch. She wished the sessions were all behind her.

"Claire, what you've told me is very significant. Girls who were abused by their fathers commonly sleep fully clothed."

"With the light on?"

Joanne nodded.

And Claire began to cry.

That evening, Nancy Childress sat in her living room sorting Richard's belongings with her daughter, Ami. She folded a pair of pants and placed it in a box bound for the Salvation Army. "You haven't said much about this new boyfriend of yours."

Ami shrugged. "He e-mails me every day."

Nancy smiled. "Be careful, honey. Sometimes work relationships can be a minefield."

"Not with John. He's so sweet."

Ami carried a box into the bathroom. Nancy listened as she called out, "Should I put his electric razor in the donation box?"

"Sure."

A minute later Ami came into the front room holding a small box and a syringe. "Mom, what are you doing with this?"

"It's drugs from Dr. McCall's office. Something to keep Richard comfortable before he died."

Ami squinted toward her mother and stayed quiet. Then she weighed the box of morphine in her hand. "She gave you this without a prescription?"

"I have a prescription." Nancy felt a twinge of guilt under her daughter's gaze. "I didn't use it, Ami. Not one dose."

Ami seemed to consider her mother's words before turning her back and returning to her job in the bathroom.

A week later, Claire fell into John's arms after unloading the burden of her past. This time, instead of defending Wally, he just listened and folded his arms around her. "It was a long, long time ago. It will take time to forgive and go on."

She sniffed. "I've started sleeping with the gun next to my bed again."

He tightened his hug. "It's okay for now."

"I feel so stupid. I tell myself I should be trusting God. I know he's my safety."

John nodded.

"But tell that to my heart."

He kissed her. She enjoyed the warmth of his mouth, and felt the stirrings of desire that she'd been shoving aside. John's breath spread out over the skin of her neck, bringing a tingle that flooded through her body. She found herself beginning to respond. She pushed forward, writhing against his touch.

But just as she did, the thought of her attack dropped in, quelling her passion and gripping her heart with panic. She pushed John away and gasped. He hung his head. "I'm sorry."

She watched him. She knew he took her rapid breaths as a sign she was hungry for more, but she knew that invisible fear had vaulted her into wide-eyed terror.

Perhaps he sensed that something deeper than pangs of conscience had taken her captive. For in a moment, his expression changed. He stepped back, but gently brushed her cheek with the back of his hand. "Don't let it bring you down today. The past is gone, Claire."

She couldn't speak. She wanted to lose herself in the comfort of his gaze.

"No one can hurt you now, baby. The bad men are locked away."

He squeezed her hand in a good-bye. He leaned forward and let his breath escape onto her forehead in a whisper. "You're safe, Claire."

That's what I'll tell myself tonight. The gun stays on the shelf. It's crazy to be ruled by something so long ago.

Or is it?

Chapter Nine

A week passed with John Cerelli counting down the days until his physician would allow him to drive. He loved getting back behind the wheel, even if it was his mother's Toyota Land Cruiser and not his beloved Mustang. His convertible had been a total loss in the crash. But completing rehab meant he could drive. Driving meant freedom. And freedom meant he could work again. Three months at home had passed with agonizing slowness, but now he could feel his attitude improving with every mile.

He frowned at the first drops of rain as he searched for the windshield wiper switch. His grip tightened on the wheel. *It was raining the night of my crash.*

Ten minutes later, he parked and headed into his office, where he was a sales representative for a company producing patient record-keeping software. He was early, anxious to get back on his Virginia circuit to monitor his clients.

His in-box had grown twelve inches, spilling into a cardboard box sitting next to his desk, and conveniently close to the trash can. Over the desk, in a rainbow of colors, stretched individual letters strung on a string from the top of his window to the opposite wall. W-E-L-C-O-M-E-B-A-C-K-J-O-H-N. A single carnation decorated the corner of his desktop.

He made coffee and returned with his first steaming mug to conquer the backlog. A few minutes later, he heard the arrival of another employee, followed by the sharp report of a woman's heels.

"Welcome back, stranger." Ami's smile was adorable.

John shrugged. "Thanks." He tilted his head toward the stack of papers. "Do you have a shovel?"

She giggled. "I'll get right on it." She leaned forward across the desk, tempting him to peer into the neckline. She tapped the end of his nose with a manicured index finger. "Someone ignored my e-mail yesterday."

John felt a stab of guilt. He had seen it, another volume of her life history. He had replied to a few of her communications in the beginning, wanting to be nice, even shared a few details of his own life as he sat at his parents' home with so much time on his hands. But Ami returned one e-mail with six more, until every response from John resulted in a dozen or more daily cute sayings or thoughts. And more and more, the tone had turned decidedly personal. He found himself torn. He loved the attention. Claire was so busy that she rarely returned e-mails. But Ami was too attentive, and lately, she was sending digital photographs. They seemed innocent enough, but trended toward the edge of decency. The last one, a picture taken at her apartment pool, looked like something from *Sports Illustrated.* He dumped the picture quickly into the trash, as his heart quickened with memories of past battles he'd fought with lust. But more often in the last two weeks, he'd found himself waiting until his mother was out before checking his mail. It wouldn't do to have his mother walk in while he was reviewing the daily load from Ami.

He cleared his throat. "Must have gotten lost in cyberspace." How could he tell her to cool off without hurting her feelings? She'd mentioned painful childhood experiences and the need for a counselor. She was fragile. He needed to be gentle.

She straightened. "Of course."

He took a sip of coffee, not knowing exactly where to begin. "Ami, about the e-mails. You really shouldn't spend so much time on me. There's—"

"Oh, I don't mind. I can type ninety words a minute and—" Her eyes paused on his sober expression. She hesitated. "It's too much, isn't it? Am I smothering you? Oh, I didn't mean to upset you. It's just been so nice having—"

John held up his hand. "No offense taken."

She looked at the floor. "Is that all?"

He nodded, but her eyes remained fixed toward the carpet. He was careful to keep his tone gentle. "That's all."

She turned to leave.

"Oh, Ami."

She looked back.

"Thanks for the flower."

"How'd you know it was me?"

He smiled. "Just a hunch."

Della looked up the drive in response to what was becoming a familiar rumble, the growl of Jimmy's Harley. As she pushed open the door and stood on the front porch, she couldn't keep a smile from her lips. He was such a boy. And retirement age looked good on him. She suspected he weighed no more now than he did as a college freshman. Trim, gray, with an attitude that said, "I'm here for adventure."

"How about a ride, Della?"

She sighed. *I'm a grandmother. I can't act like this. Besides, I'm a married woman. What would people say if I wrapped my arms around another man, even if it was on a motorcycle?*

She'd been putting him off for weeks now, with one excuse after another. With her hands on her hips, she slowly shook her head.

"Don't say it! Don't say the helmet won't fit." He shifted around and unstrapped a helmet attached to the seat behind him. "I got a new one," he said, smiling. He held it up for her to see. "It's blue to match your eyes."

"Jimmy!"

He pulled off his own helmet and rested the bike on its kickstand. He did look rather charming in his new leather jacket.

She stepped off the porch to greet him. "It's just that—"

"Wally, right?"

She nodded. "What would people say? It's not proper."

"I've lived most of my life doing what was proper in other people's eyes." He locked eyes with hers. His were penetrating, set in a chiseled face framed by silver hair. "Maybe I don't want to run my life by what other people expect."

She did want to go. It wasn't that. Riding through the mountain roads with the wind in her hair seemed like just the kind of exhilaration she needed. A life with an invalid husband and the stress of the upcoming wedding were enough to make her think twice about jumping on the back of that Harley and asking Jimmy to take her somewhere very far away.

She looked at him for a moment. "I want to."

"Well, hop on."

"I can't."

"Della, live a little!"

She shook her head.

"If it's any consolation, the face shield will keep anyone from knowing it's you. With your figure and blonde hair blowing out the back of this helmet, everyone will just think I'm off robbing the cradle." He winked.

"It's time to let the gossip mill have something else to talk about other than a serial rapist."

They stared at each other a few seconds longer before he turned and strapped the blue helmet back to his bike.

She stepped off the porch and rested her hand on the motorcycle's handlebar. "What are you doing, Jimmy?"

He squinted toward the sun. "Doing? I'm getting on with life."

"Running from guilt?" She stared at him, watching for a reaction.

His expression steeled. "She's been gone six weeks," he said quietly. "We both know if I had certain things to do over again, I'd do them differently." He hung his head. "I feel so guilty."

She nodded. "I did too. For so many years."

"Just when I was ready to tell Miriam what a cad I'd been, she was—" His voice cracked.

She took his hand. "I know, Jimmy, I know."

"What do I do? I've cried my confession to her picture a hundred times."

She stepped away from him and sat on the steps. "Find a godly man you can trust. Talk to Pastor Phil. Tell him and God your story. Let God have your grief. And let him forgive you."

He nodded slowly.

She smiled. "Then enjoy your Harley. But don't use it as an escape from guilt you haven't dealt with."

He wiped the corner of his eye with the sleeve of his leather jacket and looked away. "Why is it you seem to look right through me?"

She laughed. "Because I'm blonde."

He shook his head and strapped on his helmet. Then he started his bike and lifted his hand in a wave. "Thanks, Della."

As she watched the dust rise from a stripe on the gravel lane behind him, the receding roar of the engine prodded a longing to swell within her, a feeling she'd not felt in a long, long time.

Lucy came out of exam room A, her face blanched. Claire took the chart from her hand. "What's wrong?"

"Don't go in there."

"Why not?"

She shook her head in disbelief. "It's Tyler Crutchfield."

Lucy motioned her away from the door, frowning. "We had a temp yesterday. She didn't know the history, so she must have scheduled him.

When I asked the deputy with him why he brought him here, he said he had no idea what Tyler was in for. His only assignment was to accompany him to a doctor's appointment."

Claire took a deep breath and looked at the chart, which was made up of copies of a discharge summary from Brighton University and a few brief notes written by a nurse at the county jail. She went to her desk to read the account.

After being shot in the thigh, Tyler was transported to Brighton University, where he underwent reconstruction of his femoral artery and vein. Postoperatively, he'd almost died from a pulmonary embolism, a clot which had formed in the damaged vein in his leg and had broken loose and traveled to his lungs. He'd been in intensive care on a ventilator for three days. Eventually, he'd recovered enough to be discharged to the infirmary within the county jail to do rehab while awaiting his trial.

From the looks of his hospitalization, this must have cost fifty thousand dollars. But because he was a prisoner, the state foots the bill.

She shook her head. It didn't seem right that the state picked up the cost of care for its prisoners and ignored people without insurance like Richard Childress, who couldn't afford a visiting hospice nurse.

Lucy appeared in the doorway. "What should I do? I told the deputy to take him somewhere else. The deputy is willing but needs you to fill out some transfer-of-care form for the county."

"Why is he here anyway?"

"He's spitting a stitch." She used medical vernacular to describe a small abscess that forms around a suture. If infection forms around it, the stitch will often extrude from the wound, or "spit."

Claire sighed. "Forget the form. I'll see him."

Lucy's upper lip tightened. "Are you sure?"

"I'm the one who shot him, remember? I'd like to see what I put him through."

"Suit yourself. But I hope you don't want my help. I can't stand the thought of being with him any longer than I have to."

"Just set up a minor surgical tray with a number fifteen scalpel blade. I may have to drain a small infection."

Lucy disappeared. A few minutes later, a small light appeared on a panel on the wall opposite Claire's desk. This indicated that a patient was ready to be seen.

Claire took a deep breath and stood up, smoothing the lapels on her white coat. *I can do this.*

She entered to see Tyler sitting on the exam table wearing an orange prison jumpsuit. His ankles were shackled. An overweight deputy sat on a stool beside the table, apparently more interested in the state of his fingernails than in his prisoner. "Hello, Tyler," Claire said, purposefully raising her voice to emphasize his real name. She offered a plastic smile. "And just what can I do for you today?"

"I got shot in my leg, Doc. But you know all about that. The surgeons over at the university patched me up, but now I got some drainage through the wound." He smiled back. "So now it looks like you need to help me." He chuckled. "Isn't that a hoot?"

She wasn't amused. "Show me the wound."

He unbuttoned the front of his jumpsuit. He pulled it to the side, attempting to show the scar in the crease where his thigh joined his body.

She couldn't see.

"I need to take this off."

She traded glances with the deputy before studying the proud smirk on Tyler's face. He understood. The deputy would have to undo the shackles to allow Tyler to slip the suit off his legs.

"Don't worry," the officer said, unlocking the restraint. "I'll be right here with you."

Tyler offered a saccharine smile. Apparently sweet, but lacking the calories of real sugar.

She sized up the deputy. He seemed capable enough, but she wouldn't trust him to win a footrace when matched with a desperate criminal. A holster was partially hidden by his overlapping waist.

Tyler slipped off the jumpsuit and lowered his underwear so that Claire could see the wound. It was a six-inch scar running from his lower abdomen straight down across the top of his thigh. In the middle of the wound was a pea-sized raised area. It was purple-red. She touched it with a gloved finger and watched a small drop of pus form.

"You messed me up bad, Claire," he said. "I thought we were getting to be such good friends."

She spoke through clenched teeth. "I'll have to drain this." She stood up and nodded professionally. "This looks like a little thing, but I have to warn you, if this infection has spread down to the graft they used to reconstruct your artery, a blowout of the vessel could easily lead to a bleed-out."

His smirk melted. "A bleed-out?"

"You bleed to death. If the femoral artery isn't controlled when a blowout occurs, you could die in sixty seconds."

"A result of you shootin' me, Doc." He chuckled. "Then I guess you'd be under investigation for murder, huh?"

Claire ignored his trash talk and prepared to work.

He looked at the deputy. "Wouldn't that be a switch?"

She turned and readied a sponge with an iodine solution. As she lifted her hand to prep the skin he raised his hand. "Aren't you going to numb it first?"

Her face was steel. "No. The needle would hurt just as much as the prick of the scalpel." *And you're not worth the price of the Lidocaine anesthetic.*

She painted the wound until his thigh and lower abdomen glowed orange. Poising the knife above the skin, she glanced at the deputy. He averted his eyes to the wall and winced. The officer's cowardice was unnerving.

Claire returned her attention to the painted operative field. Then she stabbed the scalpel into the raised area to drain the infection.

Tyler sucked wind and cursed her.

"Almost done," she coached, watching the thick white fluid pour from the wound.

With her attention on the wound, she didn't notice his right hand until it came down on her arm. In a second, he ripped the scalpel from her hand and jumped from the table. Then, before Claire could even scream, he was behind her, with one hand on her chin, extending her neck so that her head lay against his cheek. The deputy, temporarily distracted by the flow of infection from the prisoner's wound, was too slow on the draw. As he reached for his holster, Tyler pressed the infected scalpel to Claire's neck, scratching a line on the surface. "One more move and I'll cut her jugular."

The officer looked up, his eyes wide, meeting Claire's.

She could feel the pain on her neck, and the wetness of a drop of blood trickling into her shirt. "Do what he says."

"Put the gun on the table with the handle facing me."

The deputy obeyed. Tyler quickly snatched the gun, throwing the scalpel aside. He pressed the barrel to her temple. "Put down the radio," he ordered. "And car keys."

Again, the deputy placed the radio and his keys on the exam table.

"Now take off your clothes." Claire gasped, but realized he was talking to the officer. Once the officer stood in only his boxers, Tyler turned his attention to her. "Now yours," he sneered. "I want to see what I missed."

Claire steadied her voice. "Tyler, you have an infected wound over a major artery. If this isn't treated properly, a bleed could be fatal."

"Shut up!" He released her and trained the gun on her forehead. "Start with the blouse."

Claire glanced quickly at the officer, hoping that he could take advantage of Tyler's attention being drawn to her.

She fumbled as she undid the buttons on the front of her blouse. With that done, she began to pull the blouse apart to reveal—

The deputy lunged forward, knocking Tyler against the wall, pushing the gun into the air. It appeared the officer held Tyler's wrist, but Tyler quickly twisted away and shoved the butt of the pistol into the deputy's abdomen.

Claire heard two muffled shots and watched in horror as the officer dropped to the floor.

"Plans have changed," Tyler quipped. He grabbed Claire by the hair and pulled her into the hallway.

Claire screamed.

Lucy stood holding the receiver of the wall phone up to her mouth, which was frozen in a circle.

Tyler squeezed off another round at close range into the phone.

Claire stumbled forward as Tyler pushed her toward her office. There, he saw her purse on the desktop. He pointed with the pistol and shoved her toward the desk. "Empty your wallet."

She shook the contents of her purse onto the desk and pulled out forty-two dollars.

In the hall, she could hear her employees' cries as they ran to the front of the building.

"Sit over there," he motioned. "Face the wall."

She obeyed and heard the rustle of clothing, a zipper, and the crinkle of her cash being slid into a pocket. He cursed her. "Maybe you'd like to take a little trip with me?" he said.

Then, hearing the front door open as her employees ran, Tyler cursed again.

"I won't forget what you did to me. I have a score to settle." He opened the back door. "I will see you again, Claire." He glared at her with eyes of steel. "Don't worry, doll. I'll be back to finish the fun as soon as my leg has healed."

With that he ran through the back door, sprinting toward the police cruiser.

She rushed to lock the door behind him, and then returned to the exam room. There, she found Lucy kneeling beside the officer. His face was pale, his chest unmoving.

Claire felt for a carotid pulse before looking up into the face of her nurse. "He's dead, Lucy," she cried. "He's dead."

Chapter Ten

That night, Claire and Della stayed at the Days Inn on University Boulevard in Brighton. No amount of convincing could have kept Claire at home that evening.

In fact, as she lay on the double bed staring at the TV waiting for the late news, she wondered if she'd ever be able to stay at home again. She looked at the loaded gun beside her bed. As long as Tyler Crutchfield was on the lam, the gun would be at her bedside. She sighed and picked up the gun, turning it over and weighing it in her hand. She had packed it away for good only a week ago. Slowly she took aim, laying the bead on the forehead of the news anchor.

Della opened the door from the bathroom. "What are you doing?"

Claire shrugged. "Just aiming, Mother."

"Put that thing down, please. It was one thing with you sleeping with it beside your bed at home, but now I'm your roommate, and I don't like it."

Claire grunted.

"You're going to get one of us killed."

"The safety is on," she said, replacing it on the nightstand. She glanced at the door. The security latch was folded over to prevent it from opening more than a few inches if someone obtained a keycard to unlock the door.

"John left?"

She nodded. "He volunteered to sleep on the floor, but I sent him home. Besides, no one knows we're here. Tyler couldn't possibly find me."

Della waved her hand toward the TV and sat on the edge of her bed. "Turn it up. Here's the report."

The anchorman brought the top story. "In the news tonight, a county deputy is dead, the result of a vicious attack by an escaped prisoner over in Stoney Creek. We go live to the Stoney Creek Family Practice Clinic where Linda Adams is standing by. Linda?"

A young reporter stood in the clinic parking lot. A yellow police tape cordoned off the building behind her. "Dave, this serene country doctor's office was the location of a brutal slaying today. The suspect, an escaped prisoner of the county jail, is Tyler Crutchfield, a patient and former employee of the clinic. Today, during a patient visit, Crutchfield overpowered his guard and escaped after killing Kevin Sandridge, the deputy responsible for guarding him. I have Randy Jensen, a deputy with the sheriff's department, for comment." The officer moved in next to Linda. "Officer Jensen, what can you tell us about this prisoner and your current investigation?"

Jensen's tone was pure business. "This man, Tyler Crutchfield, is a suspect in the rape of three women and the attack of a fourth, the clinic's current physician, Dr. Claire McCall. He was awaiting trial before an anticipated transfer to the state penitentiary."

"Can you tell us what happened here today?"

"The prisoner, Mr. Tyler Crutchfield, was seen here by Dr. McCall. During the patient visit, he somehow obtained a surgical knife and held the physician hostage until our deputy surrendered his gun. Then Mr. Crutchfield made his escape, killing our deputy in the process. He robbed the doctor of her cash and fled the building, wearing our deputy's clothing and driving a county patrol vehicle."

"Thank you, Deputy Jensen." The camera focused in on the reporter's face. "Dave, as you know, this fugitive is still at large and the vehicle has not yet been located. People in the Stoney Creek–Fisher's Retreat area are warned to stay indoors and be careful. This fugitive is considered armed and dangerous. Dave."

Dave, the news anchor, reappeared. "Thank you, Linda. It is interesting that this man was being treated by the very woman physician he tried to rape. Any clue as to why she may have agreed to treat him?"

Linda appeared on screen again. "The temp making the appointment did not recognize the patient's name. When I posed the same question to the sheriff's office, it seems that important details slipped through the cracks somehow. The Stoney Creek Clinic has a contract to provide care to the prisoners, so the prison officials were merely following protocol."

A picture of Tyler Crutchfield filled the screen, sending a shiver down Claire's spine. "Tyler Crutchfield is medium build, five-feet-eleven-inches tall, with short dark hair. He will likely walk with a limp because of a recent injury."

Claire flexed her jaw. "I should have killed him."

"Claire!"

She took a deep breath. "I'm sorry, Mom, but that's the way I feel. Some people don't deserve to live."

Her mother glared at her. "I didn't teach you that."

"Life taught me that."

Claire snapped off the TV as they started into the next story. Her mother prepared for sleep.

Claire sniffed. "What day is this?"

"Tuesday."

Claire shook her head. "I was supposed to meet with a videographer for the wedding this afternoon."

Della put her hand on her daughter's shoulder. "You'll make it through this, honey. We will. Always have and always will, by God's grace."

Claire was warmed by the gesture. "Just don't quote me Romans 8:28. I've whispered it to myself a hundred times today alone. It doesn't calm my mind."

"That's because pain is experienced here," she said, sitting beside Claire and pulling her hand to her chest. "Not here," she added, moving her hand to her daughter's forehead.

Claire nodded, unable to keep back the tears again.

Her mother hugged her. "Try to get some sleep."

A few minutes later, Claire closed her eyes to the vivid images of violence that had haunted her day.

A slumping policeman with a widening red circle on his abdomen.

The frozen image of Lucy holding the phone with her mouth open.

And a man who promised that he'd see her again.

Margo switched off the late news and breathed a prayer for her sister. She looked over at Kyle, still hiding behind the newspaper he'd lifted after two hours of TV.

In the weeks that had passed since the family reunion Kyle had gone from gift giving to sullen. His interactions, particularly with their newly teenaged daughter, Kelly, were strained, etched with too-sharp criticism or nothing, a quietness that Margo feared was a silent mist hanging above a dormant volcano.

Margo watched a pattern. He awoke early, sometimes at 4:00 or 4:30, tossing and turning, keeping her from sleep until he'd retreat to his desk to feign interest in a business ledger. Depressed. Irritable. Something was simmering beneath the surface, threatening to destroy the fragile bonds they'd made since his affair.

Was he still falling into the arms of the other woman? She cringed at the thought, wondering how far her willingness to forgive could be stretched. She took a deep breath. Coming to grips with her own need for grace had made it easier to forgive her husband's infidelity.

She tapped on the newspaper. "You alive back there?"

He dropped the paper in his lap. "Are the girls in bed?"

"Two hours ago." *You should have noticed. You should have been tucking them in.*

He grunted and began to lift the paper.

Margo stopped him, laying her hand against the sports page. "We need to talk, Kyle."

He looked up, unable or unwilling, holding his silence. She studied the man she loved. Normally athletic, friendly, and outgoing, he'd pulled in, isolated, protected.

She placed her hand against the muscles of his chest. "I need to know what's going on."

"Going on?" She felt him stiffen, his defenses going up.

She took a deep breath. "You smother me with flowers, a new van. You give me an expensive guitar for my birthday." She hesitated. "But now you've changed. You barely speak to us. You hide behind that paper night after night."

"I thought you liked the gifts."

"You don't get it. I love flowers. I love my van, my guitar." She sat on the ottoman in front of him. "But I want you to know you don't have to purchase anything for me. What is it that you need? Love? Forgiveness?"

"Margo, I— "

"The gifts were a guilt offering, is that right?"

"That's not fair."

"Or is it business? Are we in trouble?" Kyle had always been lord over their finances, rarely involving Margo in any decisions. He conducted business deals, ran his Wendy's franchise, and made investments without her input. "Did the gifts stop because the money is gone?"

He pulled his hand through his hair. "Some things haven't gone according to plan. But we'll be on track soon, I promise."

"According to plan?" She put the statement in quotation marks with her fingers. She paused. "You borrowed for a new franchise. Is there a problem?"

He shook his head. "It's not business."

"What then? Talk to me, Kyle."

His expression hardened. For a moment she looked at him, following his eyes around the room. The TV. The guitar in the corner. The new vase he'd brought home from a business trip. Anywhere but meeting her gaze.

Margo leaned forward, touching his hand with hers. "Am I wrong?" She held her breath.

He didn't speak.

"Are you still seeing her?"

His breath escaped in a snort. "No!" He fell into silence and stared at the wall behind her.

She sighed and met his silence with a forced quietness of her own.

After a minute, he looked over. "You don't remember that night, do you?"

"That night?"

"The one Claire just had to dig up, the night she went out with Shelby and Tommy." His eyes bore in on hers. "I saw them in Briary Branch together. I was out buying beer."

She couldn't follow the connection. "So?"

"Why would I remember a specific night, Margo?"

She held up her hands in surrender. She didn't understand.

"You don't remember why I was out?"

She looked at him, unspeaking.

"Remember Conner Miles?"

Memories of her own misdeeds came flooding back. Her hand went to her chin. *Conner Miles?* She sensed her own defenses rise. "That's what has you so upset?"

He stood up. "You asked me why I reacted the way I did. So now maybe you understand."

"That was a long time ago."

"Well, pardon me for having a good memory."

His sarcasm bit deep. She spoke to his back as he disappeared into the hall leading to their bedroom. "I was eighteen years old!"

He turned to face her. "I didn't bring this up, okay? I wanted to move on. But this is what Claire is digging up. Pain for me, and pain for you." He turned and walked toward the bedroom.

Margo listened to water running in the bathroom and the whir of his electric toothbrush, followed by a familiar creak of their bed.

So this is about me? He can't be bitter about Conner Miles now. She felt an old ache of guilt and shoved it aside. *Kyle is hiding something.*

She pulled a blanket from the hall closet and curled herself into their new couch. She was too angry and confused to sleep in the same bed with

Kyle. Maybe if she stayed here tonight, he would get the message that she wouldn't tolerate his adolescent behavior.

A minute later, she felt a twinge of guilt when an image of Conner's muscular form drifted into her thoughts. Her next thought scared her even more. *I wonder if that Tyler creep knows that I'm Claire's sister.*

She felt her pulse quicken as she checked the locks on the front, back, and garage doors. Back in the living room, she looked at the couch and glanced down the hall toward her bedroom. Kyle, however childish in his behavior, did seem a safer option. She shook her head. *I've still got the old McCall vinegar in my veins.* She yawned and curled up on the couch.

There, in the dim light of the living room, Margo began taking inventory. She'd always thought there would be happiness around the bend. To be free of an abusive father. To find a husband. A family. A new house. Every new goal held out the hope of satisfaction, but with the arrival of each one, it seemed that happiness slipped along in front of her, the carrot on a stick that she could chase forever and never catch.

And now, the marriage that she'd cherished seemed destined to crack. Kyle was rocky ground, impenetrable by the gentle rain of forgiveness. He seemed intent on wallowing in past sorrows, unwilling or unable to forgive himself or Margo for their infidelities.

She felt so inadequate and powerless to change her situation. The tears welled in her eyes as her aching heart began to melt. *If only I had the faith of my sister.* She shook her head and took a deep breath. *Then maybe I could believe in fairy-tale happy endings.*

Chapter Eleven

John Cerelli lowered his head onto his desk and closed his eyes, a futile attempt to block out the throbbing pain which centered beneath a jagged scar on the top of his head. After leaving the hotel he'd stayed up late worrying about Claire, and now he was paying the price for his lack of sleep.

"John?" The voice was feminine and preceded by the familiar click of her high heels.

He looked up and blinked. Ami's face reflected her concern. "Hey," he said.

"Rough night?"

He rubbed the top of his head. "It's nothing. Just a little headache."

"From your accident?"

He shrugged. "Probably."

She placed a folder on his desk. "Here's the copies for the Brighton Orthopedic presentation."

He nodded and mumbled, "Thanks," as she disappeared. He searched his desk for ibuprofen and reached for his coffee. A minute later, Ami was back, this time carrying two small burning candles. She set them on the corners of his desk and turned off his fluorescent light.

"Ami, I—" he began to protest.

"Hush," she said, moving around behind him. She began kneading the back of his neck with her fingers.

He tensed. He shouldn't let her touch him. He put his hand on hers to arrest her massage. "It's okay. I took some medicine."

"Shh. It's not a crime to let me help you." Her voice was just above a whisper.

He closed his eyes. It did feel so good.

"I always light candles when I'm discouraged. The fire reminds me of hope. Renewal."

"Fire?"

"My counselor suggested it," she said. "It's a way of looking on the bright side. My house burned when I was a child. We lost everything." Ami's fingers touched the edge of his jagged scar, lightly tracing the path through his short hair. "But something good came out of our pain. My mother met a fireman." She sniffed. "He became my stepfather."

Her hands moved to his shoulders. "Relax," she coaxed. "You're in knots."

If she wasn't so pretty, John thought, *maybe this would feel more like therapy instead of temptation.*

"So I light a little fire whenever I'm in pain, John." He felt her finger running along his scar again. "To remind myself that joy can come out of pain."

John shrugged. "Cool," he said. He reached back for her hand, giving it a little that's-enough squeeze. "Thanks. You'd better get to work."

"Sure," she said, returning the squeeze. She let her fingers linger for a moment on his scalp, then ran them slowly down his neck and across his shoulder to rest on his arm before she separated from him, leaving his skin feeling hot, afire with an imprint of her touch.

John watched her leave and inhaled the scent of the candles.

That's funny, he thought. *My headache's gone.*

Margo yanked her hands from under the kitchen faucet and massaged the ring and small fingers of her right hand.

Casey's eyes widened. "What's wrong, Mommy?"

"Just an old scar. It's nothing." She looked at the thin pink skin on the tops of her right fourth and fifth fingers. Hot water on the old burn scar could still bring tears to her eyes. She turned to her daughter. "Get your shoes on, honey. The bus will be here soon."

A minute later, with Kelly and Casey out the door to school, Margo rubbed the pain from her fingers again. It was a sensitive reminder of a regrettable moment.

She was eighteen years old, engaged to Kyle Stevens, the manager of the McDonald's where they'd worked together for the past six months. It was Friday night and the crowds had dwindled to a few teens sharing a milkshake in a corner booth.

With business slow at the counter, Margo turned her attention to cleaning the grill. A moment later, she felt his breath on her earlobe. She pulled away, giggling, thinking Kyle had slipped in before closing time. When she turned, she gasped. "Conner!"

Conner Miles flashed a Crest-commercial grin. He was on summer break from Brighton University, working the grill when he wasn't thrilling Margo or the rest of the employees with stories of college-boy antics. He paused as their eyes met. He had an irresistible smile beneath blue eyes.

Margo had watched him, even flirted with him for weeks, behavior she considered innocent enough until now. She had teased him because she thought he was out of reach. He'd talked of college girls and parties. She was soon to be married to Kyle.

But he was so hot. And a man with a vision for going somewhere out of this small town. And now they were alone, face-to-face with their eyes locked. She wouldn't be the first to break their gaze. He tilted his head. Leaned forward.

She let their lips brush. He was teasing her. He pulled away. She shivered, knowing she played with fire. "Conner, I shouldn't— "

His lips were against hers, pushing her against the counter. She resisted once before surrendering to his passion. In a moment, he'd lifted her to the counter and she leaned into him, returning his kiss full force.

"Margo!" Kyle's voice.

Conner released her and stepped back as her arms flew to the side to regain her balance. She planted her right hand on the edge of the french fryer, submerging the last two fingers in the boiling oil. She jerked her hand into the air, screaming.

She heard Kyle curse and watched as the back of his blue shirt disappeared through the back door. "Kyle!" she cried.

She ran to the parking lot after him and yelled as his car squealed into the street.

But she was too late. She sat on the curb and cried, her tears fresh and her hand throbbing.

A cry from Kristin's room brought Margo to the present. She looked at her fingers. Some burn scars lasted forever.

That morning, Claire drove back to Stoney Creek to find Lisa, her receptionist, alone in the office. They hugged. "Thanks for agreeing to answer the phones."

"Sure," Lisa said, brushing a tear from her cheek.

"Have any of our patients shown up?"

"Only Frank Williams. I don't think he has a TV, and he's so hard of hearing that I don't think he listens to the radio."

She held a list in her hand. "Fifteen others have called to reschedule appointments. Is tomorrow okay?"

Claire ran her fingers through her blonde bangs and read down the list. "Mrs. Yancy should be seen. She's worried about a new breast lump." She traced her finger to another name. "Mr. Barber was rescheduled from last week when I ran late. And I really need to see those stitches I put in Blake Alderland's foot. They shouldn't stay in too long."

They looked up as the door opened. It was Jimmy Jenkins. "Claire, I just heard what happened. I called your home. When I didn't get an answer, I came here."

The trio huddled in a small greeting hug.

Lisa sniffed. The phone rang, prompting her to pick it up. "Stoney Creek Family Practice."

Jimmy took Claire's arm and walked with her into the hall. "This office stays closed until Monday. By then, I can have security lined up to watch the place."

Claire shook her head. "I've got so many patients waiting to get in."

Jimmy frowned. "We cannot just go back to work tomorrow as if nothing happened. I'm concerned about your safety until this convict is behind bars."

Claire lifted the patient appointment list and sighed. "But I—"

"No buts. This practice ruled me, ran my life for over thirty years. I'm not going to let it do the same for you."

"Dr. Jenkins, what am I to do for five days? These people need me."

"They won't die if they don't see you this week."

"Work is the only therapy I know."

He nodded slowly and put his hand on her shoulder. "That's your style, isn't it, Claire? Work isn't the best salve, you know."

"But what—"

"Figure it out. Get out of town for a few days. Plan your wedding. Stay out of sight."

Lisa walked up as Dr. Jenkins disappeared into the waiting room. "That was the detective. They found their patrol car over in Brighton in the University Hospital parking deck."

Claire felt sick.

Lisa touched her arm. "Dr. McCall, what's wrong?"

"That's two blocks from the Days Inn."

"I know where it is."

"But I stayed there last night ... to get away from Tyler Crutchfield."

That evening found Claire sitting at her desk waiting to meet with Joanne Phillips. She sighed as she thought of the backlog of patient problems building up day after day with the office closed. That afternoon she'd read through the list of patients that had been on the appointment book for the day, making notations by the names of those she thought she could handle with a phone call.

A knock at the back door interrupted her thoughts. She looked at her watch. Joanne was right on time. When her hand was on the doorknob, she paused, suddenly afraid. "Joanne?"

"Claire? It's me."

Relieved, she opened the door. Joanne received her with a hug. "Dear Claire," she said, pushing her to arm's length and looking in her eyes. "You look great."

Claire nodded. "You're too polite."

They sat in Claire's office in front of the desk. "How are you holding up? I heard the news this morning, and I knew we should talk."

"I–I'm okay. Really." Claire took a deep breath, wondering just what she was supposed to be feeling. "I slept in Brighton last night. Knowing Tyler Crutchfield was free, I just couldn't face sleeping at home."

Claire waited for a response, but Joanne just nodded without speaking, her eyes full of concern. Claire shifted in her seat, uncomfortable to be the object of such apparent apprehension. She shrugged it off. "Right now, I'm more concerned about all these patients," she added, pointing at a pile of charts on her desk. "We've closed the office until Monday. I'll be working through quite a logjam after that."

"Don't be too afraid to take time for yourself."

"I'm not." Claire looked away from Joanne, uneasy with her examination. "I've been through so much in my life. I don't expect to fall apart over something like this."

"You're shutting down, Claire."

She looked at Joanne, who sat leaning forward, squinting in Claire's direction. "Shutting down?"

Joanne nodded slowly, exuding the kind of pity you might show someone who just lost a loved one in a car accident. "Emotionally. You've wrapped yourself in a cocoon of protection so you won't feel the pain."

"I'm really okay," she said, trying not to show the irritation rising within her.

More nodding from Joanne. "Hmmm."

What did Joanne expect from her? It just wasn't a part of her nature to curl up and mourn. Sure she was afraid, but she'd been in threatening circumstances before, and this didn't feel like uncharted waters. She looked at Joanne and raised her eyebrows. "I guess I'm getting used to this sort of thing."

"I just don't want you to be out of touch with your feelings. Don't just cover it up under a truckload of defense mechanisms. Don't be afraid to be afraid."

Claire nodded and offered a plastic smile. This was sounding a bit too much like touchy-feely psychology for her comfort.

"After a trauma, it's common to unearth hidden feelings." She paused. "Like the memories that resurfaced after your attack." She leaned back and crossed her long legs. "And now that your attacker is again free, you may have a resurgence of other memories, a reliving of emotions you experienced during the attempted rape."

"Well, so far, so good."

"Being ready, anticipating is the first step. If you anticipate something, it is less likely to trip you up when it occurs. Are you angry?"

"Angry? I—"

"It's okay to express it. This man, this Tyler Crutchfield, deserves your anger, Claire."

"I suppose."

"Anger that isn't expressed can end up harming you more than those who deserve to be the object of our anger." She leaned to Claire's desk and lifted a pen from a purple mug. She clicked the pen top as she continued. "What about your father? Are you experiencing anger toward him?"

"Some, but maybe something more like sadness. I've visited him a few times since we talked. I tried to use the visits as a stimulus to see if I could recover any more memories." She shook her head. "But I don't really remember anything else. Just the thought of my father abusing me in that way repulses me."

"It should."

"I guess I find myself pitying him more. Huntington's disease has robbed him of so much. It has changed his personality. He goes from sullen to irritated to paranoid. On the one hand he wants to die. And at other times, he seems afraid that the nurses won't get to him in time when he chokes. My mother programmed his phone to speed-dial 911 for him, just to calm him down, telling him all he had to do if the nurses didn't come was to push a single button." Claire blew her bangs out of her eyes. "Then, at the next visit, it's like Daddy has forgotten all about being paranoid and he's back to not even speaking."

"Have you given any more thought to confronting him?"

"No. I tell you, he wouldn't remember." She shook her head. "I don't even remember it all."

"You were drunk."

"I suspect he was too."

"You are quick to excuse his behavior."

Claire took a deep breath. "I've tried to come to a place of putting a lot of family hurt behind me. Digging this all up may not be such a great idea."

Joanne smiled. "Why did you call me, Claire? Remember why you called for help."

"I wanted the nightmares to go away."

"Look, I guarantee it won't be fun. But unearthing and dealing with whatever is responsible for your misery is the only way to lasting closure over these issues."

"Are you sure? Some things may be better off left unseen and unsaid."

Joanne stood. "I understand how you feel. Once a person is into the process, the pain almost always makes them want to turn tail and run." She touched Claire's shoulder. "But that's the weak way out. The Claire McCall way is straight through the pain."

And that was exactly what Claire was afraid of.

That evening, as Claire and Della stood on the front stoop of their home, Claire sorted through the keys to open the door.

Della looked worried. "Are you sure that creep has left town?"

"The police are continuing to search Stoney Creek. There are only so many places to hide in a small town. Besides, John promised he'd spend the night. We'll be farther away from Tyler Crutchfield if we stay here than if we'd stayed in Brighton."

Claire pushed open the door and hesitated. The house bulged with fresh memories from the last time Tyler was free. She looked at her mother. Della's mind seemed elsewhere. A smile crossed Della's face as she looked out over the lawn.

"Someone's watching out for us," Della said.

"What?"

"Look, honey. Someone mowed the grass while we were away."

Claire took a deep breath. Freshly mown grass scented the air. She looked at the familiar pattern. "I'll bet Jimmy Jenkins did this."

"Why?"

"He's been doing the maintenance at the office since Cyrus—er, Tyler left. Our office mower cuts a little shorter on the left side, leaving a pattern just like this."

Della's smile widened. "This would be like him. Thoughtful. Caring for us when the chips are down."

Claire looked back toward the open door and the den beyond. She took a deep breath. *I can do this. It's stupid to be afraid of my own house.* She shut and bolted the front door.

She tiptoed from room to room while her mother began clinking around the kitchen. After looking in every closet, she chided herself for her anxiety and headed for the kitchen to help Della.

Once supper was ready, Claire paged through a bridal magazine while she waited for John. Della watched *Jeopardy* and tried to yell the answers before the contestants.

Claire looked up. "I spent some time with Joanne Phillips today."

"Who is James Madison!" Della called out, slapping her leg when she heard Alex report her correct response.

"Mom."

"What is the Kentucky Derby!" Della shook her head. "He should have known that."

"Mom!"

Della sighed. "I heard you. How was your session?"

Claire put her finger in the magazine to hold her place. "She mainly just wanted to touch base because she heard about what happened. She wanted to make sure I was holding up since seeing my attacker again."

"Who is Martin Luther King!"

Claire huffed. "Are you listening?"

Della snapped off the TV with the remote and looked at her daughter. "When are you going to tell me what's bugging you?"

"Bugging me?"

Della nodded. "I overheard you talking to Margo. I know what you think about your father." She held up her finger and pointed at Claire. "I think you'd better drop this mess before someone gets hurt."

"You mean someone else." She glared back at Della. "Why didn't you tell me you heard?"

"I've been waiting for you to tell me, but I realized you wanted to protect me." She shook her head. "You don't need to protect me, Claire. I know your father. He wouldn't have done such a thing."

"My counselor thinks I should confront Daddy."

"Absolutely not."

Claire sat up. "Joanne thinks it would be helpful to bring closure to some of my past."

Della stood up. "You listen to me! I've thought long and hard about this, this ..." She waved her hand in the air. "This memory of yours. And I don't know where it's coming from, but I will not have you burdening your father with it."

"Burdening him? What about me?"

"Your father's life hasn't been a bed of roses either. Perhaps I'm to blame for some of that. But he's in no condition now to hear this type of accusation. Don't you think he's suffered enough?"

"I think my father molested me and I'm supposed to think of *his* suffering?"

"Your father did no such thing!"

Mother and daughter glared at each other. Claire looked away. Her mother was in denial. Perhaps her sympathy for Wally prevented her from accepting such a harsh truth.

Della began to pace. "This is all my fault. I talked you into calling a counselor. But it was because I wanted you to stop sleeping with a loaded gun on the nightstand, not because I wanted you to dig up some ancient misery."

"That's the way it works, Mom. Sometimes present pain is just enough like something our defenses have covered up that it freshens an old pain to rise to the surface."

Della put her hands on her hips. "And you're sure about this?" Her mother stood with wrinkled brow, suddenly older and life weary.

Claire took a deep breath. "I don't know." She shook her head. "It all seems so real." It was hard to describe. Her memories were like islands within a broad sea of merging and surging waves. "I don't know."

Her mother stepped closer, lowering the volume, but not able to hide the tension which etched her voice. "Well, I know Wally McCall. He would never have touched his daughters."

"Or have you just gotten so comfortable explaining all his bad behavior away to HD that you can't face the evidence?"

"You have no evidence."

Claire didn't know what to say. Obviously Della would never accept this. "I can't expect you to believe this."

Della shook her index finger. "If you keep this up, you will tear this family apart."

As if we're so close as it is.

They looked up as a knock at the door interrupted them. Claire jumped to her feet and looked out the window. It was John. Perfect timing. She opened the door to his smiling face.

"Am I too late for dinner?"

Chapter Twelve

Brighton University Hospital had shown interest in Stoney Creek Family Practice Clinic for years. Of course, their goal was to build a network of local clinics to secure referrals to their center. And for years, Dr. Jenkins held them off, determined to keep family medicine the community-based service he loved. To Jimmy, the university was the ivory tower and represented high-tech, high-expense, hands-off medicine. He saw himself as the front line, caring for patients cradle to grave, most of them for a fraction of the big-city cost.

As retirement loomed, he sought for a replacement, someone with youthful energy and an old patient-first philosophy. But all the new doctors wanted more than he could deliver, and the convenience of city life where salaries were high. Eventually, he settled on moving the practice out of the office attached to his home and into this new building, hoping to attract a suitable long-term replacement.

And then Claire McCall came home and agreed to fill in. He took the chance and stepped out of practice, free from the workload, but not from the burden of practice ownership. Claire was a breath of fresh air, and although she'd only just finished her internship, she seemed quick and competent. But she wasn't in a position to buy him out. She needed more training. She'd only suspended her medical training to reconnect with her ailing father and agreed to work for Jimmy as she dealt with the realities of being at risk for Huntington's disease.

So this week, when Dr. Marsh from the University Hospital family practice residency called, Dr. Jenkins responded by extending an olive branch of his own. He would meet with him and talk about a possible sale of his practice to the university. Could they meet Thursday? The university was promoting a new image. Care for everyday or specialty care for all of Virginia. Jimmy agreed. Thursday would be perfect. The office was closed, so he could meet with the Brighton University officials without threatening Claire.

He led Ron Marsh on a tour of his facility, and they stood in the waiting room to talk over a possible relationship. Dr. Marsh stroked his graying beard. "This would be a huge gain for us. We've been struggling to solidify our family practice program. An outpost with this kind of patient volume could be big."

"I want the assurances that most of the care will remain in this community. I don't want the patients to have to go to Carlisle or Brighton for X-rays or lab tests."

"Selling to us would bring more, not less, to this community. We could even consider running specialty clinics here several times a month so the people of Stoney Creek wouldn't have to travel over the mountain."

"There is one issue. About my current physician employee, Dr. Claire McCall. I want to be sure she can continue to work here if she desires."

"She's not currently boarded?"

Jimmy shook his head. "She finished an internship in surgery, but interrupted her training to help care for her father."

"We staff our clinics with board-certified family physicians only."

"But what of your residents? Certainly you could use this location for training."

"I'm sure the residents would help, but they must be overseen by a board-certified attending."

"Perhaps Claire could continue to work here as a part of additional training?"

"We don't have a current opening for any new residents. Perhaps next July." He paused, his hand still on his beard. "Didn't I hear that Dr. McCall diagnosed her father with Huntington's disease?"

"It's true. She is quite a smart young lady."

"And what of her status? Is she carrying the gene?"

Jimmy shrugged. "I don't know. Her mother mentioned her being tested, but I wasn't informed of the result."

"And you are comfortable with her taking care of so many patients? Can't Huntington's disease affect cognitive function?"

"I don't see how that has relevance here. Claire is not showing any signs of Huntington's."

"But investing so much training in an individual whose practice may be curtailed in a few years—well, it might be unfair to deny another capable candidate."

"Claire is the best resident doctor I've seen. Period. HD or not."

Dr. Marsh shrugged. "Well, we don't have any positions open now, anyway."

John took the day off, and he and Claire spent the day house hunting around Stoney Creek and Fisher's Retreat. Everything was either too big or too old. After they visited yet another fixer-upper, discouragement settled in. "I can't believe this market," she said.

John chuckled. "Let's stop at the café for a malt. Maybe Mr. Knitter knows of something coming up for sale." Mr. Knitter ran the Fisher's Café, and if anyone had his finger on the community pulse, it was him.

Claire smiled. John touched her shoulder. "What's on your mind?"

"I was just thinking how wonderful this is, doing something so normal with the man that I love." She felt her eyes beginning to tear.

"What's wrong?"

"Just that I know this isn't going to last. Our lifetime of love is going to be short."

"Shhh. Don't think about that now. This should be the happiest time of our lives."

"It is, John." She shook her head. "But maybe you don't realize what it's like to live with a constant reminder that my happiness will be curtailed." She tapped the steering wheel. "Every time I see Wally, I remember. Anytime I happen to do something klutzy, even if it's just stumbling on a sidewalk, I start to wonder, is this the beginning?"

"All the more reason to strive to make each day glorious." He touched her cheek with the back of his hand.

"Yes," she whispered.

"I love you."

"I'm trying to drive," she said. "Don't make me cry."

Twenty minutes later, with malts in hand, Claire drove toward home. She glanced sideways at the man she loved. "How long will you be able to stay?"

"I need to see a client in Richmond tomorrow. I can drive back tomorrow night if you need me."

She shook her head. "Why don't you stay in Brighton? I want to come up for the weekend anyway. I need to visit a florist and get back to the bridal shop."

"What about Della? Will she stay alone?"

"I think so. The sheriff's department has promised to keep watch. Besides," she added, "I think a little time apart will be good for Mom and me."

Claire slowed as she approached the Stoney Creek Family Practice Clinic. "That's Dr. Jenkins's car." She pulled into the parking lot. "I want to see what he's up to."

A minute later, she entered the front waiting room to see Jimmy Jenkins and Ron Marsh, a physician she knew from her days at Brighton University. She nodded a greeting. "Dr. Jenkins, Dr. Marsh," she said. "What brings you to Stoney Creek?"

He traded glances with Dr. Jenkins. "Just checking out a little business opportunity for the university."

She looked at Dr. Jenkins. "You're thinking of selling the practice to the university?"

Looking uncomfortable, he said, "What would you think of that?"

"I think it's a wonderful idea. It's win-win. You get to sell the practice, and the university gets a training site for residents and a secure referral to Brighton anytime we see anything complex."

Dr. Marsh nodded. "That's the way we see it. Shall I get our attorneys to draw up an agreement?"

"Not so fast," Jimmy responded. "Without an assurance that Dr. McCall will have a position in residency to train here, I'm afraid we don't have a deal."

"But you said—"

"Forget what I said," Jimmy interrupted. "Dr. McCall was willing to help me out of a jam. I'm not going to leave her in the cold."

Dr. Marsh stroked his chin with his hand and seemed to be studying Claire. Then he shrugged and stepped toward the door. "You've been trying to sell this practice for a long time, Dr. Jenkins. You're willing to walk away from this deal for the sake of this one doctor?"

Jimmy looked at Claire. "For her, yes."

Dr. Marsh's expression remained sober. "We've made promises to other students. We don't have approval for additional spots."

Jimmy folded his hands in front of his chest. "No spot for Dr. McCall, no deal."

Dr. Marsh spoke to Claire. "He trusts you with his patients, when he wouldn't sell to me."

"Yes, sir."

He smiled and turned to leave. "I'll see what I can do."

She stood with Jimmy to watch Dr. Marsh cross the parking lot to his car. Jimmy chuckled. "He'll come around."

She gave his hand a squeeze. "Thanks, Dr. Jenkins. For your sake, I hope you're right."

That evening, John ate dinner with Della and Claire. The conversation was okay, but Claire noticed that Della seemed quiet. She was sure that her mother was still annoyed over their talk about Wally.

That night, Claire lay awake willing herself not to think about Tyler loose and plotting his revenge. Of course, trying not to think about Tyler was a defeat in itself. At midnight, she prayed and acknowledged God's control. Trust, she'd learned, was not a state of arrival from which she couldn't topple. Trust was learned. Relearned. And relearned again through a thousand hardships.

Friday, she followed John into Brighton. While he went on to Richmond to help a cardiology practice adjust to their new e-patient software, Claire made a down payment on a wedding dress, hired a florist, and looked at two different photographer's portfolios. By the end of the day, she realized that her mother would need a small miracle not to go into debt over the wedding.

Friday evening, John and Claire rented a DVD and stayed up late eating popcorn at his apartment. In between handfuls, John asked, "What do you think about having children?"

Claire sighed. She loved children. She'd always dreamed that after establishing her career in medicine she'd have a family. But then came HD and the realization that the misery that was her father's would be hers, and each of her children would carry a coin-flip of a chance of ending up with the same fate. "John, you know."

"You always talked of having a family. Have your test results changed anything?"

Claire searched his eyes. "I would love to bear your children, you know that."

"But."

He understood. Their initial joy could turn into added responsibility for John if he ended up caring for a wife and one or more children with HD.

"I think about it all the time," he said. "I'd like to have a family."

"But what if our children have Huntington's?"

"What if they don't?"

Claire shrugged. "Equal odds."

"Your life has been worth living, even if it ended today. You've enriched thousands of people's lives, Claire. You've changed this whole town by dispelling the myth of the Stoney Creek curse." He paused. "Most of all, you've made me a very happy man."

"This means I should bear children?"

"This means that just because someone is destined to suffer from a disease later in life, it doesn't mean that the life wasn't worth living. Maybe God has a plan for the future that includes children."

"I'm afraid for you. Sometimes, in subsequent generations, the onset for Huntington's can be earlier."

"Jesus lived and died before the mean age for onset for Huntington's."

"Your point?"

"That God may have a plan for someone who doesn't have a long life."

"I don't want you to be burdened with too much. What if you end up taking care of me and a child with HD?"

"If that happens, I'll deal with it when the time comes." He took her hands. "If we are going to have children, we shouldn't wait a long time. If we have them soon, you'll be able to be a mother for a long time."

She smiled. "I want you to be sure."

"Let's elope."

"Believe me, after today at the Bridal Gallery, I'm tempted."

The next evening, with Claire on her way back to Stoney Creek, John went to cheer on his work teammates in a post-season softball tournament. It was hard for him to sit on the sidelines, but his recent femur fracture had sidelined him for the season.

John sat on the top row of a small set of metal bleachers and inhaled the warm scent of freshly mown grass. In spite of the late hour, the field was noon-day bright with illumination from the stadium lights. His team wore blue jerseys embroidered with the initials "M.R.S." for Medical Records Solutions, the parent company that produced the e-patient software he represented. He unwrapped a chili dog and dreamed of the future, watching his son play Little League on a night made for baseball.

He looked up as Ami Grandle waved and excused her way through the crowd to sit at his side. "Hi," she said, smiling. She wore an M.R.S. baseball cap and a pair of too-short shorts.

"Hi, Ami." He looked at the field where his team was up four to two.

"Missed you the last few days. You didn't come in."

"I took a day off, then I was in Richmond," he said, staring straight ahead. "The Henrico doctor's cardiology group is converting to our software." He turned his attention to a small order of french fries he had purchased at the snack bar.

Ami scooted closer and stole a fry.

"Oh," he said, holding them out to her. "Have some."

She responded by moving even closer and smiling as she helped herself. "I love softball. Did you play on the team?"

"Shortstop." He pointed onto the field to the left of the pitcher. "Right there, where Bob Estes is playing."

Bob scanned the crowd just as John pointed.

"Oooh," Ami said, taking his arm in her hands and moving even closer.

John looked over. "Ami," he said, pulling away. "I'm engaged. You know that."

She leaned into his cheek and whispered. "Oh, I know, but Bob Estes was looking at me."

He scooted away.

"Just play along," she said. "Bob has been hitting on me at work. If he sees me with you, maybe he'll leave me alone."

"I don't want there to be rumors at work, Ami."

She pushed out her lower lip. "I don't care what others say," she pouted. "Just this once," she said, slipping her arm around him and stealing another fry. "Bob's been such a jerk."

John felt her T-shirt graze his arm. Caution lights fired. He needed to get away before he started enjoying this. He stood up abruptly. "I need something to drink."

She smiled sweetly. "I'll take diet."

Chapter Thirteen

Monday morning found Claire back in the saddle and happy with the workload to keep her occupied. She walked back into an exam room to see Sarah Payne. "Your strep test is negative. I want you to drink plenty of fluids. You should be better in a day or two."

"I need an antibiotic."

Claire sat on a rolling stool and looked at her patient. Sarah was forty-two, the mother of three teenagers and the manager of her own printing business. "I know you feel bad, but it's from a virus. I've seen two other cases already this morning."

"My husband got a Z-pack when he had sinus problems."

"That was different. That was due to a bacterial infection. Viruses don't respond to antibiotics."

"So I just have to suffer?"

"Take Tylenol. Get plenty of rest."

She sighed. "I've got a business to run."

Claire nodded. "I'm sorry."

Sarah slipped off of the exam table, straightened the wrinkles in her designer dress, and huffed.

"Overprescription of antibiotics is a problem," Claire reminded her. "It creates infections resistant to medication."

Sarah waved her hand and exited the room without a reply. Claire clenched her teeth. People could be so unappreciative.

Claire walked back down the hall to find Jimmy Jenkins in her office. He was dressed in blue coveralls and a T-shirt, his attire when he came to do office maintenance or yard work. "Morning, Claire."

She smiled and laid a chart on the desk. "Mowing day?"

"Yep. How's the staff?"

"Okay, I think. Lucy refuses to put anyone in the first exam room, but on the whole, I think the crew is holding up."

"Any new word on the investigation?"

"Randy Jensen came over and briefed the staff before we started this morning. Their best guess has this Tyler Crutchfield a long, long way away from Stoney Creek by now. While this guy was incarcerated, they were able to link him by DNA evidence to several assaults out west in the Denver area."

"So that's why he was living under the name Cyrus Hensley."

"Exactly."

Jimmy stroked his chin. "I think it would help the staff to talk with a counselor, someone who could anticipate the post-traumatic stress issues."

"What do you have in mind?"

"A group session or two. Let the girls talk about their fears." He looked at Claire. "You too."

Claire wrinkled her forehead.

"I made a number of referrals to a counselor in Brighton, a Joanne Phillips. She seems to have a great reputation," Jimmy added. "I could ask her to come down."

Claire shook her head. "I'd be more comfortable with someone else."

"You know Joanne?"

Claire took a deep breath and glanced at the open door to her office. She lowered her voice. "I've been seeing Joanne myself already. I wanted to work through some issues after the assault."

He nodded. "I didn't know." He hesitated before adding, "I think that's great, though."

Claire sat in a chair. "I don't know. We haven't really clicked. She seems determined to make me deal with old pain." She shook her head. "Sometimes I wonder if she's really listening to me, or just pushing her agenda."

Jimmy sat on the edge of the desk. "Dealing with the pain in our past isn't fun, Claire. But the best counselors are the ones who take us through the pain."

"Maybe that's what I don't like." She hesitated. "But still, I don't think I want to be seeing her alone and again in a group. It could get too mixed up for me."

"I understand. Maybe I'll make a few calls. See who else I can find."

"Sure."

He held out his hand and helped her to her feet. "I'd better get working," he said with a wink.

Claire moved to the desk, where she dictated the visit with Sarah Payne. As she finished, Jimmy appeared again in the doorway.

"Have you done something with the mower? It's not in the shed."

She shook her head. "It was locked?"

He nodded.

She stood as a growing alarm tightened her gut. "There are only three sets of keys for the shed. Yours, mine, and the key I put under a stone at the corner of the shed."

"Who knew about that?"

"Only me and . . ." Her voice halted.

"What is it?"

She raised her hand to her mouth.

"Talk to me, Claire."

"Did you mow our grass?"

"Mow your grass? What are you talking about?"

"When we went to Brighton, right after Tyler Crutchfield escaped from prison. When we returned, someone had mowed the yard. We thought it was you." She locked eyes with Jimmy. "Tell me you mowed the grass."

He shook his head. "I don't know what you're talking about."

John poured himself another cup of coffee and sat at his desk. A moment later, after a soft knock on the door, Ami appeared and lifted a stack of papers from his out-box. She moved silently to adjust the location of his pencil holder and letter opener, and then turned to leave.

"Good morning, Ami," he said. "You're quiet this morning."

She glanced at him, flashing large brown eyes before closing them in a long blink and turning back to the door. "Morning, Mr. Cerelli."

"So now I'm Mr. Cerelli. What happened to John?"

"We're at work. I should treat you professionally."

He shrugged. "Whatever."

She hesitated. "If I finish early, could I leave by three today?"

He raised his eyebrows. "What's up?"

"I'd like to see my mother," she said, stepping closer to his desk. "My stepdad died recently, so she's alone."

"I'm sorry. Was it expected?"

She nodded. "Cancer."

She stood clutching the stack of papers across her chest, looking very much like a stranded child in the center of a Wal-Mart.

"How are you handling it?" he asked.

She looked at him, as if searching his face for sincerity. "You want to know?"

What else could he say? "Sure."

As she walked around and leaned against his desk, John inched his chair away. In a moment, with her hand cupped against her mouth, her voice erupted in a sob. "He was the only man I could talk to." She sniffed and swallowed before setting aside the stack of papers. "He pretty much raised me. Mom married him when I was in junior high." She shook her head. "My real dad was an abusive jerk. My stepdad loved me."

John rose to his feet, uncomfortable with the emotional volcano he'd uncapped. He'd wanted to create some distance between them, to slip past and toward the center of the room, but as he moved, she launched her body forward, enveloping him in a hug.

His arms shot straight out from his sides, and he stood there crucified with his tearful secretary draped over him, sobbing against his chest. He looked anxiously at the open door, wondering what to do. Meanwhile, Ami nuzzled her sniffing face against his neck, her breath spreading warmth over his skin.

"It's been so lonely," she said, her voice jerking between breaths.

He felt silly. Trapped. If she had been fifty and dumpy, he'd have hugged away. But Ami was young. And built to take John's mind off of work. Hugging Ami created an immediate dilemma. How could he comfort her without enjoying it in the process?

With his eyes on the doorway, he slowly folded his arms around her, and even though he tried to sink his chest away from hers, every movement seemed to be countered as she pressed against his form. He patted her back lightly. "There, there," he said softly, refusing to let his hands stay against her for more than a bouncing touch.

After a moment, he pulled his hands back in what felt like an exaggerated push-up. Managing to edge her back to arm's length, he reached for a box of tissues on his desk and held them up between them. "Here."

She blew her nose and blotted her eyes. "My mascara," she moaned.

"You're fine. Really."

"You're so sweet." She sidestepped the tissue box and brushed his cheek with her lips. A kiss, quick and innocent enough, a thank-you between friends.

She stepped away and picked up the papers she had placed on his desk. "I'm sorry to burden you. I'd better get to work."

He watched as she blotted her eyes and straightened the front of her low-cut blouse. When she reached the doorway, he called after her, "Ami."

She paused and took a deep breath to collect herself. "Yes?"

"You can leave early today."

That evening after a day of work at McCall Shoes, Della pulled into her driveway and glanced in the rearview mirror when she heard the rumble of Jimmy's Harley. Sure enough, he was in his usual pose, confident and free.

She parked and watched as he removed his helmet and unzipped his leather jacket. "Hi, Jimmy."

"What say we ride up the valley to Luray? I know a nice little café where we could have dinner."

Della leaned against her car and sighed. "You're persistent."

"That's good." He hesitated. "Isn't it?"

"I shouldn't."

He held up his hands. "We're friends. That's all. Two adults out enjoying each other's company. What's wrong with that?"

"You're a man. I'm a woman, remember? A married woman."

"You need a man to talk to, Della. I know Wally's not able." He took a step closer. "What would be wrong with a companion?"

"I–I can't." She shook her head. "People would—"

"People understand, Della. Anyone who has seen Wally in the last year wouldn't begrudge a woman who needed a man around."

She shook her head. "Friendship is only the beginning, Jimmy. I know myself."

He stood still, searching her eyes.

"You're eligible. Smart. Not bad-looking for an old man."

He smiled. "Careful," he warned.

"But I'm not. Eligible, that is," she added.

"I'm lonely."

She pushed her hand against her chest, suddenly angry at his selfishness. "And you think I'm not? I still ache for the loss of a husband," she said. "Every day. But Huntington's disease has played a cruel trick on me. Wally's not an able husband anymore, but his body lives on, binding me to a promise I made long ago." She looked away from his gaze. "For better or for worse. In sickness ..."

They stood for a moment, the silence heavy between them.

"I owe this to Wally," she said. "I can't betray him again."

He nodded and scuffed his boot against the gravel. "I'm going to have a little dinner party. A group. You wouldn't be my date or anything. Maybe you'd like to come?"

She rolled his request around, staring at this new man who had emerged since Miriam's death. With a leather jacket in place of a white lab coat, he seemed determined to squeeze something extra out of life.

"Thursday evening, seven o'clock. Casual."

She straightened. "Why not?"

That night, Della and Claire faced sleeping in the McCall house alone.

Claire pulled back the curtain. A police cruiser sat in the driveway. A second car was at the end of the lane.

Della acted nonchalant. "Someone else could have stolen the mower."

"No one else knew where we kept the key. There was no forced entry."

"Did the police look for fingerprints?"

"Yes, but Tyler's prints should be all over that place. He worked for me, remember?"

Della nodded. "So what if it was him? It doesn't mean he'll come after you."

"Mom, this guy has a revenge motive. He took the mower as a warning to me. Don't you see it? He's trying to frighten me." Claire walked to the bedroom and came out holding a handgun.

"Do I need to remind you of your decision to trust God?"

"I am trusting God," Claire said, checking to see that the pistol was loaded and sliding on the safety.

"You're trusting that gun."

Claire went to the garage and came back with a baseball bat. "Here," she said. "Come with me to search the closets before we go to bed."

"You're kidding. I thought the deputies already searched the house."

"So call me paranoid. Remember the night I was attacked? Tyler was in the house all along. He hid in the closet and came out after I'd locked the doors."

"You're scaring me."

"Come on," she said. "We'll search together."

Della tapped the bat against her open palm. "I still don't think we should be trusting in this."

"We're not. We're trusting in God," Claire said. "This is what Pastor Phil calls a means of grace."

Shaking her head, Della followed Claire into the hallway. "Somehow I don't think this was what he meant."

Chapter Fourteen

Thursday morning's schedule included two work-ins: a twenty-two-year-old camper with a weeping poison ivy rash on his arms and neck and a sixty-year-old grandmother with diverticulitis.

Claire handed Emma Robinson a prescription for Cipro and Flagyl, powerful antibiotics to fight the infection lining her colon. "I need to see you again Monday. Stay on a liquid diet until then. If you start having fever or worsening pain, let me know. I'll be on my cell phone this weekend."

Emma nodded resolutely. She'd been through a bout of diverticulitis last winter. "Thank you."

Claire exited the exam room to come face-to-face with her receptionist in the hall. Lisa was not smiling.

"Dr. McCall," she whispered. "A man is here to see you."

Claire sighed. "Tell him to get in line. How backed up am I?"

She shook her head. "He's not a patient. He said he's from the state board." Lisa held out a business card.

Claire read the card. James Dogget Jr., MD. A surprise visit from the state board couldn't be good news. A knot tightened in her upper abdomen.

"I put him in your office," Lisa said. "He's waiting."

Feeling like a fifth grader on the way to see the principal, she took a deep breath and walked back up the hall. She pushed open the door to find a man in a three-piece suit occupying her chair, his briefcase open on her desk, with her work shoved aside. He was garden-hose thin, with glasses a size too large for his bony face. He didn't stand. A smile passed on and off his face like a camera flash. "Dr. McCall?" He nodded to a chair opposite her desk. "Have a seat."

She sat on the edge of the chair, not quite believing the little general who had conquered the high ground and positioned himself in her place.

"I'm Dr. Dogget," he began, clearing his throat, "an investigator for the Virginia State Board of Medicine."

"I'm Dr. McCall," she responded. "But I guess you know that."

Another camera-flash smile. "Of course." He pushed up his oversized glasses. "We have received a letter of complaint," he said, snapping his briefcase closed. "It is a rather sensitive issue."

Claire glanced at the door before rising and shutting herself in with the suit.

He waited until she was seated again before continuing. "Honestly, we don't see this problem very often, and we debated the proper forum for this." He folded his hands into a mass of knuckles in front of him and leaned forward. "I personally thought the police should be the ones to investigate such a matter." He paused. "Murder is a criminal matter, you know."

Her jaw slackened. "What?" She lowered her voice from the fevered volume that she'd started. "What is this about?"

"My higher-ups view the board as the consummate physician advocate, and although we are ultimately here to protect the people of the commonwealth, we wanted to begin our own internal investigation before turning this into a police matter."

"I don't understand."

"Let me see if I can help." He flashed another grin, this one quick enough for Claire to wonder if it was only a weird facial tic. "I'll need to see the file of a patient, Richard Childress."

Claire shifted in her seat, immediately wondering whether she needed a lawyer, whether she should open her patient records to this power-intoxicated pencil.

He sensed her hesitation. "I can assure you that the state board has the authority to demand and review patient records. If you choose not to cooperate with us, it can only reflect in a negative way on the outcome of our investigation. The police will take little time in obtaining the proper search warrants to obtain what they need if we turn the matter into their hands."

"I–I'll cooperate, Dr. Dogget. It's just that this is such a surprise. I'd really like to know just what it is that I'm being accused of. And who is my accuser?"

He popped open his briefcase again and lifted a letter which he held at arm's length before tilting his head to look through his bifocals. "Physician-assisted suicide of Richard Childress."

"That's ridiculous," Claire scoffed. "Who is raising such an accusation?"

"A family member," he said, running his finger to the bottom of the letter. "Ami Grandle, a stepdaughter."

"Have you spoken to Richard's wife, Nancy? I'm sure she can clear this up. I only learned of my patient's death several days later when I was asked to fill out a death certificate."

He shook his head. "I have not. It is our custom as the physician advocate to hear their side of the story first."

Claire restrained the impulse to scoff. Dr. Dogget seemed more of an accuser than an advocate. "May I see what this stepdaughter has written?"

The investigator tilted his head back and forth, as if rolling the thought around his little brain, before sliding the letter across the desk in her direction. She picked it up, her hands trembling. She glanced at Dr. Dogget, whose eyes were trained on her fingers.

Slowly she read the letter.

To whom it may concern,

This letter is to inform the board of my concern that a physician, Dr. Claire McCall, has euthanized my stepfather by a willful overdose of morphine. He was suffering from colon cancer and had undoubtedly asked for her assistance in relief of his pain. Her actions, while perhaps humanistic in intent, were in defiance of my wishes and certainly are in direct violation of state law. She is a dangerous rogue who needs to be stopped. Thank you.

Sincerely,
Ami Grandle

Claire shook her head. "Excuse me," she said, standing. "I'll have my staff retrieve the record. I'm sure we can lay this concern to rest."

She stepped into the hall and motioned for her nurse. "Lucy," she said. "Have Lisa bring me the file for Richard Childress. It will be among the deceased files."

Lucy nodded and stepped away.

"Oh, Lucy, tell Lisa to offer the non-urgent patients a chance to reschedule. I may be tied up here for a while."

Lucy nodded and whispered, "I'll pray."

Claire reached for her hand. "When will I ever remember who's in control?"

Lucy's eyes sparkled beneath her gray hair. "Look with the eyes of your heart."

Claire squinted as the metaphor settled into understanding. Faith meant seeing the unseen loving Father behind the present darkness. She nodded. "Thanks."

A minute later, Lisa handed the chart to Claire. Claire, in turn, opened it in front of Dr. Dogget. "Here," she said, pointing at her last entry. "I've documented the last visit. He was getting weak. I've dictated my feelings about comfort care and a discussion we had about getting Richard a hospital bed." She flipped a page and pointed to a copy of a prescription. "Here is a copy of the prescription for morphine. It is clear that the instructions are for dosages which would be far beneath a lethal dose."

Dr. Dogget closed his hand around the file and slid it away from Claire. "If you don't mind, I'd like to examine this on my own." He turned to the first page of the chart and poised a pen over a yellow legal pad. "Why don't you continue seeing patients? I'll let you know when I'm through here."

When Claire didn't move, he held up his hands in a truce. "Look, Dr. McCall, I know you don't like this. I don't either. And hopefully, I can help clear up this mess for you." He offered a weak smile.

Claire didn't return it. Instead, she nodded and left him alone, pulling the door shut as she backed out of her office.

She plodded up the hall and pulled a chart from a door rack. A young man who wanted to play football and needed a physical. She smiled. This she could do.

Fifteen minutes later, she glanced back at her office door, still closed. She imagined Dr. Dogget cackling with glee over the open chart. She shook her head and went into the next exam room. An elderly man with a hundred complaints, all of which surfaced since the loss of his wife to cancer three months ago.

After twenty minutes of a thorough exam, and some reassurance, Mr. Bonhaver left, as he did monthly, with a quicker step.

Claire avoided looking at the office and jumped through the next three patient visits, a well-baby check, an elderly man whose urinary stream had weakened to a dribble, and a teen pregnant with her second child.

When she entered the hall again, Lucy pointed to the office. "Dr. Dogget is ready."

Claire barked under her breath and Lucy giggled. Claire pushed open the door.

He held up his hand toward a chair. "Don't be afraid of me, Dr. McCall. I'm on your side."

She sat.

"Your chart seems to be in order. There is nothing here to substantiate a claim against you."

"There is no evidence to be found, sir."

"I would assume that a physician involved in euthanizing a patient wouldn't document it."

"Assuming I am guilty, Dr. Dogget."

"I'm assuming nothing. I am merely responding to a rather serious accusation." He paused. "Were you present when Mr. Childress died?"

"No. I only learned of his death a few days later."

Dr. Dogget stared at her from above his oversized glasses. "He died the day after you gave this prescription for morphine."

Claire's mind churned, wondering if it was time to find a lawyer. She thought back to the weekend of Mr. Childress's death. "I was in Brighton that day. I was shopping for a wedding dress with my mother."

The investigator made a note.

"I think you need to talk to Nancy Childress. I'm sure she attended her husband's death. She can straighten this all out. If my patient died from a morphine overdose, it was certainly against the instructions on the prescription I wrote."

"Did you explain the dosing to Mr. Childress?"

Claire paused. "No."

Dogget raised his eyebrows. "You didn't?"

Inside, Claire's stomach knotted. She was hesitant to draw Dr. Jenkins into this. But she needed to tell the truth. She took a deep breath. "My employer, Dr. Jimmy Jenkins, is a personal friend of the Childress family. He took them the morphine I prescribed. I trusted him to give the instructions."

"Okay, I'll talk to Ms. Childress. If her testimony jibes with yours, you'll have nothing to worry about." He shut his briefcase. "But if it is as you say, why would this daughter have written such a scathing letter?"

Claire put up her hands. "I have no idea."

She followed Mr. Dogget to the front desk, and he exited through the lobby. Then she returned to her desk, where she phoned Jimmy Jenkins. She rested her head in her hand as she listened to the recording. "You've reached Jimmy Jenkins. I'm not here right now, which means I'm out feeling the wind on my Harley. Leave a message after the beep."

She sank onto her desk chair, which was still warm from its last occupant. How could things have gotten so confused? "Dr. Jenkins? This is Claire. I need you to call me about an urgent matter as soon as you come in. I'm at the office."

John sat in his favorite Brighton restaurant for lunch, a diner called Mom's Place, where the waitresses, young or old, all salted their hair and told you to eat your vegetables. The booths were seventies décor, and eight-track tapes tiled the far wall. At Mom's Place, you paid for the verbal abuse and were rewarded by generous home-style portions heaped onto your plate from casserole dishes. You wouldn't even dare ask for dessert unless you cleaned up your plate.

John lifted a steaming forkful of lasagna and inhaled. Heaven. As he chewed, he glanced at his fingernails. Once after he'd worked in his father's garden, a waitress at Mom's had sent him to the washroom to scrub his nails before she'd take his order.

Ami slid into the booth across from him. "Mind if I join you?"

"Uh, well, I was about done."

She waved her hand at the waitress. "A couple of others are coming from work. Might as well make it a community table."

John looked around toward the door. No one was following her. For the time being, it would appear that they were dining alone, something he wanted to avoid. He took another bite of lasagna, then looked up to see his waitress, a middle-aged woman wearing a name tag that read "Momma Darlene." Her hands were on her hips. "What's the idea, not warning me that you were bringing home a date?"

John reddened beneath her gaze. Her voice was loud, attracting the smiles of the other patrons.

"Starting to eat before your guest is just plain rude." She looked at Ami and took her cheeks in her hands. "Oh, you poor sweet thing. My son has no manners." She winked. "But I can see he has good taste in women. It's been thirty years since I had a killer figure like you."

Ami giggled.

"What would you like, child? How about a new boyfriend?"

"This one is fine," she said, glancing at John. "Bring me the same thing he's having."

"The lasagna? I wish I could eat it. With all that cheese, it has a million calories," Momma Darlene said. "If I ate that, I might as well stick it right on one of these hips." She looked at John and shook her index finger. "And no comments from you. You're the reason I look this way. I looked like this twiggy here until I got pregnant with you!" With that, she stormed toward the kitchen to the applause of the guests at the other tables.

John, however, hung his head. The last thing he needed was for all of Brighton to think he had a new twiggy girlfriend. He waited for the others from work to materialize while Momma served Ami and told him to eat his green salad. "It aids good bowel function," she said.

As John finished his salad, Ami pushed her lasagna around on her plate. "I'm so glad we've gotten to know each other."

John glanced around, wondering where all the spit went when your mouth gets dry. He cleared his throat and nodded, then watched uneasily as her eyes began to sparkle with tears.

She blotted her eyes with a napkin. "I've never been able to trust men," she said, her voice barely above a whisper. "Just interacting with you has given me some hope." She sniffed. "You know, that all men might not be jerks."

"Certainly you don't think all men are— "

"Not all men," she interrupted. "My stepfather was a jewel." She paused and leaned forward. "I hated my real father. It's surprising after his abuse that I could ever love a man." She let her eyes linger on his. In a flash, her expression hardened. "He's in prison."

John squirmed. Where were the others she'd promised? He looked at her. Certainly this model of physical perfection couldn't lack for men. "I'm sorry, Ami."

"You're so kind, John." She reached for her water glass and brushed his hand with hers. It seemed so accidental, but he had to fight the urge not to pull his hand away. "That's what I love about you," she added.

"Ami, I— " He looked around again and kept his voice low. "You know I'm engaged."

"I know that. And maybe that's why I'm not afraid of you. We can be friends. And I know you're not just dying to take me to your bed."

"Of course not." His voice was urgent.

"Here you are." He looked up to see Ju Phan and Bob Estes, both part of the sales force for e-patient software. Bob frowned. "Are we interrupting? We can wait for another table."

"Don't be silly," John said, hoping they didn't notice Ami's tears. "Have a seat."

John listened as Momma Darlene marched up, spouting her grief again. "What's this, you guys show up late for dinner and expect to eat?"

They laughed and ordered the daily special, meatloaf and mashed potatoes.

When Darlene served them, John handed a ten-dollar bill to Ju Phan and excused himself. To his dismay, Ami followed him outside into the parking lot.

"I just wanted to say that I appreciate you not betraying my confidence. Those guys don't need to hear of our relationship."

"Our relationship? Ami, we're friends," he said, holding up a hand. "Right? Friends."

She smiled. "Of course. I appreciate that so much." She held open her arms, offering a hug.

He stood unmoving for a moment, while she let her hands freeze in the air like a statue. "Come on, friend," she coaxed.

He returned the hug, trying unsuccessfully to keep an inch between them. Once in his arms, she kissed his cheek and pulled his ear to her mouth. "I know how you really feel," she whispered.

John backed away, releasing her. "How I really feel is that I wish you'd realize that you are my secretary, not my girlfriend."

She pirouetted on her heels and headed back to the door of the restaurant. "Oh, I understand perfectly, John. I can feel everything you think."

She disappeared, leaving him staring at the front of the restaurant, feeling exposed, wondering just what messages he'd been sending. Of course he was attracted to her. She was drop-dead gorgeous. But he was in love with Claire McCall. This girl meant nothing to him.

Except fire. And temptation.

And desire.

That evening, Della arrived at Jimmy Jenkins's house to mingle with a set of who's who in the Apple Valley. Charles Lamb, mayor of Fisher's Retreat, stood next to the grill giving Jimmy advice on how to marinate the salmon. His wife, Grace, chatted with local wildlife artist Julie Westerly. Judge F. Walter Gifford sat on a porch swing talking to town-council member Joseph Martin. Elizabeth McCall, the newly reinstated chairman of the board of McCall Shoes and Della's mother-in-law, played stand-in hostess, serving merlot to anyone whose glass was half full.

Della hadn't understood just what a few guests meant to Jimmy. Immediately, she felt outclassed and underdressed. Of course, finding herself in the same social circle with Elizabeth was new, and she found herself throwing her shoulders back and attempting to appear worthy. When the mayor retreated to his wife's elbow, Della moved in on Jimmy, talking to him in hushed tones. "Claire has been trying to reach you half the day."

He nodded. "I got her phone message. I got home after the office was closed." He furrowed his brow. "Is there trouble?"

"Claire is in some sort of quandary with the state board. Evidently, Nancy Childress's daughter reported her for suspected euthanasia of Richard Childress." Della glanced over her shoulder.

"That's crazy," he said. "Why?"

"She doesn't know. But the board is taking this pretty seriously. Some investigator was in the office today, demanding to see Richard's file, questioning Claire like she was some criminal."

"Oh, dear." He shook his head. "Euthanasia?"

Della nodded. "With the morphine you gave Nancy. The morphine Claire agreed to prescribe to protect you."

Jimmy's eyes flared. "You can't think that I would have let her do that if I'd have thought anything would ever come of it, Della. I was protecting Richard and Nancy, so they wouldn't look like they had morphine without a prescription."

"Whatever," Della huffed. "But now Claire is in trouble."

"This doesn't make sense," Jimmy said, stroking his chin. "Nancy told me that Richard died without her giving him one dose of the morphine."

"So why would her daughter make such an accusation?"

"I don't know. She's not exactly a stable person. She was very close to Richard."

"Not exactly stable?"

"She's schizophrenic. I'd heard she was doing well, but I know Nancy had some concerns that Richard's death might send her off into delusional thinking."

"Apparently."

They looked up as Elizabeth approached.

Jimmy leaned toward Della and whispered, "Tell Claire not to worry. I'm sure Nancy can clear up any concerns the board may have."

"Hello, Elizabeth."

Elizabeth smiled and lifted her glass. "Here's to your daughter and my granddaughter," she said.

Jimmy chuckled. "What has the McCall princess done now? Become the first Stoney Creek female to graduate from medical school? Solve a medical mystery that has plagued the town for generations?"

"Better than that," Elizabeth said, motioning for the others to gather around. "This is a fitting forum for announcing a new development for our town." She topped off the wine glasses. Again. "To my granddaughter," she said, raising her glass.

The mayor coughed. "What are we celebrating?"

His wife shushed him. "Let her speak."

"As many of you know," Elizabeth began, "our little shoe company has been the largest employer in this area for the past fifty years. But dwindling sales and competition from foreign companies have forced us to cut jobs, and set us on the edge of Chapter 11. Eventually, the final solution to our problem appeared: the sale of our company to a large foreign company which would have ensured a huge increase in our production and provided even more jobs to our community."

Elizabeth continued. "But with Leon's death, and apparent bad legal counsel, the deal was lost. The Japanese firm had a sudden case of cold feet and withdrew the offer."

Jimmy frowned. "What happened? What does Claire have to do with all of this?"

Elizabeth swirled the liquid in her glass. "After Leon's death, his lawyer, an oily man by the name of Alfred Pittington, pled with my granddaughter to make an appeal to Mr. Sugimoto, the official from the Japanese firm which had shown interest in our company."

Elizabeth smiled and sipped her merlot, comfortable being the center of attention. Her eyes sparkled beneath a snowcap of hair.

The judge cleared his throat. "Come on, Elizabeth. Get to the point. What are we toasting?"

"Before Leon's death, I sold him my shares in McCall Shoes, resigning my position on the board. But Claire insisted that if she was to intervene, I'd need to be reinstated to the board and allow my stock shares to be sold back to me at their depreciated value."

The judge groaned as Elizabeth paused again to sip from her glass.

"Well, about a month ago, Claire spoke to Mr. Sugimoto, urging him to take another look at our company, asking him to note the changes in board leadership as evidence that we were making progress on the issues that troubled him." She did a slow celebratory turn, holding the wine bottle in the air like a torch. "Well, today Mr. Sugimoto signed an agreement to purchase McCall Shoes. Our company is saved."

"And half the workers of Stoney Creek," the mayor added.

The judge lifted his glass. "Here's to Claire McCall." He stopped with the glass just short of his lips. "Wait a minute. Just how does Claire McCall have such influence over Mr. Sugimoto?"

Elizabeth laughed. "Let's just say she helped him through a delicate medical procedure, and became a trusted friend in the process."

Della traded glances with Jimmy and shrugged.

Margo closed the leather-backed Bible when she heard the crunch of gravel in the driveway. Kyle was home. She whispered a prayer, "Please God, not another silent evening," and crossed the room, pausing as she listened to the slam of his car door. She met him on the front porch. He kissed her and looked at the yard. "Did you mow?"

Margo looked around. The lawn that had been straggly that morning was trimmed even and short. The scent of cut grass still hung in the air. She shook her head. "I was gone all afternoon. I went to Brighton to look at a dress for Claire's wedding." She walked around the yard. Every blade stood manicured, even the grass next to the fence.

"It looks great." He scratched his head. "Kelly?"

"She's at soccer practice. She hasn't been home all day."

"It couldn't be Casey. She's afraid of the mower."

"Whoever it was did a professional job." A chill played on the back of Margo's neck. "You don't think— "

"What's wrong?"

"That maniac who escaped from prison. He used to mow the grass at Claire's office."

"You think he mowed our grass?"

Margo fought a tide of rising fear. "I don't know. But Claire said someone stole the mower from the shed behind her office. And her maintenance man, the one who escaped from prison, was the only one who knew where she hid the key."

"But why would he mow the yard?"

She shook her head slowly. "He must be sending a message. He knows where I live." She looked at her husband. "He did the same thing at Mom's. Call the police, Kyle."

He wrinkled his nose. "And say what? That someone mowed our yard?"

"Tell them that this Tyler freak is still loose. Tell them that he is still in the area."

Kyle put his arm around Margo's shoulders. "Calm down, honey. You don't know any of this. Maybe it was Henry Smith from down the street. He probably called to see if he could mow and when you didn't answer, he just went ahead and mowed."

"Maybe you're right."

"Of course I'm right. There has to be a logical explanation." He put his arm around her shoulder. "Before I call the police, let me at least check with Henry."

Margo allowed Kyle to walk her into the house.

Kyle picked up the phone book and traced his finger down a long list of Smiths. After a moment, he dialed. "Mrs. Smith? Kyle Stevens here. Just a question. Did Henry come down here to mow today?" He paused. "Okay, okay. Sure … thank you." He set the phone down and looked at

Margo. "His mother said he was out mowing this afternoon. She's not sure where."

"Why didn't you talk to Henry?"

"He's out playing basketball with his friends." Kyle walked to the window.

Margo followed, looking at the grass along the fence. Her stomach churned. Henry never trimmed along the fence.

Chapter Fifteen

As the last of the other guests disappeared, Della urged Jimmy to call Claire. "Here," she said, dialing her own number and handing him the phone, "I'll do the dishes. You talk to Claire."

She listened to the one-sided conversation as he paced in the next room. Jimmy encouraged Claire not to worry. He was sure Nancy Childress would put the rumor about euthanasia to rest. The state board would have no choice but to close the investigation.

When he returned, Della smiled. "Thanks."

He picked up a wet serving tray. "I'll dry."

"I didn't realize you were such a good cook."

"Miriam trained me." He set down the tray in his hand. "How's Wally?"

She sighed. "Horrible."

He picked up a plate. "I'm sorry."

She felt her emotions begin to tangle. She loved Wally. She hated what he had become. She enjoyed Jimmy's company. She despised that she enjoyed his company while she was still married to Wally. She looked at him, angry because of the turmoil in her soul. "Wally wants to die, Jimmy. He just lies there, trapped in a body that won't cooperate, his arms flailing about like a drowning man swinging for a rescue rope." Her hand went to her mouth to hold back a sob. "Claire and I must have talked to his neurologist a hundred times. He just keeps increasing his antidepressants as if some chemical can soothe him, but it never seems to help."

Jimmy put the plate on the counter and faced Della. As she began to weep, he coaxed her to lean against his body, absorbing first her tears and then her fists against his chest. Della hated herself for wanting this man, hated the fact that she was still unable to give into the passion she had pushed away for so many years of obedience to her vows. She knew he understood her agony. It was the quiet knowing of two people who had shared a secret for many years.

Slowly Della's tears subsided and she surrendered to rest her head against his chest. Jimmy lifted his hand to her hair and held her against him. After a minute, she raised her head to meet his eyes. When he leaned his head toward hers, she placed her finger against his lips and shook her head. "Not while Wally is alive."

Friday morning, Claire sat at her desk thumbing through Ami Grandle's medical record. Jimmy's memory about her was correct. She'd been seen in the office throughout her childhood, and her chart contained one sad entry after another. Claire read Jimmy's reports of a battered, sexually abused child who fought with depression and self-esteem. The last entry reflected Dr. Jenkins's report on a complete psychotic break that Ami had during nursing school. She had been so out of touch with reality that he had a rescue squad pick her up from the office and take her to Brighton University for psychiatric care.

Claire shook her head. Why would this woman claim that Claire had euthanized her father? Jimmy had indicated in last night's phone call that Ami was close to her father, and even wondered if the death may have loosened her grip on reality once more, but this accusation did not seem to be the fruit of a person out of touch with reality. This felt more like a calculated attack.

Claire picked up the phone and dialed the number for Dr. James Dogget at the Virgina State Board of Medicine. In a moment, she heard his voice.

"Dr. Dogget? This is Claire McCall. I called to check on your investigation. Did you have a chance to talk with Nancy Childress?"

She pulled the phone back from her ear as he cleared his throat. "I did."

Claire smiled with relief. "Good. I'm sure we can lay the matter to rest."

She listened to the silence on the other end. Then a sigh, as the investigator's breath blew into the phone. "You are anxious to put this behind you. I can understand that. But I've made no solid conclusions about this matter."

"Didn't Ms. Childress inform you that she didn't even give any of the morphine I prescribed? Richard Childress died because of his metastatic cancer, not because of me."

"Dr. McCall, if you had given a lethal injection to your ailing husband, even under the instructions of a physician, what would you say if you were questioned about it?"

Claire gasped. "You're saying you don't believe her?"

"I'm only saying that her response didn't surprise me. Either she is telling the truth or ..." His voice halted.

"Or what?"

"Or she is doing what comes natural when you are an accessory to a crime—covering up."

"This is preposterous! You have no proof of this."

"I have the testimony of Ami Grandle."

"You spoke to her?"

"I did. And her account is very convincing. She tells of her mother calling her to get instructions on how to give the injection."

"But she didn't even give it!"

"Again, Nancy's word only."

"I'll get the medicine back. I can get the unused vials of morphine from Nancy Childress to show you."

"I tried that. But she couldn't find them. She claims they're missing. And she just doesn't know where they could have gotten to." His voice carried a lilt of sarcasm.

"Then exhume his body. Have a forensic pathologist examine his body for evidence of narcotics."

"I don't have the authority to do that. I'm afraid since we've been unable to put an end to this investigation, I'll just have to turn the matter over to the police."

"This is crazy. I didn't do anything!"

"That's not my call. It's out of my hands."

Claire hung her head. "Wait. It's just Ami's word against her mother's, right?"

"Yes." He paused. "Look, Dr. McCall, if things are as you say, you should have nothing to worry about. I'm in a bind here too. If I ignore this, Ami could take the board to task by taking it to the police herself. If they end up uncovering something sinister, it will look like the board isn't doing its job."

"This Ami isn't a stable person. She's had a number of psychotic breaks when she was completely out of touch with reality."

"You know this?"

"It's in her medical record."

"Then I'm sure the police and the district attorney will take that into account when they do their investigation."

She huffed. "I can't believe this."

"I'm sorry, really I am. It's out of my hands. Really."

Claire shook her head. She felt like slamming down the phone. Instead, she took a deep breath. "Thank you," she said, before placing down the receiver. *For nothing!*

That afternoon, before five o'clock closing, Claire looked up to see Detective Randy Jensen just as he lifted his hand to knock on the door frame to her office. Her stomach tightened. *I've been expecting you. Investigating a murder, maybe?*

"Dr. McCall? Sorry to bother you at work."

"Hi, Randy." She nodded at a chair across from her desk. "Have a seat."

He sat and cleared his throat.

"Anything new on the Tyler Crutchfield mystery?"

"Maybe." He frowned, furrowing his brow.

"What is it?"

"Someone mowed the grass at your sister's place."

"Did you look at it?"

He nodded and leaned forward. "It looks just like the pattern you described from your old office mower."

"It's Tyler Crutchfield. It's a threat."

He shrugged.

"Can't you see the pattern? It's just like at my house."

"It makes no sense. Tyler Crutchfield should be miles away."

"Unless he wants to do exactly what you think he wouldn't do."

"Fair enough." He hesitated. "I—"

She watched him for a moment. "What?"

"I didn't just come to talk about Tyler Crutchfield."

Claire sighed.

"It's about Richard Childress."

"I know. The investigator from the state board told me he'd be turning information over to the police."

"So can I ask you a few questions?"

"What have they given you?"

Randy recited the report faxed to him by Dr. Dogget.

"This is really crazy, Randy. I wasn't anywhere close to Richard when he passed away. And as you see, Nancy's testimony lines right up with mine."

He nodded. "Okay, Dr. McCall, this is awkward for me. I'll talk to Nancy Childress and her daughter. If things are what they appear on the surface, you shouldn't have to worry. No magistrate would issue a warrant to arrest you based on this," he said, shaking the paper in his hand.

Claire fought back pessimism. Since when had anything gone the way it should when it had anything to do with her life? "Fair enough," she said, standing.

The officer held out his hand. "Bye."

Claire gathered her things and headed home, determined not to let this accusation, as serious as it sounded, undermine her love for medicine or the people of Stoney Creek. Medicine, after all, had been the calling that provided some sense of stability in her crazy life. As she faced the understanding of her father's abuse, the threat of the onset of Huntington's disease, and the strain of knowing Tyler Crutchfield was loose, her work stood as a refuge to divert her racing mind onto clinical tangibles. Strep throat can be cured by Amoxocillin. Helicobacter Pylori bacteria cause stomach ulcers which can be eradicated by antibiotics. These were the comforting facts that helped anchor Claire into believing in predictable patterns. Life may throw curveballs, but medical science provided research-backed, cause-and-effect outcomes.

But now, as she steered her VW toward home, she couldn't bear to think that the medical life she loved might be threatened by such a distorted accusation. There was one person she could turn to in the presence of yet another crisis. And she needed to see him tonight. She would drive to Brighton to spend the weekend with John at his parents' place. Tony and Christine expected her tomorrow morning, but she needed a dose of John Cerelli stat. She needed his ear, his compassion, and his faith in a loving Lord.

She threw clothes into an overnight bag, carried a dress on a hanger, and scribbled a note to her mother. Then she pointed her VW toward Brighton. And relief. And her lover's arms.

Della sat in a rocking chair at the edge of Wally's bed. She looked at him through the railings, a little slice of his body visible in each section. *This bed is a prison*, she thought. *Wally's illness has incarcerated him in a bed of suffering.*

She listened as his legs whistled across the sheets, now shiny from wear. "Thirsty," he slurred.

She pushed a straw in his mouth and gave him a drink of cool lemonade.

She set the tall plastic container on the bedside table and drifted to another time, another bed that they shared. In the early years of their marriage, Wally couldn't spend enough time with her between the sheets. Now his illness had robbed them of any physical union or the pleasure it afforded. Aching for the days when Wally held her, she took his hand in hers and cradled it against her chest.

"I know you're still in there, Wally McCall. I know you're still the man I fell in love with," she whispered.

Wally looked at her, but his head jerked away, his voluntary control long lost to HD. His hand pulled from her grasp, leaving her standing by his bed, her hands empty.

This isn't the life you wanted. Wally McCall was a man who enjoyed fresh air. How long has it been since you even saw the sunshine?

Is this prison?

Do you want escape?

Della sat by his bed, imitating normal life, talking as if he would answer. As if he would care. "I think Claire has picked out a wedding dress."

She listened, imagining a response.

"She asked Margo to be her matron of honor."

Della sniffed. "John won't tell her where they are going for their honeymoon." She paused, wiping her eyes. "Do you remember our honeymoon? We were supposed to spend our first night in Williamsburg, but we stopped in Brighton because we couldn't wait ..."

Wally's forehead glistened with sweat. His eyes were wide, fixed on his wife, stationary as his head twisted from side to side. Instead of joy, the memory seemed to torture him, an oasis unobtainable to a desert traveler. His mouth curled into a frown.

She leaned forward, anticipating a response. "What is it? Do you remember?"

He grunted rhythmically, as if wanting to respond, but lacking the energy to spit out the words.

She reached out to touch his hand. "I know you remember, honey."

His hand jerked away. It was an involuntary response, part of the cruel dance of HD. She knew that in her head. But the rejection stung, nonetheless.

"D–d–d."

She stood again and wiped the moisture from his brow. "I'm listening, Wally. Talk to me."

"Die." The word fell out in a tumble, but to her experienced ear, understood.

She shook her head. "God will take you home when it is his time."

He began to mumble, softly at first, then growing and accelerating as the turmoil within bubbled to the surface. Mud clung to his words, weighing them down. As he struggled to clarify his thoughts, Della extracted meaning through the muddle. "Claire can help me. Ask Claire to help."

She did not know how to respond. He'd talked of dying for weeks. It was an escape she longed for him to have, but one that she stood powerless to provide. She turned away, speaking to the wall, unwilling to view his suffering as she denied him again. "I know it's hard. I've talked to your doctor in Brighton. He has changed your medicines to help you feel better. God will take you home when it is time." Her voice cracked. She looked back at her husband. He didn't want her platitudes.

Wally closed his eyes, squeezing out a tear. Della reached to wipe it away, knowing Wally couldn't try. A rebellious finger without control could be a weapon to poke a tender eye.

She tried to steer his darkened mood toward the light. She pointed to a time when life bulged with the wonderful baggage of normalcy. "Remember when the twins were born? You were so proud." She sniffed. "They always did everything at the same time. Diapers. So many diapers. And they cried to eat together. And Clay wouldn't take a bottle, so you would feed Claire, and I would feed Clay. And then we'd change the diapers and start all over again."

Wally coughed, choking on a bit of spit or mucus he no longer had the coordination to swallow. Della winced as she listened to the wetness that rattled around her husband's hollow chest.

She chatted on, desperately trying to paint a picture of a time when life had color and meaning. After a few minutes, her palate was dry and her memories seemed a blank canvas. She held his hand for a moment, gripping his tightly so she could trail it along its pathway from side to side. A silent sadness settled over them, a blanket she couldn't throw back.

Her thoughts carried her to tougher times. His violent temper when he was drinking, and the caustic arguments with Clay as a teenager. She remembered when his personality began to change and the onset of Huntington's disease. Wally slammed doors and drawers and cabinets, all because his coordination had begun to fail him. He stumbled and balanced himself against the hallway walls, knocking the pictures of the family askew.

She looked at the hand she held, his fingers whitening from her tight grip as she dared to entertain Claire's accusations. *Is it possible, Wally? Were you ever so drunk that you would have touched your own daughter?*

She couldn't let herself accept it. She and Wally had come so far in restoration of their marriage. Yet somewhere at the edges of her mind, a nagging doubt surfaced. *What if Claire is right?* The idea repulsed her. She closed her eyes, praying that it wasn't so.

"Good-bye, Wally. I should get home."

"D–d–die," he said.

She turned and left him alone. Abandoned. Out of her care. But his voice clung to her ears. She paused at the door and shook her head, wanting something, anything else to think about, but his message stuck, velcroed to her mind. Taking a deep cleansing breath, she blotted the corners of her eyes with her hand, then proceeded into the hall. She clipped through the hallway aware of the pungent odors of urine and antiseptic, willing herself not to breathe until she reached the double doors at the nursing home's entrance and the freshness of life beyond.

John sat working with his laptop open. He reworked a PowerPoint presentation while sitting in the backyard gazebo at his parents' place in Brighton. Friday nights were supposed to be for relaxation and fun, but he needed to get the finishing touches of this project completed before Claire arrived.

He looked up from the computer screen, his eyes unfocused. When Claire called from her car just a few minutes ago, her voice was etched with stress. He'd been wanting to talk to her about Ami, to ask her advice about how to handle her aggressive behavior, but then Claire unloaded yet another problem in her life and he'd backed away from burdening her with one more crisis.

Something he'd understood from the beginning was that life with Claire McCall, while perhaps filled with hardships, was never dull. He'd seen Claire handle the tension of medical education, a malpractice suit, the traumatic death of her twin, and the knowledge that someday she would fall into the clutches of Huntington's disease. All of these, she'd met with confidence, sometimes struggling under the load, but eventually overcoming with a childlike trust in God. But he'd detected something else as she'd unloaded yet another chapter of misery. As the suspicion of foul play in a patient's death added to her current burden of dealing with her father's sexual abuse and her fears of another attack by Tyler Crutchfield, he sensed Claire approaching her breaking point. Times beyond tough threatened to crumble the rock she'd become.

He closed his eyes to pray, asking God for wisdom, for strength beyond human weakness, for the ability to see his hand of direction from beyond the veil. He prayed for knowledge to help, and for joy in spite of circumstance. Then, emboldened by a comforting peace, he prayed for God's staying hand against enemies of darkness that may be responsible for this newest threat to her career.

As he sat in the quiet, he felt her hands cover his eyes. In his absorption in his prayer, he had not heard her approach. He understood the guess-who game. He gripped her wrist, even as he inhaled her scent. She wore a familiar perfume, a light scent of honeysuckle. When he twisted his head to see her, she moved the opposite way. He pulled her hands from his eyes, pressing his lips against the back of her hands. Oh, how blessed he felt to hold the hands of the woman he loved.

She responded by leaning forward, kissing his cheek, burying her face into his neck, caressing him, and tasting him. A sudden shock of realization struck. This was not Claire! He pulled away, turning to see Ami Grandle. "Ami!"

Her eyes widened. "Who else?"

He touched his cheek, her kiss still moist on his face. "What are you doing here?"

She pushed out her lower lip and walked around to sit next to him on the wooden bench. "I needed to talk."

"But you can't just come here and kiss me like that. We're not— We're not like that."

She touched his chin. "You're blushing. You enjoyed it."

Heat stung his cheeks. Of course he liked it. She was beautiful. And he was enjoying it, but he thought he was enjoying Claire. "I—, I—"

"Why, you can't even speak," she teased, flashing a smile of perfect white teeth. She continued in a whisper. "You do that to me too."

"Ami," he countered, finally finding his voice, "I thought you were someone else." He looked away, fleeing her searching eyes. "My fiancée."

"Of course." Sarcasm edged the statement.

He scooted away. "Why did you come?"

She looked down and folded her hands in the lap of her short dress. "I'm going car shopping. I thought you should come along." She looked up at him. "You know car salesmen. They want to take advantage of pretty girls."

John shook his head. "Ami, you shouldn't rely on me to do these things. Certainly you have a brother or—"

"I'm an only child. Richard, my stepdad, would have done it. But he's—" She put her hand to her mouth.

"I know about your stepdad," he said. "I'm sorry."

She sniffed. "So will you help me? I know you know tons more than I do about cars. I know the car I want you to look at. Just go with me and tell me what you think."

"I can't. Not tonight." He took a deep breath. Why did she have to be so gorgeous? "Claire is coming over."

"When?"

He shrugged. "Anytime now."

She stood. "I need to leave."

He felt bad. She looked like a lost child. "Maybe next week."

The corner of her mouth hinted at a smile. "Soon?" She stepped to the edge of the gazebo. "My real father is being released from prison."

"Perhaps he knows about cars."

"I wouldn't ask that man for anything. He scares me."

"Why are you telling me this?"

She shook her head. "I just wanted you to know. So if I seem, well, distracted at work. ..."

"Okay."

"He's very jealous of my friendships." She turned and stepped down into the backyard. "Especially men who pay attention to me. We may have to keep our relationship quiet."

She walked away before he could reply.

"Ami!" he called.

She waved her hand above her head as she headed across the yard. "See you Monday."

Claire found him sitting in the backyard gazebo. Thanks to her mobile phone, she'd already unloaded the newest twist in her professional life. He had listened and promised to pray. With that out of the way, she could run straight for the hug she needed.

He lifted his arms at her approach. "Hi, baby."

She met his lips with hers and laid her head on his shoulder, wanting nothing more than to run away with John to some exotic land, somewhere with white sand and warm breezes and no hint of life's pain.

Taking a deep breath, she felt the tension of the week begin to melt away. She stretched out on the bench with her head in his lap and closed her eyes. He stroked her face as the minutes passed in blissful silence.

"I do have some good news," she said, sitting up. "Margo called me this morning." She paused. "Well, it's good and bad news."

He smiled. "Of course. Bad news first."

"Okay. Someone mowed her yard."

His eyes narrowed. "Like yours?"

She nodded. "Just like Mom's. John, it has to be Tyler. He's just trying to freak us out."

"Is it working?"

She frowned. "I guess. Mom has agreed to put in an alarm system. And Deputy Jensen promised that the sheriff's department is doing everything they can. They've put a patrol at our house every night."

He nodded. "So what's the good news?"

She felt her heart quicken. "With all the pressure, Margo is starting to ask questions about faith."

"That's awesome." He leaned forward. "Why now?"

"You mean, finally?" She shrugged. "She's been chasing happiness for a long time, John. And she's tasted a little with her gorgeous home, her husband, and her daughters, but ..."

"But?"

"She told me everything is falling apart. Kyle can't seem to forgive himself for his affair. Their finances are shaky. Kyle has started bringing up hurt from long, long ago. She thinks he's depressed. He's started joking about Daddy dying so they can get some inheritance."

He nodded. "He was irritable at the reunion."

She smiled. "But in the midst of this, Margo sounded as peaceful as ever. She's finally given up the idea that she needs to control her own happiness," she said, laying her head on his shoulder.

They were quiet for a moment before John turned his face to hers, letting their lips brush. Then he kissed again, harder, more deliberate, and she felt a longing begin to stir. She lifted her chin as he dropped his mouth to her neck, caressing, searching.

A fleeting memory danced across her mind, shutting down desire. Someone groping her in the darkness. Tyler? Was this a flashback from his attempted rape? Or something darker from her past, something long buried, a night she'd pushed away unable to sort or categorize? Was this a hint into a night of alcohol-related oblivion?

She pushed John away, her breath quick and short.

"Claire," he said. "I just want to kiss. I won't go farther."

"It's not that."

His eyes widened. "You're afraid. I see it in your face."

She looked away.

"Claire, what is it?"

She shook her head, willing the thoughts away. "Nothing."

"Claire."

"Old memories. Someone touching me who wasn't welcome."

John lifted his arm from around her shoulder and placed it in his lap. She read the disappointment on his face.

"John, I'm sorry."

He took a deep breath. "Me too."

"Don't be angry."

"I'm not." He struggled for the right word. "Frustrated," he said. "I want you to move on."

"Me too."

His eyes bore in on hers. "Before the wedding." He reached for her hand. "How's the counseling?"

She wrinkled her nose. "I don't know. I get mixed up. Joanne wants me to rehash my relationship with my father. She wants me to confront the past, confront my father about what may have happened." She shook her head. "Wally wouldn't remember what he did in an alcoholic haze."

"You're sure he touched you?"

She looked at the ground and nodded. "I remember enough."

"Claire, do what the counselor wants. Confront the past. I want you to do whatever it takes to heal."

"She's talking about a 'mock confrontation,' " she said, framing the last two words in finger quotation marks. "It all seems so silly." Claire looked back at John. "I don't really jibe with my counselor. It doesn't feel right."

"Digging through past hurts can't feel good, honey."

"That's exactly what Dr. Jenkins said. He seems to have a lot of faith in this counselor. She's helped him with patients in the past."

John took her hand in hers. "Then do what she wants, Claire. So we can move forward. Together."

She kissed him again, pressing herself against him one more time.

This time, he pulled away, looking down and reaching into the breast pocket of his shirt. He wore an expression of surprise as he pulled out a little piece of jewelry. She watched as he opened his hand to inspect a pearl earring.

She smiled. "For me?"

He closed his fist around it. "N–no. It isn't yours." He turned his face away, suddenly sober. "It must be Ami's." His hand touched his mouth as if to keep back the soft words which escaped his lips.

The first hint of alarm rose within her. "Ami? Who's this Ami?"

He shook his head. "Nobody. My secretary. She stopped by before you came over. She wanted advice on a car she wants to buy."

John rolled the pearl around in his hand before shoving it into his pants pocket. With his face tensed, he looked like a boy caught with his hand in the cookie jar.

"Talk to me, John. What was her earring doing in your pocket?"

He feigned nonchalance. "It must have dropped into my pocket," he said, as redness touched his cheeks. "She hugged me, Claire. She's like that. You know, expressive."

Her eyes traveled over his collar. She leaned forward and touched his cheek with her hands. There, at the jawline, she smeared away a pink smudge.

He pulled away. "What?"

She inspected the greasy gloss between her fingers. "Expressive? She kissed you?"

He backpedaled. "A greeting, Claire." He hesitated. "It was nothing." His eyes met hers. She was not about to break away.

"Claire," he pleaded. "I told her she shouldn't have kissed me. Honest." He sighed. "I've been wanting to tell you about her. She's a flirt. She comes on to me at the office. I'm not responding to her, Claire, but she doesn't get the message."

She felt her jaw tighten. "Tell me her name."

"Ami."

She spoke through her teeth. "Her full name."

"Ami Grandle."

Chapter Sixteen

Claire gasped as if she'd been punched. "No."

"What?"

She shook her head slowly. "No," she repeated, standing to pace in the little gazebo.

After two laps, she looked down at John, his brow furrowed, his mouth agape. "You don't know, do you?" she said.

He opened his hands. "What?"

"Ami Grandle is the daughter of Richard Childress. She's the one who reported me to the state board."

"No way."

Her eyes bore in on John, still seated on the white bench. "How well do you know this girl?"

He shrugged. "She seems nice enough. I mean, probably not very well. I just see her at work. Well, I did see her at a ballgame once, but that was the team from work and, well, once at a restaurant, but that was with guys from work too."

"Slow down, Cerelli. You're not on trial here." She stopped pacing and put her hands on her hips, standing over him. "What's with the blushing? What aren't you telling me?"

He looked up, shifting in his seat. After a moment he began. "Look, Claire, it's not like—" He halted and then began again. "She's just—" He paused again. "I would have told you if there was anything—" He shook his head and sighed.

"Spit it out, Cerelli."

He looked at his hands. "She has a crush on me, Claire. I've told her I'm engaged. I haven't encouraged her. Honest."

"Why didn't you tell me?"

"I've started to a dozen times. But the conversation always turns to something else, some new catastrophe," he said, waving his hands in the air. He shrugged. "I didn't want you to worry. You have enough to worry about."

Claire's stance was frozen, her hands on her hips. She thought back to a call John received that day at her office. "Does she call you?"

He shrugged. "She's my secretary, Claire. Business."

"At home?"

He winced. His silence was answer enough.

"E-mail?"

He looked down, shaking his head. "How do you know these things?"

"I'm a woman, John. This is how the relationship game is played in modern times. You like someone; you send e-mails. It's innocent enough. Not as threatening as face-to-face."

"Ami's the one who accused you of euthanizing her stepfather?"

Claire nodded. "Answer the e-mail question, John."

"She e-mails me." He took a deep breath. "Pretty much every day."

"How often?"

He winced again. "Three or four times. Maybe six."

"Every day?"

He nodded silently.

"She thinks you like her."

"I haven't tried to make her think that."

"But she believes it."

"Yes."

"She's stalking you, John. You need to fire her."

John straightened. "Fire her?"

"I'm not kidding, John." She bit her lip, knowing she couldn't reveal anything from Ami's office chart. "I can't say any more."

"I'll talk to her. I'll make boundaries."

"You'll fire her, John."

Their eyes locked. "That will be hard."

"You said she's your secretary."

"She's an assistant to the whole sales force."

Claire sat down again. "I don't like this. This girl works for you. In fact, she has a crush on you." Claire tapped her fingers against the bench. "Maybe this is exactly why she is trying to make my life miserable. I represent the competition."

"Are you jealous?"

"Maybe." She looked away. "She's stalking you. This is classic, John."

"Stalking me?" He shook his head. "It's just a crush. She's young."

"Does she think you like her?"

"She might think it, but it's not true."

"She's an erotomanic stalker."

"And you have the expertise and detachment to make such a judgment without meeting her?"

"I read about this after my encounter with Brett Daniels. Remember him?"

"Of course."

"He didn't fit the definition, but it sounds as if this Ami might. She stalks a person, whom she thinks returns all of her love. She e-mails, she watches. She dreams. It can be with a coworker, maybe someone else who has rejected her in some way." She didn't mention it, but she remembered a link between psychopathology such as schizophrenia and stalking behavior.

He nodded. "Sounds like Ami. I'll talk to the team about letting her go." He held out his hand toward her. "I'm sorry, Claire."

She stepped back, shaking her head. "It's not you, John. If I were her, I'd have a crush on you too."

"You're not mad at me?"

"I'm not mad. I'm—" She looked at her hands and closed her fist to disguise her trembling fingers. She sank to the bench. "I'm just tired, John."

She sat quietly feeling the weight of his eyes.

"Talk to me," he whispered. "I love you."

She felt her throat tighten. "What else can go wrong?" She sniffed. "I give up my dream of surgery to devote time to my father, hoping to recapture a meaningful relationship. Just when I think I've begun to understand him, to understand how HD may have been affecting him all those years—" She halted, wiping her eyes with a tissue. "I was on the verge of really coming to grips with forgiveness when I began to remember ... abuse."

"I know," he said. "I know."

"But I cope, John. You know how?" She searched his eyes. "I bury myself in helping everyone else." She hesitated. "Or I focus on you and our future together."

"Those are good things, Claire."

"That's not the point. I'm not bragging. The point is that everything I'm tempted to define my life by seems to be taken from me. Or at least tested to see what I'm trusting."

He slid closer and placed his arm around her shoulders.

"First it was my career in surgery. So I adapt, take a job here in family medicine. But now, thanks to this Ami, even that is threatened."

"Her accusation is groundless. You said yourself that the police investigation is unlikely to get past an interview with her mother."

"That doesn't matter. If this gets to the public, it's the perception that can ruin a medical practice." She reached up and ran her finger along the line of his jaw. But even as she delighted in her love for him, an anxiety bubbled up from within her soul. "I think I can take it if God chooses to take medicine from me." She paused. "But I'm not sure I can handle losing you again."

"I'm not going anywhere, Claire."

She closed her eyes, willing back the tears. She wanted to believe that John would be the solid rock in the stream of her turmoil. But she knew that forces were in play to erode the edges of her reliance upon him. Memories of childhood abuse threatened to surface each time she surrendered to his touch. And now this Ami had insinuated herself into his life. Young, full of vigor enough to e-mail, call, and even kiss the one that Claire loved.

She laid her head against his shoulder. She wanted to wrap herself in the comfort of his reassurance and rest. *He says he doesn't return her affection. So why does he blush at the mention of her name?*

On Sunday morning, Margo nudged the shoulder of her husband's sleeping form. At least he was pretending to be sleeping. It was nine o'clock and past time of rising and shining if they were going to make it to church on time.

"Come on. Get up. We're going to be late."

Kyle groaned. "Go without me."

Margo sighed. "You promised."

He rolled over to face her. "I can't."

"The girls are all ready. They want you to go."

He rubbed his unshaven chin and shook his head. "I tried, Margo. I just feel like a hypocrite if I go."

"You won't be alone."

He stared at her, unmoving.

"Maybe you should just do it for me."

A blank stare.

"Or your girls."

He yawned. "I'm going into work. I've got to get our ledger to the accountant tomorrow."

"Fine." She said the word with sarcasm. It wasn't fine. It was far from fine.

She stood and stomped her way to the doorway before turning again. "Is that the mistress I'm competing with now?"

He threw up his hands. "Mistress?"

"Your work. Is it stealing you away from me?"

He rolled his eyes. "If I get this done this morning, I can spend a little time with you and the girls this afternoon."

"Or you could spend time with us in church this morning and work this afternoon."

He tossed back the sheets and stood up. "I said I'm not going."

"What are you afraid of?"

"Afraid? I'm not afraid." He plodded toward the bathroom. "Unless I'm afraid of being a fake. That cheery gospel message may be good for you, but it's a little too good to be true for me."

He shut the door to the bathroom, leaving her alone. She stood listening to the sound of his electric razor, and then water splashing against the sink. Brushing a tear from the corner of her eye, she turned to round up her daughters.

First thing Monday morning, John walked into Carol Dawson's office, brushing past Ami, who exited with an armload of files. Puzzled at Carol's sober expression, he shut the door. "I've got a problem."

Carol lifted her hand toward a chair. "Morning, John."

John sat and took a deep breath. "I'm having some trouble with Ami."

Carol pushed a strand of gray hair behind her ear. "Trouble?"

"She keeps coming on to me. Flirting. Not respecting professional boundaries. She e-mails me constantly, even stops by my house."

He watched as Carol's demeanor shifted. "She's coming on to *you*?" The inflection of her voice reflected her disbelief.

He was taken aback. "Yes." He lifted his head. "You sound surprised."

She pushed her chair back and crossed her legs. "Tell me more."

"She came over to my house the other evening. Snuck up on me from behind. She kissed my cheek."

Carol stayed quiet, her eyes boring in on John, who felt uncomfortable beneath her inspection.

"I've not returned her e-mails. I've told her I'm engaged. She doesn't seem to be put off. She seems intent on wanting a romantic relationship with me."

"I'll need to see the e-mails, John. I need you to put this in writing."

"I've trashed the e-mails, Carol." He paused. "I think we need to fire her."

Carol tapped a silver pen against the desktop. "Are you reciprocating her feelings?"

John found himself blushing. "No." He shook his head. "No, I mean, she's an attractive woman, but no, I've told her clearly that she is only my friend."

Carol squinted. "A man can send messages without words, John."

He squirmed in his chair. "I'm not trying to send messages, Carol. I've told her I'm engaged." He held up his hands. "But she doesn't respect what I say."

Carol pushed a button on her keyboard and looked at her computer monitor. "File a formal complaint. Put it in writing so I'll have something to act on." She looked back at John. "Then I'll make a decision."

He sighed. "Okay." He stood up and hesitated. "She tells me you've asked her to help with my presentations in Richmond this week."

Carol nodded.

"I'd really be more comfortable by myself."

"You need her on this one, John. The Henrico doctor's group is expecting the nice touches that she will add."

"Can you at least talk to her? Warn her to keep things at a professional level."

Carol's attention was back on her computer monitor. "I'll see what I can do."

Bob Estes heard his name as he passed Carol Dawson's doorway. He paused and smiled. "What's up, boss?"

She motioned him in. "Shut the door."

He obeyed.

"I need your perspective on something. You're next in chain of command around here. I've got some personnel issues to sort out."

He folded his hands across his lap. "Sure."

"It's about Ami and John."

He raised his eyebrows. "You've noticed."

"Noticed? Not exactly." She sighed. "Ami came to me, very sweetly, and explained how her relationship with John had made a romantic turn. She told me she loved her job and hoped that her involvement with John wouldn't compromise her ability to continue with the company." Carol held up her hands. "I told her to be careful, and that what she did on her own time was her own business. As long as their relationship didn't affect her work, I didn't see any problem with it."

Bob drummed his fingers on his thigh and wondered why John Cerelli seemed to be the lucky guy. He nodded. "Sounds like the right kind of advice." He lowered his voice. "Did you warn her that John's engaged? I'd hate to see her get hurt."

Carol shook her head. "Not exactly. I wasn't sure it was my place. Anyway, then in comes John with a different story. He says Ami is paying all kinds of attention to him. Visits outside work, e-mails, that kind of thing. He says he isn't interested and is troubled by her desire to have a relationship. He wants me to fire her."

"Oh, boy."

"Exactly," Carol said. "What's your perspective? I know you spend a lot more time around them than I do. Someone doesn't seem to be telling the truth."

"John talks about his engagement some."

Carol tapped her pen against the desk. "Anything else? Do you see any interaction with Ami that may suggest John is leading her on?"

"I've seen them together outside work. Once at a softball game. She was on his arm. And I've seen them out to lunch together."

"What's your take?"

"I'm not sure. John talks like Claire McCall is the only woman for him."

"But his actions may speak otherwise."

Bob shrugged. "I'm minding my own business around here."

"But keep your eyes open for me. Has Ami ever been flirtatious with you?"

Bob stood up. "I wish."

Chapter Seventeen

By Monday closing time, Claire was anxious to get out. The day had been hectic. It seemed everyone in Stoney Creek was battling the same flu virus and they all needed attention at once.

As she placed the last file in her out-box, Lucy handed her a chart to initial. "Sarah Payne called."

"Another request for antibiotics?"

"No. She just wanted to tell us that she'd gone to the urgent care center in Carlisle after she left our office. The doctor there recognized that she needed antibiotics right away and put her on a Z-pack."

Claire shook her head.

"She said she felt better after the first dose. She wanted to recommend that you try to keep up with the latest drug information so that your future patients can be better served."

Claire looked up at her nurse. "And just where did Dr. Payne get her medical degree?"

Lucy laughed. "Don't let her get to you. It serves Ms. Payne right to have to spend a small fortune for her medicines."

Claire stood. "Thanks for your help today."

Lucy smiled and led the way out the back door. They parted and Claire drove out to the Childress place.

She stood on the front stoop and rang the doorbell.

In a minute, the wooden door opened, leaving Claire and Nancy Childress separated by a screen door. Nancy spoke across the divide. "Hello, Dr. McCall."

"Hi," Claire responded. "Can I speak to you?"

Nancy didn't offer to open the door between them. "Sure."

"I assume Deputy Jensen came to see you."

"He did." She smiled. "So you're too late."

"Too late?"

"To influence what I said."

"I'm not hear to influence what you say, Ms. Childress. I came hoping you can clarify a few things for me."

Nancy nodded without speaking.

"I trust you told the deputy that I was nowhere around when your husband died."

Nancy Childress stood with a stone expression, her hands on her hips. "I told him the truth."

Claire shifted her feet. "Could you elaborate?"

"If you want to know whether you're off the hook or not, maybe you should ask Deputy Jensen."

Claire didn't understand. Why was Nancy so cold? "Ms. Childress, have I done something to offend you? I'm sorry if I—"

"Dr. McCall, you seem to have a short memory. How many times did I bring Richard to your office? You saw his suffering and yet were so reluctant to give him the quantity of pain medicine he needed."

She was aghast. Every time Richard came, she provided a new prescription for narcotic pain relief. It was never the liberal quantity Nancy requested, but it was an amount Claire deemed safe and unlikely to be abused. She'd even offered him hospice care, which Nancy refused because it wasn't covered by their insurance. Claire looked at Nancy, wondering if it was her own guilt that drove her to be so nasty. "I'm sorry, Ms. Childress. I always tried to provide what I thought was best."

Nancy stood without moving, staring across the screen at Claire.

Claire cleared her throat. "There is one more thing. Do you have any idea why Ami would have thought I euthanized her stepfather?"

"Maybe she just assumed it. She knew I wanted medicine to relieve Richard's suffering. And she knew your office had provided it. Maybe she just got mixed up."

"Or could it have something to do with my relationship with John Cerelli?"

"John Cerelli? Ami's boyfriend?"

Claire took a deep breath. "John is my fiancé. He is not Ami's boyfriend."

Nancy put her hand to her mouth. "You're the one."

"The one?"

"Ami told me a woman was moving in on her territory."

Claire held up her hand. "If she's under the impression that I'm trying to take John Cerelli from her, she has it exactly backwards."

"Then this John is a two-timin' rascal."

Claire shook her head. "I can assure you, John is not two-timing your daughter. If she has led you to believe that—"

"Maybe you should investigate just how your fiancé spends his time away from you."

"Ms. Childress, with all due respect, is it possible that Ami might be deceiving you?"

"Ami isn't like that. She's sweet. Vulnerable." She glared across the screen. "Vulnerable enough for a man to take advantage."

"And John Cerelli isn't like that." She leaned toward the door separating them. "Could Ami be living out a delusion?"

"Dr. McCall, do you know my daughter?"

"No, ma'am. We've never met."

"Then I suggest you keep your judgments to yourself." She paused, her eyes locked on Claire's. "And I'd suggest you leave my daughter's boyfriend alone."

Claire opened her mouth to reply, but was met by the wooden door slamming in her face. So much for Virginia hospitality.

On her lunch break Tuesday, Claire was still stewing about Nancy's comments when she stepped into Apple Valley Video Productions. Although they had come highly recommended as the team to record her wedding, the place lacked the ambiance that inspired confidence. Tucked in the rear of a beauty salon, the video shop's every bit of shelf and wall space was covered with equipment in various stages of repair.

A man with an adolescent face and thick black glasses looked up from his desk.

Claire offered a weak smile. "You must be Josh." She paused, looking at a video monitor with her image on it. It was grainy and a bit distorted, with rounded edges, Claire inside a blurry fishbowl. She looked around and wrinkled her nose. "Where's the camera?"

The man smiled. "Here." He lifted his hand to the edge of a shelf just behind his desk.

"I don't get it."

He waved his hand in front of a potted flower. "It's a hidden camera. Here in the center of this flower."

Claire leaned toward the plant and watched her image grow. "Amazing." She stood upright. "I'm Claire McCall. I called about recording my wedding."

He opened a scheduling book. "May five?"

"Yes."

"I'll need a hundred-dollar deposit."

She nodded and pulled out her checkbook. As she leaned over to write the check, she looked up again at her image on the monitor. "Do you rent out the hidden cameras?"

"You'd be surprised at how many people want to watch other people."

"Other people?"

"Employees." He paused and put his hands behind his head. "A spouse."

The jealousy she'd carried about Ami Grandle stimulated a dark thought. She could hide a camera in John's office to see how he really talked to her. Claire glanced back at the monitor. But she could never do that. She trusted John.

She thought twice about the little pink lipstick smudge that John said was nothing. She trusted John. She wouldn't resort to spying on him.

But she'd been deceived by other men before. And John Cerelli was not like other men.

Was he?

Jimmy Jenkins spent the afternoon taking 253 digital images of a gray squirrel in his backyard. He reviewed and promptly discarded 250 of them. Then he fumbled through a beginner piano book, watered an azalea bed, and waxed his Harley. Anything was better than moping around wishing he was with Della.

But the alluring fragrance of her hair hung fresh in his memory. There was something about her, the familiarity of her scent that had brought it all back. He'd never dreamed that his feelings for her could seem so fresh, so urgent. He hadn't felt this alive with desire for years. But he knew Della regretted their relationship and there was little chance for a rekindling of old fire without Wally's death.

He finished buffing the silver tank and stood back to admire the shine. Checking the saddlebag for his passenger helmet, he decided to take a ride. Maybe he could convince Della to grab a burger over at Fisher's Café.

She was weeding a flower bed when he arrived, her smile making her look ten years younger. Wiping the perspiration from her forehead, she called, "Your mother would never have approved."

"Since when did you ever care what my mother thought?" he laughed.

"I cared a great deal. It seems to me your mother always counted on me to keep you out of trouble."

"My, how the years have twisted your memory!"

"I had to watch the clock so you wouldn't get grounded for getting me in past curfew."

He hung his helmet on the end of the handlebar. "Remember swimming up at Junction Reservoir?"

"You dared me to jump from the tower."

"You were the only girl in the class who was brave enough."

"Crazy enough." Della seemed to be blushing at the memory. Her eyes narrowed. "You knew what would happen, didn't you?"

"Never did find that bathing suit top, did we?"

"You didn't look very hard."

He shook his head. "It's been a long time since I thought about those days." He leaned his bike over on the stand. "What happened to us?"

Her eyes met his and looked away. It was a question that didn't need discussion. They both knew the answer: a Navy man by the name of Wally McCall.

Della changed the subject. "I guess you heard about Mae Simpson's wedding."

Jimmy ignored her. "Let's ride up to the reservoir, why don't we? We can pick up some chicken at Fisher's Café and have a picnic and watch the sunset."

"Jimmy—" Della stopped with her mouth open, studying his face. "I . . . You know I can't."

He sighed. "Just be my friend, Della."

She looked down. "We were never very good at that."

She was right about that. Everything about Della was all the way or nothing. There was very little gray in her black-and-white world. "Your marriage isn't really a marriage anymore, is it? What would be the crime in—" He stopped when he saw the disappointment on her face.

She changed the subject. Or was it linked in Della's mind? "Did you suspect that Richard's wife was going to help him die?"

"She made it pretty clear that she wanted to end his suffering."

"Have you ever—" She looked away.

"Helped someone die?"

Their eyes met. She nodded.

"No. At least not directly. I've given plenty of prescriptions for narcotics to terminally ill patients. But I never gave an injection to intentionally hasten death."

"If I were Wally—" She halted, her voice thickening. "I would want you to help me."

He wasn't sure what to say. He fiddled with his clutch lever.

"His life is hell, Jimmy. All he does is thrash around in that bed. They can't even get him up in a chair anymore. They try to strap him down, but with his constant movements, he ends up in danger of choking himself or pulling the wheelchair over. He can't eat regular food. He can't have a normal conversation. He can't go to the bathroom."

Jimmy couldn't seem to meet her gaze. He stepped off his cycle but didn't move closer. He was afraid. If he did, he knew she would fall into his arms.

And that's exactly what he wanted. And exactly what he needed to avoid if he was going to stay sane.

"He won't last long this way."

Della knelt in the mulch bed. "I've got work to do."

He knew his response was less than what she wanted. But what could he do? He wasn't even practicing anymore.

He watched her for a minute as she pretended that her weeds were demanding her whole attention. Then, without speaking, he put back on his helmet and drove toward town.

As he approached the hill leading to Pleasant View Home, he had a sudden inspiration.

He needed to see Wally face-to-face.

That night Claire looked at the clock with blurred eyes. Three a.m.. What had nudged her from sleep? Uneasy, she reached for the gun on the nightstand. The phone sounded again. *What in the world? Who is calling at this time of night?*

She plodded to the kitchen phone. "Hello."

The voice on the other end was feminine. Strangely familiar, but lilted with a heavy southern accent. "Hello, Claire."

"Who's this?"

"You don't need to know."

Claire shook her head, her alarm and frustration mounting. "What? Who's this?"

The woman's voice dripped with seduction. She seemed to be breathing out the words in an exaggerated whisper. "He's with me now."

"He's with you—who? Who's with you?"

"Oh, you know." *Click.*

She rubbed her eyes. Was this some kind of joke? She walked back to the bedroom and pulled a small calendar from her purse. She'd made a notation. John was to be away in Richmond on business Tuesday and Wednesday.

Was the caller talking about John? Could it have been Ami?

She picked up her cell and dialed John. After four rings, his voice mail answered for him.

Maybe he's sleeping too soundly to be disturbed.

She frowned. *Or maybe he's busy.*

She tossed the phone on the bed. She'd been tricked by men before. Most recently by Tyler, and before that by a fellow surgery resident, that psychopath in doctor's clothing, Brett Daniels. *But John isn't like that. He loves me. Doesn't he?*

Then why hasn't he fired that secretary like I demanded?

The thought betrayed her loyalty. *I shouldn't be thinking like this. It must be the hour. I'll call John in the morning and everything will be all right.*

She lay back on the bed and tried to sleep, but the phone call had revved her frontal lobes into a thousand what-ifs.

After forty-five minutes, she whispered a prayer and let God's peace wash over her soul again. *Oh, God, when will I ever learn to do this before my anxious heart spins its web of woe?*

Randy Jensen loved his job as a detective. And he hated his job. It was hours of boredom, moments of terror. But the terror made the boredom all worthwhile. It was the monthly adrenaline that kept him going amid the daily drizzle of stray dog reports and parking violations.

But something about a noisy neighbor complaint at 5:30 a.m. on Wednesday nudged him into high gear.

Randy rubbed the back of his neck. "Someone's mowing?"

"Crazy fool. I need my rest!"

"Where are you located?"

"In Stoney Creek Apartments, just behind the clinic building. That's where all the noise is coming from."

"I'll take care of it, sir."

Randy was in his patrol car and on his way in less than thirty seconds, praying that this was the break he needed. Tyler Crutchfield had just made a stupid move. If he was dumb enough to stay in town, he was doubly dumb to terrorize the ones who would recognize him. He pressed the gas pedal to the floor, lurching the vehicle into a higher gear, and sped toward the clinic.

He slowed when he was a hundred yards from the clinic building, just as a man on a riding mower disappeared around onto the side lawn. Randy stopped the car and pulled his weapon from the holster. Tyler Crutchfield had made his first mistake, and Randy smiled at the thought of making him pay.

The detective sprinted to the side of the building opposite the mowing noise, then peered around into the back parking lot and the grass beyond. When the mower appeared, he squinted just long enough to see that the mower matched the description Claire had given him. Then he paused until the drone of the mower indicated that it had turned and headed back toward the front of the clinic.

Randy sprinted for the supply shed bordering the back lot. He sorted through his options. *What if Tyler tries to run me over? I'll be forced to kill that scum.* He caught himself smiling.

He waited until the tractor turned and started back toward the shed. Then he jumped into the beam of the tractor's headlights and pointed his weapon. "Stop!" he yelled.

The tractor kept coming. Either Tyler couldn't hear him, or he'd decided to mow the officer over.

Detective Jensen fired two shots into the air.

The tractor slowed to a stop. The engine died as Jensen ran to the side to get out of the light.

"Lie down on the grass!" he yelled.

The man obeyed. "Don't shoot!"

"Hands behind your back," he ordered, pulling the handcuffs from his belt. He snapped them into place and helped him to his feet by a quick jerk on the man's upper arm.

"Easy. What'd I do? Is there a law against mowing?"

Randy spun the man around and shoved the barrel of his pistol under his chin. "Shut up!"

The officer felt his jaw slacken. "What the—?"

The man had white hair, a white beard, and skin the color of coffee with cream.

"What's your name?"

"Sol," he sputtered. "Sol Diaz."

Claire waited until 7:00 to call John. She knew he got an early start on most road trips, so she didn't need to worry about waking him. After two rings, a female voice picked up.

"Hello."

"I'm sorry, I was dialing John Cerelli."

"Oh, this is his phone. This is Ami. I work with John. He must have left his phone in my room by mistake. Should I have John call?"

"No, thanks." Claire hung up. This Ami was enjoying being close to Claire's man way too much.

Claire looked at her calendar. John wasn't due back from his trip until late that evening.

She needed an antacid. And a strong cup of coffee. She rubbed the back of her neck and thought about the video surveillance store.

Maybe I'll surprise John with a new little potted plant for his office after all.

Chapter Eighteen

It made Claire feel marginally safer to know that the mysterious mower had been apprehended. The man, Sol Diaz, apparently bought the mower from a man meeting Tyler Crutchfield's description and took his list of jobs and the advice that he cut a few of the lawns secretively as a way of applying for a new position. Sol reported that the man said he was short on cash, and needed to sell his mower so he could move closer to an ailing mother in Savannah.

Randy Jensen took it as a good sign that Tyler Crutchfield had moved on. Claire wasn't so quick to sleep without a loaded gun at her bedside. She remembered only too clearly the warning the fugitive gave as he fled the office. *"I will see you again, Claire."*

John called her cell phone at 8:15. She wasn't exactly warm to the idea of cuddly talk.

"Hello."

"Claire, it's me." He seemed to hesitate. "Ami told me you called."

"How convenient that she is able to take care of you and your phone."

"Claire, what's that supposed to mean?"

She sighed. She needed to get to work and the phone wasn't the place she wanted to have this conversation. "Ami told me you must have left the phone in her room. Just what were you doing in her room?"

"I wasn't in her room. She must have taken my phone from the restaurant table where the team ate last night."

"She called me at three this morning. Left me a message dripping with sweetness." She imitated the voice. " 'He's with me now.' "

"Honey, that's crazy. I was in my own room all night. I was dreaming of you."

"You need to fire this girl. She is after you. I don't want you working with her."

"I don't exactly have the authority to do that. I talked to our office manager, Carol Dawson. She's looking into my complaints."

"She'd better do more than that."

"Claire, she— "

"We've talked about this before. I shouldn't have to ask twice."

"I'm with you on this, Claire. The problem is, Ami puts on a different face for everyone else. I'm afraid it may come down to my word against hers."

"She is stalking you, John. If you can't see that, then you are blinded by her sweet little voice. What does she look like?"

John cleared his throat.

"Do you think she's pretty?"

"Claire, I think you're pretty. Ami means nothing to me."

"She means something to me."

"I'll talk to Carol again. I'll tell her exactly what Ami did, calling you in the night. That should convince her."

Not wanting to jeopardize their business meetings, and because he'd driven separately so he could avoid time alone with Ami, John decided to wait till they were back in the office to confront her. Thursday morning, he looked up from his desk as Ami entered. He took a deep breath. It was confrontation time.

"Ami, have a seat."

She smiled. "You sound so serious. Am I being sent to the principal's office for bad behavior?" She crossed her legs, allowing her skirt to inch upward on her firm thigh.

"Did you call Claire McCall when we were in Richmond and claim to be with me?"

She nibbled on her lower lip and looked up like a puppy caught chewing on her master's shoes. "You were with me." The lilt in her voice tickled down the scale. Playful. Teasing.

"But we weren't together at three in the morning. You're getting me in trouble."

"Can't blame a girl for trying."

"Ami, you are crossing a line. We are professionals. We aren't in a relationship outside work."

"Maybe," she said, drawing out the word. When she finished the sentence, each word was emphasized like the determined report of a stiletto heel on tile. *Click, click, click.* "I want more." She paused. One more heel strike. *Click.* "You!"

He stared ahead, not understanding. Ami's desire for him stood out head-and-shoulders above a simple office crush. What had Claire called her? *An erotomanic stalker?* "I'm engaged."

"But you're not married."

He sighed. "I think you should look for other work. It isn't working out for you to be so close to me."

She hesitated. John studied her expression. There, in spite of her playful demeanor, he saw the first hint of something that scared him. Desperation. A will to stop at nothing to get what she wanted. He saw it in a flash and then it disappeared, dissolving into a flirtatious smile.

She drew her index fingertip in a small circle on the top of her knee. "I get it. You don't want to dip your pen in the ink at work. If I quit, we can date."

"No," he said, a little more loudly than he intended. "We aren't dating!"

"John," she said, standing and walking around to the other side of his desk. "I know you have feelings for me. You blush every time I whisper in your ear."

"I'm a man." He pushed back from his desk and cleared his throat.

"I've noticed." She sat on his desk, facing him, not caring that her skirt was pushing even higher on her thighs. "John," she whispered, "Claire McCall isn't worth your time." She lifted a manicured fingernail, punctuating the air. "What was it you told me when I first came. You said you were on a roller coaster with your girlfriend."

John remembered making the off-hand comment and winced.

"I'd never treat you like that," she said softly. "I am ready to meet your needs."

His mouth was dry. He met her gaze, feeling the magnet of temptation. Her tongue touched the little dimple in the center of her upper lip. Weakening, he shook his head in resolve. She stopped the rotation of his head with her hand against his chin.

"Look at me," she said.

He obeyed for a moment, aware that his will was draining away. He lifted his chin from her hand. "No," he said. "This isn't right. You don't know me. You're obsessed."

"Obsession with a good thing isn't a crime, John." She brushed her knee against his thigh. Her eyes darted across his face, hungry, desperate.

He looked at the open door to the hallway. Where was Bob Estes when he needed him? John's thigh was on fire.

"You really want me to quit? This is the best job I've ever had."

John diverted his eyes from her legs. "I think it's best." He hesitated, then looked up at her face, trying to avoid her skirt.

Her expression darkened. "You don't want to reject me, John." She leaned forward until he could feel her breath on his face.

He searched for his voice, unable to speak through the desert dryness. "I—, I—"

"Don't do this to me, darling."

"You're not—"

"Shh," she said, silencing his protest with a finger on his lips. "You don't want to break my heart. Not now. I've been through too much." She pushed her mouth into a pout and moistened her lips with a dart from her tongue. Her lower lip quivered until she sucked it beneath an even row of perfect teeth and bit down. "We're together, you and I," she said, touching the edge of his face. "My darling John."

His voice was raspy. "No," he said, pulling his face away from her touch. "I'm sorry."

"No," she whispered, shaking her head with a quick little bob. "No," she said, a little louder.

John shook his head, matching her movement. "We can't be together."

She turned up the volume. "No. Don't do this."

He was finally getting through. He could see the tears forming in her eyes. *Those beautiful eyes,* he thought.

Her hands traced the angles of her slender neck down to the lapels of a silk blouse. Her grip tightened. Suddenly, with her eyes locked on John's, she ripped open her blouse, sending buttons bouncing from the office walls. She quickly unfastened her bra and pulled her blouse from her skirt. Then she shrieked, high and shrill, "No!"

John stood, off balance and mouth agape.

Ami shook her head, tussling her bangs. She lunged forward, grabbing him by the tie and pulling him forward onto the desk and on top of her. Her lips met his as she grabbed his shirttail from his pants.

Again, she screamed, and he felt her breath in his open mouth.

Off balance, John began to pull away. His attempt sent a potted plant and a container of pens clattering to the floor. "Ami, stop!"

Her hand gripped his back, her nails scratching a trail of pain. "Let me go," she yelled.

She pushed him back as he stumbled to his feet again. He looked up to see Bob Estes and Carol Dawson standing in the doorway. "What?"

Carol gasped.

John touched his lips, pulling his fingers away with a smudge of pink lipstick. Ami stood, the front of her blouse ripped and gaping. She attempted to pull herself together with one hand and with the other, planted a quick slap to John's cheek. She turned, and with Carol's arm around her, rushed sobbing from his office.

Bob Estes shook his head. "What was that?"

John stammered. "She attacked me."

Bob glared at him. "She told me you've been hitting on her."

"Wh–what?"

"I don't get this. You give me all that crap about you and Claire wanting to honor God in your physical relationship and then you— " He stopped and looked around. "You're a hypocrite." He walked away.

John stood, dazed.

What just happened? He thinks I was the aggressor?

John felt moisture on his back. He reached around to touch his skin and pulled his fingers away, moist with blood.

He rubbed his fingers together and pulled them apart, sticky with blood and sweat.

Then he walked to the restroom, aware of the eyes of the office on his back.

As he passed Carol's office, he heard Ami's soft sobs. He could only shake his head and open the door to the bathroom.

Two hours later, Ami answered the last of a hundred questions by a Brighton police detective and went through the humiliation of an exam by a sexual assault nurse examiner. To say it was thorough was an understatement. At the end, the nurse scraped and collected material from beneath her fingernails, placing the contents into a plastic bag which was sealed for forensic examination.

After the ordeal, she went home, turned on a CD of Creed, and put a frozen dinner in the microwave. She looked at her own reflection in the door of the microwave and puckered her lips. *John will think twice before rejecting my advances.*

As she waited for her lunch of stir-fry, she called her mother.

"Hi, Mom."

"Hello, dear. I haven't heard from you for a while. Are you okay?"

"Sure, Mother. I went to Richmond with work. John Cerelli was there too."

"You do know about Claire McCall? She claims she's engaged to him, you know."

"John has mentioned her. She's delusional, Mom. Probably suffering from whatever craziness runs in her family, that Huntington's disease or whatever."

"Just be careful."

"I'm going to have to change jobs."

"I thought you liked it there."

"I do, but John thinks it would be best. He thinks the other employees will think it's unfair if he spends any extra time with me. Once I'm not in the same office, our relationship will be able to proceed unhindered." She sighed. "I think he's the one, Mom. I really do."

"Oh, Ami. I hope you don't get hurt."

John had been sent home pending a full investigation. Carol, her face grim, had told him that Ami had resigned, and when he tried to explain his side, she waved her hand dismissively. "Save it for the police."

Pacing nervously, John called and told Claire that Ami had resigned after he suggested her conduct had been inappropriate. As much as he wanted to share everything with Claire, he couldn't bring himself to go over the details of Ami's attack over the phone. He was just glad Ami had decided to go through with a resignation. He wasn't happy about the police getting involved, but his reputation had been good up to that point, and he was confident that the event would eventually fall behind him.

Claire sighed. "I'm sorry I ever doubted you."

"It's nothing," he responded. "I don't blame you. You've been through a few losers."

She laughed. "I don't want to think about that."

"Well, I've got to make an early start in the morning. I've got to go up to Winchester to visit an orthopedic group to do a demo."

"I love you, John."

"You too. See you this weekend."

John hung up and walked to the refrigerator, where he lifted a milk jug to his lips. Just then, he heard pounding on the front door.

"Easy," he mumbled, wiping his mouth with the back of his hand. "I've got a doorbell. Don't break the door down."

He opened the door to see a uniformed man. "Mr. Cerelli?"

John nodded.

"I'm Detective Baker with the Brighton City Police. I'd like you to come with me down to the station for a few questions, if you don't mind."

"What's this all about?"

"Ami Grandle. She's reported you in connection with a sexual assault. I'll need you to come with me."

"Sure," John muttered. "Let me get on my shoes."

On Thursday afternoon following her work, Claire kept her usual counseling session with Joanne. This time Claire sat in her office opposite an empty chair with a tape recorder running. Joanne Phillips slipped her arm around Claire's shoulder and nudged her to continue. "I know it seems a bit artificial, but getting this all out in the open will help. Just say the things you need to say as if Wally were able to be sitting right here and understanding you."

Claire pressed her fist to her lips and closed her eyes. The memories flooded back. Her room. Hearing her father's voice. Smelling his breath, soured with whiskey. Feeling hands groping beneath her clothes.

"I remember you in my room." She halted, squeezing her eyes even tighter, but not able to keep back the tears. "You touched me." She stopped, trying to remember.

She felt Joanne's hand lift from her shoulder. "Go ahead, Claire, confront him with everything."

Claire took a deep breath. "You hurt me."

She leaned forward, her gut tight with anxiety. She had a flash memory of Kyle. He had brought her home. *Was he there too? Kyle and Daddy were arguing. Kyle came back to rescue me.*

"You abused me," she sobbed. "I was drunk. I couldn't defend myself. You—You—" She couldn't continue. She opened her eyes to see the empty chair and imagined her father sitting there.

Forgive him.

The impulse was strong. She wondered about her father, whether Huntington's disease may have been affecting him long ago, making him a little less able to control his impulses. Or was it only alcohol that turned a protective father into a demon?

Her accusations fell silent in the room, but left her void of the relief that Claire had hoped for and Joanne had promised. A gentle voice seemed to nudge her again. *Forgive him.*

How many months had it been since she'd started wrestling with this very issue, that of forgiving the abuses she suffered at the hands of an alcoholic father? How many times had Pastor Phil encouraged her to lay aside her grievances, knowing that her own sin had been forgotten in the shadow of the cross? Week by week since learning of the Huntington's disease gene that stalked her family, she'd clung to the comfort that perhaps some of her father's behavior may have been worsened by the loss of control he felt at the hands of his HD. With that, she'd come so far in forgiving him; she'd traveled down the road of restoration so many steps only to meet yet another horrid truth about him. She'd forgiven his drunkenness. She'd forgiven his temper, the violent outbursts, but this ... something so vile ... could she forgive this too? Or did forgiveness trivialize the pain she'd experienced at his hand?

It had been a long climb to this moment, and she knew the consequences of the choice in front of her. To forgive would not set her father free. God alone would judge him for his actions. She nodded her head. To forgive her father had the power to set *her* free.

"I—" She halted. "I forgive you."

She hesitated, barely aware that Joanne had moved to the desk and snapped off the tape recorder. Evidently, this had moved in a direction that Joanne hadn't anticipated.

"I love you, Daddy."

Claire leaned over in her chair, gripping her stomach and weeping. When she opened her eyes, she noticed that the knot in her stomach was unraveling.

Her eyes met with Joanne's and she stood to give her a hug. "Thank you." She sniffed. "You were right. This was just what I needed."

Joanne pulled from her embrace and cleared her throat. "Very good. Perhaps next time we can explore some of the problems in your present relationships."

Claire shook her head. "I don't think that's necessary."

Joanne nodded professionally, then gathered her things and walked toward the door. She didn't seem to be too excited about staying around to relish their little breakthrough.

Claire smiled. She knew the decision was only the start. There would be tough climbing ahead, but she'd taken the first step.

And because of that, she was free.

Chapter Nineteen

When Claire emerged from her counseling session, in the parking lot was an all too familiar sight—Randy Jensen's police cruiser. She walked over to his car as he stepped out.

"I thought I'd come by to ask a few questions." He handed her a picture. "Is that your mower?"

"Wow, sure looks like it." She shielded her eyes against the setting sun. "Where is it now?"

"We've taken it to a state police garage for fingerprinting. We figure Tyler Crutchfield should have his prints on it."

"But what will that prove? He drove it when he worked for me all the time."

"True, but you still can't get your mower just yet. It's needed as evidence."

She sighed.

"I didn't come by just for that. I wanted to let you know that we've closed the investigation into Richard Childress's death. That Dr. Dogget investigator is way off base in my opinion."

"Great. At least I won't be going to prison. I've got a wedding to plan."

Randy laughed. "So you do," he said, retreating to his car.

Claire smiled. One more burden had been lifted from her back.

Late Friday afternoon, with John safely off in Winchester, Claire traveled over to Brighton to retrieve her potted plant. Actually, she purchased a nicer one and pulled the "hot" one off his desk, slipping in quietly and avoiding the stares from John's coworkers.

When she entered the videography store, she was completely convinced of her misplaced loyalty. She leaned over the desk to write a check.

"Would you like to see what was recorded?"

"No." She ripped a check from the case. "I shouldn't have done it. I just want you to take the money. I don't want to see the tape." To Claire, that would be an even bigger betrayal of the man she loved.

Josh shrugged. "Suit yourself," he said, lifting the check from her hand. "We're still on for the wedding?"

She smiled. "Of course."

After her session with Joanne, she couldn't wait to get on with a happier chapter in her life.

Claire decided to surprise John by making dinner in his Brighton apartment. She wanted to share with him in person about her experience with Joanne and the good news that the investigation into Mr. Childress's death had been completed.

She used her key to get in and promptly began dinner preparations. Baked chicken, mashed potatoes, and salad were soon underway, thanks to groceries she brought with her into his sparse bachelor pad.

She set the table with paperware. Anything remotely glass seemed to need cleaning. She was up to her elbows in suds at the kitchen sink when John arrived.

He walked in slowly with a pizza box under his arm.

"Save it. Dinner's in the oven."

"Smells great. But since when do you crash my apartment? And what have you done with my plates? I had them organized on the counter."

She smiled and accepted a kiss on the cheek. "You are hopeless." Throwing a towel at him, she said, "Here, you dry."

He shrugged. "Deal."

She shared with him about her session with Joanne, and how she was so relieved to be out from under the threat of an investigation.

Rather than rejoicing, John just nodded and grunted.

She snapped him with a dish towel. "I thought you'd be happy."

He raised the corners of his mouth, a mechanical smile. "I am. Ecstatic."

He turned away, his eyes escaping hers. He peeked in the oven. "What smells so good?"

"Herb chicken. Should be done in a minute."

He nodded. "I'm going to change."

He disappeared down the hall and she pulled a CD from a stack. In a minute, sweet mellow sax provided the background.

They had just filled their plates when a knock came at the door.

John stood up, clearing his throat. She watched his face pale as he opened the door.

She couldn't hear the communication but assumed it wasn't good when a police officer trailed John into the room. John stayed quiet.

The officer spoke as Claire and John traded looks. "I'm sorry to disturb you. I'm afraid John has to come with me. He's going to have to answer a few more questions."

Claire didn't understand. "A few more questions?" She looked at John. "What's going on here?"

"I can explain, Claire. I didn't do anything wrong."

"There have been some accusations," the officer said softly. "I'll let Mr. Cerelli explain."

The officer stepped back and stared at the duo.

John took a deep breath and coughed.

"John?" Claire put her hands on her hips. "Tell me what's going on."

"Ami Grandle," he began.

"I thought you said she quit."

"She did. But she claims I assaulted her."

Claire felt her heart sink. "What?"

"I didn't do anything, Claire. I told her I thought she should quit. She grabbed me and screamed. Nothing happened."

She looked at the officer. "Go with him, John. Tell them you didn't do anything."

"We need to take a blood sample."

"What for? I didn't do anything!"

"If you didn't do anything, then there's no reason not to give a sample."

"I told you everything I know yesterday."

"Yesterday!" Claire exclaimed. "John, why didn't you tell me?"

"We want to check your testimony against your coworkers. Give you another chance."

"I don't need another chance," John said, almost pleading.

The officer motioned with his head toward the door.

Claire followed John to the front door. "What should I do?"

"Go home. I'll call you later."

She walked back into the eating area and sat down at the table, suddenly aware that the CD she'd put on was skipping. She didn't get up.

The phone rang. She sat still, listening to the answering machine.

"John, this is Bob. I was just checking in on you. What's going on? Give me a call. 820-1120."

She recorded the number of John's coworker, wondering if she should call him back. But she didn't feel like talking. Instead, she numbly stabbed a fork into the chicken and began to eat alone.

Chewing slowly, she formulated a plan. She needed facts. Why would this Ami be accusing John of sexual assault?

She understood one thing. She wouldn't be anyone's fool again. After being totally misled by Brett Daniels, she realized that men could be wolves in sheep's clothing. If she listened to John, she knew she'd be taken in by his explanation and fall into the comfort of his arms ... just as she'd been taken in by Brett. What she needed was an objective opinion.

She wiped a tear from the corner of her eye and walked to the CD player. Stuck, it quietly reverberated a dissonant chord. *Just like my life.* She switched the machine off.

After throwing her paper plate in the trash, she called Bob.

"Bob Estes."

"Bob, this is Claire McCall, John Cerelli's fiancée. I think we met at a company picnic last spring."

"I remember."

Not particularly talkative, Claire thought. "I need to talk to you about John."

Bob stayed quiet. She thought she heard him groan.

"Do you know anything about this accusation of sexual assault?"

"Look, Claire, don't you think you should get this from John? I mean, he is your boyfriend."

"I can get his side from him. I don't particularly want to talk to this Ami girl. I need an outside observer."

"I don't know. I'm John's friend and— "

"Bob, I need your help. Just tell me what's going on."

He sighed into the phone.

"Claire, he would want to tell you— "

"I'm waiting."

She listened to a ticking noise. Bob was apparently drumming his fingers against the phone.

Claire waited. Bob sighed again. "Okay," he said. "I hate to be the one to tell you this. Really I do."

She felt as if she'd been punched in the stomach. Could it be that John was yet another man in a masquerade?

"John has been seeing Ami outside work. She likes him. A lot, I think. But she's young and she says John has been pressuring her to do things—" He halted.

Claire felt her voice tightening. "Things?"

"Physical things. You know." He cleared his throat. "Anyway, this doesn't seem like John at all. I know he cares a lot about you." He sighed. "Anyway, yesterday at work, it's like he flipped. He got real aggressive with her in his office."

"Aggressive?"

"He ripped her blouse."

"You saw him?"

He seemed to hesitate. "Yes."

She'd heard enough. "This isn't like John."

"I'm sorry, Claire."

She didn't know how to respond. *Have I misjudged him?* She thought about the weird personality changes that had worried her so just after John's head injury. *I thought all of that was behind us. Is it possible that his injury changed him more than I realized?* "Thanks," she mumbled and set down the phone.

Then she twisted off her engagement ring, laid it on the kitchen counter, and fled.

Chapter Twenty

That night, Claire went room to room with a loaded pistol, checking each closet before retiring to her bedroom. Della was in bed before Claire arrived, something Claire was thankful for. She didn't exactly want to rehash her relationship failures yet again.

Until her ride home, she had kept it together, holding in her emotions until she reached the top of North Mountain. Then, with the descent into Fisher's Retreat, she began to cry, something that continued until she finished a sweep of her house perimeter to be sure things were secure for the night.

What she wanted more than anything else was a normal, happy courtship and marriage, something which she'd thought impossible after the discovery of Huntington's disease, but a hope which John Cerelli kept alive by his frequent affirmations that they should delight in their present love, to glory in the time they had together now, and to lay the future in God's loving hands.

The jerk! She supposed she understood a little of the pressure John was under. Trying to live out a chaste relationship after their previous indiscretions wasn't easy. But to look at another woman, before they were even married!

She supposed she should be thankful. Finding out such tendencies after the wedding vows would have been disastrous.

She sighed and brushed another tear from her face. Perhaps it was God's way of making it clear that a marriage commitment in the face of her Huntington's disease gene was just a bad, bad idea. She'd let her enthusiasm of being in love color her judgment.

From now on, she would concentrate on being the best physician she could be, a healer to the people of Apple Valley. And maybe, after months, she'd be able to find a silver lining in her own pain, even become a stronger, more compassionate healer because of her own suffering.

She didn't want to make a lengthy transition. She opened a notebook and began making a list of calls and cancellations she needed to make in order to put the wedding behind her. The florist, the photographer, the preacher, the reception hall, the caterer, her family, and friends would all need to be called. She would leave the honeymoon cancellations to John.

Meanwhile, John washed the ink from his fingertips in the bathroom sink. The investigation wasn't going his way. He'd been arrested, formally charged with attempted sexual battery, and stood before a magistrate who released him on a five-thousand-dollar bond. He'd found Claire's ring and immediately started to pray. He understood the rashness of her decision. She'd been hurt before. But he needed to mend some fences, and that meant some face-to-face time with Claire.

The next morning, he awoke with a knot of anxiety in his gut at 4:30. *Carol is likely to suspend me over this.* He rose and spent time in prayer and Bible study before looking at his weekly planner. If Carol didn't suspend him, he needed to cancel his schedule for the rest of the week. There were more important things at hand. He needed a lawyer. But first, he needed to see the woman he loved. He knew she'd be at the office, since the clinic offered Saturday morning hours for the working people of Stoney Creek.

He drove across the mountain, taking the white-knuckled passage toward Stoney Creek at seven miles per hour over the posted limit, and placing him in the clinic's parking lot at 10:15. He tried the back door but found it locked. *That's okay, I know the receptionist. Lisa will let me in.*

He walked around to the front door and greeted Lisa with a smile. "I'm here to see Claire. Can you let her know I'm here?"

She didn't smile. "Sure. You can have a seat."

He looked around. An old man with a large white bandage covering his foot sat next to a lady knitting what looked to be a sweater. A young woman in jeans and a Budweiser T-shirt paced the floor trying to quiet a squalling baby. Another woman sat in the corner and blew her nose loudly into a Kleenex. A teenager eyed John over a *Sports Illustrated* magazine. John selected one of two chairs on the far wall so he could avoid anything infectious.

He busied himself with a two-year-old fishing magazine and waited.

And waited.

In fifteen minutes, the receptionist called his name. "Mr. Cerelli."

He walked to the window. She handed him a note. "I'm afraid Dr. McCall is too busy to see any work-ins this morning. She did want you to have this."

John shook his head. *Is that what I am now? A work-in?*

He walked slowly to the car and unfolded the note. Instead of anything personal, it was a list of places in Brighton to notify of their cancelled wedding plans. At the top it simply said, "Could you make these calls for me? I'd like to avoid the long-distance fee."

John crumpled the note and threw it into his car.

This was crazy. She had to talk to him. He'd have to resort to the phone, although he'd come all this way to talk to her in person.

He didn't plan on canceling any wedding plans. He hadn't done anything.

But how could he convince Claire if she wouldn't talk to him?

He slumped into his car and thought forward to the next item on his list. *I need a lawyer.*

That afternoon, John sat across from an expansive oak desk in the home of William Fauls, an attorney and longtime family friend.

"I've read the police report, John. The chief's a friend of mine."

"But they've got it all wrong. She's the one who has been stalking me."

The man lifted a pen from the desktop. "Your coworkers seem to be siding with Ami's description of the incident."

"What's the next step?"

"There will be a preliminary hearing in six weeks. There, a judge will decide if there's enough evidence to dismiss the case or certify the case to the grand jury."

"How likely is that?"

"Unless we can find some other evidence, it's very likely he won't want to dismiss. It's not a popular move for a judge to dismiss sexual assault cases out of hand. So then it goes to the grand jury. If they decide there is enough evidence, they can return an indictment. Then it becomes a formal charge document."

John slumped another inch. "What's the likelihood of that?"

"Around the courthouse we have a saying, John. In Virginia, you could indict a ham sandwich."

"You're not encouraging me, Bill." He stood up and began pacing the paneled law office. His fingers trailed along hundreds of texts on the shelves. "What am I to do?"

"You say this girl has been e-mailing you?"

"Daily. Multiple times a day."

"Has it stopped since her accusation?"

"I haven't checked."

"Well, check. If she keeps it up, save them. We'll need to document all of her communication. If you can retrieve some from the trash on your computer, do it."

"Okay." He paused, then asked, "If this goes all the way and I lose a court case, what am I looking at?"

William Fauls shook his head. "You don't want to know."

Della sat in the rocking chair next to Wally's bed listening to his legs whistle across the sheets. She knew he didn't feel like talking. In the last two visits all he said was "I want to die," and even that was garbled. Sometimes it sounded as if Wally's tongue was too fat for crisp diction. Other times it seemed he just had too much spit to speak through. She thought it was because he had a hard time swallowing, so he just let it build up. The problem with that was that eventually it all ran to the back of his throat, a setup for an explosion of coughing, or if he tried to speak, he would spit with every syllable. It was best to talk and stand back or risk a spray with every word.

Della slowly told her husband about Claire and John, listening to him choke his objections to her reports of John's reckless and unfaithful behavior. "I know," she said. "It seems so unlike John. We'll just have to support Claire through this."

"Best for them not to marry." Wally's sentence was garbled, but understandable. "With H-h-huntington's it's too hard."

Della helped him slurp some thickened lemonade, and then sat back in the rocking chair to rest.

Sweat glistened on his forehead. His hair smelled of sweat. She would talk to the nurse's aide about washing it. But she knew how Wally could be. Sometimes he refused his own care, a situation that quickly became a touchy problem. How much autonomy should a patient be given when they have just given up and don't care anymore? Should a patient be forced to eat if they can't feed themselves and they don't want to eat? Should they be forced to bathe if they don't want to wash?

She stood and held his head still between her hands. She kissed the top of his head. "You need to let them wash your hair, Wall."

"I want to die."

Della wiped spit from her left cheek and bit her bottom lip. "Don't say it. You know I can't help you."

"Cl–cl–claire can help. Dr–dr–drug me."

"Oh, Wally."

She sat back down and rocked for a few minutes, but his words hung like a thick fog between them. What would be the harm in helping him die? He would be out of his misery, and she could get on with her life.

I could get on with a life of guilt if I helped him go.

She couldn't make light conversation after his request. And talking about it made her want to cry. So instead, she got up and left. At the door, she tried to be cheery, but she sounded as plastic as a credit card. "Bye, honey. See you in a few days."

It was a full week after their interrupted dinner and thirty unreturned e-mails later when Claire decided she should talk to John.

She stood in the backyard staring at the mountains, the phone in her right hand and a Kleenex at the ready in the other. "I need to hear your side of the story."

"She came into my office. I had her sit down. I told her that I thought she should find other work."

"Just like that?"

"I asked her why she had called you in the middle of the night, claiming to be with me."

"What did she say?"

"Nothing really. She said you can't blame a girl for trying. I told her we were engaged. I told her I didn't think she should be working with me."

"So why didn't you tell me what she did? You just told me she had resigned."

"She did resign, Claire. I was going to tell you, but the whole thing was so crazy, I wanted to tell you in person, and before I had the chance, the police came and—"

"Okay, okay," she interrupted. "What I really need to know is what happened."

"I was trying to confront her about the inappropriateness of her behavior. She came around to my side of the desk. Then she ripped open her blouse and pulled me down on top of her. She started screaming. In a second it seemed like everyone was there assuming the worst."

Claire didn't know what to say. She wanted to believe him, but she had heard a completely different story from two of John's office workers.

"You need to believe me. I didn't attack her. You know she's unstable. Just look at her medical record."

"I'm not basing my opinion on what she said. I—Well, I talked to Bob and Carol from your office."

"They only know what Ami told them. They didn't see her attack me."

"John, the police investigated this. They don't just arrest someone without any evidence."

"It's her word against mine. They have no evidence."

She took a deep breath. *Do I really know you? Your accident seems to have changed you more than I imagined.* "I don't want to argue with you. I don't have the energy anymore. I just need some space. I need to concentrate on my medical practice right now."

"That's been your MO all along, hasn't it, Claire? When something gets out of hand, you just avoid it by working hard. It worked when you didn't want to think about Huntington's disease, didn't it? Well, it's not going to work with this, because too much is at stake."

"Like going to jail?"

"Like losing you."

She closed her eyes, willing herself not to cry. "I've got to go, John. I'm sorry."

Chapter Twenty-One

Two weeks later, John Cerelli was feeling the pressure from his upcoming preliminary hearing. Predictably, Carol had placed him on official leave pending the outcome of his legal trouble. Bill Fauls, John's attorney, had made little progress with finding anything that could help. The best John could hope for was a lenient grand jury, but the chances of that in Virginia were slim to none. He suspected that if it went to trial, it could get very ugly with his attorney trying to bring up Ami's unstable past. Everyone was going to end up losing, with John leading the way.

Finally, he decided to follow through with moving on. He needed to make some cancellations for the wedding. His first stop was an out-of-the-way video store where he found a geekish young man in a white shirt soldering a wire onto the back of a speaker.

"Hi," he began. "I'm here to cancel a reservation for a wedding videographer."

The man looked up. "Name?"

"Cerelli." John watched him paging through his calendar. "It might be under the name McCall. Look under the May bookings."

He flipped a page. "Here it is. Want to change the date?"

John sighed. "No, the whole thing's off for now." He scuffed his shoe against the floor. "Things haven't exactly gone according to plan."

The guy looked up from his scheduling book, then leaned closer with his eyes narrowing.

John wiped his chin. *What, is there something on my face?*

"Oh man, you're the dude in the video." He shook his head.

"Excuse me?"

The guy started nodding as if a lightbulb had just switched on. "You're Claire McCall's boyfriend, right?"

John didn't understand. "Right. We were engaged."

The man held out his hand. John shook it. "I'm Josh. Maybe we should talk."

"I–I don't understand."

Josh sat on the edge of a crowded desk. "Tell me why your engagement is off."

"I'd rather not talk about it."

"Does it have something to do with another woman? Someone at work, perhaps?"

This was feeling too creepy. What did this guy know about him? "Maybe. But that's my business. I don't see how my relationship problems involve you."

"I have something to show you," he said, motioning for John to follow him into a back room. He flipped on a TV and popped in a videotape. "The image here is a bit grainy. But it's the best we can get with the small spy camera."

"Spy camera?"

"Yep. Your girlfriend rented this unit," he said, pointing to a potted plant on the shelf. "But she brought it back and wouldn't even look at what we got for her." He paused. "I bet I've watched this fifty times. This girl is so hot."

Josh pressed "play" and stepped back so John could see. The image was rounded at the edges and his face a bit blurry, but recognizable.

"Wait," John said. "Where's the camera?"

"In a plant. It looks like she put it on the edge of the desk. Too bad it's focused on you. I wish I could see the girl's face." He chuckled. "'Cause the rest of her is amazing. Just watch."

"Did you call Claire McCall when we were in Richmond and claim to be with me?"

The next voice was from off camera and female. *"You were with me."*

"But we weren't together at three in the morning. You're getting me in trouble."

"Can't blame a girl for trying."

Ami? John shook his head. "It sounds like we're in a tunnel. That doesn't even sound like me."

Josh snapped off the tape and sighed. "Okay, the audio's not great, but it's our intro-level model. The audio is better on the more expensive one." He tapped his fingers on the top of the box. "Just watch, okay?" He pressed the play button again.

"Ami, you are crossing a line. We are professionals. We aren't in a relationship outside work."

"Maybe I want more. You!"

"I'm engaged."

"But you're not married."

"I think you should look for other work. It isn't working out for you to be so close to me."

"I get it. You don't want to dip your pen in the ink at work. If I quit, we can date."

"No, we aren't dating!"

"John." Ami appeared for the first time as she came around to the front of the desk. She was visible from behind and the image cut off half of her head. *"I know you have feelings for me. You blush every time I whisper in your ear."*

"I'm a man." He pushed back from his desk and cleared his throat.

Good, John thought, his hope rising. *It shows me moving away.*

"I've noticed." The camera caught her sitting on his desk, facing him, her skirt pushing higher on her thighs. *"John, Claire McCall isn't worth your time. What was it you told me when I first came? You said you were on a roller-coaster with your girlfriend. I'd never treat you like that. I'm ready to meet your needs."*

In the video, John shook his head, but she stopped the rotation of his head with her hand against his chin.

"Look at me."

John watched the image of himself as the man in the video lifted his chin away from her hand. *"No, this isn't right. You don't know me. You're obsessed."*

"Obsession with a good thing isn't a crime, John." She brushed her knee against his thigh.

John saw that he seemed to be looking around Ami for someone in the hall.

"You really want me to quit? This is the best job I've ever had."

In the video John diverted his eyes from her legs. *"I think it's best."* He hesitated, then looked up at her face, trying to avoid her skirt.

Josh pointed to the screen. "This is my favorite part."

"You don't want to reject me, John."

"I—, I— "

"Don't do this to me, darling."

"You're not— "

"Shh, you don't want to break my heart. Not now. I've been through too much. We're together, you and I, my darling John."

"No." The camera showed John pulling his face away. *"I'm sorry."*

"No," she whispered, shaking her head with a quick little bob. *"No,"* she said, a little louder.

John shook his head, matching her movement. *"We can't be together."*

She turned up the volume. *"No. Don't do this."*

Josh slapped John on the shoulder and pointed at the screen again. "Here it comes. This is great."

Her hands traced the angles of her slender neck down to the lapels of a silk blouse. Her grip tightened. Suddenly, she ripped open her blouse, sending buttons bouncing from the office walls. She quickly unfastened her bra and pulled her blouse from her skirt.

John stood, off balance, and mouth agape.

Ami lunged forward, grabbing him by the tie and pulling him forward onto the desk and on top of her. John's body could be seen as the woman pulled his shirt from his pants.

Watching the video, John blushed. The video never showed her from the front, but it clearly revealed the woman as the aggressor.

On screen, the woman screamed.

Off balance, John began to pull away. *"Ami, stop!"*

The image bounced and blurred, then froze on an image of the leg of a chair in the room. The audio continued, but John had seen enough.

"Tell me again how you got this."

"Your girlfriend planted the camera in your office." He shook his head and nudged John's shoulder. "I only wish I'd have had your view of things." He squinted at John. "Why are you smiling, man? I'd be pissed if my girl—"

John shook his head. "Can I have a copy of this?"

"Sure," he said, shrugging. "Give me a few minutes."

Josh popped the tape and slid it into a second machine. John walked out front and waited. Five minutes later, he paid for the tape and walked toward the door before turning again. "Hey, keep us on for the first Saturday in May. You may have just saved my engagement."

John needed to get the tape to Bill Fauls as the evidence he needed to convince a judge to dismiss the accusations against him. But more important to John was to confront Claire with the images and win back her trust.

That evening, just as the sky was beginning to color, John knocked on the door of the McCall home. He knew Claire was home. Her VW bug was in the driveway.

Della opened the door, leaving the screen to separate them. "Hello, John."

"Hi, Della," he said, straining to see around her. "I need to see Claire."

She shook her head. "Maybe this isn't such a good idea. She's trying her best to move on."

"I have something she needs to see."

Della didn't look convinced.

"She'll want to see this," he said, holding up the videotape.

Della held out her hand, but John didn't want to surrender the tape and leave. "I need to watch it with her."

Della put her hands on her hips. "John, I—"

Claire interrupted, coming up from behind her mother. "What's going on?"

"Claire! You need to see this. It's the evidence I needed to prove I'm telling the truth!"

The look on her face told John she didn't understand.

"You bugged my office with a spy camera!"

She held up her hands. "I was jealous."

"I'm not blaming you. I may not like the idea, but you need to look at this."

John watched as mother and daughter exchanged glances. "Okay," Claire said, "Come in."

John smiled. "Why didn't you tell me you had my office bugged?"

Claire looked down. "I was ashamed, John. I never even looked at the tape." She walked forward and stood in front of the TV.

He went straight to the TV and pushed the video into the front slot on the VCR. "Just watch. This is exactly what happened, and your spy cam recorded it all."

John watched their reactions as the video played. Claire's hand went to her mouth as she mumbled, "Why, that snake!" She shook her head, dismayed. "I'd already turned the camera in before I heard about the accusations. Then after asking Bob Estes about it, I didn't want to see it."

By the end of the video Claire was crying. "Oh, John, I'm so sorry."

He smiled. His world was right again.

Claire fell into his arms. After a moment, he pushed her away and dug her engagement ring from his pocket.

"Here," he said, slipping it on her finger, "let's get married."

Chapter Twenty-Two

The winter passed quickly in the Apple Valley thanks in part to Claire's growing medical practice and to the need to squeeze wedding preparations in between everything else. John's case was dismissed at the preliminary hearing after a backroom meeting between William Fauls and the judge. They shared a cigar and a laugh during the closed-door session in which the judge watched the tape four times. Ami Grandle slipped from John's radar, having resigned her position after the truth came to light.

The McCall family troubles seemed to reach status quo. Margo kept attending church and wondering what was bugging Kyle, who had grown more and more withdrawn. A bout of pneumonia nearly took Wally to his eternal reward, but somehow, to his dismay and Della's, he survived. Della kept faithfully visiting, her patience wearing thin as he recovered from pneumonia only to revive his requests to die. Jimmy Jenkins kept visiting, the rumble of his Harley Davidson now a familiar sound as it thundered down the byways of the country around Stoney Creek. Della said no to his invitation to the county medical society Christmas dinner, no to an invitation to a winter gala fundraiser by the United Way, and maybe to an invitation to an upcoming spring concert at Brighton University.

Randy Jensen and the county sheriff's department kept a vigilant eye out for Tyler Crutchfield, but after three months, the trail was so cold, Claire was convinced they'd never find him. Stoney Creek Family Practice finally got their mower back after the first snow, and Sol Diaz took a job in maintenance at the Pleasant View Home, partly at Claire's recommendation that he did such a nice job mowing her home and office yards.

Claire kept up her nightly closet sweeps for two weeks, slept with the gun beside her bed for a month, and eventually settled for double-checking all the doors and setting the door and window alarms.

By spring, everything seemed to be falling into place for the perfect wedding. Early on the morning of the ceremony, the third Saturday in May, Della picked up the phone after three rings. "Hello."

"Hello, Doll." Jimmy Jenkins's voice was easy to recognize. "Did you survive the rehearsal?"

She sighed. "It was a typical McCall zoo," she said. "Grandma Elizabeth choked on the prime rib, and Kyle and Margo had a spat in the parking lot right in front of everyone."

Jimmy chuckled.

"It wasn't funny. I think Margo saw how nice things are for Claire and wishes she wouldn't have eloped."

"That's life, Della." He paused. "I know this is a busy day for you, but I was wondering if I can pin you down on next weekend's concert."

She shook her head. Jimmy was nothing if not persistent. "Jimmy, I can't think beyond today."

"So don't think. Just say you'll go."

She hesitated, her resolve weakening. He didn't let her reply before he spoke again. "Look, Della, I know you're uncomfortable spending time with me in public around here. You're married. I understand. We don't need to plow this ground again. But the concert is in Brighton."

She closed her fist in quiet determination. "Not while Wally is alive."

She listened as his breath rushed out in frustration.

"I'm sorry," she added. "Look, Jimmy, let's talk again. But right now, I've got a wedding to pull off."

Jimmy seemed to hesitate. When he spoke, his tone was sympathetic. "He's not going to live much longer."

She understood that he spoke of Wally. "He keeps surprising me."

"He doesn't look good. He won't be alive long."

"You've seen him?"

"I've visited him several times over the last few months."

The idea struck Della as odd, almost sad in a sick sort of way. Was he visiting Wally just to see how long he had to live, a pre-morbid fascination to see when she was going to be a free woman again? She didn't have time to process his motives. Perhaps he was truly interested in Wally. They were, after all, old classmates. She listened as the front door opened.

"Mom?"

"Claire's here. We can talk later." She hung up the phone and turned to face her daughter.

Claire smiled and held open her arms. "Today's the day."

Mother and daughter fell into an embrace. Della whispered into Claire's hair, "My lovely daughter."

"Did the florist add the roses I wanted?"

"It's all taken care of."

"The cake?"

"I saw it yesterday morning. It's perfect."

"Did Margo get her dress back from the seamstress?"

"The alterations are perfect."

"Linda's voice?"

"Her mother called. The strep test was negative. With warm saltwater gargles, she'll be able to hit an F with no problem."

"Did—"

Della put her hand against her daughter's mouth. "Shhh," she said, looking at her watch. "Everything is ready. Now you're due at Emma's for your hair in fifteen minutes."

Claire took a deep breath. "Okay."

"You're about to have the happiest day of your life," she said, pulling her daughter into a hug. "I'm going to see to it."

"I want Daddy to see me."

Della smiled. "Take your dress to Emma's. You can drop by the home after you get your hair done. You can model it for him and still get to the church on time for lunch at 1:00."

Later that morning, June Mason steadied the back of Wally McCall's head and lowered the end of a straw into his mouth. "Here, Wally," she coaxed. "Some of your favorite."

Wally pulled on the straw, swallowed, coughed, and made an exaggerated grimace as he tried to swallow again.

June smiled. "There," she said, retrieving the straw. "Good job." She set the jug on the nightstand. Working with patients like Wally McCall at Pleasant View had been challenging, but as a nurse, she loved the chance to spread a little joy to her patients. "Two guys walked into a bar," she said, "the third one ducked."

Wally groaned.

"What's wrong, Wally? You don't like my jokes?" She laughed. She was tugging at the edge of a rebellious fitted sheet when movement in the doorway attracted her attention. She looked up to see Claire McCall. "My oh my! Don't you look beautiful!"

Claire smiled. Her hair was braided into an elaborate updo, and she held her dress in her arms. "I came to show my father my wedding dress.

Where can I change?" She walked across the room and stood at the edge of her father's bed. "Hi, Daddy. Today's my big day."

He looked up, as his head weaved from side to side.

June took Claire by the arm. "You can change down the hall in fourteen. It's unoccupied."

The nurse watched Claire as she ushered her to a room down the hall. Claire's expression turned from sober to sad.

"What's wrong, dear? This is supposed to be the happiest day of your life."

Claire sighed. "I know. It's just such an emotional day. I wish Daddy could escort me down the aisle."

June offered a little hug. "It must be tough," she said. "But I'm sure he's glad you came by to give him a preview."

Claire nodded and stayed quiet.

"I'll leave you to change," she said, pushing open the door to an empty room. "Use the room to change back if you like." She pointed. "There's a pretty good mirror in the bathroom."

"Thanks." She seemed to hesitate. "I want to be alone with him."

"Sure, honey." June left her, but couldn't help puzzling over the bride's countenance. *She seems sadder than she wants to admit. I hope there's nothing wrong between her and John.*

A bit later that morning, Evan Harrison sat in the 911 control center in Brighton and picked up on the blinking line. "State police, 911 emergency, please state the nature of your emergency."

The other end of the phone line was quiet, followed by the sound of clothing rubbing together.

Evan wore a receiver headset, a hands-free setup that allowed him to listen regardless of his position. Nonetheless, he leaned forward reflexively, straining to hear. He slid up the volume control on the panel and looked at the digital readout in front of him. Caller identification read, "Pleasant View Nursing Home."

The rustling sound continued. For a second, he thought he heard a spoken voice, a muffled groan. A man?

He looked to his right. Tracy Greene was reading a detective novel. "Trace," he said, "listen to this." He pulled off his headset and pressed a button to put the voice through to an external speaker.

The muffled groan continued in a rhythm, "Mmm, mmm, mmmm." Another sound, a knocking, rattling noise intervened, followed by silence.

Tracy shrugged and turned a page in her book. "I can't make anything—"

"Shh!"

The duo listened as a woman's voice began, "I remember you in my room." The voice was strained.

Evan shook his head and whispered, "It's a hoax." He stopped short, as the woman spoke again.

"You touched me." Another pause. "You hurt me."

Evan and Tracy's eyes met in silent communication, not understanding. Tracy twisted her voice in an expression of question. They listened to the sound of a woman crying, soft sobs of someone in pain. "You abused me. I was drunk. I couldn't defend myself. You—You—"

The line went dead.

Tracy looked back at her book. "Weird. You'd better call the source. See if they know what's going on over there."

Sally Weathersby, RN, had worked at Pleasant View Nursing Home for six years. Now as the charge nurse on day shift, she oversaw the care of all forty-one patients. She passed the front reception desk, carrying the summary stocking reports from night shift, when Blanche Trainum motioned her over. "It's the state police," she said, holding up the phone. "He says they just got a 911 call originating from this number." She shrugged her shoulders. "I haven't called anyone from here."

Sally picked up the phone. "Hello, this is the charge nurse, Sally Weathersby."

"This is Evan Harrison, state police 911. I just got a pretty weird call. My readout says it came from there."

"What kind of weird call?"

"A sobbing woman, talking about being abused."

Sally shook her head. "That's different. I have no idea offhand who could have made a call. We do have a few Alzheimer's patients who know how to use the phone." She paused. "Tell you what, why don't I check through the assisted living section? They're the only ones capable of using a phone."

"Okay. Call me back if you find out anything we can help with."

"Sure." She hung up the phone and shrugged at Blanche. "I wonder what that's all about." She laid her clipboard on the desk. "I'm going to make rounds in assisted living."

Sally smoothed the front of her white dress as she walked, bypassing Emma Nichols in a wheelchair and Roy Brunk shuffling beside her.

"Morning, Sally," Roy said, emphasizing each syllable of her name with a tap on the floor with his cane.

"Morning, Roy." She smiled at his greeting. It was the same way he'd said her name every morning for the past six years.

She walked through the hallway, which was home to sixteen assisted-living adults. George Smith was taking a midmorning nap. Chessie Baker and Kristine Chang played checkers, and three others were watching a game show at a volume that rattled the furniture. The Stevens were walking the nature trail by the garden. Briggs Donovan and Esther Bun were arguing over a game of shuffleboard. The rest of the gang were in their rooms, and everyone laughed at the thought of making a 911 call. Everyone except Mary Porter, who took everything very seriously and promised to report any suspicious activity to Sally right away.

Sally checked with the staff nurses on east and south wing, and they reported no problems. With that, she returned to the reception desk and picked up the stocking reports.

Blanche looked up. "Solve the 911 mystery?"

The supervising nurse chuckled. "Everyone's fine. Must have been a computer glitch."

Sally poured a cup of fresh coffee and sat at her desk to begin sorting out her staffing schedules for the next month. Ten minutes later, her phone rang.

"Sally Weathersby."

"Sally, this is June over on south. Wally McCall died. I just found him while doing med rounds."

Sally took a deep breath. "Oh, boy. I'll have to call Della. This is all she needs, what with their daughter getting married today."

"She was just in this morning to see him. She modeled her wedding dress for him."

Sally put her hand to her mouth, feeling her throat suddenly thicken. She looked away from Blanche. "Okay, I'll take care of things from my end. I'll call the funeral home and Della."

"Thanks, Sally. I'll leave him in his room for now, in case she wants to see him here."

Sally hung up the phone and wiped the corner of her eye. Everyone in Stoney Creek knew Claire McCall and the trials their family faced because of Huntington's disease. If anyone deserved relief from a constant barrage of family crises, it was the McCalls. Sally thought for a minute about waiting until after the wedding to tell Della about her husband's death. *No, I can't keep this from her, even on a day like today.*

As the supervising nurse, she needed to confirm Wally's death, so she plodded on heavy feet to south wing. There, she entered the room which had been Wally's home for the better part of a year. She touched the edge of a crayon picture of a horse which had been taped to the wall over his bed. It had been drawn by his granddaughter, Kristin. Beneath the horse, it said, "Get well, Grampa." Sally smiled and thought, *It must be nice being young and naïve.*

On the bedside stand sat a Tupperware pitcher of lemonade and a few packets of a thickener which needed to be mixed with all of Wally's liquids. She was alone in the room when she realized the oddity of the silence. She studied Wally's pale face for a moment and became aware that this was the first time she had ever seen him still. The thumping of his arms against the padded bed rails, and the whistling of his legs against the sheets, sounds which were his constant shadow in life, had disappeared only in death.

She touched his forehead, still moist with sweat, and moved his head from side to side. He was cooling but not stiff. *He must have died within the hour.* She closed his eyelids and dried her hand on her white dress. Then she took out her stethoscope and listened to his chest, now a cavity empty of life. She stared at her watch for fifteen seconds, lifting his linens to check for a pulse. As she placed her fingers over his radial artery, she noticed a red circle on the sheet beneath his elbow. As she inspected further, she could see dried blood over the inside of his elbow.

Anxiety gnawed for recognition. Something wasn't right. Wally had been a DNR for months. Most of the Do Not Resuscitate patients didn't need blood drawn. So why was there evidence of a venopuncture on his arm?

Sally stepped away, suddenly spooked. A rubber tourniquet lay on the bed, partially concealed by a pillow. She scanned the room, wondering just what had gone on. Everything seemed normal at first glance. A comb and brush were on the dresser beside a collection of family pictures. One picture was facedown. Sally reached for it. It was Claire, a photograph taken at her medical school graduation. From the dresser, she looked back at the body. Perhaps a nurse had just given some medication? She made a mental note to check the record. The room felt close and eerily quiet. She walked back to straighten the covers when her shoe struck a small object and sent it skidding across the floor. It was a small vial, a medicine container. She lifted it from its resting place and gasped as she read the label. Morphine sulfate. The multidose vial was empty.

She gripped the little bottle in her hand as her stomach tightened. Shaking her head, she walked to the nurses' station.

June Mason looked up. "What's wrong, Sally?"

Sally set the vial down on the counter. "I found this in Wally's room." She paused to watch June's expression. "Did he have any meds this morning?"

"We gave morning meds with his breakfast." June leaned forward. "But nothing IV."

Sally frowned. "Has anyone else been giving meds this morning?"

"Not on south wing."

"Where's Betty?"

"Giving baths. I think she's in sixteen." June's forehead wrinkled. "What are you thinking?"

"I don't know. I'm afraid to say what I'm thinking." Sally rubbed the back of her neck. "When is the last time you saw him?"

"Let's see, I gave him breakfast at 7:30, then some lemonade at 9:00 and again at 10:00. I left him when Claire came in to show him her wedding gown."

Sally looked at her watch. An hour had gone by since Wally had been seen by staff. She took a deep breath. "I think I should call the police."

"You think someone killed him?"

"I don't know what to think."

"Shouldn't you call Mr. Johnson?"

Sally thought about calling the administrator. He would be just the type to try to brush this all under the rug so as not to spoil the reputation of Pleasant View. No, she would call the police first, and then tell the administrator what she had done.

Della had just pursed her lips to freshen her makeup when the phone rang. It was probably Claire, calling to ask her to bring something she'd forgotten. She checked her watch. She had thirty minutes to be at the church for the pre-wedding luncheon.

"Hello."

"Della? This is Sally Weathersby over at Pleasant View. I'm calling about Wally."

Della could hear the tension in Sally's voice. "Is something wrong?"

She listened as Sally sighed. "Della, I know this is a special day for you."

But? Della tapped a manicured nail on the kitchen counter and waited, knowing that with Wally, there was always a but.

"Wally died this morning."

Della gasped. She was ready for "he fell out of bed" or "Wally choked." Even "Wally's asking to see you now," but not "Wally died." She shook her head. "I—, are you sure?" As she said it, she knew it sounded stupid, a ridiculous thing to ask a medical professional, but out it slipped before she knew what to say.

"Della, I—"

"Oh, Sally, I've imagined this call a thousand times, but never did I expect that today—" Suddenly her voice betrayed her, snapping shut in emotion. "Not today." She covered her mouth as she paced the kitchen floor. She couldn't say more. It was if someone had a grip on her throat. Her eyes began to tear. She closed her fist. This wasn't the reason she wanted to cry today. Today, she was to cry tears of joy for Claire's happiness, not tears for Wally.

After a moment, she heard, "Della?"

She struggled to find her voice. "I'm here." She took a deep breath and continued numbly. "I'm on my way." She put the phone in its cradle without saying good-bye.

Oh the details that spun in circles above her head as she drove to Pleasant View. Gone were the thoughts of the wedding, the caterers, the reception, the dresses, and the makeup. Here were the morbid thoughts of a memorial service, a casket, and a suit. Or had Wally said he should be cremated? She needed to call the funeral home, or would the nurses take care of that? There were relatives to call and an account to close at the home. But in the center of all the details, one thought tortured her above the rest. What was she to do about Claire?

They had all known this day was coming. Wally had been sick for months, losing weight, unable to take in enough calories to make up for the energy-burn of limbs in a constant dance. The news would not be a surprise to anyone. "Why today, Lord?" Della said as she pounded the steering wheel.

Today of all days. Didn't Claire deserve at least one day of freedom from the shadow her father cast over her future?

Della brushed a tear from her cheek and made a decision. She would let Claire and John have one night together before telling her that Wally was dead. Of course there would have to be a funeral, so the honeymoon would need to be postponed, but she could call their hotel in the morning before Claire's flight.

Della pulled into a visitor's parking spot and adjusted the rearview mirror to see if she could rescue her mascara. She dabbed at the corner of her eyes.

Three minutes later she stood at the doorway of Wally's room and looked across a plastic yellow police tape at an officer standing in the room. Her husband's body was completely exposed, cooling on his bed. The image, as prepared as she was, took her breath in a gasp. "What's going on here?"

She looked up to see Sally Weathersby rushing down the hall. "Oh, Della, I wanted to explain."

Della sensed alarm.

She peered in to see Randy Jensen, an officer in the county sheriff's department. "Can I come in? He's my husband."

"Sorry, ma'am. This is a crime scene now. No one is allowed in."

"A crime scene?" She looked at the nurse. "Sally, just what is going on?"

"Della," Sally said, placing her hand on Della's shoulder.

Della shivered and pulled away. "No, no. Tell me what's happening." She looked back at the officer. "Why are you here?"

"Ms. McCall, we have reason to believe that your husband was murdered."

"What?" This did not compute. Della looked into the blank stares of Sally Weathersby and Randy Jensen. "My husband had a terminal illness. His death is not a crime! And this should not be a crime scene!" Della tore away the yellow tape and stepped into the room.

Immediately, Randy stepped in her way. "Ms. McCall, I can't let you do this."

She felt a hand on hers. Sally's face was etched with concern. "Della, why don't you come with me?"

Della shook her head. "Talk to me," she said, feeling her cheeks flush with anger. "Right here." She looked up the hall to see two more officers following a nursing home orderly.

Sally talked in a near whisper, "I found an empty vial of morphine and a needle puncture on your husband's arm."

Della found herself in a whirl of disbelief. Everyone knew Wally was going to die soon. Who would kill him? This was crazy. She stopped. This is what he had been asking for. Had someone finally granted his request? Had Claire—? No, it was unthinkable.

Deputy Jensen spoke apologetically. "I'm going to need to ask you a few questions, Ms. McCall."

Della collected herself for a moment and looked at her watch. "Mr. Jensen, I will be glad to answer all the questions you have, but now is not the time. You know my daughter, Claire?"

The deputy nodded and started to protest, but stopped as Della continued her determined plea.

"Claire is getting married this afternoon. And nothing," she said, and then repeated loudly, "nothing is going to steal the joy of this day from her!"

She glared at the police officer for emphasis as she continued. "Not her father's death, not this investigation, do you understand? Nothing!"

She took a deep breath, realizing she was teetering on the brink of losing control completely. The stress of the wedding, of life with Wally, of the desire to assist Claire in finding a needed respite from her own pressure had stressed her to the boiling point. Now she was looking straight ahead at the straw that threatened the camel's back. "I'm sorry for raising my voice. It's just that Claire has struggled for so long, facing the knowledge that she too is carrying the gene for the disease that has now killed her father. I cannot let this spoil her day, so with your permission, I need to get to the church. Can you just continue your little investigation here, and I will tell Claire about her father's death in the morning. I will answer all the questions you have after the wedding."

She watched as Randy Jensen exchanged glances with the other officers. He asked softly, "Where were you this morning?"

"I've been at my house all morning, doing last-minute preparations for my daughter's wedding."

He nodded. "That's all I need to know."

"That's all?"

He offered a half smile. "For now, that will do."

She felt silly for being so forward, but she needed reassurance on one item. "Can we keep this from Claire until I can speak to her tomorrow? If anyone deserves for her special day to be—"

Randy held up his hand. "I know Claire, Ms. McCall. And I know all about the trouble she's seen. There are few people in this town that don't owe her a debt of gratitude for the work she does at the clinic." He looked at the other men. "I think I can speak for these men. We shouldn't need to share any of this with Claire until after the wedding."

"Thank you," Della said. She stole another look past the officer at her husband's body. "Can I go in to see him?"

Randy shook his head. "Not until I get a forensics team in here." He paused. "Sorry, ma'am."

Della sighed and looked at Sally.

Sally reached for her hand. "Don't worry about a thing. I can call the funeral home for you. Lindsey's?"

"Yes. Use his navy blue suit."

"Okay." She nodded. "Now you go to that wedding and don't think about anything. You can come in anytime for his things."

Della nodded silently and plodded back down the hallway. She felt numb. She had known this day was coming for a long time, but it wasn't supposed to happen this way, and definitely not on this day. She had held it together until now, but as she walked by the other rooms, each one seemed to be holding a life just waiting to die. On this wing, no one could feed themselves, no one could eat by themselves, and few could carry on a meaningful conversation. Della pressed her hand to her mouth but could not hold back a sob. She sped up, needing to escape, to be by herself. A flood was coming and she wanted to be alone.

In a minute, she was sobbing in her car, not caring that her mascara would need to be redone. She needed to cry for her husband. She would go home and give herself ten minutes to vent. Then she would smile and be the mother of the bride that her daughter needed. Taking a deep breath, she pulled out on the highway, crying as she went.

Why today?

Chapter Twenty-Three

Randy Jensen watched as the forensics team from the state medical examiner's office collected their data. Wally's blood was drawn for a drug screen, his core temperature was assessed and plotted on a chart to determine the time of death, the room was dusted for fingerprints, and the rubber tourniquet and morphine vial were collected as evidence for examination.

He looked at Sally Weathersby. "I'll need a list of employees, specifically indicating who was in the building this morning."

She nodded and made a note on a small clipboard.

"Did Wally have any visitors this morning?"

"Only his daughter, Claire. She came by and modeled her wedding dress for him." Sally cleared her throat. "You understand Wally was in no shape to attend a wedding."

"I see." Randy looked around. "Any other way into this room?" He pointed at a door at the end of the hall marked Exit. "Where does that go?"

"Into the stairwell. There is another emergency exit into the parking lot from there."

"Alarmed?"

"Yes." She shook her head. "But we had no alarms this morning."

"Security cameras?"

"At all the exits."

He tapped a pen against his thigh. "Anything else unusual going on around here this morning?"

"No, except . . ."

"Except what?"

"It's funny. Maybe totally unrelated—"

"What?"

"We were called by a state police 911 operator this morning. He said he had a call originating from here this morning."

"A call?"

"Yes, the man said the call originated from here. All of the phones in the patients' rooms go through our main switchboard. He couldn't pin it down any further than to say it came through our main number."

"What was the call about?"

"He didn't say much. I believe he called it 'a weird call.' He said some sobbing woman was talking about being abused."

Randy wrote the information down. "Okay. Anything else you can think of? Anything out of the ordinary?"

She shook her head. "No."

The detective walked back up the hall and into the stairwell. He purposefully opened the emergency exit door by using the very edge of the pushdown bar. No alarm sounded. He looked above the door at a little red box. A single wire exited the box and disappeared into the wall. He reached for the wire, giving it a gentle tug. Just as he'd suspected, the alarm wire easily slid out of the wall, as it was severed just beyond its insertion.

He looked at the edge of the door, feeling the area above and below the latching mechanism. There he found a sticky residue, evidence that the latch had been duct taped to keep it from protruding and locking the door. That way, the door could be pushed open from the outside.

His gut tightened. This didn't look good.

He walked back into the hallway and found Sally Weathersby at the nurses' station. "Ms. Weathersby, I'm going to need to see the tapes from the security cameras."

"Sure," she said, standing. "Follow me."

Claire stood facing her mother in the foyer of Community Chapel and talked in a hushed voice, "Mom, in five minutes, I'm going to walk down that aisle. You need to stop crying!"

Della took a deep breath. "I know, I know," she said, fanning her face with a paper program. "How's my makeup?"

Claire sighed. "You look beautiful." She smiled and touched the edges of Della's grey-streaked blonde hair. "Just stop crying and you won't need to worry about it."

Rodney Cerelli, a first cousin to John, held up his arm to Grandma Elizabeth. "Time to go."

"Aren't you a handsome young man," she muttered, taking his arm.

James Cerelli, Rodney's brother, cocked his right arm and looked at Della. "You're next."

Claire backed up so that she wouldn't be seen. After her mother was seated, she watched as John and his groomsmen took the stage.

And then the organist began to play, "I Know That My Redeemer Lives," the hymn she had picked out for the processional. One by one, Claire watched her bridesmaids go before her. Last, she kissed Margo, who brushed away a tear, and sent her on her way.

When the organist was ready for the final verse, she sounded a repetitive cadence calling all to rise, and then launched into the final verse. Although it was organ music only, the words which Claire had memorized came flooding back as she walked.

> He lives all glory to his name;
> He lives my Jesus still the same.

She looked ahead to see John's smile, with the promise of the song ringing in her heart. It didn't matter what life would bring. Jesus was with them, unchanging.

She stepped slowly, memorizing the smiling faces. Lena and Billy Ray Chisholm were there, having reconciled after Billy stopped drinking. Lucy, her office nurse, wiped a tear away and grinned. Edna Shaffer and her grandson Stevie were there. The memory of the day Stevie came to her office with his tongue stuck in a bottle made Claire smile. Ginny Byrd, Claire's genetics counselor, was there. She and Claire had plowed a lot of ground in helping Claire come to grips with carrying the Huntington's disease gene. In the next row, Claire saw Mable Henderson, a diabetic patient, sitting next to Buzzy Anderson. In front of him was Brittany Lewis, another patient of Claire's, one with whom she shared a special bond, as they had both been assaulted by the same man.

Her heart soared with the song.

> He lives triumphant from the grave;
> He lives eternally to save.

She looked back at John and smiled. He looked so handsome now that his hair had a chance to curl again.

She paused at the second row and laid a single rose on the empty chair next to her mother. John joined her by the front row and escorted her the final steps to the altar. There, Margo helped spread out her train and Pastor Phil began, "We are gathered here today ..."

Joel Stevens had been a detective with the sheriff's department for three months. He hadn't had a chance to work a murder case before. Now, under Randy Jensen's direction, he was getting his first taste. He looked up from the nurses' station as Samuel Harris, another deputy with the sheriff's department, approached. "Joel, can we talk?"

Joel looked at the notes in front of him and nodded. Before he stood, he shook hands with Emma Johnson, a nurse's aide. "I think that will be all, Ms. Johnson. Thanks for your patience with all of the questions." He walked a few feet into the hall to conference with Randy and Sam. "What's up, Sam?"

"I just got the Drug Enforcement Agency trace on the morphine. That lot number was sold to Stoney Creek Family Medicine clinic."

Randy groaned. "Okay, tell me about the interviews. Did any of the staff see anyone visit Wally McCall this morning?"

Joel nodded. "Emma Johnson, Jane Stevens, Sally Weathersby, and Troy Johnson all saw Claire McCall model her wedding dress. Blanche Trainum, the receptionist, confirms her arrival and departure times. No one saw anyone else in that room."

"What time did Blanche say she left?"

"Somewhere between 10:00 and 10:15."

Randy rubbed the back of his neck. The security camera showed Claire re-entering the building through the emergency exit at 10:30, the precise time that Jane Stevens and Troy Johnson took a coffee break. "I don't like this. Not one bit."

Joel frowned. "We've got to pick her up, Randy. Wedding or no wedding. I'm sorry."

Randy shook his head. "I promised Della— "

"You promised Della that you wouldn't tell Claire about her father's death. But it's pretty obvious that that isn't going to be news to her."

"But on her wedding day— "

"Randy, she's a flight risk. She'll leave for her honeymoon."

"But she's been through so much."

"Boss, you taught me that an investigation requires objectivity, emotional detachment, and— "

Randy waved his hand. "I know, I know. Just do me a favor, don't make a scene at the wedding or the reception."

"We'll tail her from the reception to her hotel, okay?"

Randy nodded. "Let's go talk to the magistrate. I think Robinson is on. He'll give us a warrant."

Joel looked at his watch. "We'd better move. The ceremony has started. Her reception will be in full swing soon."

In the final moment before Claire McCall Cerelli slid into the limousine, her eyes locked with Della's, and the mother-of-the-bride makeup could not disguise the fear.

It was only a glimpse, but the communication between mother and daughter passed without hindrance, a wordless message that whispered anxiety. Claire was already in motion, and in a second she was beside John and when she opened her mouth to call her mother's name, she was met face-on with John's mouth against hers in a wet embrace.

She twisted away to wave to the faces plastered against the tinted window.

"They can't see us," John whispered, trying now to find the back of her neck.

"Mom." Claire placed her hand against the glass as the limousine pulled away from the reception.

John struggled to lift the back of her veil and her blonde hair to plant his face against her.

She stiffened.

"What's the matter?"

"Mom. Something's wrong. I've seen that look before."

He straightened, untangling his face from her hair. "That look?"

"Just now, before we left. She is carrying something. Hiding something she's not sharing with me. But at the last moment, she let down the happy mask."

"She's losing her baby girl, Claire. That's all."

Claire sighed. "I hope you're right."

"Of course I'm right." He paused. "When we're together, we're all right."

She stopped him with a finger on his lips, followed by her own mouth against his. It had been a fairy-tale wedding. She felt the leather seat beside her. "Can you believe this?" She shook her head. "Leave it to Grandma Elizabeth."

He returned her smile. "You're beautiful."

She looked out the window toward the edge of the parking lot. A police cruiser sat poised at the driveway. "Look, John. The sheriff's department is still protecting me."

He laughed. "Tyler Crutchfield will never find us tonight."

They looked as the police car pulled out behind them. "We've got an escort."

She closed her eyes and took a deep breath, trying to concentrate on how wonderful it felt to have the wedding behind her. She was Claire Cerelli!

As the tension of the wedding began to melt away, tears moistened her cheeks. "We've been on quite a journey," she gasped.

John brushed away a tear with the back of his hand. "With a few mountains behind us—"

"A few?" She opened her eyes to see his smile again. "Shall I name them for you?"

He put his index finger against her lips and shook his head. "Let's not go there, honey. This day is too perfect."

Claire nodded but couldn't keep her heart from swelling with gratefulness that she stood on this side of so much pain.

John reached into the pocket of his tuxedo and retrieved an envelope bearing an airline insignia. "For the next two weeks, it's nothing but white sand, blue water, fresh seafood, and my favorite girl," he said, running his index finger over the top of the envelope.

"Will you tell me now?"

He slowly lifted a ticket bearing Claire's new name and held it up for her to see, shrugging with feigned nonchalance. "I'm taking Dr. Cerelli to Hawaii."

"John, we can't spend—"

He held up his hands. "Hey, I used my frequent flyer miles." He pushed forward until his face was inches from hers. "If anyone ever deserved this break, it is you. The clinic never lets you rest."

She kissed him softly and felt a knot tightening in her throat. "This is so nice. This day has been perfect."

They settled into a quiet embrace, barely aware of the car's movement over the curves leading up and over North Mountain toward Brighton.

John had reserved the bridal suite at the Brighton Omni. He took her hand as they stood at the door to their room. "We need to get some rest, Dr. Cerelli. We've got an early flight tomorrow."

She leaned in and kissed him passionately, not caring that they were still in the hall. "We can sleep on the plane," she whispered. "I have other plans."

John fumbled with the key card, his anticipation nearing summit level. Since their new engagement, John and Claire had been faithful to stay within safe boundaries, knowing too well the hurt and guilt that come with compromise. This time, they had purposed to do things the right way. *Now,* Claire thought, *the time has come. We can enjoy each other the way God intended.*

Inside their room, John slipped off his tuxedo jacket and tossed it aside as he stepped forward to help Claire lift the veil from her head. His lips brushed hers lightly, and then pulled away. "I've been dreaming about this moment for so long."

"I love you, John Cerelli."

Their lips met again.

She leaned back against the door as John's kisses lingered, hungry against her neck.

A sharp knock startled Claire from her pleasure. "What?" she whispered. "Who could that be?"

"Just the bellman with the luggage." John reached for the door handle. "Your mother is the only one who knows where we are tonight, and she's been sworn to secrecy."

Claire sighed.

John opened the door. Two uniformed men stood inches from the hotel doorway. "Can I help you?"

The men looked past John. The taller of the duo spoke first. "I'm Detective Stevens with County Police. I'm looking for Claire McCall."

Her gut tightened. "I–I'm Claire Mc—No, I'm Claire Cerelli," she said, closing her hands onto the front of her wedding gown.

"I'm afraid you'll have to come with us."

Claire's eyes widened. Was this some sort of joke? Maybe John's friends had rigged an elaborate trick. But something in their faces told a different story.

John stepped forward. "What's this all about? It's our wedding night!"

The detective took Claire's hand. In a moment, she was spinning until she faced the wall. A second later, with her arm bent behind her, she felt cold metal snap around her wrists. "Ms. Cerelli, you're under arrest for the murder of Wally McCall."

Chapter Twenty-Four

A few moments later, Claire was led through the lobby of the Brighton Omni Hotel, handcuffed, and still wearing her wedding gown. The lobby now seemed crowded. Perhaps she hadn't noticed before, passing through the same foyer a few minutes ago with other things on her mind. Now it seemed that all of Brighton had shown up to gawk at the bride being led away by police. Along a side hallway, the Brighton High School prom was in full swing, and the upperclassmen rushed into the hall, giggling, pointing, and in general wanting to get a view of the action. Claire wished for her veil that she'd left behind in the room. A photographer turned his attention from positioning a couple beneath a flowered archway and ran to the door. As Claire passed, he happily snapped away, blinding her with a flash.

John trailed along a step behind her, questioning the officers. "Tell us what this is about! Someone killed Wally?" He grabbed the arm of Detective Stevens. "Please!"

The detective quickly seized John's wrist. "Do not touch me!"

John held up his hands. "Just tell us what this is about!"

The officer was stone-faced. "Why don't you ask her?"

Claire looked into her husband's eyes. The fear she saw there was not encouraging.

John pleaded, "Claire?"

She began to cry. "John, I have no idea what this is about."

"Let's go," the detective said.

The policeman stepped quickly into the parking lot toward a waiting cruiser. There, one officer shoved her into the backseat.

Claire strained against her handcuffs. "Hey," she cried, "I can't buckle up with these things on!"

The officer grunted and buckled her in before joining his partner in the front seat.

John tapped on the window, offering a laugh. "Okay, this is a joke, right? Where's the camera?"

Detective Stevens shook his head. "I wish it were." He slammed the door with John standing at the curb.

As they pulled away, she could hear John yelling, "Where are you taking her? At least tell me where you are going!" She turned to see him run for a few yards and then stop and scream, "Ahhhh!"

Claire's mind was spinning. Feeling the tears begin to flow, she tried to wipe her face on her shoulder, but couldn't reach because her hands were cuffed behind her back. "I don't understand," she sobbed. "My father's dead?"

The police officers seemed to ignore her. A plexiglass interwoven with some sort of metal reinforcement separated them.

She raised her voice. "Excuse me! Could you please tell me what's going on? Is my father dead?"

The officer driving shook his head and mumbled, "Give me a break."

His partner in the passenger seat turned to face her. "Miss McCall, you've heard your rights. I suggest you remain silent."

Claire dropped her head in frustration and sobbed to herself, "I'm not Miss McCall, I'm Doctor Cerelli."

John's mind ran from thinking this was an elaborate hoax to the notion someone had made a terrible mistake. His first impulse was to chase after the police cruiser. As he searched in his pocket for his keys, the reality sunk in. He had no keys. A limousine had dropped him off. He closed his fist in frustration and walked back to his hotel room, formulating a plan. Who should he call? An attorney? Della? Maybe he should take a cab to the county jail?

When he reached his room, he slapped the door. In his haste he'd left the room without his keycard.

He leaned his head against the door. *God, what is going on?*

Ami looked at herself in the full-length mirror and smoothed the long white gown. The day had been nearly perfect, except for when John stumbled on his vows. He always did get a little nervous in front of large crowds.

She walked to the dresser and ran her finger over the top of his picture. She was so lucky to have a man like John. But working with him so closely had been hard on him. At times, it seemed he could hardly control himself. Finally, she'd had to quit her job just so he could get some work done.

But now, all of that was behind them. Their days of physical temptation were past. She looked down at Bridgett, her poodle. "How do you like my dress, Bridgie?"

She'd left the reception before John. She expected him at any moment.

She heard the rattle of her closet door. Silly John, he was playing a game. Quickly, she lowered her veil and looked at her image filtered by the white lace. The wedding had been fabulous. Now they were alone, the moment she'd waited for, finally here.

The floor squeaked behind her.

His hand pinched her shoulder. "Hello, beautiful bride. Ready for the honeymoon?"

The grinning face was not John's. Ami's fantasy shattered. In a moment, she was falling toward the bed, seeing only the speckled light coming through her veil.

Della arrived at Pleasant View thirty minutes after the bride and groom left the reception. There, she was dismayed to find Wally's room still taped off. Randy Jensen met her in the hall.

"Where's my husband, er, my husband's body?"

"State Medical Examiners Office in Roanoke."

She shook her head. "So you really think—"

He put his hand on her arm. "Mrs. McCall, we need to talk. We're not going to have this all figured out in one day."

She studied his face for a moment. "What's wrong?"

"Mrs. McCall, did your husband ever express a desire to die?"

She nodded slowly. "He's been depressed." She looked up. "He's been so miserable."

"Any reason to believe that your daughter would have helped him?"

She shook her head. "I—" She stopped. "No. It makes no sense. Sure, he wanted to die, but Claire wouldn't help him do it. And especially not today."

Randy Jensen pursed his lip and exhaled slowly. "We had to pick your daughter up tonight. We found—"

"You what?" Della threw up her hands. "No, no, no."

"I'm sorry, Mrs. McCall. I'm sorry."

Della put her hand to her mouth. "Where is she?"

"Brighton. In the county jail."

Claire looked across the wire mesh window at Eric Robinson, a county magistrate. At her elbow stood Deputy Stevens.

Mr. Robinson pushed his glasses up on his nose and squinted at Claire through the glass. He looked to be about fifty-five and overdue for a tune-up. His eyes were puffy, as if he'd been in bed when they called. Claire estimated him to be sixty pounds overweight, and he had an ugly seborrheic keratosis on his forehead. He looked at the deputy. "Any criminal history?"

"No prior arrests. Our department was involved in another euthanasia investigation involving this same doctor."

Claire's jaw dropped. "Excuse me, but the investigation done by your department found the accusation to be completely unfounded."

Mr. Robinson wrote something on a paper. "Any plans for travel?"

"Are you kidding?" Claire shook her head. "I'm standing here in my wedding dress. I was on my honeymoon. No one has yet told me what is going on here. I didn't even know my father was dead, and now you arrest me on charges of murdering someone I didn't know was dead!"

"Ms. McCall," the magistrate began, "it may behoove you to keep silent."

"Would you mind explaining just what is going on?"

"Ms. McCall—"

"I'm not Ms. McCall!"

The magistrate sighed. "Dr. McCall—"

"I'm not Dr. McCall!"

Mr. Robinson's forehead glistened, making the brown skin lesion even more prominent. He slapped the paper in front of him. "Detective Stevens, did you or did you not arrest Claire McCall?"

"This woman is Claire McCall," he said, tightening his grip on her elbow.

Claire pulled against him. "I just got married. My name's Claire Cerelli."

"Fine. Ms. Cerelli, you've been arrested on a charge of first-degree murder." He shook his head. "And from your own admission, you are on your honeymoon. That makes you a flight risk. You will be held here without bail. The Juvenile and Domestic Relations sits Monday morning. Your bond hearing will be Monday morning."

Claire shook her head. "I have to stay here? You've got to be kidding. I'm on my honeymoon! I can't stay here."

Joel Stevens smirked. "Let's go."

"Wait. You can't be serious!"

The deadpan look on his face was all the answer she needed.

"I'm on my honeymoon. Take me back to my husband!"

The officer shoved her forward.

"Where are you taking me? Don't I get a phone call?"

The detective led her from the magistrate's office into a small room next door. "Sit," he said, adjusting a camera on a small stand. "Look here. Smile," he said, his voice dripping with sarcasm. "Nice dress, by the way."

He pointed at a counter. "Time for fingerprints. Give me your right thumb."

She complied as much as she could with her hands in the cuffs. Next, he took her into a barren hallway and swiped a keycard to unlock a wide metal door. With the door behind her, she faced a second door with a female guard. The woman looked at Claire and chuckled. "Whaddaya got, Joel?"

"Any vacancy in holding?"

The guard smiled. "For you, sure." She looked at Claire. "Don't tell me, you were at a costume party, right?" She laughed at her own joke and pulled a pair of latex examining gloves out of a box.

Claire didn't respond.

"Stand still." The woman patted Claire's dress, lightly at first, then slipped her hands along her legs with a probing just shy of intimate.

"Ouch!"

"Turn around."

Claire winced and submitted to a repeat performance as she faced the gray concrete wall.

The female deputy unlocked a second door, this one metal with a small wire mesh window.

Another deputy arrived. "Holding cell two," Bonnie said.

"I'll need my cuffs," Joel said.

He unsnapped them and Claire rubbed her wrists, but had only a few seconds until a second pair, this one belonging to the jail, was locked in place.

Joel tipped his hat. "This is where we part, Dr. Cerelli. These folks will take good care of you." He touched the female guard's hand. "Thanks, Bonnie."

The male deputy had a military cut, blond and flat on the top. He looked like he spent the best part of his short life in a gym. He took Claire by the elbow and escorted her forward, up a set of metal stairs.

"Don't I get to talk to an attorney?"

"Ma'am, it's nearly midnight. You are going to be housed in the holding area. Enjoy the view. The window overlooks booking, the central part of our fine facility. Tomorrow, they'll give you a real orientation, issue you a uniform, and move you into the general population."

The officer removed Claire's handcuffs only when she was standing in the middle of a small holding cell. He excused himself, leaving her to explore her surroundings alone.

It wasn't hard to take inventory. There was exactly one metal bed with a worn mattress and a metal one-piece commode. No pillow. No blanket. The one window without blinds was so high up on the outside wall that it gave only a view of the night sky. Claire paced the room. Two steps from bed to one wall, six steps from commode to wall the other way. On the opposite wall was a window overlooking the central hub of the jail. A few seconds after he'd left, Claire watched as Detective Stevens walked through. He made a fist and touched it against the deputy's fist he'd called Bonnie. He paused as they laughed. It was like watching TV with the sound muted. The duo seemed to be flirting. Claire tried to read their lips. The detective pointed his head to the left and then lifted his eyes to meet Claire's. The couple laughed again. Claire stared until he broke their gaze.

She looked at the mattress stains and perched gingerly on the edge of the bed, trying not to wrinkle her dress. Two hours ago, she had entered a luxurious hotel room with her new husband. Earlier that day, her heart had soared with the words of the hymn. *I know that my Redeemer lives; What comfort this sweet sentence gives.* Now she was confined to a holding cell in the county jail.

Fear, confusion, and anger wrestled for preeminence in her soul. She closed her eyes, shutting out the little room, not caring that the pain in her heart found its expression in tears. She willed herself not to understand, for she had learned that agony of soul was often a mystery that required trust first and enlightenment, if it ever came, later on. At that moment of misery, she found herself stilled by the confidence of a warrior who had tasted victory in prior battles.

She looked at her fingers, each stained with black ink. She reached for her ring finger and felt the smooth surface of her wedding band. She slowly turned it around on her finger while quietly, with a breaking voice, she began to sing.

"He lives to silence all my fears, he lives to wipe away my tears. He lives to calm my troubled heart, he lives all blessings to impart."

Chapter Twenty-Five

Finally back in his hotel room, John let the phone ring at Della's place ten times before hanging up and calling his father.

Tony answered on the second ring. "Cerellis."

"Dad, it's me. Something horrible has happened. Claire has been taken by the county police. It is so bizarre. They accused her of killing Wally. I—"

"Slow down, son. The police have Claire?" John listened as his father exhaled into the phone.

"We didn't even know he was dead."

"John, we were going to tell you in the morning."

"You knew?"

"Della took us aside right after the reception. Wally was found dead at the nursing home this morning. We all agreed not to tell Claire, because we didn't want to spoil her special day. And for that reason, we couldn't tell you either."

"Dad!"

"Hear me out. Della was planning to tell Claire in the morning, before your flight. We knew you'd have to cancel in order to attend a funeral." He paused. "Son, we just didn't want Claire to have to think of anything other than enjoying her wedding." He halted. "But this is bizarre. Why did they think that Claire had anything to do with Wally's death?"

"The police didn't say much. They acted like we knew something about it already. I asked the detective, but they showed up one minute, and the next, they were carting Claire away." His voice cracked. "Dad, I'm not even sure where they took her."

"Must be the county jail. Can you meet me there?"

"I don't have a car, remember?"

“Right. Mom and I will pick you up. And I’ll call our attorney. After defending you against Ami, Bill Fauls is getting used to sorting out this family’s troubles.”

“I can put up the honeymoon money for bail.”

“Don’t worry about that. We’ll make sure she doesn’t have to stay.”

The front lobby of the Green County Jail was spacious by Apple Valley standards, as Brighton, the county seat, boasted the largest population from Roanoke to Winchester. It was there, to their dismay, and in spite of their fatigue, that the McCall clan joined the weekend crowd. Harried parents of a partying teen argued about their son’s access to their liquor cabinet. A police officer assisted an intoxicated man through a set of double doors. A young mother tried to quiet a screaming child. And in the midst of it all, William Fauls, the Cerellis’ attorney, approached the reception window.

To call it a reception window was an irony, Della thought, as nothing about the décor spoke of receptivity.

Mr. Fauls was flanked by John and his parents. Behind them stood Della, Grandma Elizabeth, and Margo. Mr. Fauls tapped on the window.

A deputy, a clean-shaven man appearing about twenty-five, looked up. “May I help you?”

“I’m William Fauls, retained counsel for Claire Cerelli. I understand she was arrested earlier tonight.”

The man typed something on a keyboard in front of him and scanned his eyes across a monitor. “Yes, sir.”

“Where can we go to pay the bond?”

The man shook his head. “I’m afraid she’s being held without bond, Mr. Fauls.”

Grandma Elizabeth pushed her way to the front. “Young man, my granddaughter will not be staying in this jail! Name the amount and I’ll post bail.”

The man frowned. “It’s not a question of amount.”

John was about to join the protest when Mr. Fauls silenced the family with a stern gaze.

The deputy seemed to understand the family’s frustration. “It’s out of my hands,” he said. “If the magistrate issues a warrant for arrest, there had to be enough evidence to believe a crime has been committed.”

Mr. Fauls loosened his tie. “Let me speak to the magistrate.”

"I'm sorry, but Mr. Robinson is gone for the night." He paused and stood from behind a desk.

"Call him back in," the attorney responded.

"Mr. Fauls, with all due respect, you know that in charges of first-degree murder there is a legal presumption against bond. Even if I get Mr. Robinson out of bed, it won't get your client out of jail."

John nudged Mr. Fauls and pleaded quietly, "Tell him we just got married. Tell him it's important for me to see my wife."

The deputy overheard. "Sorry, sir. Visiting hours for female inmates is Sunday morning."

John looked at his watch. "It is Sunday morning."

"Ten a.m."

William Fauls rubbed the back of his neck and looked at John. "Look, I'm sorry, there's nothing we can do right now. Claire will be given a hearing before the judge on Monday. Perhaps I can convince him to let her out on bond."

The family slumped. John voiced their surprise. "Monday? She has to spend all weekend here?"

" 'Fraid so." He placed his hand on John's shoulder. "That gives us one day to figure out exactly what they have on Claire and see if we can come up with an alternative explanation for the judge. Otherwise— "

John leaned forward. "Otherwise what?"

The attorney took a deep breath. "Otherwise, Claire will stay in jail."

"How long?"

Mr. Fauls cleared his throat.

John repeated, "How long?"

"John, these cases take time. It could vary."

"How long?"

The attorney shook his head and stared at the family. "For a murder charge, the judge will set a preliminary hearing date one to three months away." The group gasped as he held up his hand. "That's not the trial, just a hearing to determine probable cause and see whether the judge will certify the case to a grand jury."

John looked away. "And she stays in jail the whole time?"

"The whole time."

Chapter Twenty-Six

John woke at 4:30 and stared at the little green numbers on the alarm clock. Instead of sleeping at the Omni, he'd collected his things and gone home with his parents. Of all the places he wanted to be on the morning following his wedding, this was probably last on his list.

The night had been a blur. There was so much he didn't understand, so much that didn't make any sense. He dressed, drank black coffee, and called the airline to cancel his reservations. He didn't mention that his wife was in jail. He thought it only prudent to say he needed to cancel because of a death in the family.

By 6:30, he was on the road over North Mountain heading for Stoney Creek. By 8:00, he was standing in the nursing supervisor's office in Pleasant View Home.

With gray hair pinned under her nursing cap, a wrinkled smile, and soft, plump hands that were perfect for soothing a crying child, Sally Weathersby looked like anyone's grandmother. But today, the smile was gone and her hands were planted on her hips. "I'm sorry, John. Nursing home legal counsel has made it clear. We are not to talk about this to anyone."

"But Claire is in jail!" He shook his head. "You've got to tell me something. We didn't even know Wally was dead until the police came and arrested her. What made them think it was Claire?"

Sally pointed at a chair before planting herself behind her desk. "Have a seat, John," she said softly. "This must be horrible for you."

John huffed at her understatement. He didn't feel like sitting. He wanted information, and so far, there seemed to be a tight seal on anything helpful coming out of the nursing staff. He looked twice at the chair before conceding. "Just help me out here. Claire is going to stay in that jail unless we can convince a judge to let her out on bail."

Sally nodded slowly and leaned forward. "I've known Claire since she was a little girl. I have no question about her heart." She paused. "And I've seen Wally suffer for the last few months. It must have been agony for Claire to see him this way."

John stiffened. Mrs. Weathersby didn't understand. "What are you saying?"

"I'm saying that no one who knew the situation as we did would ever question Claire's motives for—"

"Claire didn't kill her father!"

"John, I understand your difficulty with all of this—"

John stood. "The only difficulty I have is with you! You assume Claire helped Wally die. Did you see her?"

Sally leaned away from John as he towered above her. "Listen, John, it won't help to yell at me."

He took a deep breath and raised his hands before forcing himself to back up a step and sit again. "There has to be another explanation. If you tell me what you know, perhaps I can figure it out."

Sally bit her lower lip and glanced toward the door. "You need to see this from our point of view, John. A man has been found dead in our facility, with evidence that he has been euthanized. If this gets out, it will be very, very bad press. We may even have to close our doors."

"Claire wouldn't do this."

"I'm sorry, John, my hands are tied."

"I'm going to find out eventually. Why can't you help me?"

She shook her head. "Talk to the police. Maybe they can help you."

"Fat chance," he muttered, standing again. "Fat chance."

If anyone understood Apple Valley politics, it was Detective Randy Jensen. He frowned as he looked at the stack of pizza boxes on his desk. It was the spillover from the night crew who often ate as they worked.

He looked at the wastebasket, overflowing with evidence of Chinese takeout and Dunkin' Donuts. "Evie, can't these slobs even empty the trash?"

His secretary laughed. "They need a mother."

"Can you find Garland Strickler's number for me?"

Evie tapped her computer keyboard and wrote down the number. "Calling the commonwealth attorney on Sunday morning?"

Jensen smiled. "For this, he'll want his weekend interrupted."

Evie held up the number. "Isn't he up for re-election soon?"

He nodded. "Yep." He reached for the note, allowing his fingers to rest on hers for a moment, just long enough to test her interest.

She looked away, but not before he saw the hint of a smile. He let his eyes linger on her full figure before clearing his throat.

"I think I'll ask for his endorsement."

She smiled. "I'd like to be the secretary to the county sheriff."

"With Garland's help, it could be a reality." He winked and picked up his phone. In a moment, he heard Garland's voice.

"This had better be important, Jensen."

"How'd you know it was me?"

"Caller ID. Besides, who else has the gall to call me at home on a Sunday morning?"

Randy chuckled, hoping to lighten the bear's mood. "I know you'd want the heads-up about this. I know how important a successful high-profile case is for a commonwealth attorney up for re-election."

"Okay, you've got my attention."

"We arrested Claire McCall last night."

"The doctor?"

"Stoney Creek's one and only. You know, solved the mystery of the Stoney Creek curse, nearly killed the Apple Valley's serial rapist last year, the first woman to—"

"I know, I know. You arrested her?"

"Murder." Randy let the word hang.

"Murder?"

"It appears she gave her debilitated father an overdose of morphine."

"Jensen, are you sure?"

"Come by the office. She'll be in front of the court Monday morning. You'll want to see the evidence before then."

"Okay."

Randy listened as the attorney sighed. "What's wrong?" Randy asked.

"She's an Apple Valley jewel. Prosecuting Stoney Creek's starlet could be a political minefield."

"Handle this right and you'll have all the pro-lifers in your camp. They don't want legal euthanasia in Virginia, even if it comes from the hand of a hero like Claire McCall."

Randy turned at the sound of the door opening and saw John Cerelli enter the little office.

"Listen," Randy continued. "I've got to run. Someone's here. Can you come by at noon? We can grab a pizza."

"It's Sunday, Jensen. My wife and I eat at the country club. I'll be there at 11:00."

The phone line clicked. Evidently, Garland Strickler wasn't into niceties such as "hello" and "good-bye."

Randy set the phone down and motioned for John to come on in past Evie's desk.

John didn't smile. "I guess you know why I'm here."

Jensen shook his head. "Not really, but I need to ask some questions, so I'm glad you came by." He pointed at the chair. "Coffee?"

"No, thanks." He sat. "Why did a county detective arrest my wife last night?"

Jensen smiled. "I said I needed to ask you some questions."

"I'm afraid I know nothing of value to you. I found out last night, when my honeymoon was so rudely interrupted, that my father-in-law was dead." John folded his hands in his lap. "So what can you tell me? Why arrest Claire?"

"You knew nothing of Wally's death?"

"Not until the arrest."

"Can you verify your wife's whereabouts yesterday morning?"

John shook his head. "I'm sure she can tell you that. She stopped at Della's. She had her hair done. She stopped at Pleasant View Home to show Wally her dress. She came to the church for lunch, then dressed and had pictures taken. We got married. We had a reception."

"Did she tell you about her visit with Wally?"

John paused for a moment. "She said he cried when he saw her dress."

"What time did she show up for lunch?"

He shrugged again. "About 1:00, I guess." John put up his hand. "Look, Claire would not have murdered her father."

"I understand your concern. But perhaps you're not the one with an objective viewpoint. She is, after all, your wife."

"And what makes you think Claire did this? What evidence do you have?"

"Mr. Cerelli, I'm conducting a criminal investigation here. Certainly you understand it's not my place to discuss this with relatives of the accused."

John's face reddened. "So how can I refute your evidence if I don't know what it is?"

"With all due respect, that's not your job." Randy opened a box on his desk and inspected a cold piece of pepperoni pizza. He lifted it to his nose and sniffed before sliding the tip into his mouth. He wiped his chin and continued, "Why don't you talk to your wife? And hire a good attorney."

"My wife knows nothing about this."

Randy stood, still chewing the congealed cheese. "Perhaps you don't know your wife as well as you think you do."

Claire looked at her fingers and wondered how long it would take for the black dye to wear off. Being photographed and fingerprinted was only the beginning of her humiliation. That morning she'd been given a bottle of lice treatment and forced to shampoo in front of a female guard. She was then introduced to her new wardrobe. One-piece canvas may be nice for a hunting trip, but it did little to complement her figure. And orange was definitely not her color. She was a summer, and women with summer hair and complexion coloration do not do orange. But after spending the night in her wedding gown and sleeping without a blanket, the one-piece orange canvas jumpsuit was at least warm.

She was escorted to her new quarters in the female pod on north wing. Fifteen rooms opened off of a central common area that had a couch, a card table, and some chairs. A TV hung from the ceiling in one corner. Each room had two metal bunks and a single metal commode.

The guard unlocked the door in the metal bars that formed the front of her cell. The room was inhabited by three other women. Two African Americans lay on the top bunks. A Hispanic woman leaned over a sink in the corner. In spite of the orange jumpsuit, Claire could see that her abdomen was swollen with pregnancy. "Listen up, ladies," the male guard said. "You've got a new roomie." He pointed to the women in the beds first. "Trish. Tamika." He pointed across the room. "This is Maria. And this," he added, ushering her into the room, "is Claire."

Claire mumbled "hi" to the blank faces before looking around the room, wondering where to sit.

She leaned down to sit on one bunk when she heard, "That's mine." Maria spat into the sink.

Claire selected the other lower bunk. Here at least the mattress had a thin fitted sheet. She ran her hand over the bed. It had a plastic mattress cover that reminded her of Wally's. There was no blanket, but she noticed that Maria's bed had two.

The girls ignored her. There was no introductory exchange. She wondered how to start. *What are you in for? Murder? Drugs? Prostitution?* She sighed and lay down on the bed. She didn't feel like talking anyway. Maybe if she closed her eyes, she could sleep until Monday and her time before the judge.

She slipped off her rubber slippers, letting them drop to the floor.

"That's my side," Maria barked.

Claire complied and scooted the slippers under her bunk.

She stared at the wall and tried not to cry. It was going to be a long time until Monday.

John drove back over the mountain toward Brighton, angry and dejected over his lack of progress. By 11:00, he was back in Brighton and standing in front of the reception window at the Greene County Jail. "I'm here to visit Claire Mc—, er, Claire Cerelli."

The deputy didn't look up. "Name?" she asked.

"John Cerelli."

She tapped on the keyboard in front of her. "Sorry, sir, your name's not on the list."

"What do you mean? What list?"

"The inmate must submit a list of visitors who will be coming in advance." She shrugged. "There's no one on this inmate's list."

He shook his head. "Does she know this? She just came in last night."

The deputy yawned. "Sorry. That's the breaks. Inmates have until Friday to submit names for their visitor list. Relatives and spouses only." She held up her hands. "Policy."

"Look, we just got married yesterday. I need to see her."

"That's real sweet, sir, but I really can't help you." She offered a plastic smile. "Maybe she will put you on the list and you can see her next Sunday."

John slapped the glass with his hand. He watched as the officer pressed the button on the side of her handheld radio. "Danny, I'm going to need some help in the lobby. Potential disruptive visitor."

John glared at her and turned around. He started toward the door. He didn't know who Danny was, and he had no intention of sticking around to chat.

Sunday lunch in the female pod meant cold metal trays, macaroni and cheese, soft peas, and applesauce. The only eating utensil allowed was a spoon, so the prisoners could only dream of something firm enough to cut or stab. Claire scanned the room and carried her tray to a vacant spot at the end of a long table. The food reminded her of the fare for the edentulous at Pleasant View.

She sat across from a woman with graying hair and a spider tattoo on the back of her right hand. "Hi."

The woman lifted her head and chewed while she talked. "Stay away from the African sisters. Don't go into the showers alone."

Claire studied her macaroni for a moment. "Thanks."

"There's one phone in the commons. All calls are collect, five dollars a minute. You have to get your family to call the phone company to set it up before you call. It only allows calls to numbers that they set up."

"Oh." Claire pushed the peas around their compartment. "Have you been here long?"

"Four months." She paused. "I killed my husband." She kept chewing. "You going to eat that?"

Claire shrugged.

A woman with purple-streaked hair leaned toward her. "Eat it. It's a long time till breakfast. And I hope you like cold gruel."

Claire nodded and took a bite of macaroni. It was overcooked and needed salt.

The husband killer slurped her applesauce. "You can have visitors once a week on Sunday morning. But you have to write their names down by Friday or they won't be approved."

Claire moaned. "So that explains why my family is ignoring me."

"Why are you here?"

She looked up to see Maria struggling to fit her pregnant belly beneath the metal table.

Claire thought about an appropriate response. "It's all a mistake" sounded too wimpy for this crowd. Perhaps "I killed my father" would buy her some respect, but the guard was probably listening. Or she could say something smart-mouthed like "I heard the chef was great." Instead, she just shrugged. "I don't really know."

Her answer drew chuckles from around the table. Spider-tattoo woman spoke first. "You got arrested, didn't you? So you know."

"What I meant was, I was accused of a crime I didn't commit."

More laughter. One of Claire's top-bunk roommates called out, "We all there, sister. Everyone of us. We innocent."

Claire cringed, feeling her cheeks flush. The inmate across from her wiped her mouth with the back of her tattooed hand. "My attorney thinks he can get me off. My husband beat me. Made me crazy." She lifted her dull eyes to meet Claire's. They were unfocused and empty of luster, a muddy pool. *If one look can help an insanity plea, you've got it down.*

Maria said something in Spanish that ended in "gringo." Claire didn't understand. Another Mexican American responded with more Spanish and touched fists with Maria. They both laughed. Maria spoke again. "Okay. What's your name, Clarinet?"

This was too funny with the African Americans. The one known as Tamika put her spoon to her mouth and imitated a squeaky jazz musician.

"Claire."

"Claire," Maria corrected. "What I meant was, what did they arrest you for?"

Claire looked at the nursing-home food and told herself to be strong. *Don't let this crowd know you are afraid. As if they don't already know it.* She steeled her face and met Maria's gaze. "For killing my old man."

Sunday afternoon, Sally Weathersby looked up as Gail Norfleet knocked on the door. "What's up, Gail?"

"Have you seen Sol today? It looks like he left yesterday right in the middle of mulching the azalea beds. Left the lawn tractor and wagon out all night."

"Have you tried his home?"

"Twice. Got his answering machine both times."

Sally shrugged. "Will you ask Jake to put away the equipment? All we need is a theft on top of our other problems." She hesitated. "Did Blanche have to fend off any more reporters?"

"Other than Jennifer Eastland at the *Daily News Record*, no."

"I wonder how she got wind of Wally's death so quick."

"She was in Brighton, dining at the Omni. She said she saw the police take out Claire McCall. She just started asking questions and ended up here."

"That woman has a knack for being in the right place at the right time."

Gail laughed. "Or the wrong place at the wrong time."

"It's not funny. All we need is a media circus reporting euthanasia at Pleasant View."

Gail nodded. "You're afraid, aren't you?"

Sally looked at her colleague and nodded slowly. "I was the supervisor on. I was in charge. This happened on my watch. Mr. Johnson will be taking on heavy pressure to scapegoat someone just to save face in the public eye."

"He couldn't blame you."

"Just watch."

Chapter Twenty-Seven

Claire lay awake on her bunk until 2:00 a.m., unaccustomed to the sounds of dozens of snoring inmates and the *click-click-click* of the heels of the patrolling guards. Maria was restless too, alternately moaning softly or occasionally letting a quiet "ooey, ooey, ooey" escape her lips in front of a curse.

Claire squinted in the dim light. Maria held her lower abdomen. Claire whispered, "When are you due?"

Maria's forehead glistened. "Not for a month."

"First baby?"

She cursed. "My fifth."

"Are you having contractions?"

The grimace on Maria's face was answer enough.

"Why don't you ask to be taken to the infirmary?"

Maria shook her head. "They hate Mexicans. They won't give you any medicine."

Claire listened for the next hour as Maria alternated between resting quietly, calling Mother Mary, and cursing some poor fellow named Fredrico.

At 3:00, Maria cursed again, and began a rising "ooey, ooey, ooey," again.

Tamika rolled over, rocking the metal bunk. "Shut up."

Trish's head appeared, looking over the top bunk at Maria, who was stripping off her orange jumpsuit. "You're bleedin'!"

"My water just broke. Ain't supposed to have this baby for a month." She stood in between the bunks over an expanding wet circle.

Claire sat up. "Lie down, Maria." She put her arm around the trembling girl. "Let me check you." She hesitated. "I'm a doctor."

Maria lay down. Claire exchanged glances with Tamika and Trish. Their eyes glistened with attention. Claire washed her hands at their little sink and focused her attention on Maria. With one feel, she knew they were in trouble.

"Maria, listen to me. I'm going to need to keep my hand right where it is. The umbilical cord is coming out first. Try not to push. If the baby's head comes down any further, it will compress the cord. I need to hold the baby's head back."

Maria screamed.

"Call the guard!"

Tamika began to yell, "Bonnie! Bonnie get up here."

Maria squirmed. "I have to push."

Claire shook her head and positioned herself so her face was closer to Maria's. "Do not push, Maria! This is very important. The baby will die if the head comes down."

"My baby!"

Moans and curses echoed through the women's pod as inmates awoke to the disturbance. "Shut up!"

Tamika kept screaming for Bonnie.

Bonnie showed up a few seconds later, holding her billy club high. She rapped on the bars of their cell. "Quiet down in there!" Then her eyes widened as she looked at Claire. "Just what are you doing?"

"I'm trying to hold back this baby."

"Are you crazy?"

Claire tried to keep her voice calm. "Bonnie, I'm a medical doctor. Maria is having this baby tonight whether we want her to or not. The baby's umbilical cord has prolapsed. That means Maria needs an emergency cesarean section."

Bonnie's jaw slackened.

Claire raised her voice. "Now!"

"I'll get a wheelchair."

"No! She needs a stretcher. Call 911 for a paramedic crew. We don't have much time."

Bonnie radioed for help. Claire talked softly to Maria while they waited, all the while keeping her right hand firmly in place against the baby's head.

"Your baby has a full head of hair. What are you going to name it?"

"Olivia," she panted. "Or John."

Claire smiled. "That's my husband's name."

Tamika snickered. "How about Clarinet?"

Trish slugged Tamika's arm.

A few minutes later, a Brighton paramedic crew arrived. Bonnie unlocked the cell, and the taller of two men ordered Claire out of the way. "Let me see what's going on."

"What's going on is that you have a gravida five, para four, with an umbilical cord prolapse. If I move, this baby's head is going to engage and you're going to have a dead baby on your hands."

Maria cried, "Don't move, don't move."

"But we need to move the patient out."

"Exactly," Claire responded. "But not without me." She hesitated, looking at Bonnie. "Unless one of you gentlemen or this guard wants to take responsibility for the life of this child, I suggest you let me go with you."

The paramedics shrugged. "Can we allow this?"

Tamika scoffed at the guard. "You gonna let her out of here, just like that?"

"I'm a medical doctor. Have either of you boys managed a prolapsed cord before?"

The paramedics shook their heads. "Not me."

"Then you'd better break protocol for the life of this baby. I'm not leaving Maria."

Bonnie looked pale. She talked into her radio. "I need priority clearance to move two prisoners. Send up the in-charge."

A second deputy arrived. "They have to be shackled. It's policy."

Claire frowned. "You can't put a woman in active labor in shackles. You'll endanger the baby."

"Shut up. You're not in charge."

Bonnie shook her head. "Ned, I'll make the call. Put this one in shackles," she said, pointing to Claire. "Maria's obviously not going anywhere."

Ned frowned. "I don't like it."

Maria screamed.

The paramedics unfolded a stretcher. "Careful," Ned instructed, "We'll move her on three. One, two, three!"

Claire and Maria moved as one. The stretcher was too narrow for both of them. Ned locked the shackles in place around Claire's ankles.

She frowned. "I can't walk fast enough in these. And we have to move quickly."

The tallest paramedic put his hands together to form a stirrup. "Step up on the stretcher. You'll have to ride on it with her."

It seemed the only way, since Mr. Protocol wouldn't allow her out without the shackles. Slowly, Claire straddled Maria's right leg, so that she could keep her hand in Maria's birth canal and her own weight on her knees. Once she was on the stretcher, the paramedics wheeled them out, with one deputy in front and one in tow.

The ambulance ride was eight minutes to Brighton University Hospital, where they were met by obstetrician Phil Whitten. Claire had spent time on the Ob/Gyn service under Dr. Whitten when she was a medical student.

"Claire?"

"It's a long story."

He stood still for a moment, as if trying to process the scene. Dr. McCall, in an orange prison jumpsuit and shackles, straddling a patient. Claire's right hand disappeared in between the patient's legs. He shook his head in obvious disbelief. After a few seconds, he found his voice. "Okay, give me the bullet."

"Multiparous mother in her eighth month of pregnancy with premature rupture of membranes and a cord prolapse. She last ate at six p.m. last night. This is baby number five. One peripheral 16 gauge IV started in route."

"OR four is ready for a stat section. Let's roll."

Maria and her entourage moved down the hall en masse. The elevator was crowded, but carried Dr. Whitten, Claire, Maria, two deputies, and two paramedics. Once they were at the OR doors, Dr. Whitten turned to the paramedics and deputies. "We've got it from here."

Once Maria was on the OR table, the anesthesiologist did a crash induction and a nurse painted the abdomen with deep yellow Betadine. Only after the surgeon opened the uterus did Claire remove her hand from Maria's vagina.

She watched as Dr. Whitten delivered a healthy little boy. John.

Claire looked at her hands and slowly shuffled through the swinging door to the scrub sink. Then she turned and moved toward the exit where her deputy escort waited. Behind her, the OR door opened, allowing her to hear the cry of an infant's first breath and the dismay of the surgeon. "That Dr. McCall was one of our best medical students. I guess you just never know."

Chapter Twenty-Eight

Claire awoke to the sound of rapping on the bars at seven. She'd slept exactly one hour since arriving back from Brighton University Hospital. "Ms. Cerelli, rise and shine."

She opened her eyes and stretched. "Ugh."

"Get up. We leave for the courthouse in ten minutes."

She stood and yawned. It was funny that a little thing like lack of sleep could change your whole perspective. She found she actually wanted to stay in her miserable bed this morning. There was no time for a shower, no makeup, and only a plastic comb to fight through the tangles in her blonde hair. She splashed water on her face and decided that not having a mirror in her room might be a good thing on a morning like this. The way she felt, she'd probably only scare herself. Some things are best left unseen.

The deputy, a female of about twenty-five, had a name tag that read, "Smith." She unlocked the door and locked the shackles on Claire's ankles. As she'd experienced last night, the shackles were like handcuffs, only with a longer chain that allowed her to take three-fourths of a normal step.

Claire offered a smile and flipped her hair over the color of her ill-fitting jumpsuit. "How do I look?"

"Peachy. Now the hands." Claire obeyed by lifting her hands. The deputy snapped them into place.

Claire turned to face the door to her cell. "Trish, Tamika, it was nice meeting you."

Tamika smirked. "Hey, it's not like you will be gone long. Don't get all mushy on us."

Claire shook her head. "I'm going before a judge. I'm sure he'll let me out."

Trish huffed. "What planet are you from?"

Tamika said, "Planet White. No way a judge would let a sister out, at least not one accused of murdering a white man."

Deputy Smith nudged Claire's shoulder. "Now."

Claire lifted her handcuffs and wiggled her fingers at her roomies. "Bye-bye."

She was led through a series of fluorescent-lighted hallways to an elevator, which took her up to the glass-enclosed walkway which connected the jail to the courthouse above Liberty Street. As she shuffled forward, the irony made her smile.

Deputy Smith pushed her forward. "What's so funny?"

"It just struck me as a bit humorous. Here I am in handcuffs and shackles and we're crossing Liberty Street."

The deputy rolled her eyes. "Keep moving. We're not here for a morning stroll." Smith led Claire across the walkway and then down a flight of stairs into the courthouse.

The shackles made the stairs a challenge. They gave her feet just enough leeway to take the steps one at a time if she didn't try to land on the edge of a step. "Whoa," she said, holding her hands up for balance.

At the bottom of the steps, she saw a door. Hanging on the outside handle were two pair of handcuffs. The deputy unlocked Claire's and hung the cuffs with the rest, leaving on her ankle restraints. Deputy Smith unlocked the door. "Inside." She prodded Claire. "It's a holding cell. When the judge is ready for you, you'll be taken in."

Claire inspected the little room. It had a long metal bench along one side, a metal commode, and a metal door with a narrow vertical-covered window. Two women in prison orange and shackles sat on the bench at separate ends. Claire recognized them from supper the evening before. "Hi," she offered.

A thin woman with long, stringy graying hair stared at Claire with hollow eyes and said nothing. The other woman, appearing no older than sixteen, pushed a rebellious strand of black hair behind her ear. "Hi."

Claire sat in the center of the bench. "How long until we get to see the judge?"

The young woman spoke. "He usually takes the women at the start of the docket, around eight." She shrugged. "Otherwise we might not be seen until after ten thirty."

The older woman's forehead glistened with sweat. She shivered and wiped her face with her sleeve.

Claire watched her a moment. *Looks like narcotics withdrawal. I can guess what you're doing here.*

A long fifteen minutes later, someone lifted the metal covering from the door's only window. It was hinged at the top and squeaked when it moved. "Claire?" It was a man's voice.

She looked through the opening to see a man in a gray suit, holding up the window cover. She recognized the distinguished gentleman as William Fauls, the attorney who'd represented John during his recent trouble with a coworker. "Mr. Fauls."

"John asked me to see you."

"John? Is he here? Can I see him?"

"He's waiting outside the courtroom. The judge may or may not allow families in today. It's Judge Atwell, so I wouldn't count on seeing your family. He keeps a tight rein on his court."

Claire nodded.

"I realize it's your decision, but he asked me to represent you."

"Of course. That'd be great." She hesitated. "Do you know what's going on?"

"A little. I was hoping you could fill me in. I've had only part of yesterday to sort this out."

"I really don't have a clue, sir. I was on my honeymoon. John and I had just arrived at our hotel when the police arrested me and brought me here." She sighed. "I didn't even know my father was dead."

"Hold on," he said, disappearing from view and letting the metal cover clang shut against the door. In a moment, the cover lifted again. "Sorry about that. I needed a pen. I'll need to make some notes."

They talked across the door, with Mr. Fauls holding open the cover with one hand and occasionally with the top of his head, when he paused to make a note.

"What have you been able to find out?"

"Not much. The prosecutor is Garland Strickler. He's usually pretty tight-lipped about the evidence, but he's hinting at a straightforward win for the commonwealth. I tried probing the sheriff's department, but their paperwork on your arrest hadn't even been processed, so that was a dead end." He shrugged. "And the nursing home isn't saying anything. Their risk management people won't let them breathe a word of this to anyone, especially me."

Claire felt her stomach knotting. "When can I see John?"

"Depends. Maybe in the courtroom if the judge allows. Let's just hope we can get you out on bail and you can spend all the time with John you want."

"What do you mean, 'let's just hope'? I'm innocent. They can't just keep me here."

"Claire, maybe you don't know how much trouble you're in. In cases of first-degree murder, there is normally a legal presumption against bond."

She felt like crying. The look on her face must have prompted Fauls to soften up, because when he continued, his voice was just above a whisper.

"Look, Claire, I know this judge. He should listen to your unique situation. You don't have a record. You just got married."

"And I'm innocent," she sobbed.

He sighed. "I'll do everything I can."

"I have to get out. When is my father's funeral? I have to go."

"You may want to rethink that."

"Why? He's my father."

He shook his head. "I'd have to get a hearing in front of the judge. The sheriff will come in. He'll argue he doesn't have enough manpower for your escorts. He'll claim they can't be babysitting you with all the other work they have."

Claire started to protest, but Mr. Fauls continued, "The commonwealth attorney will argue that the judge can't possibly let you out to attend the funeral of the man you're accused of killing."

"I didn't kill anyone!"

"Look, I'd be glad to argue it before the judge, but he's not likely to let you go. If he does, you'll attend with your orange jumpsuit on, shackled, with a deputy on each side. They'll let you sit in back, but not with your husband. The media is virtually guaranteed to make a circus of it."

"Just get the judge to let me out now and we won't have to worry about the funeral."

He looked to the side down the hall. "I'll see you inside. When the deputies bring you before the judge, say 'Your Honor,' 'Yes, sir,' 'No, sir,' and 'Thank you, sir.'"

She nodded.

"I'll join you at the bench."

The metal covering clanked against the window. Claire looked back at her holding-cell mates. The older one was staring at her hands, clasping and unclasping them with a continuous tremor. The younger one was sleeping with her mouth open.

Claire slumped against the wall. Alone.

Outside the courtroom, Della, Margo, Grandma Elizabeth, and John gathered with Tony and Christine Cerelli. William Fauls opened the door and slipped out into the hall with them. "I'm sorry. Judge Atwell said no to the bailiff's request for visitors. He's allowed in a few from the media, but that's it."

John huffed. "Why? I want to see my wife!"

The attorney held up his palms. "There's nothing I can do about this, John. It's best not to press the issue. Perhaps he'll be in a better frame of mind to grant my bail request."

John shook his head. "This is crazy. This whole thing is crazy."

"Look, you can wait out here, or better yet, enjoy the spring weather and sit outside on a bench." He paused before turning to go back into the courtroom. "It wouldn't hurt to pray."

Claire padded forward wearing her orange jumpsuit and rubber slippers, shackles in place and a single male deputy escorting her with a tight grip on her elbow. The courtroom was richly paneled, mahogany or walnut, she thought, with a half-dozen benches. An oil portrait of a white-haired man holding a gavel hung between two windows on the far wall. She took a dozen steps toward a watching crowd before being directed right to walk in front of the judge. She looked up at Judge Atwell seated behind a large elevated bench and flanked by two deputies.

The judge nodded at Claire and looked at the papers in front of him. "Ms. McCall."

"Your honor, I'm Claire McCall Cerelli. I'm recently married."

The judge smiled. "Married since this document was prepared?"

"Yes, sir."

"Do you understand the charges against you?"

"Your Honor, may I approach the bench?" The voice came from behind her. It was William Fauls.

The judge looked over his reading glasses. He had a bushy white unibrow and a double chin that fell on top of his black robe. "Mr. Fauls." He motioned for him to come forward. "Are you representing Ms. Mc—uh, Ms. Cerelli?"

"Yes, Your Honor."

"Very well." He motioned again. "Mr. Strickler, you may as well join us."

Claire recognized the commonwealth attorney by his Colonel Sanders goatee. "Thank you, Your Honor."

"Ms. Cerelli, you have been charged with first-degree murder. Do you understand?"

"Yes, sir."

"Very well. The second issue we deal with during this first meeting is the issue of representation." He looked at Mr. Fauls. "But that seems to have been arranged." He leaned forward, looking over his glasses at Claire. "You are accepting representation by Mr. Fauls, I take it, and you will not need court-appointed council."

"Yes, sir, Your Honor."

"The final issue is one of setting a date for the preliminary hearing." He looked at Claire. "The preliminary hearing is not a trial, Ms. Cerelli. It is merely a hearing to see whether the case has enough merit to be certified to a grand jury." He opened a book in front of him and ran his finger down a page. "How about June 28?"

Claire gasped. That was nearly eight weeks away.

"We can be ready in one month," William Fauls responded.

Garland Strickler cleared his throat. "For a case of this importance to our community, it is in the commonwealth's interest to push the case back a bit, say the second week in July."

"You'll be ready by June 28," the judge responded. "Agreed?"

It wasn't really a question. The attorneys nodded. "Yes, sir."

William Fauls placed his hand on the edge of the bench. "I'd like to bring up the issue of bond, Your Honor."

The prosecutor coughed. "With all due respect to the court, it would set an irregular precedent to allow bond in a first-degree murder case."

The judge raised his eyebrow in a question. "Mr. Fauls, why should I deviate from a legal presumption against bond?"

"On the basis of the character of my client. She has no prior arrests. She has faithfully served her community as a physician, and, Your Honor, this is a special situation. She was just married Saturday afternoon, and was arrested before spending even one night with her husband."

The judge quickly covered a smile with his hand. "I see." He seemed to erase the grin with his hand. When he brought it down again, his face was steel. "Mr. Strickler?"

"This is exactly the reason we cannot deviate from law practice in the commonwealth. No, Ms. Cerelli has not had prior arrests, but she was investigated by the Virginia State Board of Medicine on another accusation of euthanasia. She is not only a danger to the community, but because of her recent wedding, she is a flight risk. There's no telling where she might wander off to for a prolonged honeymoon."

"Your Honor," William Fauls responded, "the accusation of euthanasia was just that, an accusation. The Virginia State Board of Medicine completed an investigation and my client was cleared. It has no bearing in this decision."

The judge nodded. "I agree. And it does not bear on the decision of this court." He took a deep breath. "Nonetheless, this will be a highly publicized case, and it would not do to begin granting bond to citizens arrested for murder." The judge looked at Claire. "Bond is denied. Ms. Cerelli, congratulations on your recent marriage. Your preliminary hearing will be June 28. You will be held in the county jail until that time." He smacked his gavel on the bench, sending a shot through Claire's heart.

"Next!"

Chapter Twenty-Nine

Ray Brown sipped black coffee and looked at Monday's *Daily News Record.* The top story made him set his coffee aside. "Local Physician Arrested on Murder Charges." "Sue! Look at this!"

Sue left two griddle cakes frying and leaned over her husband's shoulder. "It's Claire," she said, pointing to a picture of a woman in a wedding dress and handcuffs.

Ray read from the article to his wife.

"Claire McCall was arrested Saturday night on charges of murdering her father, Wally McCall. Wally, who was suffering in the end stages of Huntington's disease, was found dead in his bed at Pleasant View Nursing Home Saturday morning. It is unclear what evidence pointed to his daughter's involvement. Officials at Pleasant View declined comment. Police have also declined further comment beyond acknowledging that the arrest took place.

"It is known that Claire McCall, a physician working out of the Stoney Creek Family Practice Clinic, was married Saturday afternoon—"

Ray stopped and lifted his face. "What's burning?"

Sue rushed to pull the pan from the burner. "Oh me, the pancakes!"

He sipped his coffee and continued, "—was married Saturday afternoon to John Cerelli of Brighton. The physician was escorted by police from the Brighton Omni while wearing her wedding dress."

Sue threw the blackened pancakes in the dog dish. "Dr. McCall wouldn't kill anyone."

"Her father was suffering. Maybe she couldn't help him any other way. I wouldn't want to live like Wally." He stood up and walked to the calendar taped to the refrigerator. "I thought so. I'm supposed to inspect Claire's VW today. She wanted me to do it while she was off on her honeymoon."

Sue poured batter into the skillet. "Some honeymoon she's having."

After breakfast, Ray drove the tow truck to his shop as he had every weekday for the past fifteen years. He added water to his drip coffeemaker and settled in at his desk to do an audit of his books. After four hours, he shoved the stack of papers aside and looked up as his shop hand entered. "Afternoon, Len. I need you to drop me off at Della's place to pick up Claire's VW."

Len nodded and walked to the truck.

They drove the three miles with a typical silence between them. Sometimes they would go a whole day with the only communication being the directions Ray gave Len for work.

Ray hopped out at the McCall place and watched Leonard pull away. He thought twice about knocking on the door to find out the real scoop the paper didn't report, but decided Della probably needed her privacy now more than ever.

The VW was parked on the driveway and unlocked, the keys under the mat as Claire had indicated. As he opened the door, a bad odor greeted him. He lifted his head from the car. *How long has this car been shut up?* He opened the door wide and went to the other side to open that door as well. He fanned at the air with his hand. He looked into the backseat, expecting to see a bag of rotting fast food. Nothing. Not even a scrap of paper. He squinted through the hatchback window. The inside cover was partially displaced.

Opening the hatch, he recoiled at the sight inside. Stuffed in an awkward semicircle in the trunk was the bloody body of a man.

Della paced her small kitchen, muttering under her breath and stewing over the audacity of the judge to keep her Claire in the county jail. And on top of that, it seemed half the town had called, expressing their support for Claire and their understanding for how she had helped Wally go. Nobody seemed to really have a clue that her daughter could actually be innocent of the charges. She eyed the phone pensively, daring it to ring, and then taking the phone out of its cradle altogether to maintain her sanity.

She turned her head in response to a rapid knocking on the front door. *If that's a neighbor telling me how they understood Claire's pain, I think I'll give them something to pain about!* She hesitated to collect herself while the pounding became even more urgent. "I'm coming!"

She opened the door to see Ray Brown with his mouth hanging open and pointing to Claire's blue Beetle.

"Ray, what is it? You're white as a sheet!"

"It's, it's," he stammered.

She put her hands on her hips, feeling alarm, but also a bit annoyed to be interrupted on a day like she was having. "It's what?"

"W–Wally's body," he said. "In the car!"

Della gasped and ran ahead of Ray toward the VW. She slowed a few feet from the car and leaned forward, inching her way to see. He was right! What kind of cruel trick was this? She looked closer as the realization hit.

"This isn't Wally!" She reached forward and touched the man on the shoulder before quickly withdrawing her hand. "He's cold."

"Dead for a while, I'd say." He pinched his nose and stuck his head in over the body. "You're right. I'm sorry to scare you like that."

Della shook her head in amazement. It wasn't Wally, but it was still a crisis.

Ray took off a red cap and scratched his bald spot. "I just assumed it was Wally. I read the paper about Claire killing him and all, so I—"

"Claire did not kill her father!"

Ray backtracked. "I didn't mean she really killed him, I just meant I read about him suffering so and I understand, I mean when I saw a body and I heard Wally was dead, so I just thought—"

"Shut up, Ray," she said, walking away. "I'm calling the police."

Ten minutes later, Randy Jensen and Joel Stevens stood in the driveway talking to Della and Ray.

Randy called for a forensics team and the medical examiner. "Any idea who it is?"

Della shook her head. "I didn't look too close, but I don't think so."

"When is the last time anyone used the car?"

"Claire used it to go to Pleasant View to show her dress to Wally on Saturday morning. She left the car here after that. I haven't used it at all."

Randy looked at Joel. "Finish the interview with Mr. Brown. Don't let anyone touch the car until it has been processed by forensics and the ME."

"Where are you going?"

"To the county jail. I need to talk to Claire Cerelli."

Garland Strickler leaned back in his leather chair and looked at the calendar on his handheld computer. A high-profile case like Claire McCall's could be just what he needed to secure reelection as commonwealth attorney.

It appeared to him that Wally McCall's death was euthanasia. Wally was chronically ill. Garland had testimony from multiple sources that Wally had asked to die and had asked Claire to help him die on many occasions. A vial of morphine traced to her office had been found, and a lethal level of the narcotic was found in his bloodstream as tested in the medical examiner's office.

Just why Claire had chosen the day of her wedding as the day for a mercy killing was puzzling to Garland. Perhaps they both had agreed to wait until Wally could see his daughter in her wedding gown. Perhaps she thought the wedding activities would provide her with better opportunities for an alibi.

"Lisa," he said, punching the intercom.

In a moment, a soft knock preceded her entry. Lisa was twenty-nine and had worked for him for four years. She understood the ups and downs of politics and helped place a favorable spin on local events to make her boss look his best. "What's up?"

"I've got an important case coming up. Preliminary hearing June 28. It would be great if the pro-lifers could stage some sort of a euthanasia protest outside the courtroom for that day."

"I'll make some calls."

"Good. It would be good if you could give the media a tip as well. I want the Virginia voters to associate me with the pro-life cause. Virginia isn't ready for euthanasia."

She made a note and turned to leave. "Of course."

"Lisa," he called to her back, "handle this in the usual way. No one should be able to trace that this office tipped the media or the protestors."

"Don't worry. I can be invisible."

A minute later his intercom buzzed. "Mr. Strickler, I have Randy Jensen on line two."

He picked up his phone and said, "Strickler."

"Mr. Strickler, I've just come from Della McCall's place. We've got a second murder to investigate."

"Della?"

"No, no. A mechanic came out to take Claire's VW in for an inspection, and he found a body in the hatchback."

"A body?"

"A man. Probably twenties, but looked older. His hair and beard were dyed white. Looks like he died from a stab wound to the back. Wearing only his boxers. The ME had just arrived when I left a few minutes ago."

The attorney made a note. "Any idea how long the body had been there?"

"A couple days at least."

"So Claire McCall could have been involved in this too."

"Sure looks like it. I'm on my way to interrogate her now."

An hour later, Claire was escorted in shackles and handcuffs into a small room with concrete walls, a single table, and two chairs. In a moment, Randy Jensen came in.

"Dr. Cerelli," he said, nodding his head. "I'd like to ask you a few questions. You understand you're under no obligation to answer without your attorney present."

"Randy, please tell me what this is all about. I still have no idea why I'm a suspect in my dad's death."

"I'm not here to discuss your father. I need to ask you about another murder."

"Randy, please." She halted. "You want information from me? Then maybe you should answer some questions for me."

"A man's body was found in the back of your car this morning."

Claire reined in her surprise. "What's this about? You're bluffing."

"Bluffing? Why would I make this up?"

"I don't know. Make me think you have something worse on me, so I'll give you something helpful in your investigation into my father's death."

"Interesting theory. But, unfortunately, not the angle I was pursuing."

"Help me," she said, crossing her arms in front of her chest, "and I'll help you."

Randy sat down and leaned forward. "Okay, I'll play your game. You pretend you don't know anything. I'll tell you what you already know."

"I know nothing. What makes you think I killed my father?"

"We found the morphine vial from your office."

She lifted her hand to her mouth. "Someone overdosed him?"

Randy rolled his eyes.

"What else? You've got to have more on me than that. Anyone could have gotten narcs from my office. The magistrate would have never given you a warrant just because of that."

"Give it up, Claire. Why don't you tell me how you rigged the backdoor and dismantled the emergency exit so you could come in undetected?"

"I don't know what you're talking about."

"I'm tired of this game. We have you on the home's surveillance tape."

"There's another explanation."

"Which is?"

She didn't have it. She shrugged. "I don't know. It wasn't me."

"Okay, now you help me. Whose body is in the back of your Volkswagen?"

"I don't know."

He huffed. "When did you drive it last?"

"Saturday. I drove it to Pleasant View Home to show Daddy my wedding dress." She lifted her wrists to her face so she could scratch her nose. "I left it unlocked in the driveway at Mom's so Ray Brown could inspect it. The limo took me to the church."

"And I'm to believe you know nothing about this."

"Yes. You tell me. Who is it?"

"We will find out. If you help us, things could be better for you."

She felt like crying. "Just leave me alone. I tell you the truth, but you don't believe me."

Randy stood, shaking his head. "I wish I could believe you." He walked to the door and knocked. In a moment, he was allowed to leave, and Claire was left to cry alone.

Chapter Thirty

Early Wednesday morning, Judge Atwell looked at the morning schedule and called for his secretary. "Anita, did you pencil this in?"

"Yes. William Fauls insisted on being before the bench first thing." She set a file on his desk. "Wally McCall's memorial service is today. His daughter wants to attend."

He shook his head. "This is a waste of my time. There's no way I'm going to put the family through that."

"But what if she's innocent?"

"Doesn't matter. The family deserves a quiet service. If I send in a prisoner in shackles, the media will eat it up. Garland Strickler is likely to make a stink. The story will be everywhere, and then Fauls will want the case moved to another court, saying the jury pool in this county is biased against his client. I won't have it."

"What should I do?"

"Call Fauls. Tell him I'm going to rule against him if he insists on bringing the question before the bench."

She nodded. "I know him. He'll do the right thing."

Thirty minutes later, the PA system in the female pod produced an electronic crack followed by the monotone female voice: "Attorney visit for Claire Cerelli."

Claire looked at the others sitting in the common room. "Looks like I might get to attend my father's funeral after all."

She walked to a door and looked up at the camera and waited. After a moment, she heard the door unlock and she proceeded into the chamber room. There, a female guard put her in handcuffs as the door locked behind her. Then the guard unlocked the door exiting the chamber room and led Claire down the hall to the visitation room.

"You know the drill. When you're done talking to your attorney, signal central control by sliding the red paper under the door. They'll see the paper and radio for me to come get you."

Claire nodded and stepped into the visitation room. She took a seat on the stool bolted to the floor and looked through the windowpane at her attorney, already seated with his hands clasped in front of him. "So how'd it go? Will they let me out for the service?"

William Fauls shook his head. "I'm sorry, Claire."

"What?"

"Judge Atwell thinks your presence will be disruptive. He won't allow it."

"You told him I'd cooperate, that I'd sit quietly, didn't you? How is that disruptive?"

"Look, Claire, I didn't even argue it before the bench. I—"

"But you promised! You needed to be there for me. How can—"

He raised his hands and interrupted. "Look, Claire, let me explain. A lot of decisions are made in backrooms around here. The judge wanted me to be able to save face by not arguing the point. He let me know in advance that no argument I could make would change his opinion. Arguing it in court would have been futile."

"I wouldn't have disrupted anything!"

"Photographers would have been there. It wouldn't have been in your best interest to have your picture all over the *Daily News Record* with you in your orange jumpsuit."

"But my family would have wanted me there."

"Put yourself in their shoes, Claire. There are people out there who think you killed your father. It would be awkward for them if you attended."

"I'm not believing this," she said, shaking her head. "This doesn't have a thing to do with the truth."

"Exactly," he said, standing up. "It's all about perception." He reached for the door. "I thought I should tell you in person."

With that, he opened his door and disappeared. Claire felt her heart sink.

Then she took the red slip of paper, slid it under the door, and waited.

John Cerelli gathered with Claire's relatives and a small crowd of members at Community Chapel and listened as Pastor Phil eulogized Wally McCall.

Every few minutes, he turned and glanced over his right shoulder, hoping to see Claire. Every few minutes, he was disappointed. *She should be here by now.*

A few minutes later, John turned again at the sound of the back door opening. This time it was William Fauls. His eyes met John's. The stern look was all John needed to know. Fauls had failed to convince the judge to let Claire out for the funeral.

After Pastor Phil sat down, they sang a hymn, "It Is Well with My Soul." Then John stood and went to the microphone. "I've known Wally McCall since Claire first introduced us when we were at Brighton University together. One of the things I appreciated most about the Wall-man was his sense of humor."

A chuckle rippled across those gathered, as John's use of the nickname resurrected memories from Wally's life.

"I remember the simple joy Wally experienced from a shared joke or a gesture as small as a kiss from his bride." He looked up at Della as he spoke. "I don't know if any of you ever watched Della kiss Wally in the last few years, but it always seemed to bring a smile to his face. Kissing Wall was a dangerous experience. I think Della has had a few black eyes to prove it. But over and over I watched as Della would kiss him good-bye, leaning over him, positioning herself to ward off any unexpected blows from Wally's dancing hands. She would pin his cheeks in her hands and plant a wet one right on his lips and then make a break for it before she could be hit."

The crowd laughed at the collective memory.

"But the joy was mine, just seeing Wally's grin, knowing he had the love of a good woman.

"Many people could look in from the outside to see a man whose days were marred with suffering, a man stricken in his prime with debilitation, and accuse God of playing a cruel game." John shook his head and fought back tears. "But Wally understood that his life was not his own, that his life hung by a thread of God's sovereignty. Yes, he went through down times, he got discouraged, but he didn't shrink from the pain in his life, and he didn't shrink from his own death. I think he understood that what awaited him on the other side was glorious." He felt his voice thickening. He unfolded a paper he'd prepared to read.

"Those of you who have walked close to the McCall family know of our recent hardship. Claire's relationship with her father has been marked by significant pain. I cannot stand here today and say only positive things about a man whose life was marred by alcohol addiction. But I can say that even though Claire suffered under the hand of her father's drunkenness, she made progress in recent weeks in coming to a comfortable place of forgiveness for Wally. Yes, there were issues between them, but the months since his diagnosis with Huntington's disease have been predominately a time of healing between Claire and Wally. Was Wally a man to emulate in life? Perhaps not, but his longsuffering is admirable.

"Over the past months, Wally longed for his heavenly home. His attitude revealed his solid faith in God's promise for eternal life." John paused and cleared his throat. "And I will state publicly my dismay and disbelief at the recent allegations that Claire could have lifted her hand to hasten the death of her father." He watched as those in the small crowd nodded their assent to his words.

A few minutes later, as the family gathered at the graveside, they watched as Wally's casket was lowered into the ground.

Della leaned into John's shoulder and whispered, "Claire is just like her father, you know, stubborn and headstrong. She'll never run from pain, John, and she'll stand with you till the end."

That afternoon, Della was at the mailbox when she heard the familiar rumble of a Harley Davidson. Jimmy leaned into her driveway, the gravel crunching beneath his hog.

Della walked back toward the house as Jimmy idled up beside her. "Hi."

"Want to go for a spin?"

She shook her head and walked ahead as he stopped.

He pulled off his helmet and put down the kickstand.

"It's too early, Jimmy. I want to go." She halted. "Just not yet."

He walked with her up the sidewalk to the front porch. "How are things?"

"Crazy."

"No one ever accused the McCalls of being dull."

"I'd settle for dull."

He chuckled. "Any news about Claire?"

"No." She sat on the porch swing.

He sat beside her.

She looked away. "Do you think that Claire ..." Her voice trailed off.

"What? You want to know if I think Claire's guilty?"

She nodded without speaking.

"I think the only thing Claire is guilty of is trying to relieve Wally's pain."

"You assume that she helped him die."

"If she did, I wouldn't blame her."

"It's just so frustrating. We don't even know what evidence they have against her."

"What does her attorney say?"

"Only that Garland Strickler is acting like the trial is already underway. He acts like the case is already won for the commonwealth. He isn't giving us squat." Tears began to form at the corners of her eyes. "What if Claire did what all of us thought should be done, but were too afraid to—"

Jimmy touched her hand.

She dropped her head to rest against his shoulder and began to sob. "She's ruined her life, Jimmy. She had so much going for her."

"Shh," he whispered. "You don't know what really happened."

"I feel so helpless." Della sniffed and wiped her eyes. "And angry. I haven't even been able to talk to her."

"Now you're assuming the worst." He lifted her chin to look in her eyes. "You asked me what I thought. Tell me what you think."

"I wish I hadn't been so afraid. Then my daughter wouldn't be in trouble."

Sally Weathersby was familiar with death. But murder was a foreigner. In the space of a few days, her orientation into willful harm had come in immersion baptism.

In the nursing home, she'd seen dozens of dead patients. But they were dead from the enemies of aging. Cancer, pneumonia, and Alzheimer's stalked the halls of Pleasant View with swathlike stealth. That was normal. Death followed life in an unbroken circle. But this, this interruption of breath, was anything but normal.

Joel Stevens opened the door to the ME's office and nodded to Sally. "Are you ready, Ms. Weathersby?"

She nodded as her stomach tightened.

"This way."

She rubbed her bare arms. "Is it always this cold in here?"

"On purpose. Bodies decompose faster at average room temp." He hesitated and tilted his head toward a table in the middle of the room.

"This body was found in the back of Claire McCall's VW Beetle. How long has your employee been missing?"

"Since Saturday."

They approached the metal table with a long gray zippered body bag lying on the surface. Joel peeled back the zipper to reveal the man's face.

Sally put her hand to her mouth. "It's him," she said. "Sol Diaz."

"Are you sure?"

She willed herself not to breathe and moved closer. "It's him, all right." She stepped back and made a joke. It bubbled from her discomfort before she could analyze how crass she may have sounded. "Guess I'll forgive him for not showing for work." She halted, and her nervous smile faded. "Who would want to kill Sol? He was such a good worker."

Joel zipped up the bag and shook his head. "This man is not Sol Diaz." He paused. "At least that's not his real name."

Sally didn't understand. "What do you mean?"

"Fingerprint data from the ME shows this is Tyler Crutchfield, the man who tried to rape Claire McCall."

Back on the female pod, Claire surfed a new wave of respect which grew from saving Maria's baby. For a day, Claire thought she'd figured out just why God allowed her to be accused and sent to such a place. Maria's baby would have died without her. *Okay,* she thought, *that job's done. Now get me out of this place!*

But her pleas for deliverance seemed destined to rise no higher than the concrete ceiling, bouncing back unanswered. She wanted out. But God must have had other plans, because one night turned into two, and then another, and then the judge made it clear that she'd spend the next six weeks bunking with Tamika rather than nestling in John Cerelli's arms like she'd dreamed.

I've had enough, God. I've done nothing to deserve this.

Thoughts emerged from childhood Sunday school and checked her defense. *Hell is what we all really deserve. Okay, okay, I concede. I know I deserve hell. But I don't deserve to be in the county jail.*

Tamika made Claire tell her the story four times. Riding in the ambulance. Going with Maria all the way into Brighton University Hospital's operating rooms. Maria being put to sleep, her swollen abdomen being washed and draped. The uterus cut, its muscular wall separated, the surgeon's hand sweeping down into the uterus over the baby's head, and all the while Claire never stopped pushing back the baby until she felt the gloved hand of the surgeon from the inside.

Tamika had a new hero. "No girl in this jailhouse has ever talked to Bonnie that way." She weaved and juked to emphasize her words. " 'Now,' " she imitated. " 'I'm not leaving Maria!' "

Tamika was medium brown, wiry, and tough as cheap steak. No one messed with her, at least not more than once. She walked with Claire to the showers. She hung with her during the afternoon hour on the rooftop courtyard, and she sat with Claire at every meal. Tamika the protector. The convicted drug dealer. The abused child. The friend.

"How'd you end up here?" Claire asked during a boring afternoon.

Tamika stared off, her eyes lighting somewhere just above the razor wire on top of a fifteen-foot fence. "I didn't come from privilege, like you."

"You don't know anything about me."

"I know you's a doctor and doctors come from privilege." She salted her sentences with curse adjectives. It was as if basic words like *very*, *mostly*, or *extremely* didn't exist in the language she knew.

"I grew up poor, the daughter of an alcoholic. I dropped out of high school."

Tamika nodded like they were from the same 'hood.

Claire smiled. "But that doesn't mean I didn't come from privilege. I made my own privilege." She halted. "Or maybe God had other plans for me and I just tagged along."

Tamika finally turned her face to Claire's. "Did you really off your father?"

"Kill him? No."

"That's not what Channel 4 reports. They talk like you killed him because of his suffering." The corners of her mouth turned up with the hint of fascination. "They also mentioned that you might be inheriting some money."

"Channel 4 doesn't know— " Claire stopped herself. She'd been in jail less than a week and already, she was tempted to slip into the language of her new peers. "They don't know anything. You know the news. If it's juicy, even if it's speculation, they say it."

"I'd kill my father if he was still alive." She bobbed her head.

"How'd he die?"

"Overdose." She shrugged. "So I didn't have to kill him." She leaned forward and touched Claire's arm. "We know what it's like in the real worl'. None of us would blame you if you laid out your ol' man."

"I didn't kill him."

Tamika looked around and spoke softly. "Don't tell that to anyone around here. Everyone's fine with thinkin' you offed him."

Joanne Phillips looked at her counseling appointment book and groaned. She dialed Ami Grandle's new number and waited. Six rings before she picked up.

She sounded sleepy. "Hello."

"Ami, Joanne Phillips here. I called to see how you are doing. You missed your last appointment."

Joanne listened as Ami sighed. "I moved back to Stoney Creek."

"Your mother said you'd lost your job in Brighton."

"I quit. It was too hard working for my boyfriend."

"Are you taking your medications?"

Ami stayed quiet.

"Ami?"

"I'm thinking about moving back to the city. But I think my mom wants me close since my stepfather died. She needs me."

"I want you to come to see me. Can you come on Friday?"

"I have a date."

"Come in the morning."

"I'll be spending the day with John."

"Ami, are you talking about John Cerelli?"

"You know."

"Listen to me, Ami. John is married. You are not his girl."

"You don't know."

"Can I come and see you? You sound upset."

"Sure I'm upset," she huffed, "because you are lying to me."

"Ami, remember what we talked about in our last session? You can't keep— " She heard a click. "Ami? Ami?" Her breath escaped in frustration.

She scribbled a note in Ami's folder. "Noncompliant. Delusional. Refusing to make up missed appointments."

Chapter Thirty-One

Randy Jensen paged through Sol Diaz's job application and looked up at Sally Weathersby. "Did you guys check his references?"

"Talk to Martin down in personnel. He does the record checking on all new employees."

"I've talked to Martin. He did a criminal background check. Sol had no record." Randy began to pace the small office. "The trouble is, the real Sol Diaz seems to be alive and well, gainfully employed in Denver, Colorado. So everything seemed to check out." He slapped the application in his hand. "It says right here that he even called Dr. McCall, who vouched for his mowing ability."

"That's ironic. Get a recommendation from the same woman who helped put you in prison. How'd he ever pull it off?"

Randy opened his briefcase and pulled a picture from a file. "This is Tyler Crutchfield," he said, pointing at the photograph. He held it up next to the picture paper clipped to the corner of Sol Diaz's application.

Sally nodded. "Shave the dark, curly hair. Grow a beard. Dye it white. How'd he change his skin?"

"We found instant-tan products in his bathroom. He only used it on his face and arms."

"He was stupid for staying in town."

"Or brilliant. We never thought he was dumb enough to get a job right here."

"Why would he want to stay?"

"I think he wanted to get back at Claire McCall. He was just waiting for the right time."

"Another irony."

"What do you mean?"

"Looks like Claire McCall got back at him."

The news that the body found in Claire's VW was Tyler Crutchfield spread like an approaching thundercloud on Apple Valley with darkness, foreboding, and a sense of heaviness in the air that whispered of a storm. John Cerelli hung up the phone and poured himself a third cup of coffee.

He walked through the rented house in Stoney Creek that they had chosen to be their first together. Everything around him spoke of her and the things she loved. She'd spent hours matting and framing old photographs for the cubby off the kitchen she'd claimed as her home office. Grandma Newby sitting in a wheelchair, the woman responsible for Claire's first thoughts of a career in medicine. Next to her, a picture of a young Wally in a navy uniform. Her parents together, Grandma Elizabeth. Uncle Leon standing in front of McCall Shoes' first factory. Along a thin slice of wall next to an old bookshelf, Claire had suspended eight birthday photographs, each one attached by a wire to the one above, so that they could be viewed in order from top to bottom. In each, Claire and Clay stood smiling behind a cake. Twins with different fathers, bound in the same womb but destined for separate paths of pain.

The desk had been fashioned by Clay and revealed his eye for detail and his love for woodworking.

The bookshelves groaned with the weight of heavy medical texts, thick with knowledge of surgery and procedures, and medical journals, both medical and surgical, all reflecting Claire's commitment to excellence in her field.

Every day seemed to bring a new revelation, a new misery, or confusion. And nothing made any sense. From the little he could get from the police and local news, it was apparent that Tyler Crutchfield had been killed by a knife wound to the back. Beyond that, they were silent or unknowing.

Whoever killed Tyler Crutchfield must have known his real identity and must have known his past history with Claire, otherwise they couldn't have planted his corpse in the back of her car. But Claire didn't have a clue who Sol Diaz was.

John sipped his coffee. Or did she?

And if anyone knew who Sol Diaz really was, why call attention to Claire by putting the body in her car? Was someone trying to frame Claire?

John thought about Tyler Crutchfield working in and around Pleasant View Home for the past few months, masquerading as Sol Diaz and plotting his revenge. Could he be the one who killed Wally? Certainly he had the right access, he knew the nursing routines, and he watched Claire come and go as she visited.

Nothing made sense. Crutchfield had nothing to gain by killing Wally. Unless he knew Claire would be blamed.

John had spent the days since the wedding in a whirl of phone calls, playing detective, trying to get information from the nursing home, the police, Claire's coworkers at the office, even the medical examiner's office in Roanoke. Nothing made sense. Yet the police seemed so sure. And that frustrated him even more. They were holding out information that had bolstered their confidence in their case.

A knock at the door lifted him from his musing. *Probably another reporter. They sure haven't helped Claire's public image with their speculative suspicion.*

He peered from behind a curtain in the front room and groaned. It wasn't the media. It was Ami Grandle.

Reluctantly, he opened the door. She looked up with eyes of a brown puppy. "Truce?"

"Truce? That's what you say to a guy you accuse to the police of assaulting you?"

She glanced around. John looked past her to see an occupied white car on the curb, one he'd seen before and identified as belonging to a reporter for the *Daily News Record*. She winced. "Can I come in?"

John nodded, swiftly closed the door behind her, and peeked through the blinds at the man in the white car.

"Expecting company?"

"He's a reporter. They think I must know something about Claire and all the craziness going on in this town." He shook his head. "All I need is for them to start reporting on the young guests I entertain while my wife is in jail."

"I can go."

"You're here now. But when you leave, I want you to go out the back. You can cross the alley and go around the block. Maybe my friend out there wasn't paying attention." He didn't sit. Ami did, selecting the middle of the sofa in the front room. She crossed her legs before she began.

"I came to apologize."

John let the statement hang. After a moment, he prompted, "Well?"

She took a deep breath and plunged forward. "I've never hidden the way I feel about you." She dropped her eyes to the small coffee table in front of her. "That day in the office, when you told me I should look for work elsewhere, I—I just freaked." She lifted her eyes to meet his. "John, I applied for that job just to get close to you."

"Ami, we didn't even know each other before—"

"I've known who you were for a long time. I used to see you when you came to the medical school library to visit Claire. I was a nursing student then."

John rubbed the back of his head and turned to pace the room. He had no idea that she'd been so obsessed with him for so long.

"I watched you. I saw how kind you were to Claire." She shrugged. "My father wasn't like that."

"Ami, you don't need to say these things."

"I want to. I decided that if I ever had the chance to get close to you, I would. So that day when you suggested that I leave, well, I lost control. Everything in me wanted you to take me in your arms. I wanted your lips to touch mine. I wanted—"

John backed up a step and raised his hands. "Ami, I'm a married man now."

"I just want you to understand what happened," she sulked. "I'm trying to say 'I'm sorry.'"

"You'd better say it and go."

"These months since my stepfather died have been horrible. I've been under so much stress. That day, I just snapped. I wanted you to want me. But after I pulled you into an embrace, I knew you didn't feel what I felt." She looked down again, uncrossing her legs and tugging at her short skirt. "I needed to save face, so I slapped you. And one thing led to another. Carol insisted I call the police. I felt so bad. I couldn't admit to myself that you didn't want me." She began to cry.

John picked up a box of tissues from an end table and set it next to her on the couch before retreating to his corner again. "Am I supposed to be flattered?" His voice rose in pitch. "And what of this nonsense of reporting Claire to the board for euthanizing your stepfather? What was that about?"

"John, I meant no harm, honest I didn't. But I thought someone ought to know I had suspicions. It wouldn't be right to let a physician get away with that." She blew her nose loudly into a Kleenex. "I'm sorry it had to be Claire. If it helps, I hesitated before writing to them to report her because I knew how much she meant to you."

"Still means to me—"

She nodded and stood. "John, I should warn you. She may not be all she seems on the surface. Of course they couldn't prove anything. Dr. McCall wrote the morphine prescription for the proper amount. But it was clear how much to give to make him die."

John couldn't believe it. "You should go."

"I am sorry, John. I hope we can make a fresh start."

He peeked through the front curtain again. The white car remained. "Where's your car?"

"Oh, I walked. I live just down the street. After leaving my job in Brighton, I moved back here to be closer to my mother."

John ushered her toward the back door. She stopped at Claire's little study and looked at the pictures. "Where's your picture, John? She's got photographs of everyone else she loves."

"We were going to put our wedding photograph there," he said, pointing to an empty space above the desk.

She didn't move along and John felt each second. "My mother always talked about Claire when I was growing up. Claire, the honor student at Brighton. Claire, the first girl from Stoney Creek to become a doctor. Claire at Lafayette for surgery training. Claire, the outstanding example of everything I wasn't."

"Ami, I'm sorry."

"I wouldn't blame her for killing her father, John. It must have been horrible looking at him and knowing that's what life had in store for her."

John opened the backdoor and pointed to a gate at the corner of the lot. "It opens to a gravel lane. Take it across to the next street. You can avoid the reporter that way."

"Why don't you just give me a cup of sugar? I'll carry it right past him like I just came over to borrow from the neighbor." She smiled. "I'm just two doors down, on the corner." She started down the back steps. "Come by if you're lonely."

William Fauls had consulted with Dr. Joseph Fortenberry for as long as he'd been a medical examiner in Virginia. If the dead talked to anyone, it was Joseph. He was impeccable in his work and cool on the witness stand. If anyone could figure out exactly how and why Tyler Crutchfield had died, it was him.

His intercom buzzed. "I've got Dr. Fortenberry on line two."

William Fauls picked up the phone. "Joseph, it's been a long time."

"Fortunately for you, I don't see many cases from your area."

"I'll take that as a compliment."

"You're calling about Tyler Crutchfield."

"What can you tell me?"

"Several things. He died sometime between nine a.m. and nine p.m. Saturday from a puncture to his left pulmonary artery."

"Any signs of a struggle? Is this a clear homicide?"

"Absolutely. A struggle? Yes. Scratch marks on the chest and back. There was evidence of recent sexual intercourse." He paused. "We've got hair from his partner. Maybe a victim."

"Paint me the picture."

"Okay, with a bit of speculation, I'd say he played his hand the way he did in the past. He was raping his victim, but this one fought back. The wound is consistent with a knife plunged into his back by the hand of the victim beneath him."

"Anything interesting from the trace evidence?"

"Just some orange rug fibers and some short brown hair on his back. I can't be sure, but I'd guess his body was lying on top of an orange shag rug where a dog sleeps."

"Fingerprints from the knife?"

"It was wiped clean. I've got nothing. Claire McCall's prints are all over the car, as expected."

Fauls nodded into the phone.

"Why do you need this stuff anyway?" Dr. Fortenberry asked.

"I'm representing the owner of the Volkswagen in another case. I'm just anticipating problems from the commonwealth attorney's office over this. This guy tried to rape my client. Now he ends up dead in the back of her car. Someone knew who he was and who my client was and put two and two together."

He listened as the doctor groaned.

"What is it, Joseph?"

He coughed. "Nothing. Maybe I'm coming down with something. Let me know if there's anything else I can do."

"Thanks, you've already helped. I just don't know how yet."

He hung up the phone only to have his secretary knock and open the door, shutting it behind her. "What is it?"

She kept her voice low and tilted her head to the left, pointing over her shoulder. "It's Garland Strickler. He's here for a face-to-face chat."

"I didn't invite him."

"I know. I take it he doesn't require invitations."

"When am I due in court?"

"Not till one."

He nodded. "Send him in. Offer him coffee."

She opened the door. "Mr. Strickler, come on in. May I get you some coffee?"

He nodded. "Black. Thanks." He looked past her to William's desk. "Bill, I hope you don't mind me dropping in like this."

William Fauls pointed to the chair across from his desk, choosing to keep his desk between them rather than suggest the couch and chairs next to his bookshelves. He studied the man for a moment and tried not to think of Colonel Sanders or his secret recipe of herbs and spices. "What brings you to this territory? Looking for a job?"

"Funny." He pulled a cigar from his pocket. "Do you mind?"

"Yes."

Garland held the brown tobacco stick beneath his nose and twirled it against his moustache for a moment before slowly returning it to a small metal tube. "I'll get right to the point. I've been thinking about your defense. At first I thought you should barge straight ahead and admit to a mercy killing. The guy's life was horrible, you know? The jury would be lenient if you could produce some video of what a day was like for Wally." He shrugged. "I get the win. Your client gets off easy."

"Garland, what's this about? I don't remember asking for your help. And in case you haven't remembered, my client isn't on trial. Her case hasn't even been certified to a grand jury hearing."

"Not yet. But Judge Atwell is no fool. This case is a political hotcake. There's no way he'll dismiss." He paused. "Ever think about running for office, Bill? This case could open or shut the door."

"I'm an attorney, not a politician," he huffed. "You still haven't justified your visit."

"I'm offering you friendly, off-the-record advice, that's all. Try an insanity defense."

"But you said—"

"Forget what I said a minute ago. That was what I thought at first." He leaned back in the leather chair. "And I was glad to fight the case that way. Virginia is way too conservative to elect a commonwealth attorney who is pro-euthanasia."

"Get to the point, Garland. I can't make any decisions about this case. At the pace of their official reporting, I can't get anything from the police, and I have no idea what information you have that makes you so glad to be prosecuting her." He leaned forward, wondering if the odor he smelled actually was Kentucky Fried Chicken grease. "Why don't you bare your cards a little? I'm going to find out eventually, right? It can't hurt to tell me what you know before the preliminary hearing; that way if I happen to see something you haven't, and the case turns out to be leaky, then I've spared you the public embarrassment during an election year."

The mention of the voters seemed to make Garland twitch. It was subtle, but Fauls noted the corner of his mouth tic. Garland laughed it away. "You have no idea what you're up against."

The two quieted at the sound of the door. The secretary set a mug of coffee in front of Garland Strickler. Their conversation resumed as she disappeared.

"So why don't you help me out here? It can only prevent you from looking bad."

Garland stroked his white goatee. "We've got your client on tape, Bill."

Fauls laughed back. "A security tape showing a woman in a wedding dress. I know all about that."

"We've had her mother identify the dress as Claire's."

"It means nothing. Six identical dresses were sold in Virginia from the same dress shop."

"You've been doing your homework."

"I expect better from you. This is full of holes."

"I'm talking about another tape."

Fauls huffed. "I'm tired of the games."

"Easy, boy," Garland coached. "We've got an audio from a 911 tape. Looks like Wally had it on speed dial. Word is, he was paranoid and feared something like this might go down. All he had to do was hit one big button on his special phone to make the call."

"What are you telling me? He asked for help? The guy could barely speak a clear sentence."

"Slow down, Bill. It's not Wally on the tape. He made the call and caught his daughter doing the talking. This wasn't mercy killing, Bill. This is vengeful, premeditated murder."

"I need to hear what you've got. You're sure it's Claire's voice?"

"Sure as I can be without a voice analysis. So I'm going to need a little cooperation from your client."

"Tape her? Absolutely not."

"A judge will make her do it eventually."

"I need to see what you've got first." Fauls stopped and squinted at the politician. "You didn't come here to give me advice. You came to gloat."

Garland set down his cup. "I sure didn't come for the coffee." He paused, retrieving and tapping the cigar tube like he was bumping ashes from the tip. "I need you to talk her into cooperating with the Tyler Crutchfield investigation. Helping prosecute the slayer of such a high-profile serial rapist is only good for my office."

"His death was likely self-defense."

"So you've talked to the ME?"

"Of course. But my client had nothing to do with it."

"That's what she told you, I'm sure. But that's what she said about her father too."

"I don't see what I'm getting out of this deal. You want our cooperation. What does my client get?"

"Let her tell her side. I'll make sure she doesn't get prosecuted for murdering Tyler Crutchfield."

"You're insane. This conversation is over."

"I thought you talked to the ME."

Bill Fauls gulped the rest of his lukewarm coffee. "I did. Everything points to self-defense."

"So why didn't she come forward?"

"She didn't need to come forward. He didn't attack her."

"Call the ME again. Her hair was inside his shorts." He stood, sliding the cigar tube back into his pocket. "Claire McCall was his last victim."

Chapter Thirty-Two

Friday night John gathered around the McCall kitchen table with Della, Margo, and Kyle. Dishes were pushed aside and coffee the beverage of choice. The mood was sober and heading south when William Fauls called for John. John's disbelief was obvious. When he finally set down the phone, all eyes were on him.

John slumped into his chair.

Della leaned forward and touched his arm. "What was that all about?"

"I don't get it. Mr. Fauls talked to the prosecution today. He was able to get some more information," John said, scratching his head. "He said part of the evidence against Claire is a 911 tape. He wants us to listen to it, see if we think it's Claire." He shrugged. "He's on his way over here now."

"I don't understand," said Margo. "A 911 tape?"

"Evidently, a call was made to 911 on Saturday morning. They think it came from Wally's room, as if Wally was able to make the call right as he died." He lifted his coffee cup and started to pace around the kitchen. "There's more. He said the ME did a quick analysis of Tyler Crutchfield's body. He said it was apparent that the pattern of injury is consistent with some sort of fight preceding death, fingernail scratches, that kind of thing."

John continued in a mechanical monotone reciting the report without emotion. "He also said it looked like he had had recent sexual intercourse." He walked to the window and stared.

Della spoke. "John, what is it?"

"He said the ME found Claire's hair mixed in with Tyler's." He felt his stomach tightening. He didn't want to repeat it. "Inside Tyler's boxer shorts."

Margo shook her head. "What are you saying? That this creep raped Claire? How could they know the hair is hers?"

"I asked the same thing. He said they have Claire's DNA study for confirmation from the test they did at the Brighton genetics lab. They took DNA from the hair follicles found on Tyler's body and did some rapid polymerase test or something."

Della pushed her cup away. "This makes no sense. They're suggesting what? That Claire was raped and then killed this man in self-defense? She would never do that without telling someone."

"She wouldn't hide that from me," John said.

Margo nodded. "Unless—"

John turned around to face the table again. "Unless what?"

Margo held up her hands. "Unless she was afraid to tell you that she'd been raped on the day she was to be yours."

"Ridiculous," John huffed.

"How do you explain the evidence then?"

"I don't know. They're wrong," John said. "She wouldn't deceive me. She wouldn't hide something like this from me."

Kyle seemed to be studying his fingernails. "Maybe she snapped."

Margo shushed him. "Don't say that."

"I'm not makin' accusations," Kyle said, raising his voice. "I'm just saying that the evidence doesn't lie."

"Claire's not crazy."

Kyle slurped his coffee. "Maybe HD has affected her somehow."

John clenched his fist. "HD doesn't make people suddenly become violent, and it wouldn't make her deceive me."

"Don't blow up at me. I'm just voicing what all of us fear, that this might be the first of some ugly personality changes that HD brings."

Margo's jaw sagged. "I'm not believing this, Kyle. HD isn't like that."

Kyle returned to silence and sulked.

An uneasy tension hovered between them as they waited. In fifteen minutes William Fauls joined them and set a small handheld recorder on the table. "It's a copy, so it's not the greatest. This call came in from Pleasant View Home on the 911 line right at the estimated time Wally died. Garland Strickler is pressing me to have Claire's voice recorded for voice analysis. That's something I want to prevent if possible, but I wanted to play this for you all first to see if you think the voice is Claire's. If there's any chance this is Claire, it could be pretty incriminating for our side."

Della poured a cup of coffee and set it in front of the attorney. "I don't understand yet. Garland thinks that Wally called 911?"

Fauls nodded. "Yes. Garland thinks he has the voice of whoever killed Wally." He reached for the recorder. "Just listen." He pushed the play button.

"I remember you in my room. You touched me." The group leaned in to listen. "You hurt me."

Della and John traded looks as they listened to the sound of a woman crying. "You abused me. I was drunk. I couldn't defend myself. You—You—"

John felt like someone squeezed him, the grip on his stomach an angry clenching fist. He couldn't find his voice.

"No," Kyle whispered, shaking his head. "No! No!"

Margo's hand covered her mouth. "Oh, Claire."

It was obvious without asking. The voice on the tape belonged to someone spewing venom, poison from deep pain. The voice belonged to Claire.

For days they'd functioned within the safety of their assumptions, firm walls made up with assurances that Claire McCall could never behave unkindly toward her father. If she'd acted at all, it was an understandable mercy. Della began to cry, as the hurt in her daughter's words speared the walls of disbelief they'd constructed. With her assumptions rattled, Della's sobs broke the silence of the trance that held them.

William Fauls looked at Della, then to John, his eyes reflecting a dawning of understanding.

John nodded at the attorney. "No question. It's Claire." He shook his head and turned away, no longer able to view the pain as it found its expression on the faces of each of Claire's family. "I just can't believe it."

Kyle stood and mumbled an audible curse before Margo began to say his name. "Don't shush me," he said, pulling violently away from her hand on his arm. As he jerked free from his wife, he toppled the kitchen chair to the floor behind him.

The noise seemed to infuriate him even more. With his face flushed, Kyle kicked the downed chair against the cupboard and cursed again before fleeing out the backdoor, allowing it to slam in his wake.

John stared at Margo in disbelief. "What's up with him?"

"I–I don't know."

They listened as gravel spit from beneath an accelerating car. Margo shook her head. "He left me here. Just like that."

William Fauls picked up the recorder and moved quietly toward the front room. His demeanor spoke for him. He was an unwelcome invader in the middle of an intensely personal family crisis. He caught

John's eye as he picked up his briefcase. "We'll talk soon," he said as he turned to go.

Mother, sister, and husband studied each other for a moment without speaking. John sat again at the table. Linked in space. Linked by the love of a woman, each in the turmoil that grew from that same love. That love had exposed a raw wound that words could not touch, and that needed, in that moment, only the presence of another to feel the same pain. And so they sat in the kitchen with only the sounds of grief as communication between them, the sniffs, sobs, and sighs of brokenness enough for the moment.

Chapter Thirty-Three

Margo sat in the passenger seat of her mother's car looking out the window at the passing countryside. Daffodils were in bloom and the scent of spring drifted in, but didn't lighten her mood. Kyle had been moody for months, but never openly this hostile. She'd put up with his insecurity and forgiven the affair it had spawned, but he had reacted by pulling away as if he couldn't or wouldn't forgive himself.

Della sighed. "Let me take the girls tonight," she said. "We'll have a slumber party."

"Mom, you don't need to— "

"This is exactly what I need," she responded, obviously trying to steady her voice. She sniffed. "I need my granddaughters to take my mind off of everything."

Margo stared at the passing pine forest. She turned to face Della only when she felt her mother's hand on her arm.

"I don't blame you for being angry."

"He makes me so furious sometimes. And he always chooses your house as the time to act like such a jerk."

"Something is setting him off. A wise woman will help him discover what it is."

"He knows what it is. That's what's so frustrating. I try to talk to him, to get him to open up, but he just shuts me out. He won't go with me to church." She pulled away from her mother's hand and wrapped her arms around her chest.

They pulled in the driveway and Della pranced about in an attempt at cheeriness that galled Margo and delighted her daughters. After a few minutes, with pajamas and sleeping bags in hand, Della ushered the girls off to Grandma's.

Margo found Kyle slumped over his desk with an open bottle of Jack Daniels and an empty glass. She didn't feel gracious. She was angry and embarrassed by his earlier behavior. "Is this where you go with your troubles now, Kyle? Why Jack and not me?"

He lifted his head and looked at her with empty eyes. "Jack gives me courage."

"Courage?" She wanted so badly to avoid the easy patterns of hurting each other they'd fallen prey to. But everything in her wanted to scold him for the spineless way he shrunk from his own pain. "Would you like to explain your behavior? You had to have a temper tantrum at Mom's, didn't you? And then you dare to strand me there?"

Kyle stood up. "I don't need this anymore." He looked at his watch. He kissed Margo's cheek. "Good-bye, Margo. It's been nice."

He headed for the door. She trailed him down the hall and across the den. "Where are you going? You're leaving me?"

"I'm leaving everyone."

"Where are you going? Kyle, talk to me."

He threw his hand back toward her without turning around. "Almost time for the seven-forty."

She understood he referred to the train that crossed Macon Road between Fisher's Retreat and Stoney Creek. It always came at 7:40. But what did that have to do with anything?

"Kyle, don't go. You're drunk."

He slammed the door. She knew she couldn't restrain him. She turned around and threw up her hands. So much for an evening of restoration without the kids. She plodded back to his study, unsure what to do. Should she call the police? What would she say? *My husband's driving intoxicated down Macon Road, please stop him?*

She capped the Jack Daniels as her eyes fell to the desktop. Her heart quickened as she lifted the unfinished note. "I love you, Margo. But it's all my fault."

She shook her head, not wanting to believe where her mind was spinning to. *This is a suicide note.* She gasped and looked at the time: 7:32. Instantly, she understood. Kyle was heading for the 7:40 train.

There wasn't time to call the police for help. Her husband would be at the train crossing in a few minutes. She grabbed her keys and ran for her minivan. With her mind racing, she pulled her vehicle onto the county road and shouted an SOS prayer. "Help me, God!"

She stomped the accelerator and chose the middle of the country road, rocking the van over the small hills and willing her heart to understand. She crested a small hill and felt the van's body lift. A fraction of a second later it dropped hard and she wrestled to keep it on the road.

She slammed the brakes to regain control but found it harder to steer. The right wheels skidded onto the gravel shoulder and back on the blacktop again with a thud. She gasped and pressed the accelerator again, as her own doubts began to whisper. *What if I'm wrong? I'm driving like a fool.*

When she crested the next hill, she looked across the fields, fresh plantings of corn. There, in the distance, she could see her husband's red Corvette, and above it, the telltale railroad crossing sign. She looked at her watch as in the distance she heard the first of a long warning whistle from the approaching train. It was 7:38. She had two minutes.

She knew the whistle would sound its long repeats at Bard's Road a mile to the east, and pick up again its warning within a quarter mile of the Macon Road crossing.

She approached quickly and stopped behind Kyle's Vette. She wasn't sure what to do. Instinctively, she went to the passenger side, figuring that if she was in the car, he may not follow through with his plan. The door was locked. She pounded on the window, but Kyle ignored her, looking straight ahead. "Kyle!"

The train whistle started again. She looked up to see it approaching in the distance. She scrambled to the driver's side. "Kyle," she pleaded, "Listen to me." She began to cry. "What are you doing?"

She studied his face, which was red and glistening from sweat and tears. "Kyle," she said. "Don't do this. I love you. We need you."

He shook his head and looked down the tracks in the direction of the train. "No. I've screwed up my life. You're better off this way."

He depressed the clutch and shifted the car into first. She slapped the window in frustration and tried the latch on the door. "Kyle, don't do this!"

He revved the car as the train sounded another warning whistle.

"No, Kyle, no!" she cried. "What's wrong? I'll forgive you!"

He shook his head.

The train was five hundred yards away and closing fast. Margo ran to the front of the car and leaned on the hood. "You'll have to kill me too."

"Get out of the way, Margo!" he screamed.

She stood her ground. "No!"

He revved the engine again and she felt the vibration. "Get away! Now!" he yelled. She looked over at the approaching train and screamed.

The Corvette lurched, knocking Margo backwards. She tumbled toward the tracks as the deafening sound of the train whistle enveloped her. She felt pain. And then nothing.

Chapter Thirty-Four

Margo opened her eyes to the sound of Kyle's voice. "Margo, Margo," he cried.

She reached for him, hugging him tight as the last half of the train rushed by.

After it was gone, she recognized a sharp pain in the back of her head.

"I thought you were dead for sure."

His face blurred through her tears. "Take me home."

He touched the back of her head, gently exploring a fresh goose egg swelling. "You hit your head on the road beside the track."

"I'm alive, Kyle." She hugged him again. "You're alive. That's all that matters."

"Can you walk?"

She nodded as he helped her to her feet. He assisted her into the Corvette and turned his car toward home.

"What were you thinking? I saw your note."

"Wally's death," he said numbly. "It's all my fault."

"Talk to me, honey. I don't understand. How could any of this be your fault?"

She watched as he withdrew, his upper lip tightening into a line and his head shaking. "I've been such a jerk. I—" He halted.

They drove in silence except for his attempts to start an explanation. Several times he grunted only "I" before stopping again and shaking his head.

Margo waited and prayed, thankful that for now, his suicidal notion had been diverted because of his concern for her safety. Once home, he slid his arm around her waist and walked her into their den. There, she sat on the couch across from his favorite chair. She leaned forward to capture his eyes. "Pastor Phil taught me a verse from First Corinthians. Love bears all things," she said. "I don't care what you've done, Kyle. Love will help us make it." She paused. "Tell me, Kyle. I won't love you less."

"I let Claire believe a lie," he began tentatively, like a child sticking his toe into a cold pool.

She stayed quiet, praying that she could absorb whatever came.

"Now she's acted on the lie, and she's going to pay a huge price. I've ruined Claire's life."

"What do you mean? What lie did she believe?"

"That Wally was the one who abused her." He looked down. "It was me."

Margo closed her eyes and braced her soul against the temptation to lash out. She took a deep breath and said, "Tell me what happened."

"It was the night I saw you kissing Conner Miles." He stopped and looked up. "I'm not blaming you. This is my fault.

"I left the McDonald's pretty upset. I bought a six-pack and was going to head out to Reddish Knob. But I stopped at the Seven-Eleven near Deer Run when I saw Claire. She was sitting on the back of a pickup with Tommy Gaines, Shelby, and Grant Williams.

"I had a couple beers with them. I think Grant was slippin' Claire something heavier, 'cause she got very drunk, very fast.

"I went in to buy another six-pack and Grant had Tommy pull around back. When I returned to the truck, I saw that Grant was getting pretty aggressive with Claire. Before I knew it, he practically had her undressed.

"I told him to ease up, but he told me to mind my own business, that I hadn't been invited to his party anyway. Claire was too drunk to resist him, and it was obvious he wasn't going to stop with stealing a kiss. When he started loosening his belt, I let him have it. I punched him in the nose and pulled Claire from the back of the truck."

"How'd you get away?"

"Grant was drunk, all bravado. He swore he was going to kill me, but Tommy Gaines held him back. I just shoved Claire in my car and got out of there."

"Kyle, you saved her. So why— "

"I'm not done," he interrupted. "When I got to your folks' place, everything was dark. I helped Claire get her shirt buttoned. She was so sauced that she flirted with me. 'Margo's lucky,' she said. 'You took Margo away. Why not take me away, Kyle?'

"I had to carry her to bed. Your parents were sleeping." He stopped and shook his head. "I don't know why I did it. I guess at that point I didn't care if I hurt you. I was so angry." He stood up and looked away, unable or unwilling to face his wife. "I touched her, Margo. I didn't have sex with her, but I touched her where I shouldn't have.

"I snapped to my senses when I heard Wally get out of bed. He met me leaving her room. He yelled at me, told me to get out. I told him he didn't know what he was talking about, that I'd saved his daughter and I was just putting her to bed." He turned to face Margo. "It was me, Margo, don't you see? Claire thinks her father came to her that night, but she was drunk and doesn't have a clear memory." He sat down and dropped his head in his hands. "When she started talking about being abused, I tried to tell her Wally wouldn't do such a thing, but I was afraid to admit what I'd done."

"That's why you got so upset when I talked about that night. You weren't upset about Conner Miles, were you? You were reminded of what you'd done."

He nodded without speaking.

"My sister? It was you?"

"Yes."

She felt anger rising from within her. She raised her finger to berate him, but when she saw his brokenness, she halted. What had she just said? *Love bears all things*. She wrestled with conflicting emotions. After a moment, Margo moved to the floor and knelt in front of him. She took his hands in hers.

He looked up and asked, "Can you ever forgive me?"

"Yes," she said. "I'm not going to tell you that I'm happy about it, but I share blame too. You'd never have been there that night if it wasn't for me. And though I don't like it, I understand. She was my sister, so she was off-limits." She searched his eyes. "Why didn't you tell me this?"

"I was afraid you'd despise me. Or her. She's always been so competitive, going off, having a career in medicine. I didn't want you to have one more reason to be jealous."

She sighed. "I don't despise you. I love you. And that's what's going to get us through this."

"I've ruined her life. She thought Wally abused her, so she overdosed him."

"We don't know that, Kyle."

"You heard the tape."

"I know my sister. Sure, she thought Dad abused her, but she loved him. She forgave him. That's what love does. 'Bears all things,' remember? I think you underestimate her. I think you underestimate the power of love. In fact," she said, standing up, "after listening to what you thought my reactions might be, I think you underestimate the love of all McCall women."

At Saturday breakfast, Claire gave advice to Raynelle on her endometriosis, looked at a mole on the back of Trish's right arm, counseled Sophia on ways to manage her diabetes, and taught one of the guards about treating her gastroesophageal reflux with diet restrictions. For Claire, the chance to give a little to her new peers made her feel useful and staved off the boredom. Tamika thought differently about Claire's charity and wanted her to exact a fee in cigarettes, money, or both, but in the end, Tamika relented, and Claire kept dishing out free advice to keep the days more interesting.

But mostly, day followed night in a cycle of routine. She made a few friends, finding a link as they compared their dysfunctional families. And instead of despair, she found herself in the wonder of thankfulness, understanding that by the grace of God, she'd been given a chance to succeed. The line that separated her background from many of the other women was thin, and by an apparent mercy, Claire had fallen to one side, and most of the women to the other.

She sighed as a guard led her to the little locked conference room where she would get to speak to her attorney. She hoped that today, her one-week anniversary of marriage and incarceration, would bring good news. But it seemed that each time she took a step forward, she fell two steps back, so today, she braced for the worst.

She spent ten minutes alone, examining the small concrete cubical where she could consult with her attorney. Her room was empty except for a small counter and chair. Over the counter was a single window into an identical adjacent room. The window was framed with metal. There was a row of circular holes in the wall in the window frame to allow sound to travel around the window and into the next room. There was a small slot below the window for passing paper back and forth between the two rooms. The atmosphere was jail drab. No pictures, beige paint. When she heard an electronic lock snap, she looked through the window to see William Fauls enter the next room and sit facing her.

"Hi," she said.

"Morning, Claire," he said. He opened his briefcase and met her gaze, apparently content to study her for a moment. "How are you?"

The genuine manner in which he asked showed her it was more than a passive greeting. His eyes glistened, and for a moment, the professionalism dropped, and a gray-haired grandfather took its place. He leaned forward and spoke with his voice etched with concern, "Really." Attorney had been replaced with pastor, legal counsel with the empathy of a friend.

His compassion was disarming. The shell that had formed after her first week in jail began to crack, showing itself as only a pseudo-toughness she kept up in front of the inmates. She felt a surge of emotion, a sudden urge to cry. She pressed her hand against her lips. "I'm okay," she said, not wanting to bare her soul. "I want to talk to John. The isolation from my family is the worst."

"I talked to the phone company. They promised to set up the connection so you can call John or your mother. It should be ready Monday. You can make calls from the commons room. It's not cheap, so you may want to talk fast. Five bucks a minute, collect."

"Monday? That's another two days!"

"The good news is that you can see John tomorrow during visiting hours."

She sighed. "How's he taking this?"

"I think your whole family is pretty much shocked." He opened an accordion folder and pulled out a legal pad. "It's time for a heart-to-heart, Claire. I need you to be completely honest with me."

She didn't like his statement. "I have been."

"Truth is the foundation of the attorney-client relationship. If I'm going to know how to play this out with a jury, I need to know everything."

"I thought we weren't going to trial, remember?"

"True, but I have to be ready."

"I've told you everything already."

He tapped a silver pen on the legal pad. "Evidence has been piling up."

"Evidence?"

"Why don't you tell me about what happened with Tyler Crutchfield."

"What's he got to do with this?"

"Just tell me what happened."

Claire huffed. "He tried to rape me. I shot him. He escaped from my office. I'm sure you read the story in the paper." She stared at her attorney. "That has no bearing on what you should be working on, which is getting me out of here."

He shook his head. "He raped you, didn't he?"

"I told you, he tried."

"So what happened, Claire? He attacked you again, so you fought him off. You stabbed him with a knife."

Claire pushed her chair away from the table. "I don't know what you're talking about."

"I think you do. What I don't understand is why you would put his body in the back of your car."

"Wait a minute! Tyler Crutchfield was the dead man found in my car?"

"You didn't know who attacked you?"

"He didn't attack me!" She stood up and began to pace. Four steps, wall, four steps, wall.

Willaim Fauls held up his hands. "This isn't getting us anywhere, Claire."

"So stop playing twenty questions and tell me what you're talking about."

He sighed and patronized her. "A man's body was found in your car."

She nodded.

"A dead man. He was stabbed."

She nodded again.

"But you know all that, don't you?"

"So far."

"The man was Tyler Crutchfield."

She shook her head. "No way!"

"Yes way. He was masquerading as Sol Diaz, working at Pleasant View Nursing Home."

Louder, Claire repeated, "No way!" It was too incredible. "Sol Diaz? The man who bought my stolen mower from Tyler?"

"The disguised man who claimed he bought your mower from someone." He leaned forward. "Did you ever see this guy? White beard, dark complexion, short, white hair?"

"Once or twice from a distance at the nursing home." She picked up her pacing again. "I'm not believing this. You're saying that this guy was really Tyler Crutchfield?" She smacked her fist in her hand. "Don't you see it? Crutchfield promised he'd retaliate. So he killed my father and set it up to look like I did it."

"So how do you explain his body in your Volkswagen?"

She was at a loss for words. She held up her hands, palms up. "You tell me."

"The medical examiner has found more evidence, Claire. It looks like he was in a fight. It looks like he'd raped again."

"He deserved to die."

"I don't doubt that, Claire. So why don't you tell me what happened?"

"I don't know."

"Evidence on his body points to you. Your hair was mixed with his beneath his underwear." He paused. "Now will you tell me what happened?"

Claire felt her cheeks flush. "I am telling you the truth. You need to believe me. I can't explain what you are telling me. The lab's wrong." She threw up her hands. "I don't know."

"I don't have time for games," he said, pocketing his silver pen. "Was John involved? Was this a team effort? Did he come to your rescue and Crutchfield ended up dead?"

"Why do you think of John?"

"Who else could have recognized Crutchfield? I'm just trying to figure this out. Maybe he recognized Tyler at the nursing home. Maybe you baited him so John could finish him off."

"This is insane. You were hired to help me."

Her attorney folded his hands on the desk. "Maybe you don't understand what I'm supposed to do for you. I need to take the evidence the prosecution pulls up and explain it in a way that makes the jury feel sympathy toward you."

"I don't think you understand. I don't need sympathy. I'm innocent. And the last time I checked, I am here because they think I killed my father, not because I'm accused of killing Tyler Crutchfield."

He sighed. "Not yet."

"What do you mean?"

"Sit down, Claire. Calm down."

She sat with a thud onto the chair.

He sat back and let an uncomfortable silence hang between them. When he spoke again, she heard the same compassion he used before, but this time it sounded condescending. "You're not on trial for Tyler Crutchfield's murder. But Garland Strickler is looking at this very closely. He is hinting that he'll look the other way on the Crutchfield case if you confess—"

"Confess what? That I killed my father? That's crazy."

"I know all about the abuse, Claire. This wasn't straightforward euthanasia, was it? You wanted him to die because you thought he deserved to be dead after all he did."

"I am not believing this! You are supposed to be defending me, not accusing me!"

"I can't get you off unless you tell me the truth," he said. "Give me something to work with and we'll slant it to make it look reasonable."

She slapped her hand against the window separating them. "There is nothing to slant! I'm innocent. Period." Claire popped to her feet again and glared at the man hired to represent her.

"Look, Claire, how about if I get someone in here for a psychiatric evaluation? It would be helpful to document your troubled state of mind."

"My mind is only troubled by you."

"I've worked with Joanne Phillips for a long time on cases like yours. Can I have her evaluate— "

"Cases like mine?"

"Abuse cases. Girls who retaliated against their abusers."

Claire shook her head. "No. We're not going there. I'm innocent. I don't need a psych evaluation, especially by Joanne Phillips!" Claire pointed at him. "She was the one who started all this talk of abuse in the first place!"

"I take it you know her."

"I've already been through her counseling," she said. "Go ahead, get her opinion. She'll tell you I'm not crazy."

"Claire, listen to me. I'm not saying— "

She leaned forward over the table and locked eyes on his face. "No! You are the one who needs to listen to me! I keep telling you the truth, but you don't seem to get it."

He leaned away from her and cleared his throat, "Dr. McCall— "

"It's Dr. Cerelli!" she screamed. "Mr. Fauls," she said, imitating his sudden formalness, "you're fired."

"Be reasonable, I'm trying to help you."

She glared at him without speaking and walked to the door. There, she pounded it loudly and yelled, "Guard!"

The guard replaced Claire's shackles and walked her back to her cell, unspeaking. Her mind pulsed with anger. Why wouldn't anyone believe her? Was someone framing her? Why?

She lay down on the bottom bunk. Trisha was braiding Tamika's hair into cornrows. " 'Sup, girl?"

"I need a new attorney," she groaned.

Claire curled up and stared at the wall. *Why would there be evidence that Tyler Crutchfield raped me?*

The idea made her shiver. She'd heard of women that shut away terrible deeds in their subconscious after significant trauma. *Could it be possible that I don't remember? Am I cracking up?* Instinctively, she placed her hand over her lower abdomen. *Could I be suffering some weird post-traumatic amnesia as a defense mechanism?*

The next thought sickened her more. *I'm the only link between Wally and Crutchfield. Both were men who abused me.*

Could John have killed Tyler Crutchfield?

John picked up the phone after the first ring. "Hello."

"John, Bill Fauls here. I've got some bad news. I just met with Claire to talk to her about some of the new developments."

John listened to an uncomfortably long pause. "What is it, Mr. Fauls?"

"Claire didn't respond well. She thinks I don't listen to her." He sighed. "She fired me, John. She was pretty mad."

"Just like that?"

"I provoked her. I wanted to see if she would break down and tell me something, see if she was hiding anything from me."

"I can imagine that went over well."

"I've been wondering if I've just completely misjudged her. I asked her if she'd be willing to have a psychiatric evaluation."

John groaned and whispered, "Great." He paused while his eyes fixed on a picture of Claire and Clay on their thirteenth birthday. "I just don't understand," he began slowly. "I know what I heard on the tape. I just don't understand why she would choose our wedding day to confront Wally about their past." He shook his head. "It makes no sense. And it doesn't necessarily follow that she killed Wally, does it?"

He listened as his attorney blew his breath into the phone. "I guess not, but it's pretty damning evidence. This must be hard for you, John."

"So how did she respond?"

"She pretty much told me I didn't listen and that I was fired."

"Now what? How do I get a new attorney?"

"Look, John, I was a bit harsh with her. I'd like another chance to help. Maybe you can talk to her for me. I don't know how to make things add up. I think it would be helpful if she'd submit to a psych evaluation."

"She's not going to like it."

"Just talk to her." He paused. "I need to ask you something."

John massaged the back of his neck and listened.

"Has she ever lied to you before?"

Chapter Thirty-Five

Kyle crawled from bed, his head pounding. He looked in the mirror and groaned before pulling open the medicine cabinet and chugging two Alka-Seltzers, three ibuprofen, and two extra-strength Tylenols.

"Morning, sleepyhead," Margo said, handing him a cup of steaming java.

He inhaled the aroma and muttered, "Thanks."

He sat on the side of the unmade bed and rubbed the back of his neck. "Did I just imagine it, or did you almost get run over by a train?"

She sat beside him and tussled his hair. "You're not imagining it, Kyle. You told me everything."

He looked at Margo, studying her for a moment. Her eyes were wide, her face a reflection of calm.

She kissed his cheek. "You need a shave," she teased, stroking his cheek.

"I don't get it. I told you what a jerk I was. You know how much I've screwed up my own life." He halted, then added, "And Claire's. So why are you so cheerful?"

"Because the right road begins at a point called honesty, Kyle." She laid her head on his shoulder. "I'm not going to downplay what you did. But it was a long, long time ago. Love will get us through."

He sipped his coffee. "I love you."

"You too."

"So what's the next step on this right road?"

"Talk to Claire."

"What do I say?"

"Tell her the truth."

"She will never forgive me."

"I suppose you'll just have to take that chance."

By Sunday morning, Claire was a week overdue for some meaningful face time with John. At 10:30, a guard called eight names. The girls lined up and were escorted in single file into the visiting area, a long, skinny room lined with windows. Beside each window was a black phone. In front of each window was a metal black stool bolted to the floor. There were concrete partial-wall partitions between each stool. On the other side, the families had gathered in an identical room. The inmates rushed to the phones. Claire had thirty minutes.

Claire saw her mother and John standing at one of the middle windows. The other room was crowded with children. Most windows were plastered with two adult faces and numerous kids. The room was drab beige cinderblock with a tile floor. Everyone's voice seemed to echo, and kids on the other side were fighting to talk on the phones. Claire picked up the phone and put her hand against the one-inch glass window. John lifted his hand to touch the glass across from hers.

"Hi." She squinted to see his face through the scratched surface of the window.

"How are you doing?" John asked.

There wasn't time for small talk. "Peachy," she said. "John, what is going on? You know about the body in my car?"

"Of course."

"It was Tyler Crutchfield!"

"We know, Claire."

The volume of the phone was low and everyone in the room was talking. She leaned closer to the glass in a futile attempt to hear better. She stared at John, his face sober, his eyes penetrating. Della's hand covered her mouth but did not hide the quivering of her chin. *It's too much for her to see me this way.* An uncomfortable silence hung between them as the realization began to grip her gut. *They aren't feeling sorry for me. Do they think I killed Wally and Tyler Crutchfield?* She started shaking her head slowly. "You don't know, you don't know," she repeated. "You think I'm guilty?"

"Claire, we—" John halted as his voice caught in his throat. "We—"

"Don't do this to me. I haven't been able to talk to you for days, I'm here and I don't know why, my attorney doesn't believe me, and now you—" She halted, her voice choking with a sob.

John spoke as he and Della leaned their heads together so they could both listen. "We didn't say we thought you were guilty."

She wiped her eyes with the palm of her hand. "You don't need to say it. I can see the fear in your eyes."

Della tilted the mouthpiece toward her. "Tell us what happened, honey. What did Tyler do to you? Did he catch you when you went to see Wally?"

Claire took a deep breath and looked into their eyes, one pair at a time. "I need you to listen. I knew nothing about Tyler Crutchfield until Mr. Fauls told me about him. I knew nothing of Daddy's death until I was accused of killing him."

"Mr. Fauls told us you fired him."

"I need someone who believes me."

John sighed. "Claire, maybe it wouldn't hurt if you agreed to work with him. He's trying to help. Could you at least talk to a counselor about—"

She held up her hand. "I don't need a counselor, John. I need someone to believe me. Someone to realize that someone is setting me up."

"We do believe you, Claire, don't we, John?" Della said, nodding her head.

"Claire," John started. "We want to help. Mr. Fauls isn't such a bad guy. He helped me, remember?"

"Mr. Fauls seems to have the wrong idea. He seems to think his job is to get me off for doing something wrong. I need someone to defend me because I'm innocent."

John sat on the stool, forcing Della to lean over with her ear still plastered to the phone. "Help us understand, Claire."

She shook her head. "I can't."

John reached out and touched the dingy glass window again, his face etched with tension.

"Did you know I helped deliver a baby this week?" She watched their mouths open silently. She spoke through her tears. "Oh, no? Well, that's because I've had quite a week here that I can't share with you because the phone company won't let me call yet, and the judge wouldn't let me attend Daddy's funeral, and I couldn't see you last Sunday because your name had to be on the stupid list by Friday, and when I see you now, you both have decided that I must be in here for a good reason." Her voice cracked. She sniffed and wiped her eyes on the sleeve of her orange jumpsuit. She looked up at their blank stares, feeling like a freak at a carnival.

"Claire," John said, placing his hand against the glass in front of her. "I'm so sorry."

"Me too," she said, shaking her head. She returned the phone to the cradle and cried. "Bonnie," she called to the guard. "I need to go back to the pod."

She moved away from her seat, pausing once at the door to stare into the pleading eyes of her husband. Then she walked back into the commons, where there was an hour of freedom before lunch and afternoon lockdown.

Tamika inspected her fingernails, cut short as per jailhouse rules. Trisha slouched on the opposite end of the couch with a look that dared anyone to sit between them. She frowned and looked at Claire. "The doc's back early."

Claire nodded silently. She felt like crying, definitely not the thing to do in this crowd.

Tamika looked up. "'Sup, girl? Your new husband dis you or something?"

"Nobody seems to believe me."

"Join the club."

Claire sat in a chair and stared at the floor. "My family seems to think I need a psychiatric exam." She sighed. "It's my attorney's idea."

"I thought you fired your attorney," Tamika said.

"I did. My husband wants me to give him another chance."

Trisha yawned. "My attorney had me take those psycho tests." She grinned. "The judge says I'm not mentally competent to stand trial."

"It can only help you, Doc," Tamika added. "Even if you have to go to trial, it can help the jury understand the stress you was under."

The old woman Claire only knew as a husband killer smirked and lifted her tattooed hand. "Gets you out of this place for a few hours. It took me all afternoon to take the tests."

Claire slumped in a chair. "I'm not crazy."

Tamika nodded. "Don't matter, Doc. We knows you're not crazy."

"How do you know? Everyone else seems to have their mind made up about me."

Claire searched the faces of the other inmates as they looked away to avoid her gaze. Their silence wasn't encouraging.

Maria entered and leaned against the wall with her arms crossed over her chest.

Tamika looked over. "Maria's back!"

Trisha tilted her head at the space on the couch beside her. "Sit. You just had surgery. They make you come back here so fast."

Maria nodded. "The locked ward at Brighton University is like the Hilton. They serve you meals in bed."

"But they have to cut you open to let you in, huh?"

Claire smiled as Maria slowly lowered herself onto the couch. "How's little John?"

"He's okay." She held her hand to her mouth. "They took him from me."

"Who has him?"

"Social services." She sniffed. "I never had a chance to say thank you."

Claire shrugged. "I'd do anything to get out of here for a few hours."

Tamika interrupted. "Then you should take those tests, Doc. You're not crazy. So prove it to them."

Claire tried to smile. "I'll think about it." She walked back to her cell and lay on her bed, feeling isolated and alone. *How can it be that everyone I love seems to have lost faith in me?*

A few minutes later, Maria slowly lowered herself onto the bottom bed of the adjacent bunk. There she lay in silence, her breathing heavy.

Claire looked over to see that Maria was crying. "What's wrong?"

"I miss my baby."

Claire joined her by shedding fresh tears of her own.

"So why are you crying?"

"Nothing went right with my family. I was so looking forward to talking to John, but everything went wrong."

"I hate the black phones. There's too much pressure to get everything perfect 'cause you only have a short time. No one likes to talk in front of everyone else."

"Really." Claire smiled. Maria understood. "What if everyone is right about me? What if I've just lost it and can't remember?"

"You're not crazy, Doc. And you're not a murderer."

"How can you be so sure?"

"No murderer would spend so much time saving the life of my child."

That evening, John tried to lose himself in a detective novel, but every twisted piece of evidence made him think of Claire. He had been staring at the same page for five minutes when the sound of the doorbell lifted him from his trance.

He opened the door to see Ami with a large basket in hand. "Hi, neighbor," she said, smiling.

"Ami, I—," he started to protest.

"I've brought you supper. I know you are bachin' it, and I just imagined you over here ordering pizza night after night."

"You shouldn't have."

"Well, I did. Now make yourself a gentleman and invite me in."

"Ami, this isn't a good idea."

She barged past him. "If you hadn't noticed, I'm trying to be a good neighbor here. And I'm trying to make things right between us."

John followed her into his kitchen. She started unloading her picnic basket. A plate of steaming fried chicken, mashed potatoes, gravy, cole slaw, and biscuits soon covered the round oak table.

"Can we use your eating utensils?" she asked.

"I don't think we should—"

She shook her head and interrupted. "There's nothing wrong with sharing a meal with a neighbor when there's a crisis in the family." She opened cupboards until she found plates. She set the table for two while John inhaled the aroma of fresh biscuits.

"This isn't KFC."

"I can cook, you know."

"You shouldn't stay."

"Now John Cerelli, what would your mother think if your neighbor made all this food and you refused to share? Sit," she said, pouring tea into two tall glasses.

Ami loaded a plate, set it in front of him, and quickly put a leg along with a small dab of cole slaw and potatoes on her own. She sat down next to him.

He sighed and picked up his fork. The fragrance was heaven.

"Shouldn't you ask a blessing?"

"You want me to pray?" He was incredulous.

"Of course. I know you're a Christian." She closed her eyes and waited.

John offered a simple prayer of thanks, halting only when he felt her warm hand curl into his. "Amen!" he added abruptly. He opened his hand and grabbed his fork again.

She kept her eyes closed for a few extra moments before whispering, "Amen."

John ate too fast, emptying his plate in a few minutes, hoping Ami would speed along. Instead, she chatted about her day, her search for a new job, how she liked the neighborhood, and her mother's adjustment to life without Richard.

"Your food is going to get cold," John said. "You've hardly touched it."

"You eat like you think it's going to get away."

"It has been pretty dreary meal-wise around this place." He set another piece of chicken on his plate and slathered a biscuit with butter. She acknowledged him with a tentative smile before she looked away.

He finished his chicken without talking, wishing Ami wasn't so attractive and pushy.

"I'll leave you the leftovers," she said, moving the plates to the sink. "You know, I had a friend who got her marriage annulled. I think you can get a judge to do that if you haven't consummated your commitment." She let the last words drip from her mouth like a starving man salivating for bread.

"You should go," John said, leaning back against the kitchen counter. "Thanks for the chicken."

"Anytime," she said. "I'll come back later for my dishes."

Wednesday afternoon, William Fauls plodded past his secretary's desk and plucked the messages from her hand as he passed. She smiled. "You were right. Claire Cerelli still wants to retain you, and she has agreed to a psychological evaluation."

He chuckled. "Things must be getting boring down in the female pod."

He closed his door and hung his gray suitcoat on the back of his desk chair.

He looked at the first message from Claire Cerelli and dialed Joanne Phillips. She answered on the first ring.

"Joanne, it's Bill Fauls. I need a favor."

"I'm listening."

"I'm representing Claire McCall Cerelli. I think you're familiar with her."

"I read the paper."

"Well, I'm looking ahead, really. I can't make sense of the evidence in the case and what my client is telling me. Can I speak in confidence?"

"Of course."

"Everything is pointing to the fact that Claire killed her father out of revenge for some childhood sexual abuse. In addition, the police have opened another investigation involving Claire, involving a body found in her car."

"I saw that in the paper. What is going on?"

"It looks like the man is Tyler Crutchfield, the serial rapist who attacked Claire about seven months ago. The evidence looks like he raped Claire, then died of a stab wound to the back. It looks like a defensive wound. Either she is the best liar in the business, or crazy, or telling the truth and all the evidence is a lie."

"What's this have to do with me?"

"I need some idea about her mental status. I understand you worked with her before. What's your read of her? Can you do some additional interviews or tests as a professional opinion of her competency to stand trial?"

"Bill, first of all, you know all about therapist-patient privilege. I can't divulge information to you without a signed release of information form."

"Come on, Joanne, I'm just asking for your opinion, not a binding—"

"There's another issue here, Bill. I don't have any information for you. She's never been a client of mine."

"What? She told me she saw you when she was working through some post-sexual-assault trauma issues." He paused, tapping his fingers on his desk. "In fact, she seemed a little put off the last time I talked to her, saying that you were the one that brought up the abuse issues in the first place."

"I think you're confused. Or she is. I've never talked to this woman. Or maybe you have your answer already."

"What do you mean?"

"She could be lying to you."

"What would motivate her to do that?"

"You say the evidence points to her being raped?"

"According to the medical examiner."

"Perhaps she's having some post-traumatic amnesia or blocking everything out by some defense mechanism. Perhaps she doesn't know she's lying."

"Why would she claim to have been your patient?"

"Lots of reasons. Maybe she doesn't want to be evaluated. Maybe she's a pathological liar. Maybe she's confused and had therapy from someone else. I really don't know."

"Nothing about this case makes sense."

"Is she paranoid? Does she think everyone's out to get her?"

Bill thought back about Claire making a secret tape of her fiancé at work. "What's that got to do with anything?"

"I'm just brainstorming. From what I read in the papers, her father had end-stage Huntington's disease. I thought folks were speculating that his death was euthanasia."

"That was the media guess. But I'm thinking that was all just a cover-up. Evidence points to something a bit more troublesome, that she may have killed her father out of revenge."

"And hoped everyone would accept his death as natural, or if they suspected anything foul, at worst, they'd interpret his death as an act of love."

"Something like that. But I can't get a good read of this girl. I need to know how I'm going to go at this. Maybe she wasn't competent because of a recent trauma from a rape."

"Why don't you believe her? Everything I've heard about Claire McCall is that she is one of the smartest women to come out of Stoney Creek."

"I know that. But nothing adds up. Even her family is starting to question her."

"So what do you want from me?"

"Help me. Go see her. See if you can get a read on her."

"Get me clearance. I'll talk to her."

Two days later, Claire waited in a too-familiar conference room for Joanne Phillips. She peered through the window into the next room, a mirror-image space where her counselor would be allowed to sit during their interaction. A few minutes later, she heard the clunk of the electronic lock and looked up to see a dumpy, middle-aged woman unafraid to show the world her natural gray hair. She wore a navy suit and carried a leather satchel.

The woman smiled and sat. "You must be Claire. It's awkward not to be able to shake your hand." She laid her hand against the glass. "There," she said, "here's my hand."

Claire reached up and touched the glass where it was shadowed by the woman's hand. "Hi."

"Mr. Fauls wanted us to talk. Is that okay?"

"Sure, but I'm a bit confused," Claire said, leaning forward toward the window. "Who are you?"

"Oh," she said, with a little laugh, "I'm Joanne Phillips."

Claire shook her head. "Joanne Phillips?" She squinted her face into a question. "The social-worker counselor?"

The lady smiled. "Of course."

"The Brighton counselor who specializes in helping women who have had sexual assaults?"

The woman folded her hands. "Yes."

"The same woman I've referred patients to from my practice in Stoney Creek."

"Why is this so hard to believe?"

"Because you are not the Joanne Phillips I know. I mean, I met with you, uh, with someone who identified herself as you, for counseling after I was assaulted."

Joanne opened her satchel. "How did you contact this counselor?"

"You sent me a flyer advertising your services. I called the number on a business card."

Joanne shook her head. "I'm too busy to advertise for business. I can barely keep my head above water as it is."

"But then who—"

"What did this woman look like?"

Claire sat back. "Young, nice slender figure, dark hair, very pretty." She paused. "I thought she looked a little young for her position, but—"

"But what?"

"She seemed to know what she was doing. She helped me forgive my father."

"You say she sent you a card? Do you still have it?"

Claire shrugged. "Maybe at my desk at work."

"This is why you told Bill Fauls that you'd worked with me."

"I thought I had." Claire rested her finger on her temple. "Is it possible that there is another counselor with the same name?"

They stared at each other from across the window and said together, "Naah."

Joanne stood.

"Aren't you going to talk to me?"

"Not now. There are a few other things I need to figure out first. If I stop by your office, could I get that card?"

"Probably. Just talk to Lucy, my nurse. Tell her you talked to me. She'll help you."

"Thanks." Joanne turned to leave.

"What are you going to tell Mr. Fauls?"

She shrugged. "That someone's been messing with your life. And mine." She opened the door. Obviously this news had overtaken any obligation she felt to interview Claire.

Claire watched the woman disappear from the next room. She was incredulous. If she hadn't met with Joanne Phillips, who had she talked to?

Chapter Thirty-Six

That afternoon Claire waited through six other half-hour phone calls until her turn on the commons phone. Per jailhouse protocol, she could use the phone to make selected calls for up to one hour per week. Each number was to a relative or her lawyer, and every call was collect at five dollars a minute.

She needed more information. Too many things were amiss. She'd been frustrated and short with John. But she knew one thing. If she was going to get through this, she needed to do it with her husband on her side. She dialed his number and waited. She listened to the operator's voice. "Please state your name at the sound of the tone."

At the tone, she stated, "Claire."

Again she listened as the other end of the line opened. The operator's voice was mechanical. "Collect call from Claire, will you accept the charges?"

"No." The voice was female. The line went dead.

"Wait!" Claire yelled into the phone. "Wait!" she said softer, setting the phone back in the cradle.

A girl with purple bangs pushed her way forward and lifted the phone from the wall. "My turn, Doc."

John felt his frustration rise as he watched Ami set down his phone. "I could have gotten that."

She smiled. "Your hands were full. Besides, you were the one who offered to carry my dishes."

He huffed. "So who was it? I'm expecting Claire to call."

"Chill, John, it was a wrong number. Just someone asking if they had the Stevens residence."

He carried the picnic basket of Ami's dishes to the front door and paused to wait for her as she lingered, looking at the pictures over Claire's desk.

"Would you like to ride over to Carlisle to see a movie?" she asked.

He shook his head. "Ami, I really don't think we should be hanging out."

"We could just watch a video at my place."

"I need to be here."

"Here is fine. Would you like me to choose something, or shall I surprise you?"

He took a deep breath. "I don't think you're hearing me. I don't think we should be doing things together. That means here too."

"John, we're friends. What's the harm in friends spending time together?"

Before he could protest, she was in his face, leaning forward over the basket in his arms, with her flattering anatomy grazing his arm. "You don't need to be afraid of me, John."

His throat was dry as he attempted to find a response.

Her eyes locked on his. John cleared his throat. "I–I'm not afraid of you, but we aren't friends. Friends don't accuse each other to the police. Friends don't manipulate circumstances to destroy relationships."

"John," she said softly, "I thought I'd explained all that. Can't we put the past behind us and go forward?"

He turned away from her, but she gripped his arm with her hand and continued, "Some bad things have been happening to me. I really could use a friend."

"Bad things?" When she stayed quiet, he added, "You lost your job. Things will turn around." He shuffled his feet. "You came for your dishes. Let's go."

Ami didn't move. "I wasn't talking about losing my job." She looked away. "I was raped."

He wasn't sure if this was a weird ploy to get his attention or if she was serious. "Ami, I'm probably not the one to talk to about this."

"Who else?"

He shrugged. "A counselor. Your mother?"

"You obviously haven't met my mother." She turned away from him. "She's crazy, John. I don't think she's handling her husband's death very well."

"Look, I realize you have had your share of pain, and I think you should talk about it to someone, maybe a pastor or—"

"My mother doesn't want me talking to anyone."

John stood at the doorway in indecision. He didn't want to appear rude, but he felt uncomfortable being Ami's new confidant. He cleared his throat. "You were raped? Did you tell the police?"

She shook her head. "They ask too many questions. They drag you back through your pain. I'm not going there."

"Someone you knew?"

"No."

He sighed. "When did this happen?"

She bit her lower lip. "Last weekend."

"But all this time you've acted like everything was great. You brought me food. You—"

"I couldn't just come over and tell you this straightaway," she said, wiping her cheeks with the back of her hand. "You had just married. We hadn't left on good terms. I needed a chance to make friends with you again."

"You're a good actress."

She sniffed. "Things aren't always what they seem on the surface."

Obviously, he thought. "You need to tell the police. What if he attacks someone else?"

"I can't, John. It's too late. I know how these things work. There won't be any evidence left behind."

"Ami, you can't just ignore—"

"I've been through this before!" she screamed. "I can't do it again," she sobbed. "My father." She halted. "When I was twelve."

John shook his head. He set the picnic basket on the floor and studied Ami for a moment. She had dissolved into tears on his couch. He tried to keep his voice low and gentle. "Did you get a good look at the guy? Did he have short white hair and a white beard?"

She lifted her head from her hands and stared at John. "How did you know?"

"The same man may have raped Claire." He began to pace. "Have you been reading the paper?"

Her jaw slackened, leaving her mouth in a small "o." She nodded. "Sure."

"It was a man named Crutchfield. He was an escaped convict, serving time for rape. He had dyed his hair white and grown a white beard."

"No," she said, shaking her head and standing up. "The paper said he was a young man."

"They didn't tell the whole story. He was living under an alias, posing as an older man working in lawn maintenance at Pleasant View."

Ami's eyes were wide, her face etched with fear. "How did the man die? The paper said 'suspected foul play,' but they didn't say how he died."

"He had a knife in his back."

Her hand went to her mouth. She stumbled to the door. "No," she mumbled. "No."

With that, she fled from the house, leaving John staring at the picnic basket on the floor.

Ami fled across the neighbor's yard and up the steps to her rented house.

Nancy Childress was sitting at the kitchen table waiting. "I sent you to get the dishes."

Ami looked at her empty hands.

"Idiot!"

Ami stared at her mother. "Tell me what you did with the body!"

Nancy picked up the newspaper and feigned nonchalance. "I don't want you hanging out with the neighbor. He's a married man, you know."

"Answer my question!"

Her mother sipped black tea from a mug emblazoned with a John Deere emblem. "You covered for me. I owed you a favor. I covered for you."

On Sunday morning, Claire was let into the visiting room to face her family for the second time since her incarceration. She sat on the stool and looked through the dingy glass window into a mirror-image room. But instead of John, whom she expected, she looked into the worried expression of her brother-in-law, Kyle. She picked up the black phone. "Morning, Kyle. I wasn't expecting you."

"I know. I asked John if I could come in first, so I would have a chance to talk to you alone."

Her curiosity was pricked. She couldn't remember the last time Kyle had shown serious interest in her affairs. "Okay," she said. "What's up?"

"I came to make a confession." He shifted on his stool. "Wally didn't abuse you."

She leaned forward, not understanding.

"It was me." He halted, his face reflecting the torment he felt.

"Kyle, what do you mean? I don't—"

"Let me explain," he interrupted. "You remember the night I brought you home? You'd been drinking."

Claire felt a knot tighten in her stomach, the old guilt of her rebellion fighting for attention. "Yes," she said quietly.

Kyle looked right and left at the other family members talking to the inmates. He lowered his voice and continued. "Grant Williams was getting too friendly in the back of a pickup truck. Do you remember that?"

"A little."

"He tore off your clothes. He was intent on getting what he wanted when I told him to back off."

Vague memories played at the edge of her mind. "You took me home."

"I helped you with your clothes. You were so drunk. I put you to bed. You behaved, uh, friendly, toward me, but that's no excuse. You weren't able to say no." He looked down, no longer meeting her gaze. "I had fought with Margo. I was mad at her. I started touching you. You didn't resist me." He closed his eyes tightly and shook his head. "It never went further than that. I heard Wally getting up. I ran out of your room, so ashamed. Wally asked me what I was doing in his daughter's bedroom. I told him to back off, that I had saved you from some bad men and I was just putting you to bed." He looked up. "I'm so sorry, Claire."

Claire gasped and shook her head, trying to comprehend his words. "Why didn't you tell me?"

"When I realized you didn't remember it, I never brought it up. I never dreamed you would some day think it was Wally."

She took a deep breath as relief started washing over her soul. Wally hadn't sexually abused her. She paused, trying to absorb this new thought. "Thanks, Kyle."

"Thanks?"

She nodded. "It's a relief, really."

"You forgive me?"

"It was a long time ago. Let's let it go."

"But I—I never imagined it would turn out like this with Wally gone and you here."

"I'm not following you."

"This is all my fault. If I would have told the truth, you would have never thought Wally abused you, and you would have never ..." His voice trailed off.

"Never what?" She glanced over her shoulder at the guard and whispered, "You think I killed my father because I thought he abused me?" She was aghast. "That's ridiculous, Kyle! Why does everyone seem to think I killed my father?"

His expression changed from distress to the concern you show when someone is obviously too stupid to know the error of their ways. "They've got you on tape, Claire."

"The surveillance camera at the home, right? It wasn't me."

"I'm not talking about the video camera. Wally called 911 right before he died. They have your voice accusing him of abusing you."

She shook her head. "That's crazy! I wasn't there. It wasn't me."

"Claire, I heard it. Your attorney played it for the family. We all thought it was you."

"Look, Kyle, there has to be another explanation for all of this." She stared at him. "I'm upset that you touched me when I was drunk." She paused for effect. "But what upsets me more is that you all would dare to believe that I would kill my father."

He nodded slowly. "I shouldn't take up more of your time. John is waiting to see you."

She watched as Kyle hung up the black phone and walked out of the room. A moment later, John came in and sat on the stool. He was carrying a white envelope.

"Hi," he said.

"Hi." She so wanted to avoid a repeat of last week's frustration, but she felt the tension of little time and so much she wanted to know. She tried to keep her voice controlled. "Kyle told me about the 911 tape. Why didn't you tell me?"

"Claire, you were upset. We didn't have a chance to talk like we should." He paused. "I hoped you would call."

"I tried," she said. "A woman answered and refused my phone call."

"What? No." He shook his head and looked up meekly. "It must have been Ami."

Claire felt hot. "Ami! What was she doing there?"

He sighed. "She brought me some food. She just came by to pick up her dishes."

"She's crazy! I don't like her, John. Keep away from her. It's like she's still trying to insinuate herself into your life." She paused, not wanting to follow a rabbit trail. "John, I need to know you believe me. Can you imagine how horrible this is for me? I'm trapped in this place, and my family doesn't even seem to believe me."

"Help me understand," he said, his eyes pleading.

"I can't explain what I don't understand myself. I only know that they have evidence that they think implicates me. There must be another explanation for the tape, John. It wasn't me!"

"I believe you."

"I didn't know anything about my father's death until you did. And I didn't know anything about Tyler Crutchfield and—"

"Slow down, Claire. I said, I believe you."

"How am I going to convince them to let me out?"

"I don't know," he said. "I'll keep trying to find out what I can." He paused. "I'm praying, Claire. We'll get you out."

She sighed. "I want to believe that."

"Here," he said, opening the envelope. "I printed a few of the digital pictures of our wedding. I wanted to cheer you up." He held a picture of Claire up to the glass.

She smiled. One by one, he held up pictures of the family, the reception, and each aspect of the celebration. "Wait!" she said, looking at a picture of a group at the reception. "Go back to that last one."

John obeyed. "Do you like that one? I don't like my expression."

"I'm not looking at you. See that girl in the background? The one in the short black skirt?"

He nodded.

"That woman was posing as Joanne Phillips, a counselor from Brighton University."

"I don't get it."

"My attorney had Joanne Phillips come by the jail this week to interview me, to start some psychological tests. But it wasn't the same Joanne Phillips that I saw for my sessions. Someone has been posing as Joanne Phillips, and it's that girl," Claire said, pointing and tapping on the window.

John turned the picture around so he could see.

He touched his finger against the photograph. "Her?"

"Yes. Take her picture to the police. Find out who she is. Maybe they can identify her."

"What does that have to do with you being here?"

"I don't know. Maybe nothing. But that girl posed as a professional counselor and sought me out as a patient."

"I don't have to take her picture to the police for identification." He seemed to hesitate. "That's Ami Grandle."

Chapter Thirty-Seven

John Cerelli put down the pictures and gazed across the window at Claire. "This woman posed as Joanne Phillips? Why didn't you recognize her from the surveillance video?"

"It never showed her face, John. And your voices were too distorted for me to identify her." She turned on him. "What on earth was she doing at our wedding?"

John shook his head. "She must have snuck in, hung around the back. I did glimpse her once, but there was no way I was going to make a scene about it and ruin the reception."

Claire sat quietly for a minute. Her eyes seemed to see beyond him or through him, unfocused, a look he had seen before when she contemplated something serious. Then, slowly, her head began to nod and her eyes brightened. "John, Ami killed my father."

He straightened. "What?"

"Don't you see it, John? She's been stalking you, wanting to be in your life. She set herself up to be my counselor just to get closer to you, to find out about you." Claire cupped her hand over the phone mouthpiece. "John, she was always interested in you, encouraging me to stay away from physical contact with you." She shook her head. "All in the name of helping me work through abuse issues. And all she wanted was to drive a wedge between us."

"And how does that mean she killed Wally?"

"She recorded me making a mock confrontation with my dad over the abuse issues. She must have used the recording to make it look like I killed my father."

John's confused look prompted her to continue. "John, Kyle told me about a 911 tape where you heard me accusing my father."

"Sure, but— "

"Listen to me. Ami urged me to confront my father about the supposed abuse, and she taped the whole thing."

"So you think she killed Wally and called 911 and played your taped confession?"

She nodded her head emphatically. "Exactly. What better way to frame me?"

Claire's excitement was contagious. "I'll call Joel Stevens." He halted as another piece of the puzzle shifted into place. "Ami claims to have been raped by a man of Sol Diaz's description. When I told her that he had died of a knife wound to the back and that he was found in your car, she just freaked. She ran off like what I said scared her to death."

"Maybe he attacked her. Maybe she was the one who killed him. Then she dumped the body in my car to frame me."

"So how do you explain your hair being on his body?"

She shrugged. "Maybe it was in my car."

"Inside his shorts?"

"I don't know. Maybe Ami planted it there somehow." Claire looked at the clock. "We don't have much time."

"I need to talk to Ami."

"Talk to the police, John. She might be dangerous if you confront her. Remember what she did to you before."

"I'll be careful." He touched the glass with his hand. She responded by lifting her hand and placing it against the glass opposite his. "I love you," he whispered into the phone.

Claire nodded and wiped away a tear. "I love you."

Joel Stevens opened the formal report from the medical examiner on the autopsy of Tyler Crutchfield. He read the conclusions and looked at Randy Jensen. "I think old Garland might be jumpin' the gun on linking Claire Cerelli to the Crutchfield murder."

Randy set down his coffee cup. "What's up?"

"The ME report says two types of hair were found in Crutchfield's shorts."

"Two?"

Joel slapped the report with his hand and read from the conclusion, "Contents of pubic combing: short curly black hair with follicles inconsistent with the victim, consistent with pubic hair of possible sexual contact. Long strands of blonde hair, typical of scalp covering with follicles containing DNA consistent with individual with known genetic makeup.

See appendix one. Appendix one: DNA typing from Brighton University genetics laboratory shows hair consistent with Claire McCall."

"So?"

"So maybe this Claire Cerelli wasn't his last victim. Maybe old Garland is so anxious to secure his political career that he's getting sloppy."

Randy stood up and looked over Joel's shoulder. "The ME didn't tell us about the two types of hair when I first called."

"Maybe he didn't know that yet." He looked at the bottom of the page. "This document was just typed on Friday."

"This information still links Claire to Crutchfield."

"But it doesn't necessarily mean she was raped." He pointed at the conclusions again. "It says it was her scalp hair."

Evie appeared in the doorway. "Joel, a John Cerelli is on line two."

He nodded. "I'll take it here." He punched a button on the phone and lifted the receiver. "Detective Stevens."

"Mr. Stevens, thanks for taking my call. I have some information that I thought I should pass on. It's about the Wally McCall death investigation."

Joel sat at his desk and picked up a pen. "Go ahead."

"A woman who worked with me, Ami Grandle, made a tape of Claire McCall saying the things you heard on the 911 tape."

"She taped her? When?"

"She posed as a sexual assault counselor. She came to see Claire at her office to help her deal with issues after Crutchfield attacked her."

"What are you suggesting?"

"Only that this could explain what you heard on the 911 call. Ami must have called 911 and played what she recorded."

The detective sighed. "Interesting theory, Mr. Cerelli."

"You'd have to know this girl to understand. You can check with your colleagues in the Brighton City police. They know all about her. She was stalking me."

"Stalking you." Joel scratched his head. "And what exactly are you suggesting? Even if all of this were true, what would her motive be to murder Wally McCall?"

"To frame Claire. To get her out of the picture. Ami is very jealous."

"Mr. Cerelli, I know you want to exonerate your wife, but all of this is sounding a bit like a red herring, if you know what I mean."

John sighed. "Just check her out. At least see if she has a good alibi."

"Okay, Mr. Cerelli, I'll take it into consideration." He hung up the phone and looked at Randy. "Don't you hate it when family members try to tell you how to do your investigations?"

John looked at the phone and shook his head, feeling very much like the police cared little about the information he'd given. He walked to the kitchen, where he ate two pieces of cold delivery pizza and formulated a plan. If the police weren't interested, he'd just have to confront Ami himself.

He crumpled a pizza box and shoved it in the garbage can on his way out. A minute later, he was standing on Ami's small porch and knocking on the painted door. As he knocked, the door pushed open, unlatched. He rang the doorbell and called, "Ami?"

He turned around to see her car at the curb. *She should be here.*

"Ami?"

He skipped off the porch and walked around the house, looking for lights inside the house to see if she was home. The kitchen light was on. He tapped on the back door. "Ami?"

He waited a moment, then returned to the front porch. He rang the doorbell one more time before pushing the front door open. He stepped into the front room. A large recliner faced away from him, and from the doorway, he could see the feet of a person sitting there. "Ami?" Immediately, he sensed alarm. He walked to her side and saw her there, her complexion ashen and her chest still. She was fully clothed, wearing a wedding gown. He lowered his ear to her face. Her eyes were open and unblinking. He touched her skin and recoiled at the cool temperature. It was then that he saw a needle and syringe in her arm, puncturing the skin right at the inside of the elbow. He instinctively backed away.

Ami Grandle was dead, her body assuming room temperature.

I need to call the police, he thought.

He heard a creak of the floor behind him. As he turned to look, he felt a sharp pain on the back of his head and everything went black.

Chapter Thirty-Eight

John awoke and strained to open his heavy eyelids. A ceiling fan came in and out of focus. He sensed a dullness in his scalp and a mild euphoria. He closed his eyes again and drifted as a buzzing sensation circuited through his forehead. Waves of slumber lipped at the shore of consciousness. He was aware of the hard floor beneath him and mild pain in the back of his head. But he didn't care. Warmth seemed to flood his head, radiating into his limbs. He tried again to open his eyes and remember. *Where am I?*

"You're a strong one," a female voice said. "And from the looks of you, I can see why my daughter was so infatuated."

He tried to respond but managed only to open his mouth. His lips were uncooperative sponges, feeling strangely floppy and unwilling to curl around the words his mind imagined. After a moment, he realized he could make a smacking sound by opening and shutting his mouth. He tried to focus on the direction of the voice, but got distracted again by the pretty ceiling fan. Around and around it went, a butterfly with helicopter wings.

Sleep called to him, screamed to him, coaxing him to surrender. But somewhere at the rim of his euphoric state, an alarm sounded. He tried to force his eyes open again, but his eyelids felt fat and couch-potato lazy, so he squeezed his eyelids shut, as if the act would shrink them back to normal size. He wanted to raise his hand to his face, but his limbs were in full rebellion, unable or unwilling to do what his brain requested.

"I'm going to have to give you even more." It was the female voice again, soft, alluring, like Ami's, but older.

He looked around. *I'm in a kitchen. What happened?* John blew his breath through his boat-lips, flapping them and thinking that this was very funny, but very sad. His lips were bird wings, flapping beyond his control. After a minute more, he tried again, willing himself to focus on his surroundings. Things in his environment began to sharpen. The floor was hard, his head pounded, and the helicopter above him was a ceiling fan. He formulated the words and forced them from his mouth, willing them forward, but they seemed to lodge first on his tongue and only dribble from his lips. "Whhhooo aaarree yyyyhhoouuu?"

A face appeared in front of him. Gray-streaked black hair fell forward and tickled his face. "I'm Nancy, Ami's mom."

Slowly, a memory puzzle began to fit together. *I saw Ami in a wedding dress. She's dead.* His alarm at the recollection drove him further from the clutches of slumber. "What did you do to Ami?"

The woman sat next to him on the floor in an Indian-style position. "Ami was a very troubled girl. Very unstable. She committed suicide."

"I don't believe you."

He rolled his head to the side to study her. For an older woman, she was lean and even muscular—strong enough to give him serious trouble, even if he wasn't in his current state. He wanted to lift his arms, but they were still uncooperative.

She brushed away something at the corner of her eye and stared beyond him. "It doesn't matter if you know. You will die soon, like Ami." She nodded her head. "A suicide pact. Or a murder suicide. A troubled young woman and her married lover found together in the clutches of their sin."

She's going to kill me! John tried to wiggle a finger. His right index finger cooperated, but his hand remained glued to the floor. He needed to keep her talking until he regained strength enough to flee or fight. "Why?"

"She was getting so attached to you, John. She was going to tell you everything. She has always been weak, you know."

"You killed your daughter? You're a sick woman."

Nancy's face reddened. "You have no idea. My daughter was suffering. I didn't want her to suffer so." She took a deep breath that was accentuated by a sudden gasp, as if she couldn't hold back a sob. "She hasn't been stable since her father died."

"Her father is in prison. She told me."

She chuckled without happy emotion. "That's what we always say. It is so much easier than the truth."

"Tell me. I want to know before I die."

Nancy cursed him and ignored his request. "You think I'm a beast."

John tried to lift his head. He needed to make her talk, to keep her distracted. "You're going to get caught. I've called the police."

"You're lying."

He felt so tired. He closed his eyes for a long blink. "Tell me about Ami's father. Maybe I can understand." He paused. "Maybe I won't think you're a beast."

"Why should I care what you think? You're going to die."

John struggled to talk through clumsy lips. "But you do care."

The woman looked away, either sad from a memory or frustrated by John's persistence, he couldn't tell. After a sigh, she spoke again. "Ami's father was a beast. I told the police how he treated her. They would arrest him, put him away for a while, but he would always get out and sooner or later, he'd be back, breaking every restraining order the judge could issue." She smiled with thin lips that curved without joy. "So I did what any good mother should do to protect her daughter. I made sure he wouldn't bother us again."

"What did you do?"

She stared at him with hollow eyes and stayed quiet.

"Tell me," he said, attempting to reach for her hand.

"I don't need to tell you anything."

"I'll be dead soon. You've been keeping a secret for so long."

He stared into her face. She was softening.

"Ami loved you. You protected her, didn't you?"

Nancy looked back at him, her face twisted in anger. "Of course!" She put her hand to her mouth and began to whimper. "Ami was crying out. It was late in the night. I felt the bed next to me and knew the monster was up. I crept to my daughter's bedroom. I saw him there with Ami. I heard the squeak of the bed and my daughter's cries." She halted and steadied her voice. "I stabbed him with his favorite Buck knife." She looked at John, her eyes brimming with tears. "I've never told that to anyone."

John twitched his wrist and watched as she fingered a vial of a clear medicine and pulled it into a large syringe. *I have to keep her talking.* His arms were lead. He wanted to close his eyes again, to surrender to whatever she'd given him. "How horrible that must have been for you." He paused, straining to focus. "What happened next?"

"Ami burned down the house." She shrugged. "As far as the police knew, her father died in the fire. They found his body at the bottom of the steps." She pressed her hand to her mouth and cursed the man who'd caused her so much pain.

"Did you kill Tyler Crutchfield?"

"Me? No."

"Who then?"

"You must know by now. Your wife killed him."

"He attacked Ami, didn't he?" He strained to keep Nancy in focus. "Ami told me."

"She tells you too much. That's why she had to die." Nancy pulled her knees up so she could hug herself in a little ball as she continued. "I didn't kill him. But he deserved to die."

"If not you, then—"

"Ami. She's slept with that Buck knife under her pillow ever since—" Her voice cracked before she continued in a whisper, "I killed her father." She looked back at John. "I guess Mr. Crutchfield finally attacked someone strong enough to fight back."

"So why hide it? It was self-defense."

She shook her head. "I didn't want the police asking questions. I couldn't have that." She chuckled, but it came out sounding sad. "He thought he had found Claire. Ami was modeling her wedding dress. He was after Claire, but my daughter got what Claire deserved."

"What do you mean?"

"He must have followed me from the nursing home. I was wearing Ami's dress so that I'd look like Claire." She shrugged. "I guess I fooled him."

"You wore the dress?"

"Ami bought the same dress, dreaming of you."

"You wore the dress to the nursing home? You led Tyler here. This is your fault."

She paused, and her voice turned bitter. "You don't know how you've hurt Ami. You and that doctor-wife of yours."

"Hurt her? How?"

"You led her on, broke her heart." She held up a syringe of clear fluid.

"I did no such thing. Ami was delusional."

"You're not exactly in a position to argue."

"You were protecting her. You knew the police would find out about the dress. She killed Wally McCall and you didn't want the police finding out."

"No," she said, "my daughter was innocent."

"I know all about the tape she made of Claire, how she used it to frame her. I'm not the only one who knows."

"You don't scare me." She shrugged. "My daughter made the tape, yes, but I was the one to use it. I never meant to frame my own daughter. I only wanted Claire out of the way."

John pulled his shoulders up and wiggled his foot. He was waking up. It would be time to make his move soon, but he wasn't strong enough to run away yet. He tried to concentrate. "It was you? But why?"

"Claire McCall has been nothing but pain to my family. I can't forgive her for the way she treated my Richard. She'd never give me enough morphine for him."

"Or was it for you?" He nodded. "You were running from your own pain."

"You are a perceptive one," she said, covering a row of needle tracks on her arm with her opposite hand. She locked eyes with John. "Ami had quite a catch in you. But that doctor stole you away. She broke Ami's heart."

"So you murdered Wally to even the score?"

Nancy seethed with anger. "I only wanted to get Claire out of the way." She raised her eyebrows. "I think she knew I needed the morphine. I was afraid she was going to report me. But Wally needed to die. Just like my Richard. Pain like that wasn't meant to be prolonged."

She lifted the needle, aiming for John's arm.

"No," he said. "I won't tell. I know where Claire keeps the morphine. I can get you all you want."

"You wouldn't help me."

"Sure I would. To make it up for all the trouble you've had."

A knock at the door caused Nancy to jerk her head upright. "Ami Grandle? Open the door." More knocking. "Ami, this is Deputy Stevens with the sheriff's department. Open the door, please."

"Bad timing," Nancy whispered. "Now you know too much." She jammed the syringe into John's arm right above his elbow and emptied it into a vein. "Don't worry. This time it's four times lethal dose."

His head began to swim. The last thing he saw before he stopped breathing was Nancy slipping out the back kitchen door.

Chapter Thirty-Nine

Joel Stevens pushed open the unlatched door and nodded at Randy Jensen. He put his head in the door. "Miss Grandle?"

He looked into the front room. He saw a woman in a recliner wearing a wedding dress. "Randy!"

Randy ran by him into the kitchen. "There's another body here! It's John Cerelli."

"This woman's cold dead," Joel said.

"He's got a pulse!" Randy extended John's neck to open his airway. "He's not breathing."

Joel radioed for a paramedic unit while Randy started artificial respirations using a pocket mask.

Joel looked at the syringe sticking out of the woman's arm. "Looks like an overdose here." He joined Randy in the kitchen and monitored John's pulse while Randy kept up the ventilations.

Four minutes later, a paramedic crew arrived. Sarah Heatwole, Michael Chin, and Tim Snyder were well known to Joel from their work together with people in crisis. Tim led the trio and set down a large resuscitation bag on the floor. "What have you got?"

"Two down. She's long dead. This one still had a pulse, but no respirations. I think it's a narcotics OD."

Tim looked at John's pupils. "Pinpoint. Probably narcotics." He looked at Sarah. "Start an IV. I'll bag him. Mike, draw up an ampule of Narcan." He pinched a mask over John's face and began to force oxygen into his lungs with an AMBU bag.

Sarah slid a sixteen-gauge intravenous cannula into John's arm. "I'm in. Hand me the Narcan." She injected the narcotic antagonist.

Within a minute of injection, John opened his eyes and took a breath. Tim lifted the mask from John's face. "He's coming around."

Joel looked up as the front door opened again. A slender woman with gray-streaked black hair stood silhouetted in the doorway. She held her hand to her mouth. "What's going on? I saw the ambulance. This is my daughter's house." She looked over and saw the woman in the wedding dress. Immediately, she fell to her knees beside the recliner and screamed. "Ami!"

Randy walked toward her.

"Somebody help her! She's not breathing!" She yelled at the paramedics. "What's wrong with you? Help my daughter!"

Randy put his arm around the sobbing woman. "Ma'am, I'm so sorry. Why don't you come with me?" He tried to guide her gently toward the front porch.

"No!" she screamed. "Help Ami!" She looked down at her daughter and cried, "Oh, Ami, what have you done? Ami, Ami, Ami." She sobbed and lowered her head onto her daughter's chest. She looked up at Randy and pleaded, "Help her!"

Michael Chin knelt beside the woman. "She's too far gone, ma'am. There's nothing we can do."

"No," she wept.

"Come on, ma'am. Let's go outside where we can have a little privacy. I need to ask you a few questions."

The woman stood and wiped her eyes before looking back at Joel where he stood in the kitchen. Then she leaned on Randy and limped through the front door.

John Cerelli lifted his hand toward Joel. "Come here," he said, his voice just above a whisper.

Joel knelt by the man. "John?"

John nodded. "That woman with Randy. She's the one who did this. She killed Wally McCall. Then she killed her daughter. And she tried to kill me."

"Wait a minute. You called me today and said that Ami killed Wally McCall. Now you say it's her mother?"

"I was wrong about Ami."

"Well, she's dead, so she can't verify your story."

John's speech was thick and slow. "It's no story. Ami's mother framed Claire for murdering her father."

Joel shook his head, trying to process yet another curve. "Why? Why would she do this?"

"She hated Claire for refusing to give her large amounts of morphine for her husband. I think she wanted it for her own drug addiction. She thought Claire suspected her." He halted. "And she thought Claire stole me away from Ami."

Joel paused and studied John for a moment. "You seem to be trying to find any explanation that will get Claire off the hook and out of jail."

"I'm telling the truth."

"What evidence do you have? Your word against hers?"

Tim Snyder put his hand on Joel's shoulder. "We've got to take this guy in. The Narcan is shorter-acting than the narcotic it is countering. He could stop breathing anytime. We need to get him in a monitored situation."

"Sure." He looked at John. "We'll talk later."

"No!" John tugged on Joel's pants leg. "I can prove it." He motioned for Joel to come closer. He spoke at a whisper. "Leave me alone for a minute and step outside. If Ami's mom thinks I am still alive, she will return to silence me."

"What are you suggesting?"

"Let me give you the proof you need."

Tim knelt beside him. "Waiting could be dangerous. We need to take you to the hospital."

"I can refuse?"

"Mr. Cerelli, this could risk your life."

John struggled up so that he was leaning on both elbows. "Just do this! I'm not going anywhere until you listen to me." He put his hand up. "Here," he said, lifting the IV line. "Disconnect this and put the tip under a bandage on my arm."

The detective and paramedic exchanged glances. Joel shook his head. "This is insane."

"I'm not comfortable with this. He could die."

The detective leaned over John. "I can't put your life at risk."

John coughed. "You'll be right outside."

"And my career is over if you die."

"I'm not going to die. Fix the IV so the drug won't be going in my arm."

Joel stood up. "You want to risk your life?"

"I want you to know the truth." John coughed. "I'm refusing transport. I'll sign a release form. I'm going with you only if you work with me."

The detective frowned. "I'll give you two minutes by the clock." He walked to a small window by the back door and pulled back the curtain to create a small slit for a view from the outside. "I'll be right outside this window watching everything." He took the paramedic by the arm. "Fix his IV like he suggested."

Tim protested. "I don't like this."

"I don't like it either. But if he refuses transport, and he doesn't get more Narcan, he could die anyway." The detective watched as Tim unhooked and capped the IV and placed the end of the tubing under a large dressing on his arm. He slowed down the drip. "This won't fool anyone for very long." He stood up. "This is a bad idea."

Joel tilted his head toward the front door. "Your opinion is noted." He looked down at John. "One last chance, Cerelli. My advice is to let us take you in. Now."

John shook his head. "Leave me," he gasped. "This is my call."

Joel ushered the paramedic crew out onto the porch. The other paramedics retreated to their van while Tim lingered behind. Detective Stevens put his hand on the shoulder of Ami's mom, who sat on the porch steps talking to Randy Jensen. "Ma'am," he began, "would you like to spend a moment with your daughter? I asked the paramedics to step out for a few minutes so you could be alone with her." He spoke softly and gave her a gentle pat on the back. "Say good-bye."

Randy wrinkled his forehead but Joel gave him a subtle shake of the head to say, "Don't interfere."

Ami's mom sniffed. "I'd like that." Joel helped her to her feet. She slipped in and shut the front door.

Joel kept his voice just above a whisper and looked at his watch. "Randy, here's what's going down."

* * *

John looked through his eyelashes with slitlike eyes, feigning sleep. Nancy Childress loudly moaned and cried her daughter's name.

He felt the pull of sleep. *The narcotic is still affecting me. The antidote is wearing off. I have to fight to stay awake and keep breathing.*

Predictably, Nancy kept crying and calling Ami's name. Then she hurried to John while keeping up her charade of tears. She pulled a syringe from a small black pocketbook.

John forced his eyes to stay open. "No," he whispered.

Just as he'd anticipated, she injected the contents of the syringe into the IV line.

John held his breath and allowed his eyes to close. When his lungs were bursting and only after he'd heard Nancy walk into the front room did he dare to inhale again.

Where are they? Why aren't they coming to my rescue?

He felt the euphoric state rising. Soon he would sleep and would not remember to breathe.

Outside, Joel crouched down and peered through the kitchen window. When he saw Nancy inject the medicine, he tried the back door. It was locked. *Why isn't Randy coming in the front?*

He sprinted around the house. Randy looked up from his position outside the door. "She's locked us out!" He pounded the door. "Mrs. Childress, open the door."

"We've got to get in there!"

"Open the door!"

Inside they heard her raising her voice to a hysterical lilt.

Randy kicked in the door, splintering the wood along the deadbolt. Tim rushed in behind Randy and Joel and headed straight to John.

"He's not breathing!" Tim shouted. "Get my crew back in here." He looked up at the detective. "If he doesn't make it, I'm holding you responsible!"

Randy shouted for the other paramedics.

Tim laid his hand on John's neck. "How long was he down? He's got no pulse!"

Joel nodded and looked at Nancy Childress, who was weeping over her daughter's still form. He grabbed her by the elbow. "You're coming with me!"

Chapter Forty

John Cerelli blinked and opened his eyes. The room was bright, too bright. He waited for his eyes to adjust and decided to take inventory. He was on his back. The surface was soft. A bed? *Where am I?* He tried to close his mouth, but a tube coming through his teeth stopped him. He swallowed against the tube, which ran along his tongue into the back of his throat, and began to gag, his cough muffled into the tube. As he coughed, a shrill electronic alarm sounded, coming from somewhere close to his right ear. He looked up. An IV bag dangled above him, and a snarl of wires connected his chest to a TV screen.

"Why, hello there. Look who's waking up." The voice was feminine and belonged to a head which appeared to float just above his.

He tried to speak, but the tube seemed to have stolen his voice.

He lifted his right hand, but met resistance after moving only a few inches. *They've got me tied down! Where am I?*

"John, you're in the hospital. Brighton University Intensive Care Unit. You came in with an overdose."

A memory bubbled to the surface and drifted away. *I went to see Ami.*

Ami is dead. Her mother did it.

Her mother tried to kill me.

"John, take a deep breath."

He obeyed.

"Let's get this tube out of your throat." The floating head above him became a nurse. She pulled tape from his cheeks and asked him to cough, pulling the tube when he responded. She covered his mouth with an oxygen mask. "That should feel better."

John found his voice. "What time is it?"

"Four o'clock."

He'd lost three hours. "What happened?"

"You overdosed, John. The police found you in time."

The memory returned fresh and strong. The police had evidence that could free Claire.

The nurse touched his shoulder. "The police were here earlier. I'm supposed to call them since you're awake." She paused. "Are you in some trouble? Did you want to die?"

"No!" He tried to sit up, but the wrist restraints made it difficult. He studied her face. "You think I tried to do this? Someone did this to me!"

Her face registered disbelief. "Sure."

He shrugged. "Call the police. I want to talk to them."

The nurse undid his restraints. "I'll call Detective Stevens."

A few minutes later, Joel Stevens showed up.

"That was quick."

"I've been waiting for you to wake up for an hour."

"That long?"

"Enough time for three cups of vending-machine coffee." He held up a cup and smiled. "I don't recommend it."

"You didn't wait for me to talk about the coffee."

He nodded. "You were right. We have Nancy Childress in custody."

"She confessed?"

"Only after we presented her with the eyewitness evidence of her injecting you with morphine."

John took a deep breath. "So Claire is going to get out?"

"As soon as we show the evidence to Garland Strickler. I'm sure the charges will be dropped."

John pumped his fist. "I've got to get out of here."

"Not so fast, cowboy. You're still on a Narcan drip to counter the narcotic in your system."

He looked over to see his nurse. "When can I get out?"

"Probably tomorrow morning."

John took a deep breath and reached for the detective's hand. "Thanks."

That evening, Claire was brought back into a holding room where she could talk to her attorney across the glass window.

Bill Fauls was waiting. For the first time, a broad grin replaced his serious expression. He didn't wait for Claire to sit before he began. "I owe you an apology, Claire. When all the evidence was stacking up against you, I lost faith in you." He held up his hands in surrender. "I let you down. I'm sorry."

Claire leaned forward. "You didn't just come here to apologize."

"How do you know?"

"It's late. You have to have news."

"I do. Great news, actually." He took a deep breath. "John helped us crack this case wide open."

"It was Ami, wasn't it? She killed my father to get me out of the picture. John and I figured it out once I knew about the 911 tape she used."

"Slow down," he said. "I'm going to tell you everything. It was Nancy Childress, Ami's mother."

"Nancy? She killed Wally?"

"She's made a confession." He paused. "It looks like a pretty complicated dysfunctional little family. When Ami was a young woman, she was raped by her father. Nancy confessed to John that she killed her husband in defense of her daughter. Ami then burned their house down to destroy the evidence of her father's body."

Claire lifted her shackled hands to her mouth. "That's horrible."

Bill nodded. "I'm not sure how much her childhood abuse played into her later problems, but— "

"She was diagnosed with schizophrenia as a teenager."

"And later became obsessed with your husband. Her mother, it seems, believed Ami's version of her delusional romance with John. She believed John was two-timing Ami and that you stole John away from her daughter."

Claire huffed. "I stole John away? She was trying to steal John away from me!"

"Exactly. Anyway, Nancy had problems of her own. She was trying to cope with a dying husband and became addicted to the painkillers she was giving him."

"That explains why she was always so upset with the amount of morphine I offered to Richard."

"She was afraid you were catching on to her. In addition, she wanted you to be framed for your father's death, to get you out of the way of her daughter's romance with John. So when she found out that Ami was masquerading as your counselor and had made a tape of your confrontation, she hatched a plan to use that tape to get you out of the picture.

"By the way, I spoke to Joanne Phillips. She treated Ami with some of the exact techniques that Ami used with you. She asked Ami to have a mock confrontation with her father to tell him how she felt about the abuse."

Claire nodded thoughtfully. "So that's how Ami learned all the psychological lingo. She'd been in therapy herself."

"Now this part is weird," Bill said. "In her obsession with John, Ami had bought the exact same wedding gown and veil that you had. Nancy found out about the gown, and she dressed in it the morning of your wedding and slipped into the nursing home to kill your father."

Claire shook her head. "How does Tyler fit into all of this? John thought that Tyler may have sexually assaulted Ami."

"He was right. It appears that Tyler assaulted Ami on the night of your wedding. It was yet another rape by a convicted rapist."

Claire nodded and stayed quiet.

"Claire, Ami killed Tyler."

"Ami? So she hid his body in my car?"

"We don't think so. Nancy confessed to placing the body in your car, again in an attempt to cover for her daughter and frame you in the process. She even took hair from a brush in the glove box of the car to plant on Tyler's body to make it look like you were the victim of a sexual assault."

"She was shrewd."

Bill nodded. "I haven't told you everything yet. John went to confront Ami after talking with you."

"John? Is he okay?"

"Relax. John's fine. Now," he added. "But when he went to Ami's house, he found her body."

"Dead?"

"Yes. She'd been overdosed. From what we understand from the preliminary police investigation, it looks like Nancy killed her own daughter."

"What?"

"Evidently, Nancy felt like Ami couldn't be trusted to stay quiet any longer. Ami was confiding in John, and Nancy sensed things were spinning out of her control." He shrugged. "We may never understand the full extent that Nancy's own psychological problems and drug addiction played into this."

"So what am I doing behind bars? When can you get me out?"

"I'm working on that. The judge has agreed to hear evidence in his chambers tomorrow. Hopefully he'll agree to have you released."

Relief flooded across her soul. Claire stood up and leaned her hands against the glass. "Thank you."

Her attorney stood and touched his hand on the glass across from hers. "Thank God," he said. "Thank God."

At ten the next morning, Bonnie found Claire sitting in the common room on the bolted-down couch. "Let's go."

She looked up, studying the smile that Bonnie couldn't hide. "What?"

"There's a new prisoner in a holding cell. I want you out of here before she's introduced to the pod."

"Nancy. They arrested her, didn't they?"

Bonnie nodded. "Let's go."

"Out?"

The guard smiled. "Your attorney and Mr. Strickler met in the judge's chambers this morning. He signed a court order to release you. Bill Fauls brought it over himself."

Relief flooded her soul. She stopped to take a deep breath.

Suddenly Maria was in front of them, with Tamika and Trisha behind her. Maria hugged Claire. "God brought you to me. I know it, I know it," she whispered into Claire's hair.

Claire clasped hands with Tamika and Trish. "No offense, but I'm lookin' forward to seeing my new roommate," Claire said.

Tamika and Trisha laughed.

Bonnie pointed to the door with her head. "Let's go."

The guard led her into the chamber room and for the first time, she wasn't handcuffed before being taken through the next door.

She was led through the hallway back to the booking area. "You'll need to be processed out," Bonnie said. She followed the guard into a room where a deputy sat behind a counter. It had the feel of an old dry cleaner, with a long oval of bags hanging from an overhead railing. Bonnie looked at the number on Claire's ID. "I need eleven seventy two."

The man nodded and entered a number on the keypad in front of him. The bags began to circulate, a slow carnival ride that lurched and brought Claire's bag to the front. The man double-checked the number on the bag with Claire's jail ID. He lifted the bag from the rack. It appeared larger than any other. "It's all yours." He pointed to a door. "Changing room's right there." He paused. "Whatcha got in there, a winter coat?"

Claire took the bag and pulled it open to see her wedding dress. She began pulling the wrinkled dress out of the bag and folded it into her arms. "My dress!" She frowned. "Do I have to wear this?"

Bonnie grinned. "Yep. Our uniforms aren't for sale."

Claire slipped into the changing room and shed the orange jumpsuit. She found her shoes in the bottom of the bag. As she dressed, she felt silly but overjoyed at the thought of freedom. She walked out and pirouetted in front of the deputies. "How do I look?"

"Come on," Bonnie said, "I heard your husband is waiting."

She handed the man her orange jumpsuit and foam slippers. "I won't be needing these."

Bonnie led her through the set of double doors leading to the lobby, where Claire scanned the crowd for John. She looked back at Bonnie, who motioned her forward. "Go on outside. You're free."

Claire stepped away, timidly at first, and aware of the stares of the others in the lobby. In a moment, she walked down a set of three stairs and hit the door to the street. It was there she first saw the limousine parked at the curb. John stood next to it, wearing his wedding tuxedo. "John!" She fell forward into his embrace.

After a moment, she looked around. Della, John's parents, Margo, Kyle, and their three girls surrounded her. She hugged them all, one by one, until her own tears of joy threatened her vision. "What's this about?"

"We have a honeymoon to attend to," John said.

"We can't," she protested. "I can't leave my family now, not after Dad—"

"You can and you will," Della said, ushering her toward the open door of the waiting limo. "There will be time to grieve with us later. Right now, you have other business to attend to."

John opened the door to the limousine. "We have a plane to catch, dear."

Margo hugged her a second time and whispered, "See you in two weeks."

Claire couldn't find her voice. She nodded at Margo and wiped her tears with the sleeve of her wedding gown.

A moment later, inside the limousine, she turned to see the small crowd gathered on the sidewalk as they pulled away. She watched until they rounded a corner and then leaned her head against her husband's shoulder.

She couldn't believe it. She was free. She was with John.

And for now, that was enough.

Three ways to keep up on your favorite Zondervan books and authors

Sign up for our *Fiction E-Newsletter*. Every month you'll receive sample excerpts from our books, sneak peeks at upcoming books, and chances to win free books autographed by the author.

You can also sign up for our *Breakfast Club*. Every morning in your email, you'll receive a five-minute snippet from a fiction or nonfiction book. A new book will be featured each week, and by the end of the week you will have sampled two to three chapters of the book.

Zondervan *Author Tracker* is the best way to be notified whenever your favorite Zondervan authors write new books, go on tour, or want to tell you about what's happening in their lives.

Visit *www.zondervan.com* and sign up today!

ZONDERVAN.com/
AUTHORTRACKER
follow your favorite authors

For the Rest of My Life

Harry Kraus, M D

The riveting, emotional sequel to the bestselling *Could I Have This Dance?*

Claire McCall, MD, is haunted by the question: Does she have the gene for Huntington's Disease, the disease that disabled her father? This exciting sequel picks up with Claire moving back to Stoney Creek to work as a family physician and help her mother care for her disabled father. She rekindles her relationship with John Cerelli and—just before she's going to find out if she carries the HD gene—discovers an engagement ring hidden in his car. When John fails to "pop the question" before learning the results of the test, Claire believes he is only interested in marrying her if she does not have the HD gene. She runs away from him without learning the results of the test, or the strength of his love.

Claire copes with her romantic disappointment by plunging into her work. But a brutal rapist attacks three of Claire's patients, just as each young woman is recovering from a recent accident or surgery. When Claire has surgery for appendicitis, she herself is attacked. Only her trust in God can keep Claire safe.

Softcover: 0-310-24978-3

Pick up a copy today at your favorite bookstore!